Praise for Sara Hanover and the Wayward Mages:

"Hanover's jam-packed second Wayward Mages adventure is a hectic but entertaining roller-coaster ride. Ever since the maelstrom stone, an ancient mystical artifact, embedded itself in Tessa Andrews's palm, her world's been thrown into chaos as she is forced to defend herself from magical attacks in both her dreams and the waking world, while working to free her father from the spectral state he's trapped in, to assist her phoenix friend through his transition into a new body, and to navigate her murky relationship with the dangerous but alluring Malender. . . . Hanover showcases her boundless imagination with creative twists, outsized villains, and dynamic, magical protagonists." —*Publishers Weekly*

"Sara Hanover knows her way around the written word. . . . I absolutely loved this book. I can't wait to buy a copy and put it on my bookshelf. Hanover is now on my list of 'must buy'." —Galleywampus

"With so many fantasy books for young adults coming out, it's easy to find repetitions of the same magic systems. But Hanover's story follows its own rules, and it stands out from most of the others." —Culturess

"Plenty of action, mystery, and family drama to be had."
—Pass Me That Book

"In the second book of the Wayward Mages series, Hanover presents a realistic urban fantasy as college student Tessa Andrews adjusts to all of her magical friends and a maelstrom stone e[illegible] her left palm. . . . Fans of *Libriomancer* an[illegible] the gritty reality inters[illegible]

[illegible]ew)

DAW is proud to present
Sara Hanover's novels of
the Wayward Mages

THE LATE GREAT WIZARD
THE NEW IMPROVED SORCERESS
THE WAYWARD MAGE*

*Available June 2021 from DAW

THE NEW IMPROVED SORCERESS

SARA HANOVER

Book Two of
Wayward Mages

DAW BOOKS, INC.
DONALD A. WOLLHEIM, FOUNDER
1745 Broadway, New York, NY 10019
ELIZABETH R. WOLLHEIM
SHEILA E. GILBERT
PUBLISHERS
www.dawbooks.com

Cover art by Cliff Nielsen.

Cover design by Katie Anderson.

Interior dingbat courtesy of ShutterStock.

Edited by Sheila E. Gilbert.

DAW Book Collectors No. 1843.

Published by DAW Books, Inc.
1745 Broadway, New York, NY 10019.

First Mass Market Printing, January 2021
1 2 3 4 5 6 7 8 9

Dedicated to: Tyler, Xander, Molly, and Jocelyn.
You are the future.

CHAPTER ONE

"DO NOT GO GENTLE INTO THAT GOOD NIGHT . . ."

I NEVER USED to believe in magic, but magic believed in me and that's when the fight started.

If magic were graceful and elegant, it probably would reject me. But apparently it favors people who can barely walk and breathe at the same time, trip over shadows on the sidewalk, and fight off inconvenient face-plants wherever possible. I fall a lot, but I bounce back. Except on the hockey field where I happen to excel . . .

Take a deep breath.

Maybe Dylan Thomas said it best. I fight my hardest struggles at night. Alone. And that is partly because I'm afraid for myself. I rage. The mystical relic that embedded itself in my left palm is to blame, although I didn't have that much trouble with the maelstrom stone at first, not until it absorbed an equally magical 24-karat solid gold ring imbued with sheer evil. Now the two of them seem to be duking it out for my soul, and my dreams are a front in a no-holds-barred duel. I'm young. I can go without a few nights' sleep once in a while, but sweet heavens, this is getting old. I can't weaken. As much as I fear for myself, I am terrified for my family and friends. Nightmares are real.

Months ago, I signed up for community college, just your average kid whose father abandoned the family—oh, did I forget to mention that? Don't worry, Mom and I found him eventually. He's an interdimensional ghost living in our basement—but before that, a friend of the family died in a house fire. Now this is where it gets weird. The professor died, but didn't, because he's a phoenix wizard, and they're generally reborn in fire if the proper rituals have been held. Only he did and they weren't, so now we have a gorgeous and adorable-looking guy living with us who has two souls–his and the crusty old professor's, but little of the professor's wizardly knowledge—and we're trying to help him get restored. It has to be done because something nasty is rising in the world.

Which means as soon as the professor is successful at getting his phoenix ritual straightened out and compiled, we get to set him on fire again.

I'd like to say that's where the weirdness stops, but it's only where it gets started. Along the way to get the professor's ritual correct, I collected a motley crew of friends: a wrong-side-of-London–raised demon, an Iron Dwarf and his son, a French sorceress, and Richmond police's finest, Lieutenant Carter Phillips, who happens to be my main crush with a war hero record, a crooked smile, and the power of a desert sun god backing him. Of course, that's only one side of the equation. On the enemy side, I have an overly ambitious and therefore evil Kitsune (a Japanese fox deity that is normally good, but there's my luck), a samurai sorcerer, a pack of shadow hounds, a vengeful squad of harpies, and Malender, who has to be the most beautiful- looking being I've ever met, even though he is surrounded by a murky cloud of pure nastiness and everyone else is scared spitless by him. He is masculine, not a doubt about that, but mortal? Probably not. No one has told me what he is, but I've my own ideas, something in the realm of a lost god from a long-ago past. He has yet to disabuse me of that. Not to mention I've been warned that the bad guys will be popping up out of the sidewalk because this Great Evil is awake and presumably coming after all of us. I have been told by friends and enemies that the stone possessing my left hand is of utmost importance in the fate of the world. Peachy.

Add to that the daily consuming guilt that I put my

father into a losing situation and haven't found a way out for him yet. I'm working on it!

I'd rather face the arch rivals of my college field hockey team any day than my nightmares, because I'd at least have shin guards for armor and a sturdy stick in my hands. When I'm on the field, surrounded by my teammates, I'm a striker and the one to be feared. Go Sky Hawks!

On the metaphysical side, I've learned to duck and run.

It sounds easier than it is.

It's bedtime and that means I woke up without actually waking and found myself with stick in hand, balanced on the balls of my feet, and heard a sound that raised the hairs on the back of my neck. I stood my ground and looked at the mutated mastiff crossed with a rhino as it approached, head down, breathing a deep-throated rumble, glad for my hockey stick in this nightmare. Usually, I'm empty-handed. The thing's eyes glowed ruby red, which seems to be universal in these critters. I wondered how much that affected their actual eyesight. Like, would I disappear if I stood in front of a crimson bed comforter or something? And if I was lucky enough, was it as nearsighted as an actual rhino, which could be a definite advantage to me?

I grasped my stick in a cross-body hold and dropped my chin a little, mirroring the beast's stance. "You look like you put the ugly in monster."

It let out a massive huff and pawed the ground. A tear-inducing stink rose around it. I sniffled a bit and waved it away. "If you think I'm afraid of you, you're only a teensy bit right because you look like you could plow right through me. But I know that's not the endgame here. Someone wants my stone, and they have to have fingers and thumbs and something of a hand to take it and for it to be useful—and you don't. Meaning that you're just a big, dumb stumbling block that someone else is throwing at me."

Beastie threw its head up and charged across the grass, and I realized I might have been better off not telling it what I suspected. It cornered quicker than I figured, and its shoulder knocked me off my stride as I threw myself off to the right. I shoved my stick out and caught it between its thick and leathery front legs, sending it to its knees as it bellowed and nearly did a headstand as it stumbled to a rugged stop. Off-balance myself, I skidded to one knee and got up just a skoosh slower than Beastie did. I mean, it *levitated* to its feet. My jaw dropped. As it rushed me, I pointed to the right and rolled to the left, its reeking breath parting my hair.

In a full run, it had no chance of pivoting and hightailing it back to where I jumped to my feet. I took to my heels and did not look back, racing across the green field, which, in this dream state, might have been the local park or even the college campus athletic field, but held one singular and quite sturdy looking tree in its center. That tree had definite possibilities.

A straight line is the quickest route between two points, but a strategic zigzag seemed more effective with a few tons of dog-rhino on my heels. I could corner, it couldn't. At the last minute, I readied to leap up the tree trunk and skitter out of the way when it hit me.

What the hell was a lone tree doing out here in the middle of nowhere?

I swerved sharply away. The tree rattled and shook as if hit by hurricane winds, and flailing branches stretched out to grab me. Stray leaves slapped me upside the face. I could hear rhino-dog galloping behind me as I raced out of the tree's reach and then the thundering grew louder. I looked back over my shoulder and saw that it had multiplied into three. That brought hot anger up the back of my throat.

I slapped my hockey stick into the palm of my hand. "All right then. You won't play fair, so I won't." In a quick breath, I called out: "Lisanne, Lisanne, Lisanne. Kristy, Kristy, Kristy." And the last of my hockey teammates I would put on the field: "Jheri, Jheri, Jheri!"

In the twitch of an eyelid, four of us raced across the grass, in hockey skorts, jersey tops, and shin guards, with trusty sticks in our hands. I knew this wasn't their real selves because they didn't look stunned to be summoned, even though Jheri had on her padded goalie accessories and shook her head at me. The headshake I knew, her black curls bouncing about her shoulders, held back by a headband in our college colors. She flashed a smile at me.

I swung around, pointing at the enemy. "I need blockers."

The other three spread out to be my wingmen, sticks readied, faces determined. I don't think the rhino-dogs knew what hit them when we didn't stand aside or dodge as they charged. We wheeled around on the right side runner, split him away from the herd, so to speak, fleeter on our heels than our prey, and none of my gals were shy on high-sticking when it counted. The rhino-dog gave a gusty bellow before dropping to its flank and going limp, as swelling shut its eyes and one horn dangled by mere hairs from its snout.

The other two beasties swung about, trumpeting noisily in hopes of scaring us, I suppose, but Kristy let out her own throaty "Whuu-up," as in about to get a southern whupping. She always has a sweet romance novel in her backpack, a pert nose, pretty golden-blond hair, and a murderous stare when she's defending the playfield. No one messes with my teammates.

We ran around the field till it sucked the air out of our lungs and the stamina from our bodies—or at least mine, the other three still looked feisty—and I staggered to a halt.

"Gotta finish this." I needed to be able to breathe *and* get a few hours of sleep.

"What's the plan?"

"Turn around and run right at 'em. They'll either dissipate or knock me over, and at this rate, I don't care."

My teammates had circled me and now they high-sticked each other, wood beating in a primitive rhythm. "Can't give up, Tessa."

"Not giving up. But they can't have this unless I give it away, and I've no intentions of that. Got to stop them in their tracks." I craned my head up to look at them. Or over my dead body, but I wasn't going to tell them that. Odds were, I'd wake up. I had before.

The stone in my hand grew warmer, waking to the heat of my pulse. I curled my hand shut around it, straightened, and inhaled sharply. The line of rhino-dogs charged at us and my gals fanned out again as wingmen. I knew they couldn't be hurt but had no assurances about myself. This was an ongoing assault, and whoever or whatever initiated it had to be getting tired of failing.

As if the critters could read my thoughts, they peeled away from me and, muzzles and horns lowered, went after my teammates. Lisanne went down, rolled, and came up with an arm missing. I mean—just gone. No blood or gore, simply empty air. No harm, no foul? She looked at me, stricken, as a thin trail of blood leaked from her nose. Oh, no.

"Run! Just run! Get out of here!" Hollering, I bolted after the attackers, holding my stick like a baseball bat, ready to bash heads in. My gals took to their heels, disappearing into pink mist as they did, and I got a good swing in to cover their retreat. I hit, and hit hard, the impact singing all the way from my hands up into my shoulder. It felt like socking a brick wall. The beast didn't react like a wall, though. It fell to its knees and did a slow somersault, heels over horns, to a halt. Then it turned to ash and crumbled away.

Before it had blown to nothing, I turned to chase down a second. My breath rattled in my lungs and I whistled as I exhaled, like a tea kettle running out of steam. My second swing barely grazed the nightmare, and it had begun to pivot in my direction, its shoulder grazing me.

I have had whole trees (don't ask) fall on me with less impact. I went down, skidding across the grass, losing my hockey stick as I hit on a shoulder before splatting, arms and legs akimbo. The ground vibrated as the big boy lumbered to his feet, dug in, and charged, red eyes smoldering. I scrambled up, tripped over the lost stick, got it in both hands, and braced myself.

One solid strike between the eyes ought to slow it down, if nothing else. I bounced up on the balls of my feet, my whole body one solid ache and yelling at me *what are you thinking???*

As I struck, the rhino-dog or dog-rhino split in two instead of plowing me under and, unbelievably, my mother rose up and stood there. Dripping blood. Petite, blonde, blazing blue eyes looking up at me in bewilderment, the side of her head bashed and gashed. She put a shaking hand up to me. "Tessa . . ."

"*No.* No, no, no!" I pulled myself to a halt and stumbled back to her. I could feel hot tears stream down my face. "Mom, I didn't—I couldn't—"

But maybe I could, and had. I hadn't seen her hidden inside the beast. Had she always been there? Had she really been chasing me? I scrubbed at my traitorous eyes and reached for her. The moment her hand touched mine . . . the left hand . . . the maelstrom went red hot. I yelped, but she didn't flinch one bit. She wrapped both hands about mine in craving. She clawed at my palm, at my flesh, digging at the stone.

I twisted my arm out of her hold and shoved her away, not knowing if the thing was my mom or another nightmare or something possessed. I couldn't tell. I backed away. "Go home. Go back to sleep. Be safe. *Be my mom.*"

The apparition took a zombie step after me, and I turned to flee, running right into the branch-arms of the tree that had been after me from the very first. It sprang up and around me like a trap, sticky limbs closing tight. I dropped and rolled to the ground, breaking free of some of the tendrils but not enough. I think I screamed in fury as I tried to tear my way loose. My throat ached as if I had.

Alone again, I fought in a green jungle that hugged me tighter and tighter with every movement. Like a python, it wrapped itself close and began to squeeze. I managed a squeak for help.

A hand reached down, grasped my wrist, and pulled me up. Up, up, and away from my captor and I looked into a stunningly beautiful face that I knew well. Masculine, perfect, and utterly ageless. Michelangelo could have sculpted him.

Malender smiled at me. He rarely smiled, and the effect of that expression washed over me, like welcome sunshine on a once-rainy day.

"I didn't call for you."

"No, but how could I not come, Tessa of the Salt? I heard your distress and fear." Mal's full lips curved ever so slightly as his cheer expanded. He thought it amusing that I threw fistfuls of salt over him to protect myself nearly every time we met. Tonight, however, he didn't seem to be wearing that dark and oily cloud of malevolence he usually had. And I didn't seem to have any salt about me. Go figure. Next dream I'd have to come prepared.

He set me on my feet and began to dust me off, like some valet shedding lint from a suit, but mine were leaves and vines and angry branches that twitched and thrashed even as he brushed off the last of them. Every touch of his felt like a tiny, electric jolt, all the nerves in my body reacting. Did I like it or abhor it? I couldn't tell, and my confusion rooted me to the ground. He took me by the hand again and walked me away from the trap as it keened and wailed in a high and windy voice before it withered down to nothing but a sooty spot in the field. His grasp was firm, warm, and unsettling.

"You can't go on like this."

"I know." I hung my head a moment before looking up to meet the challenge in his eyes. "But I'm not quitting either."

"Magic has a price. Do you know what you are paying?"

"Besides sleepless nights?"

He shook his head slowly. "Far beyond that, and you need to learn what you might be giving up. Magic exacts a terrible toll."

"I don't intend to lose."

"Of course, you cannot. Because, Tessa dear—" And he took the unmovable stone gently from my palm, and beckoned with it across my field of vision. I felt a dizzying loss as he finished with, "This is the way the world ends."

I suddenly realized I wasn't fighting for myself—I was fighting for *everyone*.

I jumped to stop him.

CHAPTER TWO

LEVELING UP

AND FELL OUT of bed. Dazed, I lay still for a moment on the floor, wedging my eyes open only to see shooting stars and rainbows bouncing off the walls and ceiling. A brilliant Happy Birthday card hung from my ceiling light, courtesy of my mom, and it twirled about in a riot of color. My bedroom looked like its old self: faded wallpaper, paint chipped here and there on the crown molding, a few glossy posters extolling the virtues of various rock stars, and my bookcase in the corner, which managed to sag to one side without spilling any books. Nothing seemed hurt or damaged, and I prayed that it would be the same with Mom and my friends. Magic has its time and place, but this surely wasn't supposed to be it. I'm not magic. In fact, I'm fairly certain I'm anti-magic despite my dreams. Witness the hunk of marble buried in the palm of my left hand which is—

And I took a look.

Oh, it was still there, but—I let out a scream that only dogs could hear. It seemed to be the source of the weirdness bouncing about my room. All the colors known to the human eye arched out of my palm, punctuated by silvery stars shooting back and forth, equally bright and cheerfully determined to celebrate my twentieth birthday. I sat up and curled my fingers into a tight fist, trying to stifle the display. Nothing. Although I have to say, the optical effects had a feel to them, rather like fizzy bubbles. I promptly sat on my hand. That brought about the illusion that I was passing gas with wondrous images.

The door to my room flung open first, followed by my one and only bedroom window. For reasons about to become obvious, I sleep in a sports bra, baggy T-shirt and knit shorts, rain or shine. Reason one burst in the door and reason two hovered in the air outside the bedroom window.

Brian looked aghast at the threshold for a moment, difficult for a young handsome guy who hasn't a wrinkle on his face to make expressions with, and then he made a scholarly "hmmmm" as the dominant persona in his body took over. His other soul is about eighty and has seen a lot in his lifetime. The professor remarked, "Your birthday, I take it?" Brian is the equivalent of a personality jackpot in one body. His twentyish self rejuvenated as a phoenix wizard soul pairs with the wonderfully curmudgeonly phoenix wizard, Professor Brandard, stuck in transit to wherever. I'm helping him resolve that problem, and my mother is providing a home since his burned down. I haven't researched it, but friends we share have confided that the home situation is not uncommon among wizards of his type; phoenixes and fires having that fatal attraction, they sometimes have to couch surf. Brian may or may not look as Brandard did in his youth, broad shoulders, red-gold hair, and eyes of blue-green, with sooty eyelashes framing them. He has a dimple to the left of his mouth. The professor had a brushy mustache, so I might have missed the dimple behind it, and the wrinkles of age. Not nearly as many wrinkles, though, as his previous lives have probably earned.

Reason two, however, doesn't live in the same house; he's just floating outside it, a commanding-looking officer of the law, the youngest one in the city's history and a war hero at that, and my being twenty now makes me only four years younger than he is. I keep hoping he'll notice that there is no longer an abyss of age between us. He isn't good-looking in Brian's way; his nose is strong to match his jawline, a scar gives him an off-center cleft, and his hair is nearly black with satiny curls. Eyes of soft hazel carry a glint of humor in them, no matter what stern expression he may have on his face at any given time. Today, he was smiling and laughing at me. Carter Phillips steadied his flotation with a grip on the outside window frame. "Are you all right? I caught the scream." He tried to sound worried, but I could tell the bouncing stars and rainbows had chased away his true concern.

Both of them had the grace not to notice I seemed to be sitting on a fountain of prismatic color. I freed my hand and shook it at them. "This—this—is insane."

Brian and Carter traded looks across my bedroom, and both said, "Birthday."

"And what would that have to do with it?"

"Coming of age."

"By your standards," and I pointed at Brian, whose interior selves lined up centuries upon centuries in various lifetimes, "twenty is practically middle-aged. I thought eighteen was the coming of age, anyway, and if I were a dog or cat, I'd be ancient."

"Age is relative, you're right. But for the last century or two, the twenties have been considered coming into one's prime," Carter told me calmly.

"You were in the Marines at age twenty."

Carter looked diffident. "And discharged by twenty-two, all washed up."

"Pooh." Although, frankly, Carter was not the type to have *pooh* said to his face. He had a bearing about him that demanded respect. Being washed up had nothing to do with his discharge. Wounded and hero covered that one.

The old house's rain gutter rattled a bit as if something shambled up its side, catching Carter's attention, just as another man popped his head into my window frame and climbed halfway in, to sit down in a weathered yet still natty old suit, looking just like a chimney sweep. When he opened his mouth, the accent reinforced the impression, along with his ruddy complexion and flint-dark eyes that could snap at you. His bowler caught a bit of the sun's early rays.

"Morning, ducks," said Simon Steptoe. "Twenty, eh? Congratulations are in order," and he pulled a somewhat wilted bouquet of mixed roses from inside his coat. He twirled a finger about, indicating the fireworks as I took the flowers. "A bit of spectacular. Your doing?"

"Not exactly. I haven't the slightest idea how it started or how to stop it."

"It's your maelstrom stone." He waggled an eyebrow before looking toward Brian and Carter. "Haven't shown her how to use it yet?"

"I've been a bit busy. Lessons are somewhat ongoing," muttered the professor, "and the object in question can be quite recalcitrant and difficult—"

"Hey!" I objected.

"Not to mention," Carter added smoothly, "said object seems to have its own rules and goals dependent upon its possessor."

"You'd better be talking about the stone." I folded my arms. This changed the trajectory of the display to the extent that it began bouncing off the floor and ricocheting about with energy. A star fizzled in Brian's face, and he immediately rubbed at his mouth and nose as if someone had dunked him into soapy water. I pointed about. "This has to stop."

Steptoe hugged a kneecap. "But it's so marvelously entertaining." Stars and rainbows circled his hat like a halo and seemed intent on staying there.

Carter shook his head. "It has to be feeding off her energy, so it's depleting, and she's right. It has to stop before she drops. Question is, what started it?"

"There must be a need, deep in her psyche, that the maelstrom is trying to answer. Have you been depressed lately, my dear?" The professor peered out at me from Brian's expressive eyes. I looked away. It can be terribly confusing to deal with him/him.

"Let's see. I lost my father. Mom and I lost our house. Aunt April rents this aged and practically toppling wreck to us, and I found my dad living in the cellar. I almost didn't find him because he's a ghost now, trapped in some twilight zone between realities, and I can't restore him yet because I don't know how and the Iron Dwarf who might have had the answers died a few months ago. I liked Morty and now he's gone, and you're no closer to finishing your ritual than you were. Not to mention my hand looks like a freaking Roman candle!"

"I'd say she has issues." Carter grinned at me.

"Damn straight."

"Language, Tessa," my mother intoned from the hallway. "Having a pajama party?"

My mother could qualify as a saint. Not one loud word about three men in my bedroom at an ungodly hour, even though none of us had even known she'd come upstairs to join us. I shook a hand at her. My eyes welled up suddenly. Notwithstanding my night battle, she looked fine. She looked great! My mother tilted her head as she observed the phenomenon. "Oh. That's interesting."

Steptoe patted his pocket. "Not that they might help any, but I did bring a little birthday present for you." With a flourish, he handed over both the wilted bouquet and a tissue-wrapped package tied in a bit of shiny twine.

"Cool." I tore away at the packaging to reveal two pairs of gloves, one in a soft pastel pink and the other coal-dark, both cut from buttery leather. "Wow." They were not the sort of gloves one wore in cold weather or to drive a sports car or even golf in, but a kind of half glove. One that would neatly cover the stone in my hand and still give me a nice range of movement and touch. I pulled one on, flexing my hand about, impressed.

"They're weightlifting gloves, duckie. Thought they might be better than that brace you've been using."

"And they smell much nicer, too." My old athletic brace just about announced itself from a block away, despite my attempts to hand wash it now and then. "Thank you, Simon."

"I'd like to suggest that you get dressed, Tessa, while the others convene downstairs and I can fix a breakfast. We can discuss birthday plans and how to deal with that." Mother smiled at me, but the wrinkles at the corners of her eyes looked a little tense. I did, after all, have three men in my bedroom. Being a saint must be terribly difficult.

"Yes, ma'am."

"Good idea." Carter stepped through the window, pushing Steptoe to one side and using his shoulder as a lever. When he straightened, he stood taller than anyone in the room, and I imagined for a moment I could see him shining. Not like one of those sparkly fictional vampires, but with a kind of energy he carried inside.

I'd seen it once. Knew that it hid inside of him, and despite his all-American looks and manners, he had a touch of the totally foreign that he disguised. He wasn't a phoenix wizard like Brian, but he did have his own powers, and the sun barely burned hotter. As he passed me, he touched the back of my right hand, a reassurance, and then he was out the door and I could hear his light steps on the stairs.

Steptoe followed. He whistled as he went, a jauntysounding tune, and my mother called after him, "No lyrics!" her cheeks burning red as she left my room. I think she might have recognized the bawdy song.

That left Brian considering me.

"How did you turn it on?"

"No idea."

"Trying to work magic in your dreams, possibly?"

I didn't want to tell him what had scared me. "I don't have magic," I reminded him. "You guys are the ones with all the ability. I can block it once in a while, but so can a brick wall. Plus I know how to use salt."

The corner of the professor's mouth quirked. "That you can. Well, I'm hungry." He shook his head. "I've forgotten what it was like, but I'm almost always hungry."

"You're still a growing boy." I waved at the doorway. "I'll be down in a bit. Maybe I can wear a cooking pot on my hand or something."

"Hmmm," he said to himself as he stepped out, lost in his thoughts. I hoped they would be helpful ones.

I put my new gloves on my dresser and found an old mason jar under the bathroom sink for my roses. It might have been wishful thinking, but they seemed to perk right up the moment I sank the stems into water. Their heavenly fragrance filled the room. I love that perfume and find it disappointing that many perfect looking roses grown today often don't have a scent at all.

I showered quickly because I knew everyone downstairs had to be talking about me, and I didn't like not knowing what they were saying. It's like being in a room where you don't know the language, but you're certain what they're saying can't be good and is probably about you. And yes, that is a touch paranoid.

Sure enough, newly dressed and trailing rainbows and stars behind me like the train of a wedding gown, I entered the kitchen to hear them talking about Hiram.

"You're not talking about me?"

"That would be impolite," my mother said with a glancing kiss to my brow as she passed me on the way to the stove. "French toast and bacon all right? We thought we'd wait for you."

"Oh. Sure. So, what about Hiram?" Hiram was Mortimer Broadstone's son and heir, a brawny Iron Dwarf in the tradition of the family. He and his crew had helped remodel the cellar portion of this old house after some minor damage—Hiram had fallen through the floor, into the cellar—and we all considered him a good friend.

"There's been a power struggle among the clans," Carter explained. "He may or may not be in the center of it."

"That doesn't sound good. Or even like Hiram."

"Not all struggles are made out of our own volition." Brian stuffed a half slice of French toast into his mouth and mopped up the syrup and butter that didn't survive the maneuver with another on the tines of his fork, talking like the professor and eating like a starving youngster.

Carter passed me the plate of bacon. I managed to corral a few slices before passing it on to Steptoe.

Steptoe cleaned the platter. "Best cook another rasher," he said.

"I'm on it." My mother waved her tongs. "What exactly are we hearing about the Broadstones?"

Carter leaned an elbow on the breakfast table. Without revealing that he belonged to a Society of wizards and breaking secret protocols, he smoothly remarked, "The official mourning period for Mortimer is over, and there seems to be some jockeying for clan positions. Hiram is a logical, if young, successor. However, there is a matter that his stepmother, Germanigold, is still off-the-grid, and she may be applying pressure or whoever is holding her might. Not to mention other clans, the Sylvans, the Watergates, and the Stonebreakers among others, might be eager to step forward and take a place in the republic."

"Do we even know they have a republic?"

"We do." Carter put his plate up for seconds on French toast, deftly sliding a portion onto my plate before filling his. He pointed at my plate. "Eat."

I wasn't sure I could, what with dancing prisms and comets bouncing about. They made me a tad dizzy and their fizzles got buzzier and buzzier . . .

Brian frowned suddenly and leaned forward, slapping a hand onto my forehead. "Concentrate, Tessa! You're about to pass out."

"I . . . am?" I was already sitting; the kitchen did a little swing around me, and I shut my eyes. Instantly, my mom was there, I could feel her hands on my shoulders, and the room steadied.

"Eat."

I opened my eyes and shoved down three forkfuls of French toast, one after another, that someone had thoughtfully already buttered and laced with syrup. They tasted great and sweet. By the time I'd cleaned my plate, I felt revived.

Brian stared at me, frowning. Or trying to, a faint but earnest little line between his eyebrows. "Control it."

Steptoe dropped his paper napkin on the floor. He leaned forward to get it, his mouth somewhere near my knee, and whispered, "It should take orders." He gave me a wink as he straightened. It took a moment for me to remember that he'd borrowed a book out of the professor's library (the only room to have survived the fire, sort of) and read it. Did he still have the small treatise on the maelstrom stone? That, I couldn't remember.

I tightened my jaw and looked down sternly at my hand as I put it on the tabletop. "Stop it." I used the voice of doom, as most of us refer to parental commands that absolutely, positively *Mean It*.

The rainbows and stars sputtered out and then completely disappeared. The stone had grown warm in my hand and stayed that way as I gripped my fingers over it.

"Well done," said Brian approvingly as Carter gave me a salute with his fork—not a good idea because he flung a slice of bacon off it, which Steptoe promptly snagged in midair and chomped down with a grin.

My mother moved back to the stove where the second batch of bacon got laid out on a paper towel to dry a bit, and waved her pancake turner at us. "All done with the French toast?"

I shot a look at our three guests, squinting my eyes a bit, trying to remind them that we had a budget, and not a big one. They all demurred that another piece of bacon or so and they'd all be happily filled. She smiled in answer. I looked down at that piece of marble occupying my palm, with its ivory base and caramel, brown, obsidian, and gold flecks all swirled into it. It's a beautiful stone even when it's raising havoc. In a way, it was a shame to have to hide it with a glove.

I raised my gaze to find Carter watching. His off-center cleft adds character to his looks. "So I have to ask," he began almost apologetically, which I found funny because he's a policeman and he has to question a lot of people every day. It's what he does. "Do you remember what you were dreaming, what might have set that off? Trying to work a spell or something?"

I disagreed a little as I pretended to think backward. My dreams come on like a blockbuster movie, but I have no intention of revealing them. Not until I knew what Malender meant by magic's price and the end of the world. "Nothing that I can tell you."

Steptoe pushed himself back from the table and cleared his dishes. "Mrs. Andrews, wonderful hospitality and g'day till we meet again." He tipped his hat and left as I thanked him for the flowers and gloves.

"Steptoe has his moments," Brian admitted. "I'll load the dishwasher."

She stepped away from her counter with a smile and let him do his work after a lifted eyebrow at me, which I twitched back at her. Neither of us knew if it was the professor being polite or if his replacement was finally catching onto the current culture.

Carter cleared the table and, after licking a spot of syrup off his thumb, said, "I've got to report in. Light duty today, but there's always a job to do."

"Society meeting later?" Brian asked diffidently, but I knew the professor was inside listening like a hawk. Or whatever, ready to pounce on the answer.

"Tonight. Want to come with?" Carter's offer stayed equally casual, but I knew better. The Society would love a chance to jump down the professor's throat, but he would have none of it, confirmed by Brian's snort of an answer.

"I'm off, then." He gave Mom a light hug and waved to me. "You might get a present later in the day," he offered as he walked out the front door.

"Ooooh." I looked to my maternal unit. "Any idea what?"

"Even if I knew, I wouldn't tell."

"Damn. I mean, drat." I stood up. "I need to clean my room up. I lost one of my sneakers, and I know it's in there somewhere."

"Thank goodness for small crises."

I grinned as I passed her and headed for the stairs. Some time today, I would head down to the new cellar/basement so my ghostly father could offer birthday wishes, if he even remembered what day it might be. Visits were difficult as he did not always have the strength to materialize, and I simmered with the guilt that I hadn't sprung him from his interdimensional trap yet.

And I already felt guilty enough for having lied to Carter. Had he caught it? If he had, he hadn't shown it. Still, I didn't like coming up with alternative facts, especially not that one.

Because the last of the nightmare struck me quite clearly, with Malender standing next to me, all his unearthly handsomeness and immortal youth, piercing jade eyes and air of divine danger. He'd said to me, after telling me that was the way the world ended, "Tessa, dear Tessa. It's come to this, and you can't stop it no matter what you try."

Of course, I had to try. Then and now. And forever, if that's what it comes down to. Because he'd also said to me, "Would you rather have Magic or Hope?"

And I'd answered, "Hope. Always hope."

CHAPTER THREE

BAD TO THE BONE

I COULDN'T QUANTIFY what Malender showed me. The battlefield had started as a place that you would want to see in your dreams to refresh your sleeping self, you know? And then he is there after the monsters, saving me, and the sky is full of shapes, darting out of nowhere to coalesce in this immense darkling cloud—bugs and birds, of all sizes, coming together. Because I know him, I know what he's capable of, I'm already crying and waving my arms and pleading with them to fly away before he seizes their tiny souls and life forces. It doesn't work, and their dead bodies rain from the sky even as new recruits fly up to take their place in the formation. All this in the seconds before I plummet back to reality as I jolt awake.

So I have no idea what he has planned or what my unconscious has dreamed he might do. I propped myself up against the closet door in my bedroom and felt tears wetting my face as I sorted through the memories I wouldn't tell Carter Phillips. It's not enough to have a wizard or two on your side, and a lesser, if friendly, demon in Simon Steptoe. Or even a bickering clan of Iron Dwarves pledged to friendship. Not my mortal teammates no matter how athletic or loyal. Not enough against something like Malender. I don't know what he is other than ancient or why he tolerates my walking the earth when he could have squished me once or twice already, but there you are. Maybe, like a cat, he likes to play a little first. Not that I think cats are cruel, no, but they are curious and they do like to be clever with their paws. What Malender is, no one has told me, but they're all—wizards and demons—afraid of him. He's ancient and powerful, and he has an agenda that none of us know. Yet.

The professor might suspect, if he were in his right mind or—come to it—body, but he doesn't have all his faculties and won't until we can get his ritual together and perform it, and I am frankly not looking forward to the fire gig. We almost came to it a few months ago, but then I realized that one of the relics we'd retrieved had been corrupted by an associate of Malender's and likely to set things very, very wrong. I interrupted the ritual right as he was about to light the pyre. Brian grudgingly forgave me, admitting the ring in consideration might have made a virtual slave out of him through the greater demon it had been designed to summon. I had the feeling I still wasn't off the hook, though. I couldn't blame him. We'd been through a lot gathering his scattered artifacts and spells, and the stuff that had been easy enough for him to remember had already been brought in. Now he spent long hours in the ruins of his old house, sifting through water-damaged volumes and hoping he could remember more—something, anything, significant.

He made his research trips nocturnal, but the charred ruins of his home would eventually be demolished, and we needed to find a place that could hold the remnants of his books safely. We'd agreed our old house couldn't do it because of the danger, and Aunt April who rented to us would have emphatically agreed. She was only a little older than the house, or maybe I had that backward, but they were both octogenarians and needed to be handled delicately. If anything besieged us to get at the professor's remnant library, there would be hell to pay.

Not to mention that Aunt April had a marked gambling problem and was trying to stay clean, but little upsets drove her back to the casinos with regularity. No one wanted to be responsible for giving her an excuse.

I sighed and kicked at the bed skirt hanging from my bed. No sign of the missing sneaker. I roamed around my room, looking in corners and under objects to no avail. "Come out, come out, wherever you are, missing sneaker. I need you!"

A rustling noise answered me. I inched about, tracking the sound down to the rose bouquet given to me by Steptoe. One of the half-opened buds turned to face me.

Oh-kay. That wasn't freaky at all. I looked at its sunset-colored petals. "I don't suppose you know where my shoe is."

The bloom angled toward my closet and bowed down. "Uh-huh. No fingers, so you can't point. But you're looking at it?" Two more blooms turned about face to join it.

My closet door stood half open, even though I'd been leaning on it before. I craned my head about to look behind it. There rested my navy-and-gray sneaker, looking quite contrite. "Gotcha!"

I picked it up and waved it at the bouquet. "Thank you."

And then I promptly moved the flowers to the niche in the hallway where they couldn't do a peeping tom on any of my activities unless I was sneaking downstairs. Brian came wandering along at about the same time, savoring a last strip of bacon in his fingers. He stopped to consider the bouquet. "I think those are tell-tales. They spy. I'd be careful of them if I were you."

Suspicion confirmed.

I returned to my room, cleaned it, and changed the sheets on my bed because, sometimes, it just feels terrific to do something normal and mundane for a change. Never mind that I had to deactivate three lingering rainbows and one shooting star that had hidden themselves under the covers.

Because it was my birthday, my frenemy Evelyn came by and kidnapped me for a movie date with her. I like Evelyn, mostly, although her dad is aiming to be a noteworthy politician on the local scene, and her mother is one of those intense and rail-thin ladies that make me itch. The type of woman who sees if you fidget slightly over anything, and frowns. And then, you didn't feel at all squirmy, but all of a sudden, it just crops up everywhere until you feel like you're going to die unless you scratch away madly absolutely everywhere. I'm sure she means well. Evelyn didn't turn out all bad even with that influence: a tall, very pale blonde with a fetish for nice clothes and shoes. She stuck by me and my mom when most of my high school treated us like we were ax murderers when my father disappeared. Because it was my birthday, she even paid for my dinner and movie, but then I found the catch.

Or rather, she did. He was waiting for us in front of the movie theater. Dean Highman, in all his scruffy bad-boyness, his eyes bright with anticipation as he saw us walk up. His jeans were torn artfully at the knees, his leather jacket vintage and faded, and his knowing grin universal with bad boys.

"Oh," said Evelyn, as if surprised, and squeezed my arm. "You don't mind if he joins us?"

What could I say? "Actually . . ."

"I knew you wouldn't!" And she bridged between the two of us, her cheeks blushing, as she escorted us inside.

Conventional wisdom says, if you go to a horror movie with a friend, you go to make snide remarks and laugh at the markedly awful special effects. If you go with a boyfriend, you go to cower and hide in the safety of his arm, regardless of how bad the movie is. I pretty much sat alone and yawned while Dean comforted Evelyn and I tried not to think what kind of horror movie Malender might make. That would have scared the snot out of anyone.

We grabbed some trendy cupcakes after, and I left the two of them still squealing about the bloody end of the movie, which would surely lead to a sequel of some kind if the box office went high enough, and went home.

Dark by then, the streetlights did a little wavering dance as I walked, uncertain if they were going to stay on or black out altogether.

When the usual laws of my world look shaky, it's a warning.

I shoved my hands into my pockets, uncertain about the scenario.

Then a bright light flared from the lamppost in front of me, and a shadow jumped into existence where there had been none, a fox prancing on its hind legs, wagging three tails behind it.

That stopped me in my tracks. There is no mistaking a magical Japanese Kitsune if you've ever seen one, and I had. Before. Under trying and unfortunate circumstances. The fox goddess should be a magical being for good, but the one I'd had intimate contact with had been anything but.

"No. Way." I threw up my shield hand to let the maelstrom stone stand between me and the shadow. I didn't know what it could do—especially since it was still covered by the glove—other than attract those into power who wanted to take it off me, and yet it seemed to repel them at the same time, as if it scared them.

The lamppost swayed a bit, back and forth, and then the shadow bled away, sucking into the maelstrom stone as if inhaled or swallowed down until every dark drop of it disappeared.

"Oh, come on! Joanna, are you there?" I checked the immediate surroundings. Smart and determined and ambitious as she had been, I felt fairly certain she was done for after her battle with Malender. On the other hand, knowing what little I know of supernatural stuff, I still had the distinct impression that death didn't always mean one and done. Look at Gandalf. Kitsunes did not seem to be in the evil rank of beings, but Joanna had subverted the Japanese spirit. She'd followed in her father's power-mad footsteps, and both of them had planned to take over Malender's rule. That had definitely crossed the good intention line and things hadn't gone well. They'd almost taken me and Evelyn with them, but my friends showed up to help, and a reluctant ally of Malender's had changed alliances a second time . . . poor Remy . . . and things corrected themselves nicely. Except for the Malender-could-have-and-should-have-squished-me-and-didn't quandary, and I wondered from time to time if he kept score and thought I owed him anything, because I didn't want to be in his debt. Ever.

Searching for Joanna, her lithe frame in the shadows that still remained, I started cautiously home again, waiting for lampposts to spit her form out again. Hopefully, without her usually present samurai sword. She hadn't worn that to classes, but that's how I remember her best: Japanese features going sharp with the planes of a fox's face as she transformed into the Kitsune/fox self, her skilled hands gripped about the hilt of a very sharp katana as she did.

The sidewalk tripped me. I took a stuttering step and managed to right myself before face-planting, and as humans will do, I looked back to see what had caught me. The sidewalk looked innocently back at me. So I examined the toe of my shoe, bending down to get a good look. Maybe I had peeled back the sole somehow.

That's why the sword blade missed me.

I felt the icy slice through air over me and heard the whoosh in my ears, so I dove all the way to the ground and rolled to the side, stripping off my glove and putting my left hand palm outward to activate the maelstrom, only to see emptiness. Listening for footsteps, inhalations of breath, anything that might reveal where my attacker loomed, I moved onto the lawn and shrubbery bordering the sidewalk.

Nothing. Not a sound. Not a cricket or cicada or anything else that chirps in the early evening. It was too quiet, absolutely still. Even birds muttering their last calls before putting their heads under their wings to sleep made no noise. I put my head up to survey.

Another lamppost met my gaze. I narrowed my eyes at it, fairly certain it hadn't been at that spot before.

"Spit her out. I'm onto you."

Even as I spoke, the stone in my hand warmed a bit, and I could see a haze emanating from it, strictly defensive. I worried for a moment that the sword might slice at me again, cutting my limb off at the wrist, just to get at the stone. Never mind that the stone will only work for the receiver if voluntarily given, more info courtesy of Steptoe a few weeks back—what proper villain knows all the rules? Even takes the time to read them? After all, rule-breaking is part of their forte.

"Joanna. Show yourself and come after me face-to-face if you've the guts to do it." Not that I wanted her angry with me, but providing motivation seemed necessary, even to a vengeful ghost. If she was a ghost. Did foxes have nine lives like cats do? If so, I could be in real trouble here.

The lamppost seemed to waver or maybe it was my eyes watering. Something in the shrubbery seemed to be seriously jacking up my sinuses. A sneeze built up behind my eyes, one of those sneezes that could rattle windows. I sniffled once or twice to try and hold it. Getting to my feet, palm still held up, I moved in a slow circle. Still no sight of whatever menaced me, but even though I wasn't getting eerie feelings up and down my spine and whatever spidey senses I might have seemed to be failing me big time, the stone let me know I wasn't worried about nothing. It sensed and reacted to a threat. I did a little dance to try and shake off the various twigs, leaves, and pollen that dusted me and drove my nose crazy. Anybody watching would have thought me crazed.

To add to the effect, I began backing down the sidewalk, keeping the lamppost in focus. I'd gotten close to my neighborhood, and even farther south was the block where the professor's charred ruins stood, so I knew the territory. Which dogs would bark and which ones wouldn't. Which windows would have curtains twitch to the side as curious people took note of unusual disturbances. Even which doors would open warmly to me if I needed refuge because my charity meals run had taken place up and down these blocks. Not that I wanted to barge in on anyone, especially not if a samurai swordswoman came charging on my heels determined to commit mayhem. Shadows stretched and yawned about me as the sky darkened more and more and the streetlights gleamed brighter.

Not to mention that additional, now obviously not

belonging and somewhat quaintly designed, lamppost that edged after me.

Magic folk desire the maelstrom stone for a number of qualities, most of which I'm unaware of and cannot trigger. I've not a magic bone in me. Just a rock. For the briefest of moments, I truly wished that this was not the way of things and I could point a finger, yell "Avaunt!" like the professor, and have things react spectacularly. Of course, weak as he is, Brian drops like a log every time he does it, but he still gets the job done before he goes unconscious. It takes a lot of effort.

I decided I was so over my stalker. I began to circle it. "I never thought you'd be tiresome, Joanna, but you are. So have at it, so I can go home because my mother is holding some birthday cake for me and I'm hungry. Try your worst. You won't accomplish it, and I'm going to make you go back to wherever you came from with your three tails between your legs."

The lamppost seemed to draw itself higher and straighter.

"That's right," I muttered in what I hoped was my tough voice. "I'm waiting."

It split open with a hiss and a seven-foot-tall shadow jumped out, katana in hand.

"Now y'all are cooking with gas." I rotated my hand and remembered what Simon had whispered to me at breakfast. It takes orders. "Shield!" and the maelstrom filled the space between it and my other hand with visible armor, making me feel like Captain America and Wonder Woman wrapped into one. I met her attack.

I've been practicing, albeit with a garbage can lid. I mean, I'm ready to use anything I can get a hold of in my defense. I can use a shield edge well, and I don't lose control of this new emanation. I smacked Joanna with it even as she raised her katana for a third wicked slice, having already blocked the second one, and I drove her back as she gave off a fox's yelp. She hopped back a step before doing a twisting leap in the air that was sheer kung fu poetry—and she did it without wires.

I could see her face in the gloom of her manifestation, her brows tight in concentration, her lips thin, her dark hair drawn back in a ponytail, and she looked not a day older than when Malender had vanquished her. She would forever be twenty, I realized, while I would grow older and older and someday slower.

I intended to make an impression. I charged forward with my shield, to meet her when she landed, and took a leg off just above the kneecap with a swipe. It didn't feel like I hit a shade, and it sounded like the ripe thunk of maimed flesh but without the blood as a spray of charcoal ash hit the air. She let out a sound of pure anguish and while I hesitated, feeling bad, she pivoted on the leg she had left, and whipped her katana around. I braced myself and blocked the sword's edge, but it knocked me to my rump.

She must have expected me to react as I had earlier, by rolling out of the way, but I kicked back onto my feet and caught her off-balance as she prepared to dispatch a target that wasn't there. She'd already grown a near transparent, shadowy leg back.

I wasn't there, cutting my shield through the air, its leading edge between her head and shoulders, hitting home. Her head rolled.

Three tails twitched at the rear of the shadow, and then Joanna disappeared.

The lamppost swallowed her up as it had before. Then it, too, faded from view.

I didn't drop my hand though I did manage to take three deep breaths. Not like that wasn't too weird for words. Holding the shield close to my chest, I took a sideways step and then noticed the sound hadn't yet returned to the evening. Nothing had resumed being normal.

Tilting my head, I said, "All right then. Bring it on."

Invited, he stepped into a bright arc of natural, real, streetlight illumination and it haloed about him, emphasizing his unearthly looks and his pretty decently built body. He did not carry that vicious-looking, oily miasma of a cloud surrounding him, but shadows hid him and I didn't know whether that was good or bad. Malender smiled, crinkles at the corners of bright blue eyes. "Happy Birthday. You're doing well."

"I've got salt on me." I never went anywhere without one of those mini shakers in a spare pocket.

He raised an eyebrow. "I'm sure you do. I hope you didn't mind my little . . . test . . . to see how you are faring."

"What's a little attack between friends?" I tightened my left hand on my shield and pushed my right hand into my pocket, seeking the salt shaker. He either hadn't really been in my dream or decided not to mention it. I decided not to, either.

He laughed. "I am pleased to be called friend."

"Just a saying."

"My apologies for Joanna slipping her leash, as it were."

"I'm sure it was an accident."

"Of course." Malender took a small step backward, his eyes squinting a bit as if looking at something too bright. "I will see you again?"

"Not if I see you first."

Laughing, he slipped away, disappearing into wings of darkness that folded about him.

My stone let the shield slip away, but my nerves stayed tight until I turned the corner for home, our weathered old house with its porch light on and—glory be—a nearly equally vintage car sitting in the drive.

With a bright red bow on its hood.

CHAPTER FOUR

BEEP! BEEP!

I PLOWED TO an astonished stop. Our porch light shone thinly as the old bulb toiled valiantly though it was due to burn out any day now, and I wondered if I looked at a mirage. True, mirages were generally found in the desert and involved people dying without water and seeing things, but I could have been imagining this red, shiny, ancient Corolla . . . couldn't I? After all, I'd seen Joanna pop in and out of a lamppost not two blocks from here.

And it had a suspicious resemblance to a car I'd noticed about and around Professor Brandard's house before it had been hauled away and disappeared when he'd been a regular customer on my meals route. Before the burning of nearly everything else he owned. So, if the past owner had been the professor, it stood to reason the current owner would likely be Brian. He didn't have a license yet; in fact, he had little in the way of authentic ID except a passport we'd found in a safe deposit box that had assumed his picture the moment he held it and opened it up. I was highly dubious a magical passport would give him the skill or right to drive. Still, here sat the car. I was even more dubious the impound yard would have sent it with a saucy bow crowning the hood. I scarcely dared to breathe as I crossed the yard to our driveway and stood next to the vehicle, which had been waxed and polished within a micron of its little metallic hide.

Cupping my hands around my disbelieving eyes, I leaned to the window and caught the odometer: 32,306 miles. Practically brand new. I stepped back and kicked a tire. Lots of tread on those babies, and plump with air. I would have popped the hood, too, but that entered the realm of the ridiculous as I had no idea what to do with a car engine beyond adding water and oil to the appropriate places. Oh, and I have a good idea where the battery sits, too. Beyond that, though . . .

The porch light flickered as the front door clanged open and multiple figures ran onto the porch, crying, "Surprise!" They surrounded me, and we jumped up and down in a group hug, with Mom saying, "Isn't it great?! It's yours, all yours. I am paying half the insurance, the other half is your job, and Carter got it from the impound, and Brian paid the fees, and everyone contributed to getting it tuned up and polished . . . do you like it?"

"What's not to like!" I disentangled myself and hugged the car a moment. "But, Brian, are you sure?"

"It couldn't be in worthier hands." He smiled. "You'll be needing it."

That held an ominous echo and put a slight chill in my warm and fuzzy happiness. I pushed it away. "Thank you, guys! This is awesome."

Carter stood back, not indulging in the hug, but allowing himself a crooked grin, and he tossed me the keys. I immediately opened the door and slid in. The smell of new leather hit me. How did they manage that when the professor had been smoking either his pipe or cigar in here for the better part of ten years? Obviously, magic had its good points. If we couldn't get him restored, maybe we could go into the car detailing business, getting rid of tobacco smoke, and baby sour spit up, and dog accidents.

I popped the trunk and hopped out to see it.

Nice and clean, except for a small canvas duffel. I opened the flaps to see a baker's dozen of Steptoe's famous flash-bangs waiting inside. Ammo! "Fully equipped, too!"

"A distinct advantage," Brian noted, "unless you get

rear-ended, and they go off. In that case, well, that's why you have insurance."

My face hurt from smiling so wide. "Wow." I closed the trunk (carefully) and went to retrieve my bow. "This is getting hung on my bedroom wall."

Mom told me, "We've cake and ice cream waiting."

"Where's Steptoe?"

"He delivered his duffel and said he had a spot of business to take care of."

"Oh. Well, he's already wished me a happy birthday. We'll save him cake."

Mom's smile wavered. "I had trouble convincing him of our good intentions. He wanted to take a piece with him, to be sure."

"That cad!" I laughed at Mom's expression and locked an arm with her as we walked back to the house. "What's insurance going to run?"

"Not much, actually. We can handle it."

"That's good." I hugged her. "This is absolutely the best. You know how much I wanted a car."

"I know. I wanted to get you one sooner, but two cars in the family seemed expensive. The university has been nagging me to get my paper finished. The dean has been dangling a full-time job in front of me, but only if I get my PhD finished, and until then, well, money is tight." Her expression thinned out, and I got the impression she hid her worry from me.

I knew she wasn't nearly as close to that goal as she needed to be. "You can go to that writing boot camp they hold."

"I can, and should, I know. It's the time, honey. I just never seem to have enough time."

"Well, now I can drive myself places and do the grocery shopping and banking."

"You have college to think about."

"Right. I'm sure I said 'go to classes' in there somewhere."

She hugged my shoulders. "We'll see," she said, sighing a bit as we entered the kitchen and then she stopped cold. "He didn't!"

The beautiful cake, white-frosted with chocolate underneath, stood on its platter, with a large piece clearly missing.

"It looks like he did," Carter said as he followed us in.

"This is absolutely—I told him to trust me—we wouldn't forget him—and look what he does!" She marched to the counter in outrage and pulled out her cake knife, gripping it with white knuckles as if she would hack up Simon Steptoe if he dared make an appearance. Mom inhaled deeply. "We'll just have to make do with candles on what's left."

It sat as a fairly ginormous cake, as cakes went, and I suspected we'd all have more cake than we could eat, even with the trespass. She put the cake knife down firmly and reached in a drawer for a box of candles.

As soon as she brought them out, the vision of the cake wavered. Then, with a poof! the missing piece reappeared with a "JK" iced in thin chocolate drizzle as the cake stood restored. She began to laugh. "That scoundrel." She began to plop twenty candles into place.

So we blew out candles and sang silly songs (Brian knew a few from ages past about getting older that made all of us blush) and ate cake and ice cream till no one could move from their chairs and still have enough for the now infamous Steptoe and maybe a surprise visitor or two.

I stood up reluctantly.

Mom tilted her head at me. "Where are you going, hon?"

"Downstairs. In case Dad is around."

"Want company?"

"Not tonight."

She said softly, "Tell him I love him."

"Yes, ma'am, I will." Because I knew she still did, despite all that he'd put us through.

The stairs had, at one time, been hidden and incredibly creaky when discovered. Illumination came from the massive hole in the floor when Hiram fell through to a forgotten cellar. Old shelves had held mysterious jars floating with viscous liquid and objects too vague to be identified. Then there had been the cupboard in the corner where I'd unearthed the maelstrom stone.

Now, of course, it looked bright and glossy, like a modern day ice cream parlor, and the only shadows left were stark silhouettes in the corners. It still smelled a little musty, though. Aunt April had never told us about this old cellar and I wondered what she'd think if she knew it had been renovated. I didn't think she'd mind. When we moved on, which we would someday, it would only make the old place more valuable.

Unless, of course, we'd laid a new floor over more family secrets. That might perturb Aunt April.

I sat down on the bottom step. "Hey, Dad. I know time is a little distorted down here, but it's my birthday, so I came down to say hi and thank you." I folded my hands, absently stroking the new glove over my left hand. Good thing Steptoe had given me two pairs; I'd almost lost the one glove tonight already.

A slight chill swept over the stairs. I couldn't see anything, but I could hear a thin and reedy voice in my ear. "How old?"

"Twenty. Can you believe it?"

The breezy tone whistled slightly. "I've missed so much."

"Mom says for me to remind you that she loves you."

"And I love the two of you."

"I haven't found the way to bring you back yet, but I'm working on it." I looked around the basement. "Maybe I could bring his books and stuff here after all. The professor needs to clear them out."

"Dangerous." The cold gust touched the side of my neck.

"You're probably right on that one. We could rent a storage unit, but I haven't got the money, especially now that I have to pay insurance—oh! They got me a car!"

"Nice." The word, long and drawn out and weary sounding. I could tell that my father had just about reached the limit of his communication tonight. I hadn't talked to him in weeks, so I wondered for a moment what he'd been doing that drained him so much.

"Go rest, Dad. I'll be back after a while."

"Goooooo."

And then the chill evaporated, and I stood up and made my way back to the kitchen where the dishwasher hummed with a load of dessert plates and forks and dinner plates and everything had been tidied. An heirloom cake lid, slightly dinged and silvery, rested over the leftovers. Guests had gone and family was treading lightly in the rooms upstairs and I could hear the wood flooring creak softly as they did. I went to join them.

The next morning I fell out of bed again.

I huffed a long breath, irritated with what seemed to be a habit, but no rainbows and stars greeted me. Instead, the whole house moaned and groaned and shook as if gripped by an earthquake. The windows shuddered and the eaves rasped. Quake? Really? I felt and listened for a moment as my home moved uneasily, and then I grinned. I threw clothes on, washed my face, and wrestled my hair into a ponytail before thundering downstairs while the house settled, its joints still scraping uneasily. As I'd passed the tell-tales sitting in their vase in their niche, I could see their flower faces were all aimed downstairs, letting me know the center of the house's troubles. But I already had a fairly good idea.

"Hiram!"

Mortimer's somewhat taller, just a tad thinner, and much handsomer son turned in the foyer and smiled up at me as I leaped down the last of the stair steps. "Well met, and I am sorry I missed your birthday." The house settled as he steadied his Iron Dwarf mass.

"That's all right. We still have cake."

"Cake sounds desirable this morning. Might you have a stout cup of tea to go with?"

"If we don't, I'll make you one."

I squeezed past Mom to the stove where the kettle made little puffs of steam, getting ready to whistle, as she'd already put it on to heat. "I'll get that."

She took a plate, fork, and napkin to Hiram as he sat down carefully. The chair complained a little as he made certain to center his bulk upon it. I made a note to watch yard sales and see if we could get him his own stout perch. The Iron Dwarf swung a twine-wrapped package onto the tabletop.

"For you, lass. The clan wanted this for you."

I made sure the tea held nearly the color of coffee before I set his cup and the sugar bowl in front of him. He didn't take milk in it like Simon did, and he smiled as he reached for his drink. "Go on. Open it, then."

The package nearly opened itself as I unknotted the colored twine and pulled the heavy paper open. What lay inside took my breath away. "What . . . are these . . . they look . . ."

"Bracers," he said. "Wrist cuffs, aye. Won't turn bullets away . . . well, they might, but I wouldn't depend on that. They will turn away most blades and keep you safe. If you put them on a windowsill in the sun, those yellow gems there will soak up the light and glow in the dark for a while, at need."

I looked at them, nearly speechless. "What? Really? Get out of here!"

"Really."

I picked up the bracers and examined their beauty. "Not gold." They couldn't be. Bronze, maybe.

"Not exactly," Hiram smiled around a forkful of chocolate cake.

I tried one on and flexed my arm about. "I look like a freaking superhero!"

"Aye, that's the thought of it. Not for the looks but for the use of them. They're armor, and they're meant to help keep you safe, and to aid you in the art of war."

My mother sat down too quickly. "War?"

"Well, not war, Missus Andrews, forbid that, but encounters. Of a magical and other sort. At need, as it were." Hiram quickly devoured two more forkfuls as if to shut himself up as much as enjoy the dessert. His cheeks puffed out.

I put on the other bracer and stretched my arms out to test their weight. Definitely could feel their presence, but it wasn't like carrying a bowling ball in each hand,

and I considered them thoughtfully. "Thank you, and thank everyone for them. They have an old look to them."

"They have a history, that's for certain, but not one I can relate here and now as I'm not much of a scholar." He'd swallowed hastily before answering and now reached for his napkin. "I'll ask around and get the stories for you."

More than one story? "Cool."

Hiram beamed. "I am pleased you like them. It would be advisable to wear them as often as you can. They need to learn their wearer; that much I know."

"Interesting."

"Necessary," he countered, before looking away from my mother's hard glance and busying himself with his tea.

"Did you see my new car in the drive?"

"I did. And it's yours now?"

"Yes. Want to come sit in it with me, soon as you've finished?"

He caught my look. "Ah. I'd be honored. Taking me for a drive?"

"Not yet. I've work to do around here and finish up for class, but soon. I just want to sit in it."

Hiram inclined his head gracefully and made short work of his treat, dusted his hands after he surrendered his plate and thanked my mom, and followed me out the door.

It still felt strange to open the car up with keys that belonged to me. I sat in the driver's seat and watched Hiram make his way to the passenger side. He slid in and settled comfortably, and the old car, bless its steel hide, settled a little on its shocks and struts but didn't complain too much. He fit well.

"I thought so."

His auburn eyebrow rose. "What?"

"The front seats are mismatched. Yours, if you may note, is bigger, wider, and deeper. This used to be the professor's car and it looks as if he customized it a bit so he could drive your father around."

"Ah." Hiram took stock. "Yes, so it would appear. It

fits me well, although cars are not my favorite mode of transportation."

"Horse and buggy?"

"Of course not! SUV." Hiram winked at me. "I'm glad you brought me out here. We have to talk, and I needed a bit of privacy."

"Me, too."

He waved a hand at me. "Ladies first."

I took a deep breath. "There's never been a good time to ask this, but Mortimer once mentioned he knew my father . . . and possibly what had happened to him. He did some work in my world that included debt collection, and both my aunt and my dad had gambling problems."

Hiram inclined his head. "He could very well have known both of your family."

"Would he have had any idea how my dad got sucked into the ghost zone?"

Hiram sat very still for a long moment. I could see the muscles along his jaw tense and release, tense and release, before he finally answered. "That I cannot tell you."

"Don't know or can't disclose?"

"They are not the same thing."

"I know that," I told him seriously. "I don't know if you're bound by any kind of oath or pledge or rule, but I've got to find out what happened so I can undo it."

"You have a dilemma, then, because I can't help you. I will, however, do what I can to help you find out what you need to know."

Disappointed, I sat back in the driver's seat. Hiram spread his hands apologetically. "It's the best I can do, Tessa, for now. My sources, however, are widespread. There's that, at least."

It didn't feel like enough, but I thanked him anyway. We sat in silence for a moment until he noted the low mileage and a few other features, praising my birthday surprise.

Finally, I asked, "What did you need?"

He looked at the floor boards. "A deed, if you will.

A quest, of sorts. And it's not as a payback for your bracers. Those are a present, freely given. They are yours whether you tell me yay or nay."

A quest? "Tell me."

"You've heard, no doubt, that we are in a bit of turmoil."

"Your clans?"

He nodded.

"It's been mentioned. How serious is it?"

"Not very, yet, but it could become fatal at a moment's notice."

I could hear the dismay in his voice, and I patted his knee. "Fighting?"

"All-out war." He looked up. "We can't have that. There are few enough as 'tis, and with Malender returned, we need to be united and focused."

"Is he the Great Evil?"

"We don't know. Many think such. He is powerful, and he does cause a great deal of consternation. Truth to tell, Tessa, he is not remembered all that clearly, for there aren't many records of him and his purposes. We are long-lived and keep good journals, but he existed in the misty first years of our civilization before he disappeared."

I thought of my dream of him, and all the souls he took for his own power, and a cold shiver ran through me. Hiram didn't notice, though, wrapped in his own worries. I'd promised to listen to him, so I pressed. "So, what kind of quest is it?"

"Something has been taken, something very valuable and important—not just to my clan, but to all magic peoples."

This felt like pulling out fingernails. Or teeth. "Okay, but why me and what is it?" And my palms began itching before he answered.

"It is best that you search for it because you have no personal stake in it. And yet you're nearly one of us, so you can understand how important it is. Also, the last possessor was female and it will return mostly easily to a female hand."

"And it is . . ."

"The Eye of Nimora."

I recoiled. "You want me to find an eyeball? Ewwww."

"No, no, no. I mean, yes, I want you to find it, but it's not an eyeball. It's a ruby. Large as a goose egg. It did have its own 24-karat setting, but it could have been removed."

"A ruby? Like in emeralds, sapphires, and rubies?"

"Aye."

I tried to imagine how much a ruby as big as a goose egg would be worth, and failed. I'd google that later. "What are the odds it's still in one piece? That someone wouldn't have cut it down into several priceless gems? A jewel thief likely would have done that first thing to make it easier to fence."

"If they knew what they had, they wouldn't dare."

"Hiram, this is the real world here. And who is Nimora and why don't you ask her what happened to it?"

"She's been gone for a millennium, but her memory remains as the gem."

"Mystical, okay. Who had it last and why would anyone want it?"

"I'll answer the last question first: the Eye sees truth. I don't have to explain that one to you; the value is clear, and we Iron Dwarves have used it to help rule fairly for centuries. Among all our peoples, uncomplicated truth is even more rare than egg-sized rubies. It keeps our interactions fair and just. Some tribes are incapable of simple honesty. The elves alone are—"

"There are elves?"

"Aye. They don't lie, but neither do they tell the precise truth. They're a very slippery people to deal with, and then there are those who live and die by magic whether human or immortal. To them, truth is a blade that slices both ways. Vampires are a law unto themselves—"

"Vampires?"

"Very few and rare but generally extremely powerful despite their rarity."

"I can imagine."

"You're better off if you don't." Hiram shifted and the whole car moved with him, rocking up and down and side to side. "We Broadstones carry the justice system in our hands, and the Eye of Nimora is crucial. We have a trial coming up for which the Eye is desperately needed."

"Okay, then." I felt a little dizzy. "Who had it last?"

"It was a bride price from Mortimer to Goldie."

"Morty gave it to your stepmother?" My voice climbed. I had experience with harpies, interactions that I hadn't liked at the time and vowed never to repeat. It had been a harpy who'd killed Morty, and I knew that Hiram knew that well.

"Yes."

"Whatever for?"

"To prove his love to her, and his trust in her."

"And she absconded with the thing when she disappeared."

"We're not sure. It might have gone first or slightly thereafter or with. That's part of what we need to find out. And we need to find Germanigold to know. And then we need to find the Eye of Nimora before any more tribes learn it's gone, and our whole system breaks down. When she was by my father's side, the system stayed whole and workable despite the fact she was a harpy, with no one the wiser that she actually held the gem. She gave up most of her life for him. The Eye of Nimora saw for us as it's meant to do, and we had no problems even though it was Goldie's."

"But she was technically one of you."

"Exactly."

I thought of the day I'd come to deliver one of the professor's meals and I'd overheard Mortimer talking with him. I hadn't know who or what he was then as I eavesdropped from the kitchen, only that his rich and profoundly bass tones filled the professor's small house and he'd wanted the wizard to find his wife, who'd been taken. And the professor had refused to interfere. I'd wondered why then and now.

I also wondered if the professor in Brian's head would

remember—or tell me. I thought some more before saying, "So this is just a little quest."

Hiram looked at me. "Why, no. This is deadly important."

"I was being facetious."

"Oh."

I crossed my wrists in the air over the dashboard, wondering if my new bracers and I were up to the task at hand. My mother would be sternly against it, and Carter would probably have conniption fits, but I thought I could guilt Brian into backing me. After all, if he'd gone after Goldie when first asked, a great deal of what followed might not have happened. Despite all the manipulations I began to plan, I still felt like a superhero. I heard Hiram swallow tightly. I thought of his friendship and his father's friendship and made a corporate decision.

"I hate to ask, but we're going to need some operating funds."

"I am prepared to offer you—" and he named a princely sum that would cover my mother's salary for the next two years, if we were frugal, and both of us knew how to squeeze a dollar until the ink ran out of it. She could go on sabbatical. She could finally finish her dissertation and get a tenure track job with more money, benefits, and stability. She could publish. I could give her one of her dreams. I didn't for an instant feel sorry for the Iron Dwarf clan because I knew they had very deep pockets and they could well afford a dozen of me doing the job.

"So you'll . . ."

"Do it? Of course." I patted the steering wheel. "Looks like I got a car in the nick of time!"

CHAPTER FIVE

SHAKESPEAREAN THINGS

"HE ASKED YOU and not me, so I fail to see how your question is relevant."

I braced my elbows on the kitchen table and stared, not at Brian but at the long, tall, and cold glass of sweet tea in front of me. As a girl of the South, I am prepared to swear that iced sweet tea is our mascot. I drew my initials in the dewy condensation coating it. "That last book you made me read can be boiled down to 'every single thing is relative.'"

"That's what you got out of it?"

"Pretty much."

"Good. That was, indeed, the lesson. It will apply, later on, to sympathetic magic if you wish to study it—"

"Which means that my question is. Relevant," I added.

"Ah. Well, then, my answer is no. I don't care to get involved."

"Professor, your mouth is writing checks that Brian's going to have to cash some day."

"Are you suggesting I'm leaving my future self with karma that must be paid?"

"Actually, he's your present self. Go look in the mirror. And yes, Brian is going to have to deal."

"He'll be equipped."

I shook my head. "Not if you burn all his friendship bridges first. And besides, you're just sulky because Hiram didn't ask you first."

"I am not sulking."

"And you don't even know what he asked me to do. I should think you'd be curious." I took a satisfying gulp, eying him over the glass. He reached for reading glasses he no longer wore and settled for brushing hair out of his eyes and glaring at his hand.

He stared at the ceiling for a few minutes before looking back at me. "I do admit to being curious."

"Listening won't commit you. But you might know something that I need to know."

"That is true. My experience in life far exceeds yours."

"By several centuries."

He pursed his lips. "At least. All right. Talk away."

Now it seemed to be my turn to squirm a bit. The professor guessed he'd had a listener to at least part of a private conversation those long months ago, but we'd never discussed it. I tapped a finger on the table. "I think it starts with Mortimer and Goldie."

"But you're not certain."

"No. I mean, there's a lot of history with people like Morty that I didn't even know existed. But Goldie was taken—"

"She disappeared."

"Morty told you she was abducted."

"He may not have wanted to believe the truth." The professor watched me steadily with Brian's guileless face, but the eyes held a shrewd glint to them. Narrowed, even, as I admitted I'd eavesdropped on him, at least the once. His mouth tightened.

"I'll give you that one. I may find out more when I investigate—"

"You're not getting involved with the harpies!" His professorial voice rose.

"It may be part of the job."

"They killed Mortimer."

"Yeah, and as far as I saw, he dealt a pretty mortal blow in return. I don't want to wade into that mess, but it seems to be part of the problem. An object is missing.

They may have it or know where it went, so I need to know how to contact them."

"I don't think I'll be telling you that. Maybe you'll have better luck with Carter or Steptoe." His tone of voice suggested that I wouldn't, not if he got to them first and warned them off. I etched another initial into the side of my glass.

"I know at least one of them will not only want to give me information but will come along with me. I'm certain Steptoe will be as interested in the Eye of Nimora as Hiram is, and the Iron Dwarves want it back. That's where the harpies come in."

The professor sat back in his chair, stunned. "It's missing?"

"Yup. Evidently, that's the cause of the trouble in the clans at the moment. It was the dowry for Germanigold, and she either took it with her when she was kidnapped or told someone where to find it or . . . well, that's what I have to find out."

"Bride price? Oh, Morty. My dear, foolish, lovestruck old friend." The professor hung his head down, in mourning.

"Not so foolish. The marriage allied two tribes together and rather successfully for . . . how long were they married?"

"Three short decades."

I mentally tried to age Hiram in my mind as the son from Mortimer's first marriage, and couldn't and gave up. Everyone involved in magic seemed to have a phenomenal lifeline. You would have thought the opposite would be true. "From my point of view, that's not shabby."

"Pifff." He straightened up. "You're positive it's the Eye of Nimora?"

"Egg-sized. Ruby red. Missing. Truth seeing or something like that. Needed for trials." I ticked them off on my fingers.

"That would be it. Although its usage is not widely known and you should not be disseminating that information." He got up abruptly and went to the fridge to pour his own glass of tea. "He has no business involving you in tracking it down."

"All I need to know is how to find the harpies."

"You're going to the nest?"

"If that's where I'll find them, then, yes, that's where I'm going."

He added some sugar to a tea that was already sweet enough that the spoon could stand by itself straight up in the glass, and made a bit of noise stirring it in. "I have to go with you."

"I doubt they'll let you in. They seem to have this Amazon thing going on."

"True. I'll stay in the car, but I'll be prepared to help if you need it."

"How far are you going with me?"

He gulped down half his drink. "All the way, if necessary. I wouldn't mind seeing the Eye of Nimora for myself before we, ah, return it. If we find it and survive."

"That's the spirit!" I beamed at him and finished the last sip of my drink just as the side door clattered and Mom yelled, "I'm home!"

We both went suspiciously quiet as she entered the house.

Realizing even the hobbits had a fellowship considerably larger than two participants, I mulled over my options about other arms I could twist to join my endeavor. Simon would jump at it, but I had to consider that his self-interest would probably come first, although he'd been helpful in the past. I thought him trustworthy, but the professor and Carter disagreed with me, and I couldn't exactly blame them. Minions of Steptoe had frightened and pressured the professor into making a hasty escape via fire and put him into this predicament in the first place. Neither party had confessed to me the reasons for the unfortunate misunderstanding, but I'd find out, sooner or later. As Shakespeare used to say, the Truth Will Out. Or maybe I'd just find the Eye of

Nimora and take a look for myself. A few minutes with a relic like that might possibly straighten out several puzzles in my current life.

Carter would be the most difficult because he held a full-time job, but then, I kept nearly full-time student hours, so I wouldn't be out at all times of the day or night anyway. His hours seemed a bit more problematic. He didn't work eight to five, or even night shift, anymore but had gone into an undercover operation he wouldn't discuss. It left him often with batches of time and just as frequently with no time at all. He wouldn't be much happier than the professor about what I'd promised to do, but he'd understand when I explained the opportunity it would give my mother to earn the price Hiram had quoted for the job. Wouldn't he? He'd been on our case from the beginning when we finally reported Dad missing, and I knew he'd kept watch on me when he could. He'd been little more than a rookie then, fresh out of the police academy and home from the Middle East, and now he was an officer, making his way up the ranks very quickly. I'd like to think it's because our city recognizes a good man when they see one, but I could be very naïve about politics. The Society had placed him as a liaison, of sorts, so he held a position created specifically just for him without anyone in the police being aware of the politics. He knew we needed the money. He'd understand the lure of the job.

I'd appeal to that goodness when I saw him, hoping it would be soon. I admit to crushing on him, despite our age difference, but he'd never led me to believe he'd noticed it or would take advantage of it. In another year or so, that gap wouldn't be so noticeable and I'd throw myself at him and hope he would catch me. Evelyn was of the opinion that I shouldn't wait, and she might be right, but I'd had enough of guys who would offer me a pity date and then ask for benefits that were never implied or offered! I would bide my time with Carter.

So if I could depend on Carter and Steptoe, and I didn't even have to ask Simon because he generally went where the rest of us did, that made four of us for the investigation, three with considerable magic weight. Add in my maelstrom shield and awesome bracers, and we should be able to get the job done. Probably.

"Are you kidding me?" Carter asked, one hand full of carry-out coffee cup and the other with a card in an envelope, as I met him in the front yard, the sun slanting low over the roofs. "You're putting together a team? A team for what?"

"It's my job to ask the questions. Are you in or are you out?"

"With this group? I don't join until I know what's going on. So." He fell in step with me. "What's going on?"

"I got a job offer, and it's a really good one, and if I complete it successfully, I'll earn enough money that Mom can take time off and finish her dissertation, so it's important and I need your help."

"What kind of job takes a team, especially one like ours?"

"It's a recovery. For Hiram."

"For—oh, no. You are not going after the Eye of Nimora."

"You know it's missing?"

"I do. In fact, it was the subject of the Society's meeting last night. What surprises me is that you know." He sipped. "I take that back. Obviously, Hiram told you. What pisses me off is that he asked you to recover it."

"Oh, not recover. Just find."

"Usually retrieval is involved in a case like this."

I looked up at him speculatively. "That sounds as if it might make the whole job thing a bit more difficult."

"Try impossible, and over my dead body."

"But I'm counting on you! I've already got the professor and Steptoe."

"Then they're both in it for themselves, not you. Forgive me, Tessa, but neither of those two men is the charitable sort. I know you think well of them, but they have a background that stretches for centuries, and not an altruistic one. The professor probably thinks he can apply it to his current restoration problem, and Steptoe undoubtedly thinks he can make a profit on it after he uses it to blackmail a few select associates."

"Cynic."

"Realist. Which you need to develop if you're going to dabble in my world." He swirled his coffee before taking another hit.

"I don't dabble, and I can't help it if the stone dragged me in."

"Oh, you were in up to your neck before that thing implanted itself in your hand. Look at the company you keep!"

I looked up at him through my eyelashes. "Does that mean you're not going to help? If you're the only one I can trust?"

"Any cake left?"

"Maybe a piece or two."

"Good. I haven't had anything but coffee all day and I need to think straight. Oh, and your birthday present is in my car." He handed me the envelope and his car keys.

"Oooh! What is it?"

"It's something which may or may not become yours."

I blinked. "Then how is it my birthday present?"

"Well, it's conditional. Go introduce yourself and we'll see how you get along."

"How I . . ." I shut up and marched myself to his car. There, sitting on the front seat, was a creamy yellow pup. Labrador, if I knew my dogs, and he wasn't a small puppy, but a medium one, maybe already about four months old.

"A dog! You got me a dog!"

"Not necessarily."

"You talked to Mom about it?"

"I did, and she said yes, provided you take care of it."

The universal answer for all mothers. Our last dog had disappeared with my father, and I missed him dreadfully, but we'd made a pact not to get another dog, circumstances as they were. However, if she'd said "yes" to Carter, all bets were off.

I opened the car door and the pup swung around to

look me steadily in the eyes. Not many dogs do that for long, as if they're born to look away, but this guy didn't.

"So what's the story?"

"He's a police recruit who didn't work out."

"Awwww. Sniffer no good?"

"No, he's great at scents. It's more his attitude."

The dog and I watched each other. "Attitude? He's not a coward, is he? Doesn't look like he could be."

"Well, he didn't get good grades in aggression, but that's not exactly it, either."

Those big Labrador eyes gazed soulfully into mine as if waiting for me to say exactly the right thing. "He looks perfect to me."

The dog sniffed once or twice, scenting me. For a Lab, though, he seemed terribly restrained. They were bounders, until trained and disciplined. Enthusiastic and playful. Energetic. This guy sat on the car seat like he was hatching eggs.

"What's his name?"

"Scout. If the two of you don't work out, I have a rescue that will take him until he finds a situation." Carter stood behind me, waiting.

"Why wouldn't we work out?"

"Long story, we don't know why he hasn't bonded with anyone. It's as though he's waiting for something or someone to come along, and then he'll give his heart. Doesn't matter what sex; we've had all sorts of trainers and officers work with him, and he's stayed aloof."

"Oh, that can't be right. Look at his eyes. Who's a good dog? You, that's who. You don't have to wonder if you'll ever find out. You're a good boy, Scout."

The dog whined slightly and moved from the passenger seat to the driver seat. I put my hand on his head and rubbed one of his ear flaps. Scout wriggled and put his nose into my maelstrom hand. He gave a chuff as if he smelled something not quite right.

"I know," I told him. "That's a little off, but I think it's temporary. At least I hope it is, and the rest of me is pretty normal."

He surged forward suddenly, butting his head into

my chest and leaning into me, making small puppy noises as if very happy to have been found after having been left alone all day.

"And there it is," Carter said.

And so it was.

CHAPTER SIX

PEE MAIL

SCOUT LEAPED OUT of the car when I gave him the okay signal, hit the ground running, and didn't stop for ten minutes, overcome with true puppy joy. I grinned and Carter laughed to watch the tornado circling the yard, sailing over the back fence, soaring in return, and then racing up and down the city block itself. When he came back and sat down on my feet—not next to them, but on them—his tongue lolled out, and he gave a big, doggy grin up at me. I had to reach down to massage the top of his head.

"He'll grow up to you," Carter said.

"And the department said okay?"

"Absolutely. I wouldn't have brought him for an introduction otherwise. It wouldn't have been fair to anyone." Carter bent over and massaged an ear as well, while Scout nuzzled him. As he wiped his hand off on his pants, he gestured toward the house. "Might as well take him in."

Scout led the way, his sleek tail curved like a scimitar and waving happily, as he trotted in front of us. Carter told me that he had a Labrador-sized crate in the back seat of his car, along with sleeping pad, a forty-pound bag of kibble in the trunk, and stainless-steel dishes. Also a harness and leash and collar. I hadn't noticed any of that, my eyes full of puppy.

I realized that Scout wore nothing on him now. "Why no collar?"

A pause before Carter answered, "He's not too fond of them."

Interesting.

The door opened before we got there, and my mother appeared to Scout's delight as he jumped up and down in front of her and then sat, squirming a bit, as if presenting himself for approval.

"You brought him."

"And he seems to fit right in."

"Good. It'll be nice to have a dog about again." She bent over to scratch that sweet spot on his chest that dog lovers know about, and he moaned a little in appreciation before she stepped out of the doorway to let him inside. "I have long lunch hours this semester, so I can come home and let him run about. No need to crate him all day."

"Nice to know. I'll go get his things."

Mom pointed at me. "Go open the garage door. For now, we'll store them in there. I think there will be room in the mudroom for his crate, but we may have to rearrange a few piles of boots and junk first."

I came back in to find Scout sitting warily at the threshold of the kitchen, eying Steptoe and Brian, with them trading a hard look right back at him.

I patted Scout on the back of the head. "That's Simon Steptoe," and I pointed. "Chaotic neutral. He used to be chaotic evil, but he's trying to redeem himself these last few centuries. Sitting there is Brian Brandard, lawful chaotic. He's two men in one, but they're both pretty straight arrow. You already know Carter. He's lawful good, and I'm the daughter, and Mary there is daughter's mom and professor and doctoral student. The only one not here is Hiram, an Iron Dwarf, and since his clan is made up of judges, I'd say he's probably lawful neutral. That should do it? No, wait. My dad is a ghost who lives in the basement, but we hope that's temporary. I have no idea how to classify him."

Steptoe sat back, looking as though he was biting the inside of his cheek, and Brian blustered about in his chair, his own face flushed, while Carter made a noise into his hand that sounded like a choked laugh.

"Am I right?" I looked about the room.

Steptoe cleared his throat. "More right than not." He put his hand out. "Here, laddie, give me a sniff so you know me."

Ears back a little, Scout approached him, snuffling up his hand to his elbowed sleeve and back again. The pup then rolled an eye at Brian and shoved a nose into his kneecap, before heading to the stove and lying down in front of it, tail thumping tentatively.

Mom handed out the last piece of cake to Carter, and we all sat about and told her a little bit about Hiram's request. She seemed to sense she wasn't getting the full version. She checked her watch before telling me, "I've got papers to grade and my syllabus to update, so why don't you tell me what you're not telling me. Let's unpack this little situation first before I have to disappear. I want the rest of the details, the stuff you're avoiding telling me."

I tried not to wince. She has these steely blue eyes that see through me. "It could be dangerous. I'm not sure, which is why I'm taking a posse with me." Her eyes reminded me of something, nagging at the back of my brain, but I couldn't pin it down, so I shoved it aside and watched my mother's expression.

"Mmmhmm."

I held my left hand up. "But I've got the stone now, and I'm pretty good with a shield, and these guys can take care of themselves. Most of the time."

"So you're tracking down something that's lost for Hiram. What exactly did he lose? What is the Eye of Nimora?"

"A ruby the size of a goose egg."

Her tone went up despite her projected calm. "What?"

"So, we have the supernatural element as well as everyday human greed possibly involved." I shrugged a little.

"There's something supernatural about the red egg?"

"Supposedly."

"No supposing about it," Steptoe objected. "The thing's a bloody oracle. Ow!" and he stopped talking long enough to glare at Brian, who'd evidently kicked him under the table. He folded his hands on the tabletop, stuck his lips together, and looked unhappy. His bowler hat sat a little askew.

Mom hadn't needed the hint anyway. "Annnd . . . others will be after it, too."

"Could be. It's not widely known that the thing is missing, though. We have a head start, so that should help."

She assessed each of us, one at a time. "Of course, all of you know that if anything happens to Tessa, I will do more than hold you personally responsible. I will pull out all your teeth and then make you even sorrier you still exist. There is no force in heaven or earth greater than a protective and angry mother." She looked like she meant it.

"No, no, no," everyone said. "We'll take care of Tessa," or words to that effect, putting their hands up in the air. When things calmed down to a dull roar, we discussed our game plan a bit, which was to say, we really didn't have one except that I intended to find out the beginning of the trail.

Also, we talked about moving the professor's library from the remains of his burned-out home to a more secure location. Steptoe offered one but got turned down before he even finished his sentence. Carter mentioned vaults that the Society held for such emergencies and also got rejected, although he did get to end what he said before everyone else said: "No!" I proposed the basement and got another end-all glare from my mother. Brian merely shook his head to that, saying, "Not unless I have no other choice."

"I do have, my dears, a low impact alarm system set up 'ere in the 'ouse. If that makes a difference."

"Low impact?"

"I think," Brian said, "he means the tell-tales."

"You spotted them, did you?" Simon gave a half grin.

"It would have been hard not to. Interactive roses are most uncommon."

"True, but I thought it might 'elp us all keep a watchful eye on our Tessa."

I sat up straighter in my chair. "Hey!"

Brian shrugged. "Not to mention that said alarm is in extreme fatigue already, trying to keep up with the pup's activities."

How the professor knew that without having gone upstairs to take a look, I had no idea, but I got this mental image of my vase of "roses" wilting everywhere.

Steptoe sniffed. "Not my fault. Someone has to take the creature up and introduce it."

"Or remove the tell-tales."

"I like them," I put in edgewise.

"See?" Steptoe looked around the table in triumph.

I knotted my eyebrows at him. "Although you could have warned me what they were and where to set them up in the house."

"I thought you'd figure them out soonest, ducks. You've always been a quick study."

I couldn't think of a rejoinder and decided just to shut my mouth. I did as suggested, taking Scout upstairs and letting the tell-tales and dog sniff at each other before coming back to the kitchen to a group that looked a little guilty as if they'd been talking behind my back.

The group disbanded shortly after that, and my mom disappeared into her office. Carter stood and dusted his hands off.

"Need some help with the mudroom?"

"Sure."

Carter followed me out. We propped open the back door, and I opened up the garage as he went to unload his car. He toted the forty-pound bag of kibble over his shoulder and let it drop in the corner. I didn't recognize the brand. I tapped the colorful paper. "Where'd this come from?"

"This stuff is locally made by a small-time guy. It's his own formula. No grains but rice, lots of meats, and fresh veggies, mixed up and baked into a kibble. It's a little more expensive but worth it to keep the dog healthier, and I think it helps with the cancer."

My heart did a panicky thing. "He's got cancer? How could you not tell me that before?"

"No, no. But we don't want him getting it, and that's a tough new thing with some breeds now. So when you need a refill, give me a call and I'll bring in another bag for you."

My eyes speed read the ingredients. "Bison I can see, but alligator?"

"Surprise, huh? The dogs seem to like it. I rarely see dishes that aren't licked clean."

"I wonder if it tastes like chicken."

"We should find out someday but not by tasting his kibble. In the meantime, you need to get a heavy-duty bin with lockable lid to store this in, or the varmints will eat it all. They'll find a way to get in the garage if they can. This stuff is like candy to them."

"Good for them, though."

"Yeah, but I'm not paying to feed raccoons and possums." Carter threw me a smile as he ushered me out of the garage and closed the massive door after us. The old wooden building protested and yowled a bit at the joints as he did, and he knocked on one of the support beams. He checked the side door and made sure it fit well into its frame and could be locked if needed. "These old places."

"I don't know which is older—the house or Aunt April."

"She's that old?"

"Can't tell under that immaculate hair, can you? And she doesn't walk bent over or use a cane, but I can outrun her, so she does show her age a little."

That made Carter snort. We stood in the threshold of the mudroom. "This place is a mess."

"Don't hold back. We Andrews can take it."

"How did you let it get to this? I thought this area was all cleaned out when Hiram fell through."

"We don't come in here. We've always just used the side or front doors, even though this is closer to the driveway. So, sad to say, we can't take credit, and when Hiram and the crew just redid the middle, this stuff all piled up next to the walls."

"Okay, then. When's the trash collection?"

"Wednesday and yes, this is the week of the month when they get the big stuff if we leave it on the curb."

"First things first. This wheelbarrow goes outside, in the corner of the yard. In the garage if we still have room after cleaning up all this stuff, but definitely in the yard."

I peered. "There's a wheelbarrow under that?"

He pointed at a substantial metal brace holding a half-inflated tire. "I'm betting there is."

I hefted an armful of rags from the pile. A mouse darted out and raced off through the door before I could even jump. Carter raised an eyebrow.

"We're going to have to work on your reactions. If that was a shadow assassin, you'd have been skewered."

"B-but–"

He shook his head. "No excuses."

I dropped the rags on the floor. "What if there's a nest in there?"

"As the professor might say, this would be a good time to learn nesting behavior, especially since you intend to go after harpies. Theirs is definitely an avian culture."

"I'm getting some plastic trash bags." And I stomped off. Lightning retorts, if not reflexes!

He had the wheelbarrow–yes, it was one, if old and dented and rusty–halfway out the door when I came back with a box of lawn bags. I kicked the assorted rags around a bit but no more streaking squeakers emerged as I bagged the trash up. I threw the filled bag out and onto the driveway. I emptied the shelves of another sagging bookcase of some sort while Carter busied himself taking each load out to our trash.

As to the bookcase–this had been a good piece of woodworking once, but now the bookcase wood had grayed and faded so that I couldn't even tell what variety of tree the planks had come from. I spit on a finger and tried to rub the dirt off with no success and ended up wiping my hand on my jeans. The open shelves on the top ran halfway down, and little post office box drawers finished the bottom. Maybe this had come from an old corner of an even more ancient library? I opened each drawer up cautiously, worried the rest of the mice might be up to playing Pop Goes the Weasel on me. I couldn't see the back of the furniture, but there might have been a hole or two back there. Twine filled one drawer. Some brittle two- and three-cent postage stamps another. Most were empty.

And then I came to the one that didn't want to open. I checked it over closely. No lock. Just stuck. I tugged on it. Really stuck.

I ran a fingernail around the rim to see if I could tell why it had gotten wedged in. No luck, but the wood didn't seem to have swollen excessively around this one drawer. Nor was it crooked where the others had been straight. It simply didn't want to open.

I pulled my glove off. Set the stone to the front of the door and said, "I will you to open."

Not that anything like that has ever worked for me before.

Glove or no glove, filth covered my hands. I batted them against my thighs and tried to pull the drawer open again. Nada.

"Look," I told the recalcitrant furniture. "I really want to see what's in the drawer. No matter what it is. Well, not if it's an angry mouse."

No yielding.

Carter came in, and I handed him some more trash bags quickly, putting my body between him and the now-empty cabinet. For some strange reason, I didn't want him to see the drawer I'd been working on. Mind you, the last stubborn bit of furniture I'd fooled with had held the maelstrom stone. I ought to know better.

"Almost done." Carter nodded at me.

I looked around the mudroom. To my surprise, we were. A pile of old boots and galoshes leaned up against one wall. "I'll go through those later and give what we can to the thrift shop. None of those are ours."

"Sounds good." He hefted the bags and returned to

deposit them outside. Alone again, I put my hand on the cabinet. "Last chance." And, left hand firmly on the brass pull, I gave it a jerk that would have won a tug-of-war contest.

The drawer came out so fast it dumped me on my butt and scattered the contents on my chest. Sputtering, I grabbed for paper so old it had yellowed inside its brown leather cover. The book, no; it had so few pages it qualified more as a pamphlet, composed in readable but faded ink. It reminded me of the Declaration of Independence on display at the Library of Congress. Brilliant, defiant, old, and priceless . . . and, sadly, fading away. I scrubbed at the cover. Fubject of Darke Artes.

Wonderful. Someone's book of curses? It not only looked prehistoric but smelled like it, too: musty and mildewed. Old enough that capital S's looked like funky F's? That might date it back several hundred years. And what was it with old books of magic? Brian had his ancient journal and Steptoe had those few scraps written about my stone. I rubbed my thumb over the cover, and a chill slithered its way down my spine.

Carter's shoes scraped on the driveway as he approached, and I shoved the thing inside my shirt. Friend or not, there were times when the Society came first, and I had no intention of his confiscating the thing until I'd gotten a better look at it. After all, I had found it.

Scout put his nose out to see what we were doing. "Not dinnertime." He wagged his tail anyway and I got a chance to really get a good look at him. Undoubtedly Labrador retriever, but something told me he wasn't purebred. A little slimmer in build, a little sleeker in the head, a little lighter on his feet. I folded up my legs and sat down next to him, waiting for Carter to return.

His long and lanky form filled the doorway, hiding the midafternoon light, his shadow spilling over the two of us.

"So let's talk about the dog."

He leaned a shoulder against the door. "You don't have to keep him if you don't want him."

I threw my arm around Scout's neck. "I want him. But I think you know more than you're saying." Pup and I rocked together for a moment, and Carter gave us a look that was almost longing.

He sat down on the floor, too. Noticed the empty postal drawer resting there and stowed it back in the cabinet, sliding it into place. It made a little click as it did. I took note of that—darn thing had been locked in, after all. I gave Scout another hug to hide my interest.

"He's not all Lab."

"I guessed that. From his reactions and his looks."

Carter shifted. "Not sure what he is. He and two littermates were left in a basket outside the police kennels. The other two just seem to be dogs. But this one," and he reached out to rub under Scout's cream-colored chin, "this one has always been different."

"Very intelligent."

"Yup. Older than his age, in some ways. And, he gets this look in his eyes, as though he not only understands what I'm saying but anticipates the consequences. A friend in the Society took a look at him about a month ago and gave his opinion on his heritage."

What is it about magic users that they can't seem to give straight answers? I bit back my impatience.

"And?"

"Maybe some elven hound in him."

"Seriously? How do we know for sure?" Not only were there elves somewhere, but now they had dogs?

"We don't, unless the person who bestowed him on us tells us, although it should be apparent in about twenty years, regardless."

"Twenty years?"

"He won't age like other dogs."

Scout put his cold, wet nose to my neck and I grinned, thinking that having him around a long time was actually kind of reassuring to hear. "Any side effects?"

"He seemed to agree with your assessment of your friends, so I'll grant him a certain awareness of magic and its affiliations. That, along with his excellent sense of smell and natural speed and agility, will give the pair of you an advantage."

"Hear that?" I told Scout. "We're going to make a great team." He licked my chin in agreement.

"Eventually. Both of you have a bit of growing to do."

"Gawd, I hope not. I'm already taller than most of the boys in my classes."

Carter pulled a face, and I couldn't tell if he was trying not to laugh or wince. "There could be one problem, though."

"Which is?"

"He might not be the gift we think he is. He might have been stolen from a litter and discarded hastily, to hide him."

"What litter? Someone might, sooner or later, come back to get him?"

He inclined his head. "Exactly."

"I won't give him up easily."

"No, and since he's obviously bonded to you, he won't go easily either."

I examined his face for a moment, looking at the planes of it: an ordinary yet well-defined face, not breathtakingly handsome like Malender though undeniably good to look at. Yet there was an expression hidden in his warm brown eyes. If I had to interpret it, I would say it was . . . concern. What had him worried?

"What's wrong?"

His breath hitched slightly. "What makes you think anything is wrong?"

"I just feel it."

He shrugged. "I can't be around predictably for the next few weeks. Maybe longer."

"Aha. You can't keep tabs on me."

"Something like that." He reached out and wiped a smudge off my chin with the ball of his thumb.

"And where are you going to be?"

"I've an undercover assignment that is going to be very unpredictable."

Now my breath caught slightly. "Dangerous?"

"It could be. I won't bring that home to you, though, so don't worry."

"I'll worry if I want to," I answered him. "What is it, anyway?"

"I can't tell you that."

"Ordinary stuff for the police or magical stuff for the Society?"

"Not that either." The corner of his right eye twitched ever so slightly.

My jaw dropped. "Both? Do they know? Are you like a special paranormal investigator now?"

Carter sighed.

"You don't want to tell me."

"I can't tell you."

I leaned forward. "Is my not knowing going to protect me better or worse?"

He blinked. "All right," he said. "I'll give you this. If, at any time, you hear of or run into a Nicolo or a Nico, walk away. As quickly as you can."

He meant it. Every word of it, and he wasn't going to give me any more detail than he already had.

"All right," I agreed.

A long pause stretched into what could have become an awkward silence, but Carter filled it by leaning very close, tilting his face slightly, and my heart did a quick flutter because I realized he was going to kiss me.

And he did, his lips warm and possessive on mine, his hands coming up to my shoulders to brace me as I closed my eyes and gave into the warm feelings rushing through my body like a sea tide. My knees would have given out if we'd been standing. I kissed him back when he started to pull away slightly, and the moment lingered on. I could feel a heat in him, not the heat of a living being, but a fire, banked and waiting, as though a sun resided deep within, and I thought of his magical power. Awe washed through me just before he pulled back.

He touched a finger to my mouth. "Was that all right?"

"That, Carter Phillips, was about damn time."

He laughed, stretched and got to his feet. “I work tomorrow, so any sleuthing for Hiram will have to wait until Tuesday afternoon. After practice? And stay out of trouble, all right?”

“Of course!” I rumpled up Scout between the shoulders. Who couldn’t stay out of trouble for a couple of days?

CHAPTER SEVEN

A SEA OF TROUBLES

"TIME TO MEET the neighborhood," I told Scout as I put his harness on him, noting that it came in an adjustable size, because this guy was not going to stay at his four-month-old size long. Especially not eating the way he did. His stainless-steel bowl reflected a licked-clean surface, as bright as any mirror, right back at me. The handsome blue-and-green-plaid harness stood out against his golden-cream hide, and he swiped his tongue across the back of my hand as I finished with the buckles.

"You're going to meet some of the nice people on my charity run. I don't deliver meals anymore. I passed that on, but I still visit a lot of my customers. They're older but fun. And, it's just after dinnertime, so they'll be serving dessert, maybe. Sometimes they have cookies."

Scout's ears perked up alertly.

"That's right, I said the word. Not saying it again." I snapped the leash into the harness and grabbed a windbreaker from its hook in the now clean and utilitarian mudroom. I hoped the cool breeze would chase the blush from my cheeks—Carter kissed me!—and I could keep my feet on the ground. I still felt a buzz about my lips, a pleasant, tingling feeling. Scout gave me a quizzical tilt of his head as if wondering the same thing. "Let's go."

He took off, pulling me with him. We compromised on a slow jog with frequent stops to check the pee-mail around the various trees and shrubs. Two blocks away, we came up to Mrs. Romero's house, a tidy little bungalow that always had a wreath celebrating one season or another on its door. She'd knitted me a sweater early in our relationship, a knitted commodity I had plans for at the annual Ugly Christmas Sweater party. She heard us clattering up the porch, Scout panting, and came out, wiping her hands on a dish towel.

"Tessa! How good to see you. It's nice having our regular back, but I do miss your visits! She drives and it seems like she whisks in and out so quickly I barely get to say hello. I just put a batch of cookies in the oven. Can you wait till they're done? Come on in." Without waiting, she retreated and went back into the house. Scout made as if to lunge after her. I pulled on the leash.

"Careful with the treats. She often leaves out or doubles ingredients."

He shook his head at me in disbelief.

"You'll see." We followed inside.

She sat in her little living room, smiling, the dimples in her cheeks flashing as did the ones in her petite hands. Her knees were dimpled, too. When I first met her, I'd wanted to trade my Aunt April, who is tall, lanky, and a little mean-spirited, for this porcelain doll of a grandmother. She had her own family, though, and I suspected they would do battle to keep her.

"So tell me about the pup."

"Just got him. This is Scout, mostly Labrador retriever—"

"Good dogs, they are. One of the most popular breeds in the States. Energetic, though. I bet he needs this walk. Look at that tail!"

"I thought I'd bring him over to get acquainted."

"I'm honored."

She held her hand out. He sniffed it, more than politely, although I suspected he was checking out the cookies. He rubbed a paw over his muzzle as he lay down at my feet. "Told you," I muttered quietly to him. He looked disappointed.

"I just thought I'd check on you and see how you're doing."

"Oh, fine, fine. The weather's turning now, and my

arthritis will be bothering me again soon, but what a relief to get out of the summer. Of course, in another month or two I'll be complaining about the cold!" She let out a cheerful laugh. "How's college?"

"Fine. It's too early to predict, but we're hoping the team makes finals."

"Splendid, but don't forget the scholastics. Thinking of driving the route again?"

"I don't think so, got a small car now and need to pay insurance and gas. I need a job that pays. You know how that goes. I miss everyone, though."

"And we miss you—" A rattling buzz went off, and she bounced to her feet. "Oh, the cookies! Sure you won't have one?"

Scout looked up at me with big brown eyes.

"One or two would be great, but only a couple. Got to stay in these jeans."

"Of course, dear." She came out of the kitchen with a little baggie full of warm goodies steaming inside. The pup's ears went up and down several times as if he was tasting the cookies by scent, and he probably was.

Scout gave a satisfied chuff as I hugged her good-bye and left. I pulled a cookie out, breaking it in two. "This way, we'll both only be half-poisoned. Last time, I swear, she put a whole salt lick into the batter."

He gobbled his down while I nibbled cautiously, and the sugar cookie tasted great. "Remind me to tell her this is a good recipe." Pleasantly surprised, we sauntered on down the street.

His tail cutting the air like a curved saber behind him as we jogged, we both enjoyed the cooling afternoon air. Mrs. Sherman, another delightful widow, occupied her rocking chair on the porch and waved happily at us. Her brilliantly red bouffant looked as perky as usual. "Come on up here and let me see that fine beast you have."

She leaned over as Scout bounded up next to her. "And who's a good dog? You are!" She smiled at me. "A wonderful looking pup. Yours or have you taken up dog walking?"

"Mine." I omitted the birthday present part, because I didn't want her to jump up and go rummage for something to give me. She had a spare room that she used for crafts and such, and wrapped presents in a rainbow of tissue papers amid boxes of scraps and half-finished projects. Last time I'd won the jackpot and gotten a nice bottle of lilac-scented toilet water, but I didn't want to press my luck.

I gave her a little hug. She looked fine, except for some tired bruises about her eyes. "Sleeping all right?"

"I'm at the age where any sleep is welcome." She patted her bouffant wig.

I smiled sadly down at her. She really hadn't been the same since I'd brought someone into her home who'd possessed her, even if only for a short while, and I didn't know how to take the last of the nightmares away. Brian and I had been working on it, though. Maybe another visit to the remnants of his library would offer up a spell book that could solve the problem. I hated leaving her unsettled and decided a distraction might help. "So what's the gossip?"

She watched as I took the top porch step. "I don't like to carry tales," Mrs. Sherman reminded me. She got around her aversion to gossip by averring that she told nothing less than the truth she'd witnessed herself.

We talked for a few more minutes until Scout nudged my sneaker. The smell of fresh cookies still hung about me as he nagged.

"Better go. It's getting late. I'll stop by again soon."

"You do that, honey. It's always a pleasure seeing you." The worried look in her eyes told me differently. I vowed to get the professor off his duff as soon as I got home. I couldn't let Mrs. Sherman continue to suffer because of something I accidentally brought into her life.

I fed Scout another treat as we headed down the block to the professor's ruins. Early evening slanted across the homes, sidewalks, and streets in blue-gray shadow, and I watched the streetlights as we walked, wondering if Joanna might make another appearance.

Asking about the occurrence now would only point out to the guys that I hadn't told them about the incident earlier, and upset all three for different reasons. I'd lost one father only to gain three father/older brother types in his place. I didn't want to encourage Carter to occupy that position as well. Concerned boyfriend should be his speed. I glanced down at Scout.

"Smell anything odd?"

He shook himself all over and dropped back a pace or two so his heavy tail could thump across my calf, which I guessed meant negative. I had no doubt, however, that he was as intelligent as Carter claimed. This was one pup I was going to have a lot of trouble staying a step ahead of. We'd slowed from a jog to a walk, which was fine with me, as my legs had begun feeling the burn. I have good legs, thanks to months of bicycling the charity meals route and running for the team, but I hadn't been terribly active for a few weeks now and could feel it.

Out of the dusky shadows, the great gaunt, charred bones of a building appeared. Months had not bleached away the smell of smoke and fire, despite summer rains and sun and wind. It came to the nose almost as fresh as it had that first, awful night when the professor had called me for help, gasping, "Fire." I angled toward the backyard. Daylight had fled completely, but I knew the place almost as well as I knew my home. Night didn't hide much from me.

Scout planted his butt on the walkway. I tugged on the leash. "Come on."

He tilted his head as he looked up at me but didn't move.

"It's safe. Almost. I'm just going to duck under the tape—" and did so, dragging him after me, the warning tape thin and nearly colorless and practically fragile looking as we went. Inside, the floor crackled under each step. I could understand why the fire department pressed for demolition even as red tape held it at bay. We went cautiously, sidling along until hitting the interior of the house where the professor's library and study had almost escaped damage.

Almost because it hadn't, not really, but the wards there kept it mostly intact, some roof and partial walls, with smoke and water destruction not nearly as bad as the rest of the house, almost as if this room were an egg and the rest of the nest had collapsed about it in protection. I took out my phone and tapped on the flashlight app. Its illumination swept the various bookshelves where edges had been nibbled at by flames, the barest of touches. Some of the books had sagged into moldy lumps from both fire hoses and rain, but a good number of them survived. Their titles, already nearly unreadable because of sheer age and difference in language, blurred as I attempted to make sense of them. Scout whined lightly before giving a sneeze and leaned in his harness. He wouldn't be happy until we left.

I stripped off my gloves. "I'm here because the professor and I have to right a wrong. He'll be back to claim all of you soon, but right now, I need to help Mrs. Sherman." How do you know if a pile of wrecked books is listening to you? You don't. I just hoped the professor hadn't left any death traps behind.

My beam of light flickered and made as if it, and my phone, might expire on the spot. I shook it. "Don't you dare."

It flared strongly, its light centering on a bookshelf just off the floor where only three items remained. I knelt to examine them. Their titles reflected back at me, all short and sweet: *Aftermath*, *Clean Sweep*, and *Remedies*. I plucked all of them up and straightened. My phone flickered a last time before the flashlight app went off. I couldn't get it to work again although the rest of the phone seemed fine. The omen seemed obvious.

"All righty, then. Thanks. I'll be back soon to rescue the rest of you."

Scout couldn't wait to pull me out of there. We came out the back of the house, across the remnants of a screened-in sun porch and rickety steps. In the depths of the backyard, the grass waved high as a sea. Scout plowed through it as he might two feet of snow, bounding up and down in the blades. The redwood arbor and arch beckoned at me, reminding me of late spring days when the professor himself and I used to sit while he ate his dinner and we discussed history and the city and other odds and ends. He'd had a lined face, wrinkled as much with laughter as wisdom, a thinning gray hairline, a bristly chestnut-and-gray mustache, and ear hairs that sprouted everywhere, and he'd lectured me at end from this patch. I'd no idea that the history we'd argued about, or at least a chunk of it, he'd experienced personally.

A little surprised no one had made off with his wooden patio furniture, I sat down. Across from me was the massive chair, more like a throne, which Brandard had procured for Mortimer's Iron Dwarf frame. Scout snuffed it all about with great interest.

"They say scents can last a really long time when they're embedded in a substance, so what you're getting is the essence of the Iron Dwarf Mortimer Broadstone. He was a great friend of mine and the professor's, and Hiram's father."

The ruined house groaned faintly and creaked, but it had nothing on the noises my house could, and did, make, so I ignored it. I rubbed the arm of my chair. "This is redwood. You won't see it much in Virginia because we use pine and other woods. Redwood comes from the west coast. It's a protected wood, so we don't build from it very often, but the professor says it has warding qualities, so he had this shipped in. It's like a guardian wood. Like, mmm, rowan from England and such. He can explain it better, so I'll have him do it when we get home. Like it? I can't smell it, but I see its beauty."

Scout wrinkled his nose. He turned his head, looking behind me, then back at the house, and his lips lifted away from his teeth as he began a low and warning growl. Though still a half-grown pup, he looked menacing.

Shit. I'd forgotten all about Joanna. I inched about

in my chair, the tiny hairs on the back of my neck prickling, wondering who had caught up with me.

"Not my friend," a hollow voice said softly as a blurry figure emerged out of the very ashes of the sun porch. "Not a true friend of Mortimer's."

I swung about completely. Not Joanna. Not anybody—yet. The apparition continued until disclosed in all its dimensions. I cleared my throat. "Maybe both were a little selfish, but I don't think I've ever seen better friends." I approached the sun porch cautiously, cloaked in night and soot as it was.

A half moon appeared just above the rooftops, throwing a little illumination across the backyard. It revealed a statuesque woman in leather corset and leather skirt, with battle weapons strapped about her waist. A gasp died in my throat.

A harpy. Her wings must be folded tightly behind her, so I couldn't catch the full glory of her plumage and coloring, but she looked down at me with a severe frown. I had half a second to wish I'd worn my bracers.

"Think you that you know my Mortimer better than I?"

"Your Mortimer—are you Germanigold?"

"Once upon a time, as you might say it."

I faced her. "Where have you been? And, no offense, you don't look like you're all here, as it is."

"I have been where I still am, held by enemies. If I were not imprisoned, you'd see me in all my winged glory but they've been taken from me, and illusion is all that's left."

And a drama queen, too. I put my hand down to stifle Scout's growling, as her hollow voice did not carry well enough for me to hear as clearly as I would like. His hackles stood up like a ridge under my fingertips. "Do you know we're looking for you?"

"Are you? I can't imagine why you haven't found me if you are. Perhaps you all need to exert a greater effort."

"Nobody but Mortimer seemed all that interested, frankly. Being a harpy and all."

Hard to tell in the moonlight, but she might have

paled. Her mouth twisted unhappily. "I do not think I deserved that."

"Nor would Hiram. He's asked me to find you."

That brightened her face just a touch. "Hiram? He thinks of me?"

"Yup."

"A good man. He had an excellent role model in his father. His mother as well, may she sleep in peace until the great day."

"If I may ask, what are you doing here?"

"Haunting Brandard's ruins? Trying to reach that worthless, irascible old man. I had no idea he'd been burned out."

"He's gone, too, although not quite the way of Morty."

"Dead?"

"Revived. But not successfully."

"By the gods. Tell me he's not a zombie."

"Oh, no. No, no. Nothing like that." The thought that Brian could have become a zombie made my legs go weak. Scout butted up behind my knees to bolster me. "Just incomplete."

"Then he'll be looking for all his goods. Mortimer told me once he'd scattered them, having mastered them, so that no one could steal his knowledge from him and misuse it."

I edged a little closer. She didn't look like a haunt, nothing transparent about her, and if Germanigold projected her form, she did a great job of it. "Did Morty share a lot with you?"

"We were husband and wife."

I smiled. "And he adored you."

Her eyes glistened. "Yes. Yes, he did, and I loved him back." She put her chin up as if blocking a weakness. "I came to extract vengeance for his death."

"Mmm. Awkward. I saw it . . . and couldn't stop it . . . but it was a harpy who stabbed him."

"In self-defense. The attack was reported to me."

"Then you were lied to. They attacked us in Central Park. Took Brian . . . the professor . . . off. There was a skirmish getting him back. The leader, I don't know her name, but she had steel-colored hair and magpie wings, stabbed Morty from behind. He pulled the sword out and got her in the gut when she jumped him again. It was swords and daggers everywhere as I pulled Brian out of there." I ground to a halt, my throat tight, my words thick as the sorrow flooded me and made it nearly impossible to tell her what had happened and my last sight of Mortimer. Of the look he'd thrown me. The victory he'd eked out for himself, after betraying us at the beginning. But he'd gotten Brian back, and the relics we'd come for, even if it cost him everything. I swallowed and couldn't get anything else out.

She reached out, and I felt the faintest touch on my shoulder. "There was a time," she said sadly, "when I could have known without a doubt if you told the truth. Now I have only my own senses, but they tell me you do." Her eyes narrowed. "Which means I have been lied to again, by someone else."

She stood close enough that I could see the wings folded tightly behind her, as softly golden as the sunrise, feathers gleaming through night's veil. But more than that, I imagined I saw the strong woman shining through as well.

"Mortimer's memory deserves the best," I said, voice still tight. "Who lied to you? Where are you being held?"

She made a sharp movement with her head. "A Society judge. It will be difficult to pry the truth from him, and very dangerous to face them. He must be a betrayer to all, but only you and I know it. His name is—"

A sharp clang rang out and with it, her form disappeared in mid-sentence. The air thundered about me, as the displacement slammed shut, and the burnt timbers of the professor's house trembled in her wake. I swayed back.

"Wow. That was an exit."

Scout made a rumble. He nosed forward, among the tall grasses, retrieved something, and brought it back to me.

A beautiful feather, gleaming like molten gold in the moonlight.

At least I had proof. Now all I had to do was decide how to investigate a magic Society who thought itself above human rules. And yell at myself for not asking her about the Eye when I'd had the chance.

CHAPTER EIGHT

A TISKET, A TASKET

SOME DAYS YOU think you make it through free and clear and others you get nailed right away. Nobody said anything until after the dinner dishes were done and the laundry folded, but when I started up the stairs to get ready for bed, the professor was waiting for me on the steps. He wasn't smoking, but he had a pipe in his hand that he kept turning over and over. Normally, I can tell when he's dominant just by the way Brian speaks. The pipe was just another one of his tells. The professor likes a pipeful now and then while Brian is a nonsmoker.

Brian, when he's home and in charge, is rather like a left coast surfer dude, easygoing and sometimes a little clueless about the big picture. He's not dumb or anything, just doesn't have a keen edge. The professor is much more well-spoken and grouchy and cynical and would never say "cool" or let things slide. In fact, Professor Brandard never lets anything slide if he's interested in it. Getting his attention when he doesn't want to give it, however, can be a completely different matter.

"You were trespassing again."

I stopped as he peered up at me before taking the stair step one down from his position. "I swear, how is it you know things?"

"For one, I can smell the smoke on you. It has a subtle reek that never seems to clear."

I sniffed my hands and shrugged. All I could smell

was dog as I'd just put Scout to bed in the mudroom. "Teach me, O wise one."

"Teach you? I ought to have Mary paddle you. I've told you the house is dangerous and you shouldn't go traipsing around in it alone."

"Just because the second story has collapsed onto the first story, and there's not much left except the study, I don't see the problem." I blinked at him.

"It has magic seeped into its very bones. I lived there a very long time and made sure of that. It was my shield and my comfort."

"And now it's your excuse."

He looked up sharply from the pipe in his fingers. "Beg pardon?"

"I have a duty to fix Mrs. Sherman and you tell me you might have something on it that will help, but you won't come with me to retrieve it. You tell me that it's not right to sift through the debris just yet. It's dangerous. It makes you melancholy. It's a reminder of your current situation." I ticked off the most popular excuses. Then I untucked my T-shirt and pulled the three slim books from my waistband, dropping them in his lap. "And it was the books you smelled, not me. I think."

"Nothing happened when you took them?"

"I explained you sent me because we needed certain information. Really weird, I had my flashlight app set on my phone so I could see, and these three lit up. Then the app refused to work, and I thought my whole phone had bricked."

He blinked. "Your phone morphed to brick? That's not one of the wards I had set up . . ."

"No, no, not like that. Just nothing worked right for a few minutes."

"I see."

I don't think he did, not really, but he'd obviously decided it wasn't important to the current topic. He tapped the books. "What are we fixing on Mrs. Sherman?"

"She's the one who got possessed, remember?"

"Oh, yes. Unfortunate."

"It's like PTSD, but she doesn't know why. She looks worried and has trouble sleeping. I can't leave her like that. She doesn't deserve it, just because she got caught in the middle."

"Right, right. We should do what we can. Well, there may well be something in here we can use. It's the ingredients that worry me, not the execution."

"Execution?"

"Method. No, many of my ingredients I had stowed in the root cellar and I know that is gone, burned away before that corner of the foundation caved in. I'll have to look for something simple and perhaps substitute a few herbs."

"I'll take Brian to the garden supply in Home Depot. Lots of herbs there. The university has an arboretum, too." I didn't like the idea of swapping out important elements. We might end up with inedible cookies or explosive spells.

"Do that. In the meantime, it appears I have some reading to catch up on." He stood and paused, one hand on the banister. "Anything else to tell me?"

I debated a split-second, but he caught me thinking.

"Out with it! What other mischief have you gotten into tonight?"

"First, not tonight but the other night, I saw something."

He gave me an exasperated, stone-cold expression.

"The streetlight just split into shadows that shouldn't have been there. Not to mention the lamppost shouldn't have been there either. Anyhow, I saw Joanna in her Kitsune form, three fox tails and all. She attacked me. Now, after what happened last spring, I thought she'd been gathered up and removed."

"Illusion?"

"Her katana seemed real. I think she'd have taken off my head. I know she tried."

"Hmmm. What did you do?"

"Brought up a shield. Solid. I actually held it in my hands, like the real thing, and I could use it like you taught me. I took her head off with the edge."

"Did you now?"

"It felt and sounded like it."

"Excellent. That news makes me feel a bit better about our prospects searching for the Eye of Nimora. Not the attack but your defense." He rotated about on the stair.

"Will she come back again?"

"Likely. And just as angry, no doubt. I couldn't tell you for certain without seeing the materialization. The supernatural being what it is, as such."

"Do you think Malender captured her spirit?"

"Could very well be. He was there, was he not? That night at the country club when you faced the two of them."

"Yes."

"And Joanna and her father had tried to gain enough power to vanquish him?"

"That seemed to be their game plan."

"There are other options, but it seems most logical it would have been Malender, displeased with their attempts to supplant him. Then he will have taken steps, not only to stop them, but to make an example of them."

I thought about it. "Ouch."

"Indeed. Let that be a lesson for you. Always be very circumspect about your allies and your enemies."

I made a note before adding, "That's not all."

He raised an eyebrow at me now. "More?"

I decided not to tell him about Malender that same night, so I went with option two. "Germanigold made an appearance at the house. By projection."

That staggered him. For a moment, I thought he was going to plop back down on the steps. "Goldie?"

"That's what she said, and although her wings seemed pinned back, they were golden-ish by moonlight. She didn't have use of them."

"Why?"

"Why what?"

"What was she doing there?"

"Looking for you. I think if she'd found you, there

might have been a problem because she seemed very upset about Mortimer."

"It was her sister who killed him."

"I don't think that was the point."

He gestured impatiently. "I disagree. If she'd come to curse me or take her vengeance, her actions would be entirely misplaced."

"He had asked you for help."

"And I refused it for a very good reason. I loved Mortimer like a brother, but he did not always hold the best of judgment. He should never have married her."

"But he loved her!"

"Precisely. He put her in mortal danger when they joined. It would have been better for all if they had merely loved discreetly."

I tried to take that in. "Hiram seemed to think the marriage good for both tribes."

"He would be one of the few thinking that. And witness the disaster occurring now. I rest my case." He jabbed his pipe at the air. A long moment of silence fell between us. "Was that all you talked about? You said her wings seemed pinned. That's not usual for a harpy."

"I know. She didn't seem to be all there, even though Scout perceived her and growled a lot. She was talking to me when someone or something yanked her away suddenly."

"She disappeared on you?"

I explained, "She wasn't really there in the first place."

"She's still being held, then. It would have taken quite an effort for her to project. I didn't think she had that much strength in that kind of power. Interesting."

"I told her we were looking for her."

"Pity. We could have used the element of surprise."

I blinked. "Wouldn't you like to know if someone were coming for you if you were being held against your will?"

"We don't know that she is."

"She told me so! And she got pulled away."

"And you've never in your life been lied to?"

"Oh, come on, Professor. That happens all the time."

"Sadly, it does." The corner of his mouth quirked a little. "What I mean to say is that she might have been abducted and then joined with her takers and then changed positions yet again, regretting a rash decision."

"Right."

"It happens. Look at Remy."

"Oh." Now my mouth pulled unhappily. "Maybe she didn't trust the Society."

"Very wise of both Remy and Germanigold if they don't."

"Do you trust the Society?"

"Do you see me marching in and saying, 'I surrender and I need your aid?' Never would I ever, as you might say."

I laughed softly. "You're catching on."

"Slang. It will be the death of any near immortal trying to blend in. That, and computer identification. We are preparing, you know, to hide ourselves once the AIs take over."

"And that's another thing." I got up, tired of craning my neck to look at him. "Germanigold says a judge has her."

"A judge." He paused. "A Society judge?" He shook his head vigorously. "Then that's another matter altogether. You'll call Hiram tomorrow and tell him you cannot look for the Eye. He'll have to hire someone else. Don't worry about Hiram; there will always be someone foolish enough to do anything for money."

I avoided the pipe as he jabbed it toward me. "I promised."

"You can't keep a promise if you're dead."

"Dead?"

"Does Remy still live? Not that we know."

"But Joanna and her father killed her, not anyone in the Society."

"If you wish to believe that they thought about going after Malender on their own, and that they were strong enough to do it and succeed, then you haven't been listening to what I've been trying to teach you. They were likely manipulated, and for decades. Tessa, like any structure or organization holding great power, there is also considerable corruption. And neither you nor I have the ability to weed it out. Not at the moment, and possibly never."

"What about Carter?"

The professor's eyes narrowed as he considered. "Carter is a shrewd young man. He can take care of himself." He started upstairs. "Tomorrow, you'll tell Hiram our decision."

I smiled up at him. I would do no such thing.

Besides, I had classes and practice.

I miss Homeroom. At our high school, it started the day as a beginner class. You could wake up, finish your coffee or toaster tart, trade homework, and listen to the news of the day. In college, as it should be, you're on your own. Hopefully, you've learned enough by then to survive. Evelyn found me wandering the edge of campus, wondering if I really wanted to go to class, and how to crash a Society of magic users, and grabbed me by the elbow. My thoughts staggered to a halt.

"Where have you been?"

"Usually, you can find me at home on the weekends. Y'all know, doing laundry and projects and helping around the house. Oh, and I celebrated my birthday Saturday. You might remember that because you sort of took me to the movie."

"*Phone.*"

"Wasn't near one." On purpose, actually, because I didn't want to hear about her evening with Dean the bad boy. Really didn't want to hear about it.

"Tessa, you can't ghost me now. I need to talk to you."

Seriously? I didn't want to hear details. Plus I had this momentary thought that she had no idea about ghosting, and I ought to show her one of these days, but I decided against it. The news that my long-missing father was alive, after all, but only barely, might not be understood. I needed a distraction.

Fishing my car keys out of my pocket, I dangled them in front of Evelyn's perfect nose. "Guess what I got."

"OMG. A car? What kind? What color?" She grabbed the key ring and her extreme excitement bled away. "This is not a keyless remote."

"No, it's an older car."

"Oh."

"But it's red. Ish. Faded a little but pretty red. No rust. New tires. And, it's all mine. It should get me wherever I want to go."

She dropped the keys back in my hand. "If you ever go anywhere!" Evelyn nudged me with a tiny laugh, so her words wouldn't sting too much. That's my girl.

The loudspeaker came on. "Tessa Andrews, report to campus security."

We looked at each other.

"What have you done?"

I held my hands up. "Nothing, I swear."

"Go, go." She pointed. "I'll see you later."

We shared English, but I, on the other hand, took chemistry to try and have some freaking idea of what the professor talked about when he discussed his version of alchemy, not that I expected anyone would ever turn lead into gold. Maybe security wanted me because I'd parked in the wrong place? Or maybe I'd downloaded the wrong permit off the Internet last night.

Thinking of the professor and alchemy, I felt fairly certain he wasn't calling to see if I'd contacted Hiram yet and given up the job. At this point, the only plan I could come up with involved getting in neck-deep and hoping the others would come wading in to help me out of any trouble I might be in, since he would insist on backing out. Not a good plan, a few rough spots here and there—like maybe getting imprisoned right along with Goldie—but I thought it workable. The hardest part of it would be getting it implemented without getting stopped immediately.

That's why helping Mrs. Sherman would be a great

smokescreen. It needed to be done, and as soon as possible, and it would shield the rest of my movements. If that didn't work, then we had getting my dad out of the ghost zone successfully. I'd bury him in pleadings and research.

The professor would never know what hit him.

I headed to the security office.

CHAPTER NINE

SOMETHING WICKED. OR ROTTEN. OR BOTH.

A COUPLE OF suits waited for me as Norma, the senior secretary, waved me into the administration office as campus police delivered me. The so-called perp walk had been a little awkward, and I still had no idea what I might have done. The impulse to back out and run washed over me, and curiosity tried to cancel it out. Why would anyone use security to get me to Administration, unless they wanted to be certain I'd respond to a summons? Who were these two impeccably dressed people and what branch of law enforcement did they represent? The woman wore her hair glossed back into a French knot, her trousers creased, dark stockings covering her ankles, and her shoes so modest in height I almost wondered what the point was in wearing heels. The man looked a little sleeker than she did in what I felt sure Evelyn could identify as Armani, although he wore his Maui Jim sunglasses perched on top of his head, and he didn't have a handkerchief popping out of his chest pocket. I wouldn't have been surprised if the handle of a Glock did, frankly. And they both looked like Northerners. From DC, if I could guess.

Administrative Dean Moreno beamed at me. "Come in, Tessa." He beckoned a welcoming hand at me, indicating for me to take a chair. He occupied the back of the desk, nearly as wide as he was, and behind him a small curio cabinet held the pennant of his own college and the trophies his team had won in football, and an imposing picture of him as a linebacker. I think he kept them not only for the memories but as a warning he could hold a student accountable if necessary.

He meant for me to sit down in my chair, but I really wanted to wield it like an old-fashioned lion tamer. I perched on it cautiously, feet gathered under me, calculating where and how fast I could run. And if I might need the maelstrom stone as I did. By the pricking of my thumbs, to paraphrase both Shakespeare and Ray Bradbury, something wicked looked my way. Again, I regretted not wearing my bracers. I would have to remedy that, and soon.

"Good morning," the male suit intoned. "I'm Agent Danbury and this is Agent Naziz."

"Agents of what?"

Dean Moreno looked appalled for a fleeting second. He forced his smile to return. "Forgive the caution; Tessa has been through some traumatic times. Tessa, your academic record and test scores have drawn some attention and, it looks like, the offer of an internship."

"My test scores?"

He tapped a folder on his desk. "This first quarter."

They didn't look like scouts from a major university nor were recruiters usually titled "Agent." Since my mother taught locally, I had a fairly good idea what academia looked like, and these two definitely did not fit the mold. And since when did anyone scout off first semester grades? I decided to play, anyway.

"So you're from MIT or Stanford?" I looked from Danbury to Naziz.

"Not exactly. We're from a private university which has a campus on the edge of Richmond, and from time to time, we take in interns to work in our offices and library. It's a great opportunity for higher education, and provides a modest income as well."

Dean Moreno folded his large, fleshy hands. "Sounds promising."

"Oh, more than that," Agent Naziz offered. "We

have international connections that will reflect on her resume in the future." Her eyes sparkled gleefully in tandem with her smile.

If I had a future. The maelstrom warmed a bit inside my glove, but whether it woke on its own or my nerves alerted it, I couldn't guess. "I'm a bit confused. Do I take a class on your campus or assist a professor or do administrative work?"

"A bit of all three. Twelve to twenty hours a week, depending on how ambitious you feel."

"What sorts of classes are available?"

"Anything you might be interested in. We do suggest you study courses that might not be conventionally available at this college level, to round out your education." Agent Danbury leaned forward, his posture conveying keen interest and ambition of his own. They wanted me at their private university, but I couldn't figure out why. Nor how they'd found out about my so-called great scores. I knew I hadn't earned a perfect on the SATs or any of the other tests given in high school. Good, but not perfect; that was my general performance level. Nor had we gotten far enough into field hockey season for them to be scouting me.

Or perhaps they sensed the maelstrom stone as strongly as it sensed them. I fought to keep from curling my hand shut as if I could hide it away, wishing I had the professor or Carter or even Steptoe whispering advice in my ear. I realized everyone waited in silence for me to say something. I had the feeling I sat in the sales office at a used car store where the offer was today, and today only. "An interesting offer. Have you got brochures I can take home for my mother or more information on your website? I discuss everything with her."

"We don't extend an internship like this to just anyone," Agent Naziz said crisply. "It would be a mistake to turn it down without thinking about it."

"Oh, I'm not turning you down. I just don't know about it. Committing for a few quarters seems like a big step that I don't want to take without my mom. And what if it interferes with my team practice and schedule?"

Danbury pushed out of his chair and onto his feet. He put his hand out for a shake, his left hand, and he gripped mine tightly. No doubt he felt the stone in my palm, glove or not, and he looked into my face with a confident expression. "I think, when you investigate and consider us, you'll make the right decision. We can do a lot for you, Miss Andrews, and your family."

He waited at the office doorway while Agent Naziz pulled a few colorful pamphlets from her purse and handed them to me. She also shook, but conventionally right-handed, and smiled. "I look forward to seeing you. We can arrange a campus visit whenever you want, to help in your decision." She paused as she joined Danbury. "Oh. And you might be interested to know the hourly wage," and she named a figure well above the national minimum wage. It staggered both me and Moreno as the two suits left his office.

He managed another beaming smile at me. "Well. How about that?"

"I don't know," I told him frankly. "How did they learn about me?"

"Nobody said a word here, but I know the national grading company that handles the scores occasionally puts out advance word about exceptional students. You might remember some of the essays you did? The optional work?"

That set off a little light bulb. I'd had a packet of forms that few other students had gotten, but I thought maybe my mom's school had brought a special set for me because they did offer discounted rates for family and dropped all the way down to free if the employee had tenure or other qualifications. I'd processed them and promptly forgotten about them, graduating high school in January and soldiering onto community college last spring, when everything odd began happening in my life courtesy of the professor and his dilemma.

Looked like I'd been wrong about her university, though. These two, wherever they acted for, most certainly did not represent her school. I studied my brochure as I gathered my backpack and made ready to leave.

Red-brick and ivy-covered buildings. Quaint sidewalk pathways throughout the campus. Smiling students. A few professor types in long black robes in the background, no doubt going to classrooms—hey. Wait a minute.

Nobody at Mom's workplace wore robes except for graduation services twice a year. In fact, most of them dressed little differently from the students, my mother being an exception as she continually tried to make a good impression on the staff.

What was this place?

I flipped the pamphlet over. The page reflected blankly up at me.

"Well," Moreno muttered. "What do you think?"

"Don't know."

"Keep an open mind, Tessa. Now, if you don't mind, you've got classes and I have another appointment."

"Yes, sir. And thank you. I'll let you know." A smile flickered across my face, and I left before the unbetter part of me started to rant at him about the lack of support to either my mom or myself when my father disappeared. He'd been vice principal at my high school and had frowned more heavily than most at me whenever we'd crossed paths. My mom and I had both held the title of probable ax murderer, here and around town, for months until the next city scandal popped up. Scorn and pity, in equal measures, and I was pleased to duck out of it all as soon as I could. Hence the early graduation.

Norma put her hand out as I passed her desk. "Everything all right?"

She never changed. Her light brown hair stayed twisted and pinned in its updo, her seemingly starched blouses always had clean cuffs no matter what office work she'd been doing, and her pencil skirts always ended mid-calf. She wore fashionable but sensible shoes, and her manicured nails were finished off squarely so they wouldn't be susceptible to chipping or breaking. I think Moreno had been hired by Sky Hawk, just to poach Norma and bring her with him. When a student came in who lacked cafeteria funds or owed back debt, she had a cash drawer always full of just the right amount needed, no questions asked. No one went hungry at our high school. A lost or stolen or maimed textbook got replaced without recriminations. And whenever I'd needed to hide somewhere, away from reporters with cameras who wanted to know why my father disappeared, she always had a secure corner office available. I had no doubt she worked similar miracles at Sky Hawk.

I waved the brochure at her. "I'm just baffled."

"Life can be like that."

"Seriously." I tapped my paper. "Ever heard of these people?"

She took it from me. "Silverbranch Academy? Can't say that I have." She flipped through the five pages, ending up at the back, where the brochure now proudly proclaimed internships and scholarships available for the qualified. Diversity encouraged. And so forth. Norma put on her reading glasses and studied it closer. She returned it. "As they like to say: Google it."

Oh, I intended to. "As my mother would say, it merits consideration."

Norma winked at me. "That's our girl. Now get on with you, classes start in about"—she consulted her watch—"forty seconds."

I skedaddled.

Despite my promise to scour the Internet on Silverbranch, I held doubts. That blank page suddenly popping up with encouraging propaganda? It reeked of the professor's brand of wizardry. For that matter, as I thought back, so had the two agents. I rubbed the stone under my palmed glove. Not only my shield, it seemed to be my b.s. locator.

In English, my teacher said not a word about the supposedly outstanding essays I'd written in the past, even if they'd attracted Silverbranch. Evelyn sat behind me, slender enough she could cross her legs at her desk and still have seated a squirming toddler on her lap with room to spare, and sent little texts to me whenever she thought she could get away with it. A row closer to the teacher's desk and podium, I had trouble reading what she sent, let alone replying. I drew enough attention from Mrs. Gill that I caught the privilege of diagramming not one but two very complex sentences. I managed to pull it off with only one correction from her.

Out of Mrs. Gill's domain, I caught Evelyn by her earlobe.

"Ow!"

"Stop texting in class!"

"It's important."

"Dean the wonder boy can wait till lunchtime."

Her cheeks pinked. "Maybe."

"I know, and maybe I'm just a little bit jealous."

"I didn't think of that."

"Then you need to. Save me a seat for lunch, and don't you dare invite Dean over if you want to talk about him."

She agreed, and we split up again. I had a break before my next class and ducked into the library for research. As I suspected, the Internet provided pretty much the exact same pictures that the brochure offered up, along with two glowing recommendations from former students, and a "Study Overseas for a Semester!" opportunity. I went through the tabs, not finding anything substantial or even interesting until I caught the barest glimpse of a familiar face among students crossing the picturesque grounds. It wasn't even a glimpse, really, except I knew that face. Crushed on it, misplaced cleft and all.

A younger, paler, but just as compelling Carter Phillips strode along those hallowed halls of Silverbranch Academy.

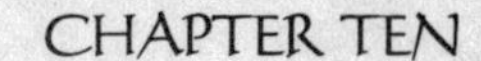

CHAPTER TEN

WHAT DO I SPY WITH MY LITTLE EYE?

I'D SEEN PICTURES of Carter in his military gear, tanned and face grizzled with beard, and this barely caught image of him at Silverbranch showed him thin, pale, and clean-shaven as though he'd been ill and recovering. He fit in with the other students, which I now noticed ranged from my age to middle age. He'd been gravely wounded, though, which accounted for his early exit from the service, although I imagined knowing now what I did, that pressure brought by none other than the Society on the Department of Defense to give him an honorable discharge because they wanted him saved for other purposes aided. I imagine that he'd hardly known what he was then or what he could do. Had Silverbranch helped or hindered him? As for the wound, he had no lingering effects that I could see, but I studied the barely seen personage on the academy website. This shot had to have been taken right after his release. So that begged the question: what was he doing there, and did he have anything to do with the agents waiting for me today? I hoped he didn't because I didn't particularly like those two and how they operated.

If he did, why didn't he tell me to expect them? Nothing I saw on the monitor screen would give me the answers I had to have. But if I wanted to check out the Society and find who might have taken Germanigold and where, this seemed my perfect opportunity. She'd said a judge, though, and my intuition, otherwise known as Andrews family common sense, told me that he was likely a rogue within the Society. Unless the lot of them were malevolent, but Carter wouldn't be a part of it if they rolled that way, so this abductor had to be operating outside their laws. Or I hoped he/she would be. The professor's dislike of them did not mean that they were corrupted. He disliked a lot of people. But I'd have to be very careful about anything I did, and I might be alone in doing it.

Without allies. That made helping Germanigold seem a much tougher problem. I could possibly convince Steptoe to help. He might like a look at that Dark Arts booklet I'd found in the old cabinet in the mudroom, but I hadn't had a chance to look at it yet myself. Steptoe had a way of convincing others to give him items he wanted, even if they didn't feel like it. I might be so persuaded but not until I'd had my own good look at it first. There were questions needing to be answered, like: Who had the booklet belonged to and why? I couldn't see either my dad or Aunt April tied to it, but then, a lot of odd things had been happening in the past few months. What if it held the answer to the question of my father's predicament?

Learning that magic existed was the proverbial can of worms being opened, and boy, did they wriggle out everywhere. Also, being worms, it stayed extremely difficult telling the good ones from the bad ones. Sometimes it appeared strictly situational.

Which brought me back to Steptoe. Going without him seemed only slightly riskier than going with him. He, undoubtedly, would have his own opinions about the august magical body, but he'd do it stealthily behind me and I, hopefully, would be none the wiser. Simon could be, and had been, like that. Still, he'd had my back on several occasions, and if I were going up against a judge on the Society no less, I'd need that alliance.

So Steptoe would be invited.

And Evelyn. I definitely needed a wingman. Steptoe had ways of moving about relatively unseen, and he actually had a jacket that could function as a cloak of invisibility, although I had no idea of its limitations. Magic was not a bottomless well. It had to be fed and coaxed from what I'd seen. If I used it, who paid the price, him or me, and what would the cost be? So he could follow according to his skill and hopefully not taxing that wondrous item, while Evelyn would give me the perfect disguise of two coeds interested in transferring to a unique academy.

She could keep up a stream of seemingly inane patter that would make both of us appear conventional and clueless. She was no more harmless than I was, although her skill came mostly from her background of having a father extremely well connected in law enforcement and politics, and she could wield her stilettos with deadly results. I'd seen that firsthand. Also, she had good instincts about people. After all, she'd stayed friends with me when everyone else seemed fairly certain I might have dropped my father down a sinkhole, never to appear again. She had money to burn, but that didn't motivate her whatsoever, although she occasionally forgot that others didn't. If I could find an angle that would keep Dean away while she came with, we'd have a date.

It ended up being easier than I thought.

Her sandwich sagged in her hand. Sprouts looked ready to tumble out in a green waterfall. "And this academy is a university campus?"

"Yes, with all the handsome privileged guys you can count. Never mind, forget I asked, you always outshine me. People will be looking at you and not me and Dean will be jealous, probably. Maybe you shouldn't come with me, after all. Besides, you're doing well here at Sky Hawk. I doubt you'd want to transfer."

She put the sandwich down carefully, so as not to bend or chip a nail. The cafeteria noise around us seemed to mute as she centered all her concentration on me. "A little jealousy does a relationship a lot of good. I should look valuable, not desperate. I want him to know he has to appreciate and pursue me if he wants me. I don't wait around for just anyone."

I wasn't so sure about that, but, "Then you'll think about going with me?"

"You couldn't keep me away!"

I smiled at her. "Great! When shall we plan this? Don't forget, I've got a car now. I can drive." She had a car too, a neat little older BMW, but her parents didn't let her drive on school nights. She was an adult, but as she'd told me more than once, she picked her battles with her parents. Being chauffeured wasn't that difficult on her.

We decided on Wednesday as we both had short days, athletic practice intruding, but we'd take a day off to do our academy scouting. If anything, her spot in cheerleading was even more athletically demanding than my field hockey team. Perfect, because now I had to figure out how to reach Steptoe. I had no direct way of signaling him, we'd never arranged anything, but I had a feeling the tell-tales might get through to him if we didn't all get together on Tuesday night.

Monday after practice I ate dinner, did the dishes, and disappeared to my room to finish assignments and study the curious booklet. Preoccupied with her new class and the various glitches in her university's web setup, my mom left me pretty much alone, and the professor took the opportunity to sneak out. He came back, trolling the smell of smoke and ashes down the hall that even I could scent, and Scout and I decided he'd either gone to a cigar smoker's convention or he'd been back to his house, sifting for whatever he could find. As Evelyn would say, not my circus and not my monkey. Scout curled up to my bare feet as close as he could get, and I enjoyed his puppy warmth. He'd greeted my return from school with wild, enthusiastic leaps and running about the yard in great circles, finishing with a jump into my arms that knocked me over. We both agreed that I needed more training as he would only get bigger, heavier, and possibly even more enthusiastic in the future. I needed to be prepared.

The found book looked even more fragile than I remembered. Paper crackled under my fingers as I gingerly laid the book out, wearing my gloves to protect them and the article from oils and contaminants, although a silverfish ran out of the thing only to be thoroughly squished by me before it got very far. I wiped my desk down with a shudder and a tissue. I wanted to shake the thing before I opened it any further, but it didn't look like it would survive it. I settled for spraying it with air freshener. Trust me—air freshener is a pretty good bug spray and smells tons better.

Scout didn't agree with me and sneezed twice before abandoning my feet and crawling in under the desk away from the mist.

The fading ink proved to be only part of the difficulty in reading each page. I also ran across a major language barrier even more than S's being written as F's. Mrs. Gill of college English fame had lectured, albeit very briefly, about the changes in the English language since we'd become a nation. I hadn't listened a whole lot because, frankly, it didn't seem interesting. Now I wished I had. I sat in my chair and looked at a page whose unfaded half I could see made no sense. The faded half couldn't be interpreted at all. I went over and over it until my eyes blurred. This was worse than writing in lemon juice and putting it over a candle flame to make it appear like we used to do in summer camp.

The professor could probably decipher it if I wanted to show it to him or explain where I'd gotten it from, but I didn't care to. Not yet. It was mine, my secret and my discovery. When, and if, I started showing it around, I would lose it. Even if I shared it, I would lose it, and chances would be good that Brandard would take it from me. That was the way he operated. He liked to hoard his magical items and seldom explained the purposes of any of them. He was sneaky like that, quiet but self-serving . . .

I stopped trying to read and raised my chin. Nasty thoughts whirled about my head.

My eyes ached and I rubbed them carefully, and then reached for my lukewarm glass of sweet tea, which had been forgotten on the edge of my desk.

What had I been thinking? Miserly, closed little thoughts, even bitter ones. I shut the booklet. Without even knowing the words it held, or spells, or curses—whatever they were—it affected me. Dark Arts, indeed. Suddenly, I wasn't even sure I wanted the thing in the same room with me.

I looked down at Scout. "What do you think?"

Scout thumped his tail on the floorboard at my query, but he raised his head to look at the desktop where the booklet was and peeled his lips back from his teeth. I didn't think he was smiling.

"I agree." I stood up and went to my closet, where I found a nearly empty shoebox. Nearly because it had one shoe in it. The other undoubtedly rested in a pile of shoes in the corner. Dumping the other shoe into oblivion, I dropped the booklet in the now empty box, rubber-banded it, and tucked it under my arm.

"Time, I think, for your evening break, and a visit to the garage."

Scout jumped to his feet, and we trotted out to the backyard, did our various duties, his in the grass and mine in the garage hiding the box on the tool shelf, pushed to the back, and then we returned to the house. I found Mom in the kitchen, hand-squeezing some orange juice so as not to make much noise. She gave me a tired smile and fixed a glass for me. We clicked juice glasses.

"Bedtime?"

"Just taking Scout out."

"He's not sleeping in the mudroom, is he?"

"Nope. I mean, he starts off there, but he's an escape artist. He usually ends up on the foot of my bed. But he is when you go to work, right?"

"Yes. At least, I think so. But the catch on his crate seems to be broken. I keep finding him in it, door unlocked, when I come home, with little things around the house misplaced here and there."

We both looked at the dog. The pup hung his golden head and licked the evening dew off one paw carefully.

"We'll see how it works out," my mother said, still staring at Scout.

His ears flexed, but he kept his head down, ensuring that his paw was immaculately clean.

"Right." I snapped my fingers. "Let's go."

We went. I had Tuesday to get through, and two teachers to make excuses to for missing class, and then a strategy meeting on the Eye of Nimora.

Steptoe wore his bowler hat to the meeting, its dark felt sprinkled with raindrops from a light drizzle outside. He'd folded up an umbrella when he came in the door, leaving me a bit confused. Why the brolly when he had a hat and vice versa? The reason came to me immediately. Either one or both was not quite what it seemed to be, in tune with Simon's entire persona. I determined not to handle either without knowing what they were or could do just in case I could set them off—lessons learned the hard way.

Mom had cleared the dining room table and set up a pitcher of sweet tea, a carafe of hot coffee, and a tray with cream, sugar, glasses, mugs, and a dish of cookies. I was helping bring chairs into place when the house did a familiar shimmy and shake, and I could hear a deep voice at the door.

"Hello the home!"

"Come in, Hiram, come in."

He entered cautiously, I could tell from the shuffle of his steps and the noise of something hitting the various doorways between here and there. When he finally appeared in the dining room, he held that ginormous redwood chair in his arms, a bashful look on his broad face. "All right if I bring this in to sit on? It seems a waste just sitting there in the professor's backyard." It seemed he had read my mind.

"No, no, ah—there. Put it at the end of the table there, and we can shift it easily to the kitchen whenever you come by." Mom recovered adeptly and pointed where she wanted it. Hiram obliged and sat down with an enormously pleased and tired look.

"I've been around and about all day," he explained. "Don't know how my father did it, all his responsibilities and stonework and such. A mason's job can be tiring."

Mortimer did much more than masonry, and Hiram knew that I knew that, but I liked his sharing with me.

My mother smiled back at him. "How about a Coke?"

"That would be quite wonderful." He waited till her shadow had followed her out of the room before doing his own pointing. At me.

"I hear you're backing out."

"I'm not."

"The professor says . . ."

"Too much, and he's not the boss of me. If he doesn't want to be in on this enterprise, fine. But I promised you a deed, and I intend to keep to that promise." Our financial situation certainly wasn't any better, and now I had a car to support. Besides, I had a lead too good to overlook. I filled a dessert plate with cookies and put it next to him. "Things any worse?"

"Tension is growing. Word is getting out that we no longer have possession of the Eye, and that means the docket of cases we have coming up is subject to postponements, arguments for dismissal, and all manner of problems. It is discouraging, Tessa. We've been handling judgments for centuries, and there's always been some disagreements and appeals, but this is far beyond the norm. It's as though no one trusts us to do what we know is right and fair without that cursed jewel to tell us. It was naught more than a tool, but no one will abide that. We have a very important matter coming up, and the elves will stomp right through us and Justice if we let them, and they're insisting we set a date for the trial, regardless." He stopped with a huff, his hands gripping the end of the chair arms tightly. I could see now just how Morty had worn grooves into it over the years.

Steptoe listened without comment, but his eyes snapped alertly as he took it in.

"I don't know much about elves. Are they normally trouble?"

"This bunch of them are little more than organized hoodlums."

"Elven Mafia? Wow." I shook my head. "We'll get it

back, and we'll also prove to them that the Iron Dwarves can be Just without it."

His jaw tightened. "From your lips to immortal ears."

"Now have a cookie, or my mom will know something's wrong."

He took one and was licking the crumbs off his fingers when she returned. Carter came in on her heels, a harried look on his face, his dark brown hair sticking out as though he'd just run his fingers through it or maybe even pulled it in frustration.

It apparently took one to know one. Hiram tilted his head. "Bad day? You look madder than a wet hen."

"It's a rule that everyone lies. It gets tiresome." Carter patted himself down as if looking for something, found it in a hip pocket, and nodded to himself in satisfaction before pouring himself a cup of coffee. "Cookies any good?"

"Delicious," Steptoe and I said together. I added, "Help yourself."

He did, and everyone looked fairly content by the time my mother bowed out to get refills as the oven dinged. "Third and last batch," she warned. "On the counter cooling. If you don't mind, I'll leave you all to whatever planning you're going to do. I have work to do and maybe even a little writing tonight." She waved as she disappeared.

I looked around the table. "But the professor's not here. We need to wait." I tried to remember when I'd seen Brian last and failed, although I did remember when he'd come in last night smelling like his burned-out house or maybe a really bad cigar.

Hiram put his empty cookie plate on the table and stayed leaning forward, his eyebrows beetled. "I cannot be waiting long. Not tonight or any night because there's trouble in the halls at home, and it's not going away until it's handled. If you can't help me, best tell me now, so I can find someone who can."

"We're all in, Hiram. I know that's not a guarantee

we can do what has to be done, but we will try our best. Right?"

Carter had been tapping on his phone and glanced up. "Right."

Steptoe managed to mumble, "Too right, lad, too right," around a cookie or three. I wondered if I should fix him a ham sandwich or something. The man acted as though he never ate until he got here.

I decided to give Hiram a pinch of hope. "Actually, I have a bit of information. Germanigold has been sighted, and she is in one piece but not as free as she'd like. She might be able to give us an idea what happened to her and maybe the Eye as well."

"You've talked to her!"

"Not precisely as it was her projection, but I think I might be able to, in the flesh, soon. She supposedly wants to cooperate."

"That would be quite helpful." Hiram rubbed his brow. "That's a bit of encouragement."

"She wouldn't be about holding back on you to get even?" Steptoe reached for a napkin and dabbed at the corners of his mouth. He eyed the rest of the cookies on the plate speculatively.

"Simon, why don't I fix you a sandwich? I've ham and cheese."

"That would be delightful, ducks."

"One for everyone?" I glanced around the table.

"If you don't mind." The gentlemen all smiled happily back.

"Not at all." I fixed a plate of sandwiches, noted for Mom that we needed more bread and ham on the refrigerator shopping list pad, and opened a bag of barbecue potato chips to go with the sandwiches. Scout stayed by me hopefully. I brought the goods back to the dining room where everyone sat up cheerfully and fell to, and I caught Carter sneaking bread crusts to Scout.

No professor. I looked to Hiram. "When did you talk to Brian, anyway?"

"Oh, early yesterday. Ran into him when I was, erm, liberating the patio chair. Just a wave, he seemed busy."

"No one since? I heard him come in late but nothing after."

"Busy," said Carter around a mouthful of ham, and Steptoe echoed.

"He can't be that busy if he wants to stop me from doing something stupid." I put my hands on the wooden tabletop. "We're going to have to go look for him. Maybe he got trapped if part of the old house fell in."

Carter sighed, reaching for his phone. "Don't do that."

"Why not? If he's in trouble, he needs us."

Carter flashed a picture at us. "He's not in trouble. He's in jail."

CHAPTER ELEVEN

A HEAPING HELPING

"JAIL!"

Carter tried to explain. "I'd hoped to get him out before anybody noticed, but it seems not." He held his phone, face out, to us.

We all leaned forward to take in the picture on the phone, a mug shot pose, with Brian looking scuffed up and outraged, with an even angrier professor glaring out of those aquamarine eyes.

I reacted. "Holy moly. Good thing he doesn't have his blasting stick."

The stick in question rested depleted in his bedroom. He occasionally took it out while we studied, and I could see the clear crystal in the handle which had turned completely obsidian and useless in our last battle progressed, degree by degree, clearing to a charcoal but far from the diamond-like beauty it had been. I found it encouraging that the infamous weapon could be regenerating, but the professor growled every time I suggested it. The last time I saw the cane, he had it resting as a bookmark in the creases of the *Remedies* book that I'd brought out of his scorched library. Talk about breaking the spine of a book! That nonchalance about one of his tomes made me even more certain he must have returned to his study to ferret out more of his research titles, regardless of the fact the house remained taped off and out of bounds. It hadn't stopped me, and I knew it wouldn't slow him.

"What happened and where?"

"Early this morning, according to reports, at his place. I found out about it around noon while working another case and have been trying to intervene without being obvious about interfering. It's not been easy; he has a number of people very upset."

"The professor? Never."

Carter wrinkled his nose at me and my sarcasm. "He got into a fight early this morning with an arson inspector. Arson has been cleared, but the other fire officials didn't get by so easily. He's charged with aggravated assault and battery."

"Why?"

"They tried to escort him off the premises and explain that the lot will be bulldozed next week so the insurance agency can begin with rebuilding. They insisted on it being too dangerous to enter, and he insisted on going in to retrieve his items. Acting on public safety, they tried to restrain him. Of course, he doesn't wish the building knocked down before he's done with it. I'm told he reacted very aggressively."

"Whoa." I knew Brian could throw a wicked punch if he had to, and the professor had the crusty personality that would provoke it. "Wow. Can we get him out of that?"

"He assaulted a city worker who was doing his job. It seemed to have been quite a brawl."

I huffed and thought for a few seconds. "If the prof was in his own body, we could plead diminished capacity or old man distress and goofiness or something, but not looking like Brian."

"Actually, we still can. There is a great deal of stress in being shipped off to a foreign country and relative and then losing nearly everything in a fire."

"Oh. Is that what you're doing?" I watched Carter's expression.

"Trying to. There are a few others who'd found out he's been jailed and would like to block that, at least long enough to sift through the ashes themselves." Carter wouldn't quite meet my gaze.

"Society?"

Simon grunted softly. "Of course. Who else? I might do it, too, but I've chosen a different alignment this time around. So." He put his hands palms down on either side of his now empty plate. "Looks like we do a bit of looting ourselves."

Carter elaborated. "We're going to have to go in and recover what we can and store it here, until we can find a property easier to ward. We can't hesitate on this."

Hiram scratched his temple. "The basement here would hold. We built in safeguards, just in case, hrmmm, Tessa might need them someday. A so-called safe room."

We'd been rejecting Aunt April's house out of hand for weeks, but this changed everything. "Really? But you didn't tell me!"

He smiled out of the corner of his mouth. "You don't strike me as the kind of lass who thinks she needs to be protected."

"Well, I don't, but magic stuff." I shrugged. "That's a whole 'nother thing, right?"

"So it would seem."

Simon asked of Hiram, "What did you do?"

"Trade secrets, Steptoe, but I do suggest you don't go down there unless you must. You might become very uncomfortable."

"Oh." He looked aggrieved. "That really wasn't necessary."

"Not against you, but you do keep company with odd fellows."

Steptoe fell silent, his chin down.

Scout put his paw on my thigh, and I slipped a bread corner down to him, complete with a sliver of ham. "Back to the house in question. Can we get in now or is the place surrounded by the SWAT team?"

"We wouldn't use the SWAT team, but yes, we can get in. I'll have permission to retrieve what few valuables are left." He checked the face of his phone. "I should have received notification already."

Hiram tapped his fingernails on the arm of his chair, sounding like a miniature hammer at work. "Then we go with or without permission. Our first duty tonight, before we consider how and who to approach over the Eye. Immediate actions outweigh the planned campaign."

"Agreed."

The men all got to their feet at once, bringing Scout up with them, the pup evidently having some idea that the game was afoot. I stood up much more slowly. "Before we charge out the door, guys, I need to tell Mom we're going."

Simon tugged on the hem of his coat and bowed. "Most certainly, ducks. We'll be at the curb." I could hear the English accent in his words.

Mom sat at her laptop, reading glasses slid down to perch almost at the end of her nose, blonde hair pulled back in a loose ponytail that had fallen to the nape of her neck and then coiled around one shoulder. Looking at her, I caught a momentary glimpse of what she'd looked like maybe twenty years ago and why Dad had thought her pretty. She still was, if older. I wonder if she saw Dad when she looked at me. She held a finger up, pushed the save button, and smiled at me. "Meeting over?"

"We have to go salvage what we can of the professor's library. The building is coming down completely soon. Can I use our moving boxes?"

"Of course." She flexed a hand. "Is there much left?"

"Not really. We thought we'd stow it in the basement."

"Okay. Then I won't be alarmed when I hear you all stomping about."

I leaned over and kissed her forehead. "I'll try and keep 'em quiet so you can work. Later, gator."

She began typing again, and as I left the room, I thought I faintly heard, "After a while . . ."

We had three cars to utilize: my little Corolla, Hiram's SUV, and Carter's plainclothes sedan. All had fairly good trunk space, but we piled the empty boxes into Hiram's vehicle, along with two tape guns and two extra rolls of tape. Having just moved, well, a little over two years ago, I had a fairly good idea how to make boxes out of flattened cardboard and all the tape required to do so. It's an art. Really.

Scout stayed at home, after a little protest and bribery with doggie treats.

Steptoe asked to ride with me. As soon as the car doors closed and we sat alone, he said, "All right, ducks. The tell-tales told me you told them you needed to speak with me privately. What is happening?"

"A little reconnaissance, private, is required."

"Oh. You, me, an' who else?"

"Evelyn Statler."

"That rich gal you and me rescued last spring?"

"That would be the one."

He considered my words. "Who are we spying on?"

"I'm not totally sure who they are, but it's the Silverbranch Academy."

A pause while he thought. Then, "What about them aren't you sure of, and what are we looking for?"

"I think they might be Society, or in league with them at least, because they came out of nowhere and are interested in my academics. Listen, I have good grades and all that, but I'm no blooming genius, yet they're suggesting I consider transferring. I could lose college credits doing it, and I've no good reason to even try." I held my left hand up. "I think word about the maelstrom stone has spread."

"Does them no good if they try to force it from you."

I started the car and put it into gear. "I'm hoping they know that. I have no desire to lose a hand over this."

"You won't if me or Carter are with you." He fastened his seat belt hastily as the warning bell began to sound. "I won't say you're right about Silverbranch, but I won't say you're wrong, neither. But if you're worried, why are you going there?"

"Because I think someone there knows about Germanigold."

"Bloody 'ell—she's that close?"

"Possibly."

"Her nest is in Maryland, not far from DC. I was just beginning to think we'd have to traipse all the way up there again." He looked pale.

"You don't like long trips."

He wiped his forehead. "Some of us, not all mind you, but some of us have centers. Centers which keep us close and are not wise to wander too far from."

"And where is your center?"

"Here, in Richmond." He turned his head to stare out the window, and I sensed he wouldn't say another word.

"I was hoping," and I turned the corner carefully, "that you would tail me and Evelyn the way only you can do, without being seen and all that, while we snoop around." He'd gone all the way to New York with us, and I hadn't noticed him in trouble then, but he'd been rather pale and tired since. Helping pull Evelyn out of trouble could have weighed on him further. How did a lesser demon recharge, anyway?

"It's a good thing the professor is in jail."

"You think?" He never would have allowed me to go hunting after Goldie. We pulled up in the professor's darkened driveway as night began to close seriously about us. I checked to make sure I'd gotten the lights switched off.

"He would have a conniption if he thought you was poking your nose into Society matters like, especially where Goldie is concerned. Now, it's not that he doesn't trust her, but he feels a bit guilty about letting Mortimer down and all that, not to mention the Society itself, if they took her, did so as bait."

"You don't think they took her for the Eye?"

"'Twasn't known on the streets that she had the Eye till recently, if at all. Which means she likely weren't taken for that, but now she might be leveraged for it. Tricksy folk will use every advantage they have." Steptoe unbuckled his seat belt and got ready to bail. "And, luv, you'd better make darn sure you don't get added to that when we go in to look. You cannot allow yourself to be taken."

"You'll come with us?"

"I daren't not, one way or t'other. Come on, now, we've work."

I made up boxes, a good dozen of them, while the

others set up light stands with flashlights and a few other, magical, considerations. Orbs of illumination are not a tremendous amount of help without walls, ceilings, and such to reflect their light upon, but they're better than nothing. Carter's police-issue flashlight had the strongest and widest beam, so they set it up in the study itself, and we hauled the boxes into what had once been a hallway where they sat to be loaded.

Before going into what was left of the room, Carter put up a hand. "Parts of this area are still warded, but it's an intricate working that I haven't time to unwind and, frankly, we're bound to set off a trap or two." He tapped each of us on the head. "Protection ward. Actually, more of a deflection. The trap will still go off, but hopefully next to you or behind you. So, freeze and then duck if you set anything off."

We went into the room one by one, sending Hiram in first to test floor strength, knowing that all of us might collapse what was left of the fragile building, especially with the weighty bulk of an Iron Dwarf. After a few minutes I couldn't smell the soot and char anymore, although I sneezed every time we cleared a shelf. Hiram found himself a good, solid spot in the corner, where two great bookcases intersected, and began to unload whatever whole or decent remains of manuscripts could be found. I cleared a shelf of charcoal briquettes, basically, with two crisp pamphlets the only items left. I couldn't sit on the floor, so I settled for squatting, but when I tried to move away, my left hand went to the shelf and stayed there. I tried to tug myself loose and couldn't. The maelstrom stone might have been Thor's legendary hammer, fastened in place. I couldn't move it away but I could push it deeper along the shelf. Pondering, I tapped it. A hollow sound answered me.

I balled my stubborn fist up and crashed it into the back of the bookcase. My knuckles stung as my hand sank into a hollow, but now the stone would let me pull back. I cleared the splintered boards away from the hole as I did. A row of spines met my eyes.

A whole hidden bookshelf sat behind the first. And

it was full of items. Books, rings, crystals. Not a lot, maybe a dozen, but a potential treasure trove. I wondered if the professor had remembered them, and if he had, why he hadn't gotten them out?

Or, for all I knew, every bookcase in the room was a façade for the real thing. I looked over my shoulder to see that everyone had stopped working to see what I'd done.

"Should have guessed." Steptoe began working on his shelves as they emptied, but he found nothing similar.

Hiram, though, found two solid display cases at the foot of each bookcase in his area. And a ward.

Behind him, the floor exploded as he stood on the brink, tipping dangerously backward. Carter leaped across and steadied him. Steptoe and I grabbed boxes and the two tossed relics to us, which we promptly packed. Four additional crates' worth of goodies sat near the fire-shadowed threshold when we finished.

We got five more salvaged boxes out. I set off a ward that sent arrows *thhhp*ing through the air, narrowly missing Carter's broad shoulders. Steptoe tripped another, but he threw his jacket on it and all we heard was a muffled boom as his jacket billowed up in the air. He caught it, shook it out, and put it back on. Then he did a slow turn on his heels. "Looks like we're done."

Indeed, it did, as the flashlight beam wavered on the room, and shadows jumped up and down to catch the light. Carter thumped a hand on the end of the massive desk. "Except for this."

The great oak monstrosity crouched there like a mammoth animal, ready to stampede if angered. I blinked at it. A certain familiarity tugged at memories of dreams.

"Surely, the professor would have gone through that first."

"Who knows? I can see someone's been through here, but we've boxed up a lot, so that someone must have been awfully picky."

"Or looking for something in particular," Hiram offered.

"Or that."

"We've all set off a trap. Are we still protected?"

Carter considered. I could see him reaching back in his mind before he inclined his chin. "Another fifteen minutes or so."

I wondered how he calculated that. Not by sunset or moonrise. Maybe the protection he'd set on us had its own limit, and he'd divided that by the four of us. An uneasy shiver crawled down my spine. I don't like having to depend on something I know very little about.

We gathered around the desk. Hiram did a quick survey for hidden drawers and panels by judging the various depths and hollows of the structure. He did find one hidden drawer, lined in dark velvet when he pulled it out, but it was empty. I couldn't tell what had been stashed in there although there were indents on the fabric.

Carter looked, and his eyes narrowed. "Bones," he muttered. "And what would the old guy be doing with bones?"

"A valued pet, mayhap," Steptoe answered. "Who knows?" He pulled a file drawer out which divulged a stash of empty hanging folders. Whatever had been filed there then did not reside there now.

We got down to the last center drawer, long and short in depth: the pencil drawer, it's often called. It yielded a map, which Carter took carefully and wrapped one of the empty folders about it for protection.

Hiram checked his watch as did Steptoe. Hiram wore his on his wrist, one of the shiny metallic tech innovation watches, while Steptoe took his out of a vest pocket, on its chain, and flipped the cover open. What each found on their timepiece, they didn't say.

Carter wiped his hands on his trousers. "I'd say we've done all we could."

"Without knowing all the nooks and crannies, I agree."

"We can't just let them knock the place down."

Warm and strong, Carter's hand rested on my shoulder and squeezed a little. "We don't have much say in that. This is a battle we've won, here, and that will have to do. I should be able to get Brian out tomorrow morning and he's going to have to make a last stand to be allowed to search the ruins. I know he doesn't remember much, but someone's been through here and we have to hope it was him."

Scout met us at my back door, butt wiggling as much as the tail wagged, and he followed us in and out each trip we took with a box. I taped them shut and stacked them in the far corner of the basement. He snuffled them, sneezing as he did, and then sat and looked at me.

"I know. They belong to the professor and may be important. There may even be something in there to help me get my dad back."

One of the boxes fell off its stack, startling the pup, who flinched and skittered away. I picked it up and put it back. "I know, Dad, I know. We're working on it."

I left the basement while a cool breeze swept around me in an ethereal hug and Scout looked warily over his golden shoulder.

The others had left already, but Steptoe waited in the kitchen, dusting bits of dust and lint off his dapper suit coat. He looked up.

"Now we go back."

"What?"

"There's something there that only one of my ilk could sense, and it's waiting for us."

"Ummmm . . ."

"Coming or not?" he challenged as he plucked my car keys off the table.

CHAPTER TWELVE

CURSE WHAT SHADOWS LAY

SCOUT STAYED HOME again, out of protest, but I told him he had to guard. He looked dubiously at the door to the basement and then at my mother's workroom, went over to her door, and lay down, chin on his paws.

"Good boy."

His tail thumped once, but then he looked away from me and closed his eyes. He didn't watch as I put my bracers on.

Steptoe sat in the car waiting, rubbing his thumb over the cover to his pocket watch. He put it away when I got in and started it up.

"What do you think it is?"

He shrugged. "It could be something living or another object of some kind." He rubbed his chin uneasily.

"What's wrong?"

"You're not afraid to go there alone with me?" he answered.

"You've proven yourself."

"Not to all."

I said emphatically, "To me."

"I'm not used t' being believed or befriended. I haven't deserved it for a while, but I've moved myself in this world, I have, and I'm trying to find the good side of things. It's because you accept me, the others do. You cannot know what that means to me."

I didn't answer that, only slightly understanding because my recent experience wasn't the same as his, but close enough, and I knew he needed to talk.

He stared out the window at the dark neighborhood as it slid by. "I was responsible, you know."

"I know. I was there. But it was those two who work for you that scared the professor into regenerating without his ritual. You hadn't told them to kill him." No, but in fairness to my memory of the night, he had told them to bring him the professor's head, horrifying me. That was only if the unthinkable happened, which it had, but I hadn't known that then. Steptoe's minions, or at least one of them, had gone in for the kill. I couldn't hold Simon responsible for that, and as awful as the "off with his head" bit seemed, I knew now that it was one of the ways to resurrect the phoenix wizard if they had to. As for Brandard's overreaction and immolation—"He thought they would kill him," I said aloud.

Steptoe's nail scratched the stubble of his beginning beard. "Too eager they were and too stupid to heed what I'd told them. An' one of them, I'm certain now, had another master 'e answered to first. He attacked the professor. I hadn't sent them in to use fisticuffs and beatings. I was only hoping to persuade him a bit. The other one, though, had different ideas and orders."

I considered who that might have been and offered, "Malender?"

"Mayhap. I can't be sure who. There's others about, Tessa, who oughtn't to be. Old ones, ones that used to be great when times were different, wanting to rise up again. They want to send the world back into darkness. Primitive times."

I thought about running to the fire that night, to hear voices railing in the night, Steptoe so thick with his cockney accent I could barely understand him and the two cohorts scarcely human at all arguing with him. I'd been scared of him, myself. He'd been hopping mad, and all I'd known was that he seemed to have directed the professor's death. I knew better now, but I didn't know everything and wasn't sure I ever would. The professor, trapped inside Brian, still hadn't all his memories or wasn't sharing if he did. I couldn't think of what it might be that Simon Steptoe needed so desperately from the professor.

"If the world is tipping . . . aren't you on the wrong side?"

That brought Simon around to face me, as I pulled into the long driveway and stopped the car.

"It would seem so, eh, ducks? But it's where I want to be, this time around. Where I need to be. And wot kind of friend bows out when you need him?"

"Nobody I want to know. So." I pointed out the window. "Ready?"

"Not quite. The eleventh hour is best for what we've in mind. Wait a few, then we'll go in." He patted his vest pocket where he'd stowed his pocket watch and seemed to be mulling something over. "I want you to know what I was pestering the professor about. Told you I was centered here, right?"

I nodded.

"Centered is a polite word that guv'nors use. I'm chained, but it's a long chain. Not sure 'ow far it stretches but it'll do me a fair bit of harm to get to the end of it, as it were."

"What gets you free?"

"Don't know. Yet. I thought the professor might know. That's what I was about that night, trying to get him to tell me." Steptoe paused for a long moment. "He's the one that chained me, see?"

"He did?"

"Seems likely. Don't it?"

I thought about it before answering, "Probably. But he doesn't remember or doesn't want to remember."

"See? You understand."

"He wouldn't help Mortimer either."

"Crusty old git." Steptoe sighed. "So I don't know what it is that will free me, or even who, to be sure, did it, although Brandard's the best guess."

"What do you know?"

"I know I'm shackled to that church, the famous one, at t'other end of town."

My eyes widened. "St. John's Church? The one where Patrick Henry gave his 'Give me liberty or give me death' speech?"

"One an' the same. A movin' piece, it was."

My town is steeped in historic places and that one ranks among the top. I'd been there a handful of times on school outings, feeling all patriotic as we were traipsing through. "Wow. You're sure?"

"Ironic, is it not?"

"Considering we're talking about liberty, I'll say." I gestured. "I can't see how we can search St. John's for your curse, though. Especially if we don't know what we're looking for."

"Too right." Steptoe's vest pocket sounded a little chime from the watch he carried there. "Eleven. Let's go." He paused outside the car, one hand on the fender. "Tessa."

"Yeah?"

"I take it back. I have a pretty good idea what was taken from me that ties me down here." He looked a tad embarrassed.

I waited.

He cleared his throat. "Lyin' comes a bit too easy to me still."

"Change takes a while."

"It does. I had a tail once. Barbed. Demon-like."

I couldn't help it, I glanced behind him. He showed no sign of having had a tail once. "Must have been hard on the suit."

"Glamour, lass. Does wonders for a dapper man." His mouth pulled wryly. "And now it's gone. I know. There was a battle, a bitter one, and I was already thinking I'd taken the wrong side, so I went down."

"You got defeated on purpose. That made you some enemies on both sides."

"You have the right of it." He shifted. "Woke up without my tail and bound to old Richmond."

"That must have been a long time ago."

"'Twas. I stayed in hiding for near a century while I regained my power and worked on my humanity. I saw things. Learned them. Decided what to make of them. Looked to the Light and found out there's good and bad everywhere, so it begins and ends with one being. I do what I can, but it's a struggle. You called me chaotic good. There are times, my girl, when the chaos rears up and wants to take me with it."

"One day at a time."

He said, "But there's another lesson here. If you're looking for something, it helps to have a piece of it already. So I'm looking for meself, as it were."

I thought of the feather Goldie had left me and the possibility that just opened. "Does it call you?"

"Sometimes." Steptoe saw the expression on my face. "The professor didn't teach you that?"

"No. Not yet, anyway."

"I need to have a word with the old man, then. He's been neglectful."

"But if you're bound to St. John's, wouldn't your . . . erm . . . tail be there?"

"Not that I've found. The thought finally came to me that I might be wrong about the binding, so I sent my lads to shake the professor down about whatever he knew. It might not have been me tail, and it might not have been him, though it seemed most likely. And this happened." He indicated the ruins of the old house.

"We'll find it," I told him.

"Thanks, luv. I knew you might be tellin' me that, as one friend to another." He took a deep breath. "Well, we'd best get on with it."

The ruins seemed to be waiting for us.

We approached the place quietly from the backyard, me on edge thinking we were asking for trouble and Steptoe because he had all his senses primed to find what he thought he'd detected earlier. Whatever it was. I hoped we wouldn't find anything, except if it helped Steptoe, I was in.

A low fog had come rolling in, just enough to cover the backyard with mist and dew, and make the place look spooky. Tendrils reached up as if to grab whatever they could, before dissipating and dropping back down into the condensation. It broke apart reluctantly as we waded through.

My voice dropped to a whisper. "This can't be good." I shook a vine of fog off my ankle.

Steptoe agreed. I didn't feel much better to hear him whispering as well. I stripped my gloves off and stuffed them deep into my jean pockets. I could feel my stone growing warm in the palm of my hand. My bracers set off a faint but comforting candle glow about them.

"Setting up a shield?"

"If we need one." I tapped the bracer.

"Good idea, that."

A wave of fog rolled up and caught him, knocking him down and covering him almost instantly. Steptoe bounced up with an indignant sputter.

"Are you all right?"

"Pass your hand through this naughty bit of cloud, and I will be."

I swept my left hand through the mist circling around us, and it shredded away. I thought I heard a faint hissing as it did.

"You've had your bit of fun. Now show us what you wanted and we'll be on our way," Steptoe announced.

Curling away from us, the fog climbed the last remaining pillars and then across a surviving and sagging eave of roof, framing an entrance. I watched the performance warily.

"I think we're being invited inside."

"Not until we know what we're dealing with." Steptoe put his hand out in front of me, in case I started to go without him, and frowned into the night. "Show yourself."

It might have been the wind, or maybe the faint and far away howl of a dog, but something answered. "Only to you, Shimon."

His name, in an olden accent. He growled softly in answer, still holding his arm out to protect me. "Bring up your shield. Now."

I did, the metaphysical one and the actual one that I'd dispatched Joanna's Kitsune with, balancing it in my hands. Simon's intense gaze moved to view it, and his eyes widened slightly in surprise. I twirled the shield in answer.

"At least he's taught you something."

"Damn straight. I just hope we won't need it."

"Remember when I told you about masters. This one used to be mine."

And the mist erupted about us.

I fought without knowing what I struck at. It had body and substance and could hurt me even as I hurt it, but I never saw it. I kicked and used the shield to slice and dice, wielding it right and left without a target. But it hit, and hit hard, and something wet and slimy spewed around us. The grass, already slippery, became nearly impossible to move on without sliding, so we anchored ourselves, back to back, and battled.

Steptoe held his brolly like a sword, having fetched it out of nowhere, or maybe the inside flap of his suit coat. It hummed with the pitch of a nest of angry hornets as he swung it. The noise settled in my eardrums, annoying and lethal. My shield developed a whine of its own, no less lethal as I used it, but growing ever heavier.

I tired just swinging it, and whatever in me that manifested it, well, it seemed to be draining. I went to one knee and couldn't get up. Whatever it was we fought had tentacles to spare. And stink, too. Something gaseous and marshy, backed up by sulfur and brimstone. I gagged as the greasy smell coated the back of my throat.

Steptoe felt me slip. He let out a string of curses that I could only translate if I was fluent in gutter speech of old London, but they didn't need to be interpreted. Then, boom! Boom! Boom! He tossed out a handful of flash-bangs, and the fight exploded out of private and into the neighborhood night, loudly and in vivid color.

As did our opponent. Between us and the ruins, something ghastly off-color grew. And grew. And grew until it towered over us. I pulled my shield up and over my head.

Steptoe answered it by slamming his umbrella point first into the ground, where a massive crack opened up, flames edging the ripped earth. The crevice threatened to swallow both of them up. He ripped off his suit coat and threw it to me, before turning about and launching himself at the rippling monstrosity to hug it tightly. He took a leap, pulling them both into the chasm in the ground.

Flames roared up, and then the gap closed with a snap and all went quiet. Very quiet.

"Steptoe?"

Not that I expected an answer, though I would have appreciated one.

I stayed on one knee for a very long minute, blinking, covered in slime, and wondering if Steptoe would come back. If he could come back. The brolly had gone in with him, but I clutched his jacket in one hand and my shield in the other. He would expect, perhaps, that I'd go after him. I clutched his coat closely, in case something would rise out of the wisps left along the ground and try to snatch it from me. Nothing more happened, though I could see lights from nearby houses snapping on, one by one. We hadn't gone quietly, at the end.

I ran home. Covered in ichor, I had no intention of inflicting myself on my new-to-me car. I'd come back for it in the morning. Safely, more or less, in my yard, I hosed myself down, dancing in the chill of the water. Scout watched from the window of the mudroom door, nose pressed to the glass, my only witness.

Two thoughts slammed into my brain: now we had to rescue Steptoe as well, and two, would Evelyn and I be able to pull off a visit to Silverbranch without him?

CHAPTER THIRTEEN

GRATEFUL IS AS GRATEFUL DOES

"WHY DOES EVERYONE keep saying I should be a little grateful?" Brian paused long enough to mop up his fifth fried egg with his third piece of raisin bread toast and stuff it in his mouth. Scout watched him with absolute fascination, brown puppy dog eyes going from plate to lips and back again. Or perhaps the intensity came from waiting for a miss, but I hadn't seen even a close one yet.

"Perhaps," my mother stated, "because a thank you is due."

He flicked a glance at her, shrugged, and reached for another piece of toast.

"Carter called in a few favors to get you out without charges."

"I didn't ask him to, but perhaps if he'd done his job properly in the first place, there wouldn't have been an incident to worry about."

I put a hand out and shoved the toast plate away from him. "Those were fire department and city personnel. The police don't employ them. The place has been cordoned off for months, and we've been lucky to sneak in so far."

"My house should never have been scheduled to be razed."

"Professor, it's totaled. Maybe you need a reality check."

"Reality check? The reality is that I have a lifetime

woven in there, knitted into the very fabric of my home, in every stick and stone and bit of metal used to fabricate it. I can't afford to lose it. I don't want to lose it."

"Then maybe you shouldn't have set yourself on fire."

The fork clattered out of Brian's hand as he shook it at me. It hit the table, and a half a piece of raisin toast went flying as if catapulted. Scout leaped after it like a Frisbee disk and chomped it down happily.

"It's not your place to lecture me, young lady."

"All we're saying is that Carter went to a great deal of trouble to get you out of jail, and a little gratitude would be nice. Instead, you're making us think he should have let you cool off a few more days."

"Bah. I need to get my things out of there."

"There's a restraining order against you."

"What?"

"You can't enter your property."

"Why—why—who ever heard of such a thing!"

Mom slid another egg out of the frying pan and onto his plate. "The paperwork came early this morning before you were released. It's for your own safety. For everyone's safety, really." She eyed me briefly. She hadn't missed the fact that I'd made an early morning jog to bring my car home. No questions were asked, but I deserved the sidelong look she gave me.

I took a breath. "I should let you twist in the wind."

He squinted at me.

"We boxed up what we could find of your library and brought it home last night. It's all sitting in the basement."

"All? How could you know what was all?"

"Well, we found the hidden bookcases, so I think we have an idea."

His jaw tightened. "And who is we?"

"Me, Carter, Steptoe, and Hiram."

His gaze swept me in examination. "And you're still in one piece?"

"Carter put a protection on us, a displacement. It didn't last long, but long enough."

This time he set his fork down carefully, but somehow a slightly burnt edge of crust managed to slip off his plate and float off the table. It never made it to the kitchen floor. "My desk?"

"We went through that, too. The map of whatever it is, we put in a folder in the box marked 'books and map.'"

"Hmmm." Brian chewed and swallowed. "You all seem to have thought of everything."

"Look, we know we probably didn't get everything, but we got most of it, and Hiram says the basement is a kind of safe room, so it's protected for the moment. I seriously don't think we can go back to your house."

"Perhaps I cannot, but why wouldn't I be able to send you?"

"Because something is there that Steptoe is familiar with, and it's got tentacles and it's stinky slimy. It attacked us."

Brian nearly choked. "Perdition."

I added the kicker as my mother turned an alarmed expression toward me. "And it's got Steptoe."

"Really? How on earth?"

"He threw himself at it to protect me."

Brian dabbed a napkin to his lips, finally pushing his plate away. "Thank you, Mary. That was most appreciated. As for Simon, that is most astonishing."

"It is not." I defended my friend. "He's done it a number of times before."

"Oh, not that he guarded you, but that she sent someone after him. His change in allegiance has evidently not gone unnoticed."

"Why wouldn't it be noticed? It seems obvious."

"Steptoe comes from a world where the long game is always played, and it can last for centuries. Simon's reformation can be measured in decades, as I count it, and probably hasn't registered with other powers. No, the thing came to my place and no doubt came after me. The two of you just happened to be in the right place at the wrong time, and he resorted to desperate measures on your behalf."

"You know, not everything is about you."

"No, but many things are, and it seems to me that this one might well be. Zinthrasta can be counted as an enemy of mine even as she once used to be a mistress of Steptoe."

"Zinthrasta?"

The professor made a slight face. "The glop is one of her trademark minions. You described it accurately?"

"I left out the fog."

"Definitely a glop." He stood to carry his plate over to the sink, rinsed it, and put it on the counter to wait for the dinner dish loading. "I should check the boxes over before making any decisions of any kind."

I fetched a tape gun from the mudroom, along with a cutting knife. "Right behind you."

He raised an eyebrow. "Perhaps I wanted privacy."

"I can always call the police department and tell them you're still belligerent."

"Brat."

"Professor."

He opened the pantry door leading to the basement, and I clattered down the stairs behind him. Scout followed.

I expected the fire stink to fill the room, but surprisingly it didn't. One of the boxes had leaked a small, inky puddle onto the new tile floor, but on examination, it turned out to be fine ash that had filtered out of a crack in the box. Brian examined it closely with an odd expression and ran a finger through it, sniffed it, but said nothing to me of why that might have happened. I wondered if he knew, himself. Scout didn't alert to it, so I decided it might be nothing, although I'd learned in this new reality that hardly anything was nothing. There was always something and often a nasty surprise.

The box that had fallen off and gotten restacked had jumped the pile again. I stood and looked it over to see if we had written anything on it to ID its contents, but nothing stood out. Brian located his "Map" box quickly and put his hand out to me.

"Scalpel."

I slapped the box cutter across his fingers. "Scalpel."

He sliced the tape open quickly and returned the box cutter before kneeling down to examine his rescued treasures.

Brian in his new reincarnation stood tall, carried himself with broad shoulders and, when occasionally shirtless, had six pack abs to admire. The frizzled, thinning hair of the professor was gone, as was the bristly, almost alive mustache and the thicket of hair from the canals of his ears. So his current resemblance did not remind one of a dragon unlike the other persona. I saw it now, though, as if the great mythological beast found his hoard restored. He ran his hand over the box's contents.

"If you say 'my precioussss,' I'm outta here."

"What? Oh. Hmmm." And Brian smiled slightly. "It would give you a start, wouldn't it? But all of you did an admirable job. I doubt there is much left for me to salvage."

"You're going back?"

"Just for a quick sweep. Just in case." He put a finger alongside his nose. "I have my hidey holes, you know."

His finger left a charcoal stripe along his face and I ducked my head, trying not to laugh.

"I'll go with you."

"Best not. If the glop is fixated on associates of Steptoe as well, it will come after you."

"What about you?"

"It dare not."

"Taking your blasting stick?"

"I might, although that will tax its recovery. No, there is something in this box that will aid me a bit." He tapped the cardboard before reaching in and pulling out a copper bracelet. Without telling me what it was or did, he fastened it on.

I thought of Steptoe's suit coat and how he'd stripped it off and tossed it to me, shoving his shirt cuffs up his arms, before throwing himself at that thing charging at us. It was and wasn't part of him. I very rarely saw him without it and I knew it had, at least twice, provided invisibility. But other than that, and truthfully that was enough, I had no idea what else it could do. I also didn't want to try it out here, in front of the professor. What if he took it from me, for my own good? Magic users seemed notorious for looting each other's items. Or using it made it unusable for another time when I might need it? Yet I had questions. What if I could find Steptoe through it?

"Tell me about using a part of something to find the rest of that something," I said to the professor.

Elbow-deep in a second box, carefully shuffling through items like a card shark stacking a deck, Brian lifted his head and stared blearily at me once or twice to get me in focus. "Hmmm? That would be a form of what we call sympathetic magic. More or less."

"Why more or less?"

"It is a convention which believes that compulsion or influence can be had over an object through a similar or connected part of it. The hair of a dog might rule the dog, for instance."

"Might?"

"I've found it's not a reliable magic."

"Oh."

"Why do you ask?"

"It was mentioned to me, and I hadn't heard of it, and they then said you were behind on my studies."

He scrunched up his nose. "I believe in learning actual magic and then, when one is a master, one can dabble in learning about fakery."

"So . . . voodoo is fake?"

"No, no. But that involves another matter altogether. What I've been attempting to teach you, Tessa, uses will, disciplined and educated and imaginative. It's a finer art than herbology or learning spells by rote or making sacrifices to harness another's power, often demonic."

I stared at him. Then made a sign of passing my hand over my head. He, now purely Brian, grinned.

"I know, right? Welcome to my life." He dipped back into the container and many rustles followed.

My mother bellowed down the staircase, "Tessa! Classes!"

I hit the stairs. "And welcome to mine."

Evelyn dressed in camos for the day, shocking me and nearly everyone else, although I could place a bet and win money that girls would be dressing in camos in every classroom before the week was out. She did look fetching, thin with curves in the right places while I simply wore jeans and a long-sleeved cotton shirt with the cuffs rolled up and my sneakers. She nudged me.

"What do you think?"

"About what?"

"The outfit, duh. I'll blend in if we need to do some spying."

"Ah. Stunning." I shifted my backpack and tried to look admiring.

Despite the professor and Brian's viewpoint on sympathetic magic, I hoped to try it out. I had Germanigold's feather in my backpack and with any luck, could figure out a way to utilize it while on the computers in the library. Google had magic of its own: information. Tons and tons of it, some of it real and some of it so far from the mark it made fake news look credible. I just needed enough time to sift through it all. "I'm just going to get a look at the campus. No spying involved." Not for her, anyway.

Evelyn pouted for about twelve seconds. "I can go home and change at lunch break."

"Why? You look adorable." I thumbed open my phone. "See? You're already trending on Instagram."

"Am I?" She peered at my cell and laughed. "Guess I'll go as I am."

I shelved my phone. "Good. Did you look up the academy last night?"

"I did but, well . . ."

"What?"

"I think you deserve better."

"Evie. Thank you. But the place looked like a brain trust to me."

"Oh, no doubt of that. But it's small. It seems to be

quite conservative. I don't know—I should think you'd want to spread your wings and fly."

I pondered telepathy and wondered if she'd honed in on my plan to find Germanigold at Silverbranch. Despite the suspicious use of words, I decided there wasn't a chance. She can be good people, but often Evelyn considered herself first and a lot more frequently than she considered other people. It wasn't her fault; she'd been taught to do so by her image-conscious parents. I patted her shoulder. "Thanks for the thought."

"Welcome. See you later."

We split in the hallway.

By the end of the day, the Internet had vomited wordage all over me, and I decided that I might have been better off not knowing most of it, because my early impulse of simply holding the feather and willing myself to be able to find Goldie and free her seemed the best, most positive, not to mention sane, way of rescuing her. Philosophers are sometimes right: the simplest solution is often the best. My only worry now seemed to be getting Evelyn out of the way at the critical moment in time when I hoped to accomplish the feat. Turning her around in a circle three times, taking a blindfold off, and pointing in the direction of the nearest good-looking guy didn't seem feasible. Not that it wouldn't work, but she might be a bit annoyed at the blatant manipulation.

One doesn't want Evelyn Statler or either of her parents annoyed at them. Especially her father, who will probably be elected mayor in November.

I could, however, probably convince her to decoy for me in a dire situation. I'd just have to think of what it could be if/when I located Goldie.

We linked arms and walked to the parking lot where my shiny, only somewhat faded red car waited for me, along with Dean the bad boy leaning on its fender. He had a new haircut, faded on the sides with a luxurious curling wave on top. He'd found a vintage athletic jacket from somewhere and had that on, along with hip-hugging jeans, a black shirt, and shoes too cool to bother lacing up, even if they tripped him somewhere down the block.

He reached for Evelyn. "Hey, babe."

As fast as she could be, Evie dodged him. "Not now, sugar, I've got a road trip with Tessa."

"But we had plans."

She poked her finger into his chest. "You had plans. You forgot to ask me, and I'm going to be busy. Maybe tomorrow."

"Maybe tomorrow I'll be busy."

"And pigs will fly. You'll wait for me if you know what's good for you." Evelyn tossed her head again, light blond hair rippling over her shoulders, and a dare-me look filled her eyes.

"Now go on. We've things to do." She turned him about and gave him the tiniest of pushes away from the car. I watched him stride away with that super confident "I'm the shit" strut alpha males must practice from the time they hit 12 until they need a walker. "Mmm-mmm," Evelyn murmured. "Isn't he something?"

He definitely thought he was. "You're lucky. Now, get in the car and buckle up, buttercup!"

The temperature had dropped considerably in the afternoon and made her camo outfit look like genius while I rummaged around in my car's trunk praying for a stray jacket or hoodie to be stuffed in among the textbooks. Nothing turned up. I would have to brave the autumn weather in shirtsleeves and made a note to put contingency supplies in the car.

Evelyn tapped my shoulder. "Ready?"

"Pretty much." I turned. She had a windbreaker hanging from her fingers.

"Thought you might need this."

She could read my mind! Acceptable, for the moment. "Where'd you have this?"

"Stuffed deep in my backpack. Sorry it's wrinkled."

I took it and shrugged into it. "Good job. I see I picked a super sidekick."

She tossed her head. "Partner."

"You've just been promoted."

She dropped her pack into the trunk and away we went.

* * *

The edge of the Silverbranch Academy bordered a small, unnamed creek that ran into Richmond's main river, the James, which is a massively important waterway, some 340 miles long. The campus' little fellow looked very unimportant in comparison, although it did set the Academy apart from the farmlands nearby. As the car crept into the visitors' parking lot, the sky darkened with growing clouds, and trees thrashed to and fro in the wind. "My," said Evelyn. "It's getting busy out there."

Looking through the windshield, I caught the distinct impression that the coming storm might not come from Mother Nature. Would that make me paranoid?

Evelyn grabbed her handbag. "Let's go." There are accessories she wouldn't be caught dead without. Her pack, not so much but her purse and phone, always.

I sat. My purse these days is a small, heavy-duty, and lightweight backpack. I couldn't find a comfortable shoulder bag that held Steptoe's flash-bangs and a quart-sized carton of salt easily enough, not to mention the other necessities. Picking the pack up, I hefted it over my shoulder.

"Administration is that way. They said they'd have a pass for us."

Much as I'd wanted to sneak in, the open country around made it impossible as well as unwise. Although forest blended in and out of farm acreage, the campus stood out easily. Down the road, a near-primeval forest awaited, but not here.

Stepping outside, the wind whipped Evelyn's hair about her face, blinding her for a moment. She stopped and tried unsuccessfully to tuck it in place. I dug in my pocket and handed her a scrunchie, and she quickly bound it back.

We headed to Administration, skittering like other students and various fall leaves along the sidewalks in a hurry. In the gray afternoon, the blaze of climbing ivy turning red, gold, and orange lit up many of the buildings while the more modern ones held mirror images in their glassy sides, giving the whole place a small but classy and dynamic look. I wondered if any of it was illusion.

We blew into the main hall with a clatter of double doors and staccato of Evelyn's bootheels on the tile flooring. I glanced down. Marble. Marble flooring. For the briefest of moments, I wondered if Mortimer and his Broadstone clan had done any of the work here. Quite possibly. No, make that probably. His people were said to be masters even among masters, and this stuff looked like quality, understated elegance. I smiled down at the floor. For another brief moment, I thought I could feel warm wishes reflected back at me.

Fortified, I tapped the back of Evelyn's hand, and we forged down the hall toward Admittance.

A receptionist smiled up at us, perky and not much older than either of us at first glance, although a look at her clothes suggested she had never left the Fifties or maybe she just liked being retro. While Evelyn stared at her, thinking, I introduced myself.

"Oh, we have your visitor's pass right here. Customarily, we let you take a walk around and then meet back here for a little orientation film, and a question and answer session."

"Sounds perfect." I took the pass. Under my glove, my maelstrom stone flashed red-hot, and then went icy. I guessed it just neutralized something in the paperwork, although I had no idea what and decided to get moving before the ageless receptionist figured out something had gone wrong.

Evelyn waved cheerily before joining me. She whispered, "OMG. I think she's 80% Botox."

"Really?"

"Has to be. Did you see her clothes?"

"Yup. I thought maybe it was rock 'n roll day here or something."

Evelyn snickered. "She wishes. Okay, where to now?"

"A quick look at the classroom halls even though we're going to have to hurry between buildings and hope it doesn't start raining."

"I'm game. My jacket is probably warmer than yours."

"And not borrowed."

"Right."

A small but detailed map had been printed on the backside of the pass. I could see a silver star neatly marked "You Are Here" at the Administration building. I showed the map to Evelyn. "Hey! They've got a Starbucks. We can stop for coffee."

"We're going to need one."

As we stepped back outside, the wind swirled up, much colder and uninviting, and it tried to slice through our clothing. Evelyn glanced up at the sky. "It almost feels like snow."

"Seriously?"

"I know, I know. It can't be." She pulled up the hood on her jacket and tied it tight under her chin. "Yours has a hood, too, in the collar."

My numb ears felt much better as soon as I got protection in place. We hurried from one building to another, sometimes with students and professors, but mostly alone, as class times didn't coincide with our visit. We peeked into a number of classrooms, saw nothing remarkable, and Evelyn complained in a disappointed voice, "Doesn't seem that different from Sky Hawk."

And it didn't.

"There are dorms," I said helpfully. "We don't have dorms."

"Oh! Right! Maybe the good-looking guys are in the common rooms, studying." She dug an elbow in my ribs.

"Sorry about that. They were in the brochure. Maybe we can sue for false advertising?"

She giggled, which seemed to lift the brooding atmosphere a bit, as we ventured to the nearest dorm.

If this was a den of magical learning, I hadn't seen it, other than my stone's reaction to my pass. Nor did I have an inkling as to why Carter Phillips had enrolled here, however briefly, or what he might have studied. If there was a glamour here, disguising the place, it was impenetrable. Notwithstanding the pass, I detected no magical activity, but I told myself I wasn't the best detector ever. I should have brought Scout. The concrete pathway evolved into rather clever stepping stones as we approached Birch Hall Dorm. The vibrant autumn-painted ivy covered this building in huge waves. Behind it, however, I could see red brick, old-fashioned glass-paned windows, and numerous chimneys adorning the rooflike turrets on a castle. It looked tremendously old and a bit pretentious and very New England-ish charming, tucked away in the heart of Virginia. Two immense silver birch trees ruled the front lawn to the main part of the dorm.

A handful of students charged out of the doorway as we neared to step in, and a girl to the rear of the group stopped, her gaze catching sight of me with pass in hand. She was a ginger, and freckles dotted her face, making it merry looking. She laughed and waved the others on.

"Visiting?"

"Yes."

"Bloody weather for it." Her accent couldn't quite decide if it were English or maybe Irish without the brogue. "You should go to the library. Definitely the library. That's where everyone gathers." And she was off, rather like a headstrong pony, catching up with her herd of fellows.

"Library?"

I shrugged. "She did recommend it." We located it by the map and also by the students headed toward it, in handfuls and singles, seemingly unmindful of the weather.

We started toward the building, off to the northwest, when I happened to look back, over my shoulder, a recent habit. Anything could be following us. There, in the shadows of Birch Hall, I could see the gardens of the courtyard behind with three lovely statues celebrating water, earth, and air. Only the air statue looked disturbingly familiar.

My backpack tugged a bit. I shoved my hand inside to find Goldie's feather doing a frantic jig.

"Ummm. How about you head to the library? I'm going to double back and see if I can find the girls' bathroom in the dorm."

"You can't wait?"

"It's been all day." I danced a little on the stepping stones. Shoving the pass into her hand, I promised to catch up with her immediately. "And save a guy for me!"

Evie waved me on, shaking her head and chortling.

I legged it back toward the dorm, ducked around the south wall of the building and headed to the courtyard. There, face-to-face with the statue, I could see the unmistakable resemblance even though I'd met her in the darkest of night. The feather practically flew out of my backpack into my hand where I held it, with absolutely no idea what to do with it.

I could see that part of her wing statuary seemed chipped, missing a piece. Could it be that simple? Stepping forward, I angled the feather down into the gap and completed the wing.

Goldie turned her head toward me with a gasp.

CHAPTER FOURTEEN

FLY SO FREE

THE SKY BURST open, with a sheet of lightning striking nearby and sending its ozone smell crackling across the little courtyard. Seconds later, rain began to fall in torrents and with every wet drop on her body, the stone melted away. I couldn't help but watch until both of us stood, drenched and free, and facing each other.

Goldie smiled as she stepped down off the dais toward me. "What enterprise. You have my profound gratitude, Tessa Andrews, and—"

The sound of a single person clapping interrupted her. We both swung around and she flung her wings up in genuine fight or flight reaction. I gestured at her. "Go! Go on, get out of here!"

"Oh, she can't do that, Miss Andrews. You've freed her, but I still have a binding." And the clapper moved into view, his features sharp and his stature a little on the short side, his suit far more expensive than either of the agents who'd visited me, and his bearing one of absolute authority. My heart sank a bit. If this was the judge in the Society, he knew his magic and I didn't. My only move was to strip my gloves away and stow them and worry about freezing fingers. My stone flared up again, though, instantly warming the one hand. I clasped them together to share. Under my shirtsleeves, my bracers caught the same slight heat.

Lightning hit again, and thunder rumbled loudly, right overhead, so I knew the strike had been somewhere on campus. Maybe at the library? I hoped Evelyn had the good sense to stay inside. Or maybe it was worse in there? Did they know about me all over Silverbranch?

The gentleman drew closer, and I could see a flicker of caution in his movements. Okay, so he knew about harpies being warrior women with a lot of ability, and maybe he thought I could do more than I actually could, so he took care. Goldie shrugged, trying to bring her wings up again, and shuddered when they refused to answer to her.

She fell to one knee with a groan. Her head bowed. I nudged her. "Get up! We're not done fighting yet!"

The gentleman laughed harshly. "She is. The moment Mortimer was taken from her, she surrendered." He stopped watching Goldie and looked to me. "What about you? What does it take to break you?"

I refused to think about it. No names in my thoughts, in case he could somehow perceive them. "I don't quit. Not in the driving rain, not standing all alone. I can't fight the way you can, but I don't quit." While I talked, I dug the toe of my sneaker under a loose stepping stone in front of me. As any teammate on our field hockey team could tell him about the way I played the game, rain or shine, I'll drive down that field and put my stick down your throat if necessary. If we needed points, I determined to be the go-to girl. Guys on the ice hockey team came out to watch and get pointers from me on roughing players without getting penalized.

Goldie gave another low moan, so quiet I barely heard it even though it gave me goose bumps when I did. I could feel her tremble next to me but refused to look at her. I had my attention centered on the man across from us. The stepping stone loosened obligingly. A heave rippled through her body.

"You know my name. Do you have one?"

"I have many. At this campus, they call me Maxwell Parker. Judge Parker, if you will."

"You give it out so freely, I gather that's not your true name. You don't think I can harm you with it."

He flashed white teeth, smiling.

"You would be foolish to try. I can reach out and

touch any of your loved ones that I wish. Your mother. Your father. Your rather silly friend Evelyn. Not to mention the others which I already have in my sight—Broadstone. Steptoe. Brandard."

My heart did a quick step when he mentioned my father. I wondered just what he knew about the situation or if he was bluffing. I noted he'd left Carter off the list. Had Carter covered his activities, or did Parker think that the Society had swallowed Carter hook, line, and sinker?

"You can't touch me." Maxwell Parker raised his hands to create some magical havoc.

"You'd be wrong." I kicked my foot up, and the paver came up in the air where I caught it neatly and swung, my maelstrom stone smacking into it soundly, batting it directly at him. My hand and wrist stung like fire. He didn't dodge in time. My aim caught him right in the temple and he dropped, well, like a stone.

Goldie lunged to her feet as he did, her wings gone, and her body entirely human, encased in that Amazon leather armor. She got to him first and tied him down. Stuffing a handkerchief from his pocket into his mouth, she looked up at me.

"Nice going."

My hand smarted. I shook it off. "I manage. The question is: are you rescued or do we have something else to do? I'm game, short of slitting his throat."

"Pity, because that would accomplish a great deal, but I understand your reluctance." Goldie stretched. The rain had slowed to a very light sprinkle, and the drops ran over her as though her human skin operated like ducks' feathers and was water repellent.

I watched her before getting it. "You're a shapeshifter. Harpies are shifters. Took me a while, with everyone talking about where your nest is located and such."

"Yes. We perform best half-and-half, human head and arms, the rest winged and avian, but we operate back and forth." She winked at me. "My wings are tied to some spell Parker has concocted, but I can get around that, given enough time."

"It took you a while to shift."

"Yes. Side effect of his working. I expect it to wear off if nothing else, sooner or later."

"We should make it sooner." I joined her and looked down at the judge. "He's really Society."

"Oh, yes."

"Is everyone else like this?"

"A few are worse. His is a secret malady, though, or he'd be thrown out. And he doesn't want that. It would cut his power until he learned to adjust it. Right, buddy?" She poked him. His eyelids fluttered.

"I say we dump him in the creek and see if he floats, sorta like they used to do with witches in Salem."

"That is an idea." Goldie grinned at that.

Not a particularly good one if I wanted information out of him, though. I thought I could hear shouts and laughter in the distance.

"We need to go, and now. Can you leave this place, or are you centered here?"

"I can leave." She patted the judge down one more time, found something of interest in a side coat pocket, and slipped it down her corset cleavage. I had a momentary mental picture of all the men I knew watching her action closely. I shook it off.

Opening my backpack, I took out Steptoe's coat. "The best way to get out of here would be to do it unseen." I also got my phone out, texted Evelyn to meet me at the car PRONTO, and put my phone on silent before putting it back in the little pocket most backpacks had reserved for cell phones and other important goodies.

I turned the coat inside out and began, very carefully, to see if I could stretch it apart, just as I'd seen Simon do it. It resisted. Fabric is fabric, right? Except when it isn't, and I didn't think this was, not entirely. I gritted my teeth and prayed I wasn't exhausting its magical capability but this felt urgent. "I know what you can do," I muttered at the object. "So get with the program."

Judge Parker began to thump on the ground, kicking up small puddles of mud and water.

"What are you doing?" Goldie brushed sopping wet hair from her face impatiently.

"Working on something. Simon says . . ." I halted. No. Really? As easy as Simon says . . .

I took up the coat again, determined to stretch it enough to cover both of us, chanting Simon says with every pull. With great resistance, it began to grow in my hands. I turned it about, stretching and shaping it until it could cover both of us. I stood next to her and flung it overhead, catching the other edge. "Let's go. Match your pace to mine. We can't be seen."

I hoped.

Being on the other side, it seemed impossible to tell. I couldn't be sure until we passed a loving couple on the walkway, immersed in each other and laughing in that intimate way people in a relationship talk to each other, and they didn't notice us at all. Or the rain.

Of course, that could just have been being in love.

I took a moment to text Evie.

We walked each other across Silverbranch to the parking lot where I opened the car door and shoved both Goldie and the suit coat into the back seat. It wavered for a moment, but I pointed at it and said, "Stay."

It did. I couldn't see either of them at all, but could feel the car bounce a little as she settled on the rear seat. Evelyn came running up, her clue to hurry because I had the car started and in gear. She threw herself in.

"What is it?"

"A little trouble, nothing serious, but I might have accidently assaulted one of their professors."

"What???" She let out a screech to match the squeal the tires made as we left.

"It was him or me."

"Really? What happened? One of those sexual advance things?"

"No, more like a field hockey hit gone wrong."

She winced.

"He caught it in the head."

"Caught what?"

"One of those nice stepping stones on the path. That's what I get for showing off my athletic skills."

"Oh, jeez, Tessa. Are you sure you didn't kill him?"

From the manic glare in Maxwell Parker's eyes as he struggled to get loose, I was pretty sure I hadn't. She reached over to pat my knee. "You probably didn't."

"Thanks."

"De nada." Evelyn paused, and her breath slowed. Then she said, "There are two, darkened by cloaks, hidden by shadows—you think they are one and the same, but they are not. An abyss separates them. Choose well."

Goldie gave a strangled sound from the back seat as I sat up straight on the driver's side. "Evie?"

Silence.

"Evie, are you all right?" I wondered if the students of Silverbranch had put a hex on her or something.

She shook her head then and answered, "My hair is going to frizz something awful by the time we get home!"

And then all of us sank into our thoughts as the rain got serious and noisy. What had she been gibbering about, and was it serious? Because she didn't seem to be all there when she'd said it. I wondered if the Society had reached through her to threaten us and decided things were bad enough from time to time without imagining worse.

We made good time getting away from Silverbranch and caught up with the leading edge of the squall. I put the headlights on, but they did a poor job of cutting through the dark curtain of advancing night and pounding rain. Evelyn shivered. "Got any heat in this thing?"

"Sure." I eyed the dashboard. "Somewhere."

I'd taken my eyes off the road. If I hadn't, I wouldn't have seen the small dead things falling along with the rain. But I did. My heart skipped a beat. I did hear the profound silence of nothing but the wind howling and the rain pelting the ground, and the car schussing through the growing puddles. It fishtailed as we hit unexpected slush and maybe a patch of ice.

The car drifted in answer to my pull at the steering wheel and I jammed my foot on the brakes. I tried to counter the movement, remembering centrifugal forces and those driving movies that were mandatory viewing, but none of my efforts helped. A huge tree keeled over right in front of us, branches thrashing and immense roots going bottoms up. Evelyn made a tiny squeak deep in her throat, and someone muttered, "Athena have mercy" from the back of the car.

No mercy to be found. I wrenched the steering wheel about. The car skewed around in a circle and then accelerated in the opposite direction, directly at the massive tree blocking the road. I had a moment to wonder if we had working air bags and if Goldie had buckled in, when the car spun around yet again. My wrists weren't strong enough to keep the steering wheel straight, and I felt as if we'd been jolted into a bumper car ride with no control. About then, I decided this was no ordinary skid. Solid shadows assailed the car, and the headlights died out without even a flicker. Then the car itself quit as it hit the fallen tree, hard.

My door popped open as if it had never been latched, seat belt snapping loose, pitching me into the rain and onto the road, and I lay there for three seconds to catch my breath.

Then something truly immense leaned out of the tree toward me. It was darker than the night and the storm, as if it were the thing that swallowed all universes and suns. My feet, still hung up inside the car, caught on my backpack strap, and as I flipped over to crawl away, I dragged my pack with me. Before I could free myself and get to my feet, the thing in the night took me by the elbow, jumped me to my feet, and kicked the tree off the road. My little car rolled into a small ditch at the side, and I heard nothing from either Goldie or Evelyn.

The nightmare holding onto me shrank to almost human size.

Malender leaned into my face and said, "We need to talk."

CHAPTER FIFTEEN

WHO'S ON FIRST

MALENDER TOOK MY breath away, his leather and lace like a cavalier from centuries gone, and his eyes a rich, deep, jade color set off by curling sable lashes. They weren't emeralds, but something smokier and deeper and far more mysterious. Rain glistened off his so-black-it-shone-purple hair, and he had never been baked, tanned, or wrinkled by the sun. Moonlight illuminated him, as the streetlights had not the last time I'd seen him, and I soaked in his beauty. I would want him to the ends of the earth if he were not encased in a boiling, oily, and distasteful cloud. Or if people would stop saying terrible things about him in warning. Or if Carter Phillips did not exist.

And then, because my brain seemed to be spinning, I remembered seeing him with blue eyes and no cloud. How had I not remembered his green eyes? Did they change color according to his mood? Or had it truly been him? Had Joanna's master been someone entirely different who knew how to mimic Malender? Who would dare such a thing?

Goldie climbed out of the backseat, Steptoe's coat peeling off her as she did, and it gave an eerie note to her appearing out of thin air. She swayed a bit as she stood, and then her eyes widened. "You!" She jabbed a finger at Malender.

I edged in front of her. "Take it easy, Goldie."

She put her hand on my shoulder, turning me out of

harm's way, and I could feel her wings flutter. "He is not to be trusted, or trifled with, or ignored. You have no idea what you are dealing with."

Oh, I had some small idea, but as soon as Goldie and I could have some private time, I intended to find out what she knew about tall, dark, and awesome.

He curled a lip and pointed right back at her. "Do not meddle where you have not been invited."

"I may not remember your weak spot, but I—"

Malender snarled a word, and Goldie was jerked off her feet and stuffed back into my car. The door slammed after her.

"You didn't . . ."

Malender's attention swung back to me. "A lesson for those who would interfere with me."

"She's not . . ."

"Of course not. Would I stuff a dead body into your vehicle?"

"The thought did occur to me."

"You do have some self-preservation sense, then."

Evidently, only just enough. I gathered up my backpack and clutched it to my side, struggling for a breath because I suddenly could not quite breathe. With his free hand, Malender waved a bubble around us, separating us from the real world and all that it contained, but everything around us grew intense: sight, smell, sound. He smelled like cedar and leather; the oily substance had no scent at all but it gathered at the back of my throat as though it would pool there to choke me, and I could hear my heart beating loudly. I cleared my throat in rapid succession, but nothing rid me of the greasy stuff although I noticed the cloud seemed far less encompassing than it had been, almost as if Malender had found a way to outrun or dissipate it. It wasn't at all like the nasty cloud of the glop that took Steptoe out, but just as bad in a different way. I thought I'd gag in front of this beautiful being, so I clamped my lips shut and tried to think of other things. Like, why was he holding me by the back of my neck, a foot off the ground? I stabbed a finger downward.

He slowly lowered me and let go.

"Do your eyes change color? And is that cloud like a cloak, sometimes here and sometimes not?"

His jade gaze narrowed at me. "No. But when I said we had to talk, I envisioned myself doing the talking and you listening, to provide an answer now and then."

"I thought I had something important to say, but—" I managed a smile. "Sure. What do you want to talk about?"

"You are stirring things about which you know nothing."

"Your little plots or someone else's? And if I am screwing around in yours, I might remind you that I have friends and tend to help them when they have problems."

"Friends would not lead you into trouble."

"Sometimes they don't have any choice—none of us do, if there's a difficulty." I looked him up and down and could not quite contain the smile that pulled the corner of my mouth. "And, mister, if anyone looks like trouble, you do."

His nostrils flared ever so slightly. "You are a child." The cedar smell grew sharper, as if tied to his temper.

"By your standards, we are all barely more than a second old, I'm sure. I don't function by your standards. You take care of friends if you can. Out there, somewhere, is a little car with one of mine in it. I don't know if she's hurt or safe, and I'm not happy to be standing here with you in this—" I circled my hand around.

"If you wish to stand in the rain, I can arrange it." The bubble opened up, and the storm flowed in as though I stood under Niagara Falls, drenching me immediately. He, of course, stayed high and dry.

"Thanks."

"Don't mention it."

He looked almost happy, so I decided I wouldn't complain. I fiddled with my jacket and brought out the aforementioned hood Evie had told me about again. My hands brushed over the backpack bulge of the ginormous salt container I hauled around every single day, just for contingencies like this. I decided I wanted to hear a bit more of what he had to say before resorting to drastic measures.

"So. I've irritated you enough that you must want me to stop doing something, but I can't if I don't know exactly what it is. I've got a full plate right now. What portion are you suggesting I dump down the garbage disposal?"

"What a quaint way of putting it." He waggled a few fingers, and I got dry head to toe, but the pelting storm didn't stop, of course, and I quickly got just as wet all over again. A distinctly amused twinkle settled in his jade eyes.

"I'm not going to abandon my family and my people."

"I'm not suggesting you abandon them, precisely. Perhaps guiding them would be more accurate."

"Oh. You want me to push them over a cliff you might be suggesting?"

"Nothing that harsh."

"What then, and who?" I shook inside my jacket, rather like a wet dog shakes, vigorously, and just happened to soak Malender as well. "Not that I'll take your advice, but I'd like to know what's up." I listened in vain for a siren, indicating that help of some kind might be headed the way of my little car and its occupants. Tired of Malender's little lather, rinse, and repeat exercise, I held my maelstrom hand up over my head, Immediately, its shield covered me, keeping the wet out and bringing a comfortable warmth in.

A flicker of surprise went through his eyes. Had he not noticed this before? I could have sworn he did when Joanna attacked me. Didn't we discuss the shield work? Yes, we had. But I don't think I'd told him there were other attributes I had begun exploring. Perhaps not. And even more perturbing, it might not have been him I'd even talked to, in which case, I'd just done something very stupid by exposing the maelstrom to him and whoever the not-him might have been. Both of them. If there were two of them. My thoughts boggled a bit, and I hesitated about keeping the shield up. But neither did I want to catch my death of cold.

"You were saying?"

He moved a pace, as if getting me centered in his

sights. “You’re not magical. No, that’s not correct. Few people are as magical these days as they were centuries and centuries ago, so you might have a dash or two in you, but strictly speaking, you’re not magical.”

The words stung, but I didn’t want to let him see that. I made a face. “And proud of it. I do things the hard way.”

“Oh, magic isn’t easy. Far from it. But even though you’re not magical, you reek of it as if you waded in it every single day. You attract it.”

I flashed my palm at him, adding, “Hello, I have the stone, and I live with a late, great wizard.”

“If they were onions, I could smell them on you.” Malender took a step forward, seriously invading my personal space, and I fought to not step away. He was trying me, and I knew it. “But they are not. Still, there is that in you that attracted them.”

“Returning to . . . people need friends.”

“Professor Brandard had a world full of friends. He turned his back on them.”

I thought of Morty. “Not all.”

“Enough that, in these days, in this place, he needs all he can find.”

“We all do.”

“Do you speak excuses for him?”

“Actually, I thought I was speaking truth to power.”

Malender laughed lightly. “Not with Brandard. I think more of you than that. You have a very good idea of who he is and how he operates.”

“The professor is a crusty old dragon who has had his hoard greatly disturbed, and he doesn’t like it. Nor does he particularly care for visitors treading upon his grounds, but he knows he’s been mortally wounded and that he needs help and he accepts it.”

“Well.”

That stunned Malender quiet for long enough that I wondered if the prof actually could be an old dragon. I stood, arm raised and hand over my head, and also wondered how much longer I could hold the pose. “So I take it that he is one of the people you want me to step away from? I won't do it, but it would help if you could be a little more definite about it."

"The professor needs to come to me if he wants to solve his problem."

"You?"

"Me."

I shut my mouth carefully, gathering my thoughts. "Oh-kay. You want me to pass that along?"

"I do."

"Why don't you approach him yourself?"

"He's still rather fortified. It would set off a draining and senseless struggle. Also, it occurred to me that the message might mean more if he trusted the messenger." Malender leaned a shoulder against something that I couldn't see and disconcerted me as I waited for him to go off-balance or fall and, of course, he didn't. "He would be wise to want my help."

"And what could you do for him?"

"Brandard and I come from similar roots, though mine are much more powerful than his. Still, I understand him, and if you could reach the old man inside the young one, he might tell you the same. We have dueled much, in the past, oft on the same side and oft against one another. He remembers me."

No kidding. He warned me against Malender. I don't think his memories were as touching as Malender thought, similar origins or not.

"You're a phoenix wizard."

"Oh, no." Malender smiled briefly. "I am the Fire."

That explained a bit. None of it sounded the least bit persuasive, though.

Malender pressed. "If you tell him I intend to help, he might listen."

"Might is the operative word here. What's it going to cost?"

"That's between me and Brandard."

"Now, see. You want me to offer a bargain, but you won't tell me the terms."

"What we negotiate you would never understand nor need to know."

I tilted my head. "I don't understand life, death, and the weight of a soul?"

"My price should not be that dramatic."

"Then you're shortchanging yourself, because while Brian looks like a nice, easygoing surfer dude, the professor is all piss and vinegar and hard to get along with. Anything you partner with him to do is going to be difficult. Just a warning."

He put his hand to his chest. "You're worried about me? I'm touched."

"I'm worried about the east coast because, if the two of you tangle, I'm thinking we're all dust."

"Hmmmm." He still looked pleased. And unbearably handsome.

"Anyone else you want me to offer a deal to?"

"No, but you should walk away from Steptoe and the Iron Dwarves and Silverbranch."

I counted on my free fingers. "I can keep Evelyn."

His nose wrinkled slightly. "If you can bear her. She is more in the realm of a—What would you call her?"

"Sometimes a bestie and sometimes a frenemy. She's fluid that way." A pang went through me at assessing Evelyn so harshly, but I didn't want Mal to notice her too closely. I thought of my words as camouflage over her true value to me.

He shrugged. "That is a world I do not understand. It's your choice."

I straightened. "I have news for you, Malender. It's all my choice. I have no intentions of leaving any of them behind for any reason, and most certainly not because you suggested it. I trust them, and I don't trust you."

"Trust has nothing to do with wisdom."

"The heck it doesn't. It's one of the foundations of freedom."

"I don't have your trust?" He bent his head down to look at me closer, his face creased in a touch of sorrow. The laughter at the back of his jade eyes faded a bit.

"Not really. Have you given me reason to?"

"Do you wish to make a deal with me for this trust?"

"No." A few drops of rain began to slip past my shield,

and I knew the stone faltered because I tired. I didn't really want to be standing out here when it gave way entirely because I didn't want to let Malender see a weakness. I sensed a hesitation in him.

Then, without warning, a young buck stumbled into our bubble, his three-point horns still covered with velvet, the pupils of his eyes wide in the night, and as quickly, Malender's hand shot out and grabbed him by the throat. I thought he would simply push the deer out and away. He did not. His hand closed tightly.

The animal kicked his hooves out and thrashed, trying desperately to back up, his rear outside the bubble in the rain and gaining little traction on the soaked ground. Mud splashed everywhere but not a spot hit where I stood. I moved, though, for his striking grew intense with frantic hooves slashing for freedom.

"Don't hurt him!"

"Do you think he happened here by accident? He's a tribute, sent by the forest. And he's been claimed. What I do is a mercy." Malender's fist closed. I could hear the jackhammer of the stag's heartbeat and smell the anguish surging through his body. The deer made a strangling noise, and foam fell from his flared nostrils and open mouth. The sound of his snorting and breathing grew faint. The fog that cloaked Malender billowed darker and grew thicker.

Softly, for the animal and not Malender, I murmured, "It'll be all right. It will." Like a subtle flame, his spirit rose inside him, and began to climb out of him, a glowing bit on a string, aiming for freedom. I tried to tear my eyes away from the awfulness eating away at him, the darkness flowing from Malender's hold into his body.

"Don't do this."

"He's already been committed, but I don't expect you to understand." The cords on Malender's neck stood out as if he struggled, but his voice stayed in velvet tones meant to reassure me which were patently not working.

The stone in my palm bit at me in a surprising and

sharp pain. I flicked my hand as if to shake it away. A white light cut through the air and across the string that held the deer's spirit. It leaped away from him, springing up as if it were the buck itself and leaping over a fallen log or a thicket or a troublesome fence, a jump into freedom. Malender, his face carved into hard lines, did not seem to notice.

I could see the buck stop fighting and begin to tremble. His hindquarters got loose and wobbly and he would have fallen, but Malender detained him too tightly. His legs collapsed and he no longer stood but that his captor held him in the air. His lungs heaved for breath and abruptly stopped. The wide, frightened eyes went all white. As the life left the deer, I could sense it flowing into Malender, and yet . . . and yet . . . I had cut the soul loose. I had helped it somehow, hadn't I, by setting its spirit free? I closed my eyes a brief second, remembering all the thousands of starlings which could fall from the sky when he struck and absorbed the very essence of life from them. This was both the same and far worse. I did not think of it as a tribute but a needless slaughter. The lathered warmth of the deer's body turned cold and chill.

I stood frozen in place, afraid to move. This was the being I dared to sass? To share time and space with as if he were one of us? I'd forgotten what I'd been told. What I'd learned. The death of the deer gave me a grim reminder.

The carcass hung from his hand and then, inexorably, turned into ash without flame or heat, and floated away into nothingness. *I am Fire*. Fire consumes, and if unchecked, will consume utterly. Stone returns to earth and water recycles continuously, but fire—fire must engulf utterly. His act chased the words out of my mouth, the breath from my lungs, the thoughts from my mind.

"Odd, but to be expected these days, I suppose. He had no soul. No matter. He fought well enough. The tribute was accepted. I cannot explain it, Tessa, but you have not seen what you think you've seen here." He did not seem pleased.

"I just saw you strangle an animal to death and then incinerate it."

"He was dying when he blundered into us. I tried to ameliorate his struggle. But I cannot expect you to understand."

"Explain it."

He shook his head. "Believe it or not, I am not willing to risk you by telling you more right now. One day when this cloud about me is gone . . ."

I couldn't move until he dusted his hands against his leather pants and took his own deep breath and tried to push his cloaking darkness away from his shoulders. He no longer smelled of cedar but death. He closed his eyes for a long moment. The fear stink of the animal, and the sweat of the near-silent battle, and the stench of its dying clung to Malender. That oily cloak about him seemed excited and exhilarated, giving me a vibe that clawed at the back of my throat and made my heart race a little. But his words struck me. He didn't like it. He didn't want it. Was it part of him or some kind of curse that had been lowered over him? He straightened and, I swear, stood four inches taller, his eyes more vibrant when he opened them.

"As I said, the professor needs me. And, unfortunately, I believe I have need of him, but only if he is restored. We are both hungry, almost infinitely hungry, but that should not be. We can help each other beyond that. So I allow your interference but only to a point. Believe that."

After what I'd just seen, I had no doubt. I managed to inhale, coughed on the odor, and swallowed my repugnance down. I took a step away from him and bumped into the inside of the bubble, reminding me I, too, stood trapped even though he'd ripped my part of the ceiling away. How had I forgotten that he was fear and the night and the abyss without hope?

"You seem unconvinced."

Wavering, I shook my head.

"Then I offer this to you, gratis. A onetime boon to prove my trustworthiness. You've been troubled by . . .

what is it? A glop?" He laughed then, genuinely, as if the name greatly amused him. He waved a hand negligently. "It is removed and Steptoe can be gathered up."

He would offer this? And what would he gather in return? Whose life would he devour? My throat dry, my lips reluctant to unseal, I surprised myself by speaking again. "Gratis?"

"Absolutely gratis. There is little worth in a demon of chaotic good, anyway. He trades away most of his ability amid enemies."

I wanted out and away. My mind galloped ahead with that goal. "I'd argue that with you, but frankly, I need to get home before I worry my mother, and she has been through enough on my account."

He waved. "Go then. We'll talk again." Malender brushed a bit of hair from his forehead. "A blessing of salt, Tessa?"

He wanted salt? Then, by George, I'd give it to him. I clawed the huge container out of my backpack and rained it down on him. That cloak seemed to quail and even develop holes, shredding at its edges, under the cascade of crystals.

Malender winced. It hurt. It seared. I could tell that, but he stood solidly and then put his head back and faced upward into the crystals as they bounced off the planes of his face. The cloak shrank closer about him as I poured. Did I feel sorry for him?

Not if I could help it. The world's most beautiful being had a core of ugliness I could not tolerate. I turned to run. The bubble burst.

The rain came down in pounding, unrelenting wetness, the road reared up under my feet, and my little car gave a forlorn honk as its lights and motor roared to life. It heaved itself out of the ditch as though an invisible someone with a winch towed it out, and settled back on the pavement, ready to go.

I jumped in. The airbag hadn't gone off, but Evelyn shook herself awake, one hand to her jaw.

"What did we hit?"

"A tree. I pulled it off the road. Ready to roll?"

"The sooner the better," came a faint voice from the back seat. Goldie sat up, shrugged off the invisibility coat, and she leaned up front. She held a hand to her temple and said, with a touch of pain in her voice, "We should hurry."

I had forgotten that Judge Maxwell Parker and the hounds of Silverbranch Academy might be hot on our heels. I put the car in gear. "Rolling!"

CHAPTER SIXTEEN

WHAT FOOLS THESE MORTALS BE

I FELT LIKE I'd met the devil himself at a crossroads and he'd offered me a bargain for my soul. I'd turned it down, hadn't I? At least, that version of it. I didn't hear any ominous banjo or fiddle music in my head strumming like a madman played, so I must have. Evelyn turned in her passenger seat, eyes on Goldie in the back, but said nothing. I reached over and patted Evie on the knee.

"I picked up a hitchhiker."

"I can see that. What I don't remember is when or where."

"She helped me move the tree off the road. You were pretty fuzzy then. I think you might have hit the dashboard or maybe the window."

Her slender hand rubbed the side of her head. "Okay."

"Goldie, this is Evelyn Statler; Evie, meet our new friend, Germanigold Broadstone."

"Pleased." But Evelyn did not offer a handshake. She slumped back in the car's seat, looking a bit dazed. "Someone tell me why she is wearing Wonder Woman's Amazon armor."

"Actually, she is wearing mine, but this is an outfit designed for a fencing and saber group I belong to. My motorcycle petered out and I was walking the road when Tessa spun into the tree. I was glad to help."

Goldie settled back in her seat then, Steptoe's jacket

now right side out and folded neatly on the bench beside her, reminding me of Malender's "boon."

He'd said without strings. Really? I'd agreed to it gratis, right? I wasn't sure I would take him up on it, after what I'd just witnessed, but could I leave Steptoe helpless? No. So, sometime tonight, after I dropped Evelyn off safely and did whatever I could for Goldie, I'd swing by the house and pick up Steptoe. If I could find him. If the ground hadn't swallowed him into a sinkhole miles deep. If he wanted to come back.

My hands wrapped themselves about the steering wheel. Should I bring Brian along? Would he help or hinder, or would he simply start sorting through the ruins of his home one last time and let me do what I had to do? And when would I tell him what Malender suggested?

My brain felt too fried for decisions. I decided just driving would be complicated enough for the meanwhile, especially in the rain, until we reached our first destination.

Evelyn stumbled out of the car. Her home, a two-story, Montpelier colonial, rose out of the storm, lit from every corner like a rescue beacon. I got the feeling that her parents wanted to be certain their daughter couldn't miss it. They could be insanely protective of their only child, which made me feel mildly ashamed for leading her astray now and then. I leaned out after her. "Tell 'em it was from hockey practice. You accidentally caught an elbow. Put ice on it!"

"I will. See you tomorrow."

Walking like a drunken pirate, she made her way to her front door, fumbled at the doorknob, and eventually got inside. I shifted to ask Goldie to move up, but she was already climbing into place. I could feel her staring at my profile as I switched on the car heater.

"You seem to have a rapport with Malender."

"You'd be right."

"I should have come to your defense."

"He just wanted a talk." I spent a moment digging my gloves out of my still damp jeans and pulling them on. They'd stayed almost dry. I flexed my fingers and steered away from the curb.

"I should ask how you know of him and how he knows you."

"He attacked us while we were on a search for some of Professor Brandard's magical relics. I fended him off with salt. This seems to amuse him, and he shows up every once in a while to keep tabs on me. I don't know why except that he wants to keep tabs on me. He's even helped out now and then."

"He might be building a debt in which you owe him." She searched my face a moment before leaning back and shaking her head. "He doesn't own you."

"He'd better not!" I paused. "I haven't made any bargains with him and don't intend to. I don't even know what he is."

"He is the best and the worst of us."

"Now that tells me a lot."

Goldie scoffed mildly. "None of us know his secrets. None of us still alive, that is. If you wish to remain among the living, never turn your back on him and never seek to learn what he is about. We might wish that he'd never awoken this century. Last century was dire enough without his being in it."

"That bad, huh?" I could believe it.

"Yes."

"But you have heard of him."

"A tale told to frighten the foolish."

"What kind of tale?"

"One of violence and revenge, generally." Goldie brushed her hair from her face.

"He unnerves you," I guessed, but I didn't know her well enough to know when she felt unsettled. She was a battle harpy, after all, and it should take a lot to make her feel off-balance, but it seemed Malender had.

"Your friend Evelyn."

"Yes?"

"Does she often prophesy?"

I choked a bit. "Prophesy? Her? Now you're just messing with me."

"I'm most serious."

But she wasn't. Germanigold couldn't be. I loved Evie in my own way, and there's no doubt she had smarts, but a prophet? No. Flat-out impossible.

"A change of subject, then." I glanced at her. She stared out the windshield as if searching for something she would never find and I wondered if she thought of Mortimer.

"If you must."

"I must. Hiram has asked me to look for the Eye of Nimora, and it seems you were the last one in possession of it."

She flinched as if I'd stuck a needle in her. "The Eye is missing?"

"Yes."

"It can't be. I had it hidden away, safe and secure. It's vital to the clans."

"Word is that it's gone."

"No." She shook her head in finality. "I'll take you to it."

I looked at the dashboard clock. "I have something to do, but first I need to check in with my mother."

"No phone?"

"I can use that, but I think she'd rather see me and inspect me head to toe and make sure I'm mostly in one piece, the way things have been going around here. And I'd like to change shoes. These are squishy." I wiggled my toes and my sneakers made awful sounds. "And we have to make a stop on the way to wherever."

"Another stop?"

"Steptoe needs a hand."

"Oh. Is that why you have his coat?"

"Something like that."

She folded her arms over her corset. "Maybe we could grab a hamburger and fries, too. I'm hungry."

"Deal." Who knew harpies ate fast food?

Someday if I ever get to be a mom, I hope I can do it as gracefully as my mom does. I let Germanigold know that my mother knew quite a bit more of magic than most people, although I didn't share everything with her. We came in bearing gifts, fragrant bags of fresh fries and three char-broiled hamburgers, medium rare, with crisp lettuce and homegrown tomatoes crowning them, and we ate. She gave one or two curious looks at Goldie, settled when we told her who she was (and even gave Germanigold a sympathy hug for Mortimer's passing) and shared our dinner.

Oh, she had questions. I could see them bouncing around inside her head, but she wouldn't pester me with them now, not in front of guests. They could wait until later. She had this unwritten rule about hospitality that few people dared to break, and I didn't intend to start.

Goldie did answer a few of those queries without being asked, out of obligation or explanation, I couldn't tell. "Mortimer married out of the Iron Dwarf clan when he married me," she told my mother, passing the information around even as she handed over the ketchup bottle.

"I gather that was unusual."

"Very."

"That must have been difficult for both of you."

"It was, then. There are few of us in the unknown races, and mixing blood is frowned upon. We were narrow-minded then and not much different today. What we are accepts differences minutely, big changes even slower." She wiped her fingers on a napkin. "I loved Morty. I'm fairly certain he loved me as well. Because our life spans are different than yours, there were years, even decades we spent apart, but we never lost touch and we never lost how we cared for each other. That might seem strange to you."

My mom smiled a bit. "A little, but understandable, given the circumstances. And you had no family?"

"No, ours was a second marriage. Morty already had the children he wanted, and we couldn't have any together. I had sister-eggs set aside for my future." Goldie blushed slightly, a pretty rose hue to her fair skin. "My apologies, I might have said too much."

Her expression flashed a bit of surprise before going

back to neutral, and my mom leaned forward. "You're among friends here."

"Thank you, I've noticed that. We're a different people, even from each other, and it can be difficult to understand one another." Goldie reached out and covered my right hand with her left. "You have an outstanding daughter."

I sat, still drying, my brunette hair recovering as it lay over my shoulders. "I look like I've been out standing in the weather."

They both laughed. Goldie gathered herself. "We have another mission or two this evening. I can drive if you're worried about Tessa."

"I do, and that would be nice." Mom looked at me. "How far are you going and how late will you be?"

I shrugged at Goldie. "How far?"

"Toward the coast. Maybe a three-hour roundtrip? Plus getting Steptoe on the way."

Mom frowned as she checked her watch. "It would be eleven when you get back. Late, but if you stay off your phone," and she looked down her nose at me as if she still had her reading glasses on, "you should still get to sleep about the same time." She added, "And don't you think you should take Brian?"

"No," we said together.

"All right then. I'm not sure he's in. He can be very quiet."

He could, but he mostly wasn't. When the professor was in charge, you could hear the bluster all the way to the rear fence. My mother looked down. "What about Scout?"

My pup looked up, hope glistening in his brown eyes. Goldie shook her head, very slightly.

"Nope, not this time. I need you to guard the basement," I told Scout.

Goldie let her curiosity out when we'd finished, washed up, and said good-bye.

"What about the basement needs guarding?"

"Some of the professor's goods."

"His stuff survived the fire?"

It seems she was familiar with phoenix wizard rituals.

"Not much, but a few odds and ends." I felt a little uneasy telling her, so I skimped on the details. I could remember the conversation I'd accidentally eavesdropped on, and he hadn't had much confidence in her then. He had his prejudices, though, and I gathered true love was one of them.

Goldie dropped the car keys in my hand. "Drive to Steptoe and I'll take over from there."

The house looked still and grim as we pulled up and parked. New bright yellow "Danger Do Not Cross" tape wrapped about the place, fluttering in the evening breeze. The clouds had thinned out while we ate, and the moon peeked from behind one, its glow getting stronger and stronger. If Brian wasn't at our place, he could be here, doing last minute sifting through the wreckage. With my worry about how he felt about Goldie, I didn't want to run into the wizard, but neither did I want Steptoe to stay captive if I could free him.

Carrying his jacket in hand, I took Goldie around through the side yard, after whispering to her that we needed not to attract attention from the neighbors. We stopped short when we reached our objective. The backyard looked as if it had been bombed. Not the professor's little arbor area, but the grassy lawn leading off the sun porch, away from the house toward the deep rear footage, yawned with holes everywhere. Gophers would have been in awe.

I'd fled, but Steptoe must have put up more of a battle than I'd seen, surfacing and being pulled back down again and again with each crater. I gulped at the sight and held his coat to my chest. Had he even survived? Or had Malender had a bit of fun at my naiveté?

I whispered at Goldie's shoulder. "Brandard might be in the house, but I don't think we should disturb him."

"I'll keep watch. Tackle him if necessary." She gave a half-grin as if she hoped it might be necessary.

I went to the center of the area and, down on one knee, stripped my glove off and put my hand stone downward onto the ground at a yawning edge of one of the bigger holes. Nothing happened for several long breaths except I could feel my pulse slow to a reasonable heartbeat. Rain had made the grass slippery and cool, and an odor rose from it that carried the familiar stink of the glop. I wondered if it roamed below and would reach up and grab me. A sudden fear of grasping tentacles ran through me. Dust-bunnies-under-the-bed nightmares had nothing on this beastie.

Just in case, I drew both legs up under me so I could dodge or dart if I had to, and the maelstrom heated a little. Goldie watched me briefly and then took her own alert stance, cued by mine.

The ruins creaked a little. I couldn't see a light within, so I didn't know if Brian moved through there or not. I watched it warily for a few moments and trained my sense of smell in case the glop stench got markedly stronger. It did not.

"Simon Steptoe," I whispered lowly. Three times, right? I repeated it two more times. "You're free. Come meet me."

The stone in my palm does not loosen, ever, but it can pulse now and then. It's not a pleasant feeling, but at least it reacts, and it did now. Like a heartbeat, pulsating and quickening, like a creature waking up.

"Come on," I urged. "Wake up, my friend."

The ground rippled under me, like a carpet being yanked up. I fought to keep on my feet, and Goldie merely jumped up and hung in the air for a moment as if her wings held her aloft. She didn't manifest her feathers, but her body reacted as if she had. She lowered after a breath or two.

The dirt buckled under me. I jumped back with a muffled squeak, startled and expecting the glop. Instead, a very pale hand reached up.

I reached down and grabbed it, thinking that it had better be Steptoe. I said so. "Steptoe?"

Cold but alive, it yanked and pulled me down to the grassy blades, chin to the ground. I gritted my teeth and pulled back, rearing up, playing tug o' war with whatever/whoever lay below. It gave, bit by bit, inch by inch, until I could see a man's head and then his shoulders and shirtsleeves and arms, and he spit out a mouthful of roots and dirt, sputtering.

"Keep hold, luv!"

"I'm not letting go."

Steptoe peered up at me, one eye closed by a terrible swelling, and muttered, "I might."

"No, you're not. Come on. I've got your coat and things to do tonight."

Our voices: hushed and urgent. Our hands: tight and clinging. I dug in my heels and reeled him in as though he were a prize 175-pound catfish until he floundered to a stop in front of me, heaving and fighting for breath. I slapped him on the back once or twice until he rolled over, looking at the sky.

"Stars," Steptoe observed. "Thank the heavens. That's a bit of all right." His accent thickened.

"Get up and thank everyone later." I helped him up and dusted him down, mud and earthworms sloughing off him. "I should have brought towels. You're a mess."

Goldie fell in behind us as I marched him to the car.

"Give me my coat." And he wrenched it from my hands with a little half-growl, a tiny red light in his black eyes, a reminder of his feral beginnings. I hoped I hadn't saved the wrong being. He snapped his coat in the air. A long hair fell off it and I grabbed for it, shoving it into my pocket.

Steptoe took a deep breath, wiped the back of one hand across his mouth, smudging a bit of dirt at the corner, and hugged his clothing a second. The moment he shrugged the coat on, he stood clean and dapper looking and dry, if weary beyond words. Even his swollen eye looked nearly healed.

"Just pour me in and I'll get a few winks."

Goldie held the door for him, but I don't think he even noticed her before stretching out, somewhat, on the compact back seat and falling asleep, his arms crossed over his chest to hold his suit jacket tight.

CHAPTER SEVENTEEN

FLOCKING TOGETHER

STOPPING FOR GAS didn't wake Steptoe even when Goldie switched to driving with much noise changing seats, filling the gas tank, and slamming the door shut. She raised an eyebrow at me. "Consorting with demons?"

"He doesn't look like it to me. I think of him as a very well-dressed chimney sweep." I found it hard to believe what others claimed about him, although I had not the slightest idea what he could be, otherwise.

She twitched a quick glance at him. "Really? I guess there is a slight resemblance. It's the dialect, I suppose. There had been rumors that he'd slipped his chain from Zinthrasta and gone chaotic good, but I hadn't believed them."

"But it can happen?"

"Oh, yes. Usually for two reasons—a demon genuinely feels remorse for some of their acts and wishes redemption, because they've seen the consequences of their behavior and it's frightened them, or, more often—it fits into the game plan of their master and being the trickster comes naturally to them. The jury is still out on Steptoe's true motivation."

"So the tribes are wary about him."

"Wouldn't you be?"

"Other than flash-bangs and the coat, I haven't seen a lot of what he can do, but he has grit and he's helped me, often without even being asked. I judge him on that if I have to judge him at all." I paused, with a short wonder about the tell-tales at home.

"As long as that works for you."

That's rather the way I've treated all of them since being introduced to the professor and then Brian succeeding him. I wasn't sure if there was another method to go about it. How many strange things can you see in a day and accept? I changed direction.

"Did you know Morty well?"

"I was his wife." The headlights of passing cars played over her face with light and dark shadows as she concentrated on the highway.

I decided to push through her short answer. "It seems dumb, I know, but sometimes people know each other and sometimes they don't. I had questions I never got to ask him, even though he suggested once he might have answers for me when we had time. We never got that time."

"Hmmm. We were close. It's possible I might be able to supply a few for you."

I flipped open my mental notebook. "It's a family problem, and I didn't realize it myself, but it started with my Aunt April. Dad's aunt, actually, so that makes her my Great-Aunt April, and she is somehow the reason my father disappeared." Actually, I was the reason, but I didn't feel like disclosing our nasty argument.

"Sounds complicated."

"It is. Aunt April likes to gamble. To the point where she is seriously addicted. Maybe it's for the adrenaline, I don't know, but my father found out and stepped in to help her. He ended up losing my college fund, his retirement, and our mortgage. I don't think he was necessarily that bad a gambler. Mortimer mentioned something about identity theft. Then my father got involved in something that, more or less, disappeared him. Everyone thought he'd just abandoned us, but it's more than that. He haunts my house. He seems caught between here and there." I ran out of words, and she didn't ask for a better explanation.

"Mortimer knew him through the work he did occasionally outside the clan?"

"Said he did."

"And your father's name?"

"Not memorable. John Andrews. John Graham Andrews." I turned my face to look outside the window, feeling my nose sting and my eyes well up. I had him, but only barely, and if I couldn't find the solution to bringing him back from whatever dimension he ghosted in, I should let him go.

"I'm afraid he said nothing to me, at least, not recently."

I let out a puff of breath.

"No, no, don't get discouraged. That doesn't mean the end of it." She patted the steering wheel instead of my arm. "Morty kept journals, very detailed ones. He wanted them passed to Hiram, but I doubt if he even told his son they existed. He could be private like that."

"Wouldn't they have been found?"

"Doubtful. I, however, have a good idea where they would have been stowed. The only difficulty there is the clan letting me back into Broadstone Manor to retrieve them."

Knowing what I currently did, I muttered, "Good luck with that."

"The nice thing about luck is we generally make our own, particularly if we prepare. Getting the Eye will greatly help to convince them to give me entrance. Once we do, the rest will open up."

Harpies were optimists? News to me, but I'd take it. I needed it.

A soft snore sounded from the back seat. Steptoe, I'm sure, had never heard a word.

I leaned my head against the passenger window glass, and I think I fell asleep myself.

"We're here."

I rubbed my eyes open and could hear Steptoe stirring and fussing around. Here seemed to be pitch-dark, off the road, and the only things the car's headlights illuminated were loblolly pines, which were everywhere. I cranked a window down to smell and hear the ocean. "We're at the beach?"

"Yes."

"Awesome." I hopped out, kicking sandy soil as I did. The soft roar of waves hitting a shore I couldn't see yet surrounded me, as did the heady smell of salt and something I couldn't quite identify.

"Don't wander. There's quicksand and sinkholes hereabouts."

"Bummer." I spread my arms and turned about cautiously. If I could get to the shore itself, I could run along the sand, see the tide coming in or out, with that fluorescence edging waves sometimes held. From very far away, I thought I could hear a horse whinny. "We're at Virginia Beach!"

"Nearly."

"Thought I heard one of the wild ponies on Chincoteague."

"Possible but not likely. More probable one of their tamed herd mates here on the coast. We're at the edge of Westmoreland State Park, Colonial Beach." Goldie had the trunk open on the car and arms inside, searching about. "No shovel?"

"No," I answered deliberately. "Are we burying someone?"

She ignored me. "Should get a camping shovel. And a hatchet. Just in case." Goldie closed the trunk lid and realigned her armor a bit. "We'll just have to make do."

Disappointed I wasn't closer to the wild pony island refuge but glad to be out of the car and just about anywhere else, I trotted after her. Behind me, I heard a car door open and close. After a few moments, Steptoe caught up with me.

"Wot's up?"

"Treasure hunting."

"Oh? Indeed." And Simon hummed a few cheerful bars but shut up when Goldie threw him a look over her shoulder. Something decided to take a bite of him and he slapped the back of his neck. He shot a glare at her as if she'd sent it personally.

Maybe she had. I gathered there was little love lost between harpies and those of Steptoe's ilk.

She took us around what might or might not have been the edge of the park, which was a huge amount of acreage for camping and other recreation and sped up when we neared what looked like a logging road with a cabin waiting at the end of it.

Had been a cabin but now looked like a catastrophe. Even in the night, with nothing but a crescent moon to shine down upon it, it looked like little more than a pile of logs, tossed here and there, on what might have been a foundation. Goldie made a little sound as she came to a halt.

She stood, shoulders slumped a little, and muttered what sounded like "Stupid fucks" to me, but I decided not to ask her to repeat it. Finally, Goldie turned to me. "They've demolished my camp."

"Looks like it. You didn't have your, ermm, sister-eggs stored there, did you?"

"No. No, those stay at the main nest and no one would bother them. An egg is considered pretty much a blank start, and needed in our clan, as our population ever dwindles. No, the notion of who the mother and father are wouldn't taint the egg. This was done to get to the Eye of Nimora. Damn them." She strode forth then, angry as a harpy could get, which was pretty angry. Both Steptoe and I decided to stay out of her way and took a lesser path.

I could understand her feelings, having been through the destruction of the professor's home with him. And having lost my own home when we'd been evicted. I remember my mother crying as she ran her hand down the inside of my closet door where she had penciled off major markings in my height and the year of my age and the calendar as she did. We took a picture, but it never seemed quite the same. I suspect she cried for a lot of other things, too, as we shut our door for the last time. We didn't drive by again for months and months and when we did, she was shocked to see it had been "flipped" with all new landscaping and painted white with a forest-green trim, looking nothing like what we'd left behind. That made it both better and worse for me. It didn't look the same, so it didn't remind me. At the same time, there seemed to be a gigantic gap in the beginning of my life.

Goldie went to a side shed, pulling aside a door lying on the ground, and knelt with a hissing breath. It, too, had been shredded as I studied what was left. What could reduce a building to splinters? It hadn't left tracks, whatever it was. She got up and paced about, then went to a knee again, running her hands carefully through nails and shards as sharp as any sword.

When she faced me again, I really didn't want to be there, but I made an effort to stand still. Very still.

"Gone. It's gone."

I squelched that tiny voice at the back of my head that wanted to say, "Told you so" and kept quiet.

"Someone knew its worth and where I was likely to have kept it. I'll return to my nest and ask among my sisters. We have to find it. Mortimer gave it to me as a wedding present, but I always knew the day would come when I'd have to return it and counted on that. Now someone has shattered my pledge."

She looked back at the scattered timbers for a moment before adding, "I can't rest until it is restored to the Broadstones and its taker is punished."

"Impressive," Steptoe commented. "But it's likely to have been one of your sisters."

I hadn't dared say it, let alone as flippantly as he made it sound.

"Whatever it takes." She turned and, with a half-shout, half-groan, unfurled her wings. She ran her hand along them, testing the flight feathers, and looked to me.

I had to ask. "Still bound?"

"Yes. But I would leave you here, if I could. We've both work to do."

I rubbed my maelstrom stone. Brought back to mind the deer's spirit which I had cut loose to free it from Malender. Took several steps to close on her, and examined her wingspread. My stone pulsed a little, and I held it up to show her. "This might work. And it might not."

"Work how?"

"Slicing you free."

Goldie frowned. "Have you done it before?"

"I've cut things with it before. I can see this shining coil running along here," and I put my left index finger out to what I had found and plinked it. She shuddered and gave a gulp, laid her hand over her stomach.

"I felt that."

"Hmmm." Maybe, in the moonlight, I was seeing her essence tied to her winged ability. I moved my hand away. And then, at the lower boundary of her wing, I could see a dull red rope, a nasty looking thing, that pulsated in time with my stone. "Oh, no. I think maybe this is what I need to cut." I plucked at that. As I did, her wings folded as if in fear, collapsing away from me, and she shuddered.

I didn't intend to let the serpentine cord disappear on me.

"Careful," Steptoe warned.

"I know." I unwove a bit of it and showed it to him. His black eyes reflected the sickly glowing crimson.

"That would be it. Not natural to the shining beauty of the harpy's true self."

"Goldie? Give me permission?"

"Go for it." She held her breath.

I pulled as much of it free as I could gather and then cut from the bottom of it, not far from the base of her spine. Then I just sliced and diced, watching it disintegrate as I did until nothing seemed to be left of it. The stone sputtered a bit as I finished.

"Well done." Steptoe patted my shoulder. "All right? The stone protects your left hand, but your right might be takin' in some of that nasty bit, so hold hands. Rub 'em a bit, to clean 'em."

I did. Goldie hugged me. "I will send word!"

"Right and, uh, be careful."

"Always."

She took flight then, with a jump and a rush, her great wings beating in a glory of white and gold, and she disappeared into the moonlight.

"Wow."

"Gorgeous, ain't it? I could never understand why harpies could be so harsh and bitter." Steptoe stood with his head tilted back a moment before turning. "Road trip?"

"Home. Where should I drop you?"

"Home. Yours, that is. I have a little place next to the garage if needed."

I looked at him.

"Well, I do."

"I've never seen it."

"You're not supposed to."

"Does Scout know?"

"He must certainly does. I bribe 'im with dog treats not to tell anyone."

I rolled my eyes. "Remind me to remind him what a guard dog is supposed to do."

"But I'm friends. Almost family. Ain't that right?"

"Yeah." I kept pace with him as we found our way back to the car. "Definitely right."

"Good. Put out your hand."

I looked at him quizzically. He dropped something into it. "What—"

"That there is called a clue, I believe."

When I got the car door open, I examined it in the light. "It's a feather."

"Black swan, mayhap. Although it could be taken for a harpy feather. But lookit this," and his stubby nail pointed out a harsh thread wrapped around its base.

I squinted at it. "It looks like a hair."

"Horsehair, I'd say, for tying the feather in place."

I let thoughts run through my mind for a minute until it made sense. "So someone wore feathers as a . . . what . . . a disguise?"

"Dropped feathers as evidence. That was the second one I found. First was this 'ere." And he showed me the long, black feather.

"Now this one looks like the real thing."

"As meant."

I took it from him as well. "If she'd seen it, she'd have gone after her own sisters."

"Which, I imagine, was the intent."

"Good thing you found them. She's going after them anyway, but not to get even."

He tapped the side of his nose. "And didn't jump to conclusions."

"Right." I turned the odd feather over a few times. "Would sympathetic magic work on this?"

"Likely to take you to th' bird they plucked it from, not the ones who did this deed. Although this," and he scraped his nail against the horsehair. "Is a clue in itself. But I cannot tell you it will lead anywhere."

"I need to know more about Hiram's enemies, it seems. And Goldie's." I yawned. It would be a long drive home, and I needed to stay alert.

But then Steptoe discovered the car radio and the heavy metal golden oldies channel.

CHAPTER EIGHTEEN

CRUMBS

BRIAN WANDERED IN just as I parked the car to the side of the driveway, a hobo bag slung over his shoulder. He stopped to look us over. Steptoe hugged his sack of late night drive-through goodies and disappeared on us, but the professor didn't seem surprised or unsurprised to see him. He fell into pace with me. As we went through the door, I tapped his bag. "Finished salvaging?"

"It seems so. I can only hope you and the other helpers did a fair job. The current situation prohibits my returning again." He sighed heavily.

"I'm sorry."

"Can't be helped."

"I think we did all right by you. Critique us after you've been through all the boxes."

He gave a diffident tilt of his head. "Would it surprise you to know that I can sense most of my belongings, the cardboard being little or no barrier? I have a fairly good idea of what's been found without opening them."

"And?"

"Not enough," he said heavily. "Not nearly enough."

"But better than nothing, right? Which is what you could have been left with."

"True. Unutterably true."

"Is it not enough because we overlooked things or because the fire and water destroyed stuff?"

"I would say that, after tonight's inspection, that we've salvaged what we can."

I liked the fact that he included me and the others who'd been trying to help. We paused at the kitchen; its only fixture on was the small light in the cooking vent over the stove. That meant Mom had gone to bed. "I ate on the road with Steptoe. Need me to fix you something?"

He sniffed. "Did Mary make biscuits before she left the kitchen?"

It did smell of fresh baked goods, with a hint of cinnamon and peach. "Possibly. Can't guarantee what it would have been."

"A cup of tea would be nice."

So I fixed him a cup of tea, added a big dollop of honey and a half-shot of brandy, and pushed it over to him. He took a deep inhalation of the aroma before sipping at it. "Ah. Perfect."

"Thank you. And look. There are, indeed, biscuits." I plated him one, wrapped a second in a napkin for myself, and put the others away for morning.

When he pushed away the cup, he went strangely silent, and finally gave a big sigh, turning to look at me. The fiercely intelligent glint of the professor in his eyes did not show, and I sensed that Brian faced me.

"Finally," he said softly. "The old guy doesn't like to give me much time."

I wasn't certain if he expected sympathy, so I answered, "He's trying to solve problems."

"Yeah, I know. But he doesn't think about me much. Sometimes I think he's jealous."

"Jealous?"

"I have the age and health he needs."

"What about you?"

"I'm not jealous. I think. Just a little terrified." He pushed his teacup a little. "What will happen to me?"

"He'll do the ritual again, and you'll have all your wizardly capability back." Tactfully, I did not mention he might go up in flames again. I could see where that might bother him.

"I've been reading his journal when he rests. He

wouldn't like it if he knew, but even if he decides to hide it, I should be able to find it. Anyway, he usually doesn't change much from lifetime to lifetime. This is strangely different. For both of us." Brian leaned forward. "Frankly, I think I'm done if he rejuvs successfully."

"You learned that from the journal?"

"He's never had two souls before. He thinks . . . he thinks it's corrupting him."

I put my hand out and wrapped my fingers about his free hand. "You're not like that, Brian!"

"I don't think I am. It worries me a little, you know?"

"I can understand that. I don't know how, but I'll help however I can. You're a good guy. The professor is used to being a little selfish. Old confirmed bachelor and all that. We'll work on him."

"Thanks." Brian stifled a yawn as he pushed away from the table. "I don't want to disappear into nothing, you know?"

None of us did.

Upstairs, I found Scout sound asleep in the middle of my bed, ignoring his own dog bed in the corner. I booted him out, which cost me very hurt looks from very big puppy dog eyes, and then was instantly forgiven when I broke apart the biscuit to share with him. He scarfed up every single crumb. I considered going back down for seconds, but weariness sank in, so I crawled into bed after promising myself I'd have a biscuit for breakfast.

Scout returned to sleep immediately and I followed after, thinking of what big birds had long black swan-like feathers until I dreamed of them chasing me across a park, pecking at my ankles.

Scout woke me far too early, his puppy eagerness to go outside and check out the new day, plus decorate the back yard, a necessity. I stumbled after him, mouth engulfed in yawning and breathing, my body sort of tromping around behind my mouth. Field hockey practice was going to be agony today. Double agony for having missed running earlier in the week.

Luckily, on a Wednesday, no one seemed to be very ambitious, not even the teachers. As I drifted from class to class, I had the thought that Silverbranch might well come looking for me at school. My inner self scoffed at that—witnesses!—but the back of my neck itched anyway. The feeling someone watched trailed me all day until I finally drove Evelyn home, me dirty and grubby from field hockey and she a little sweaty from cheer practice and then her gig as a trainer. I looked ridiculous, but she glowed. I sighed as she leaned back through the car door. Her bruise even looked healed, which I could only be grateful for as I didn't want either Statler parent after my head for harming their princess.

"See you tomorrow."

"Right. Game day Friday night."

"I have to be at the JV game, sorry."

"Of course. Go, boys!" I shook a fist at her in fake ire at the guys getting the cheerleading.

"Both teams should be in the finals."

"Mine, too." I couldn't say if I'd be able to join them. It depended on my penalty status. Evelyn shut the door and pushed herself away, waving and making the "call me" sign.

I felt a little more human after a shower and change of clothes. Downstairs, I had the fixings out for an immense pot of homemade spaghetti, as it was Mom's late night at her campus, with a student appointment or two scheduled for her office hours. She'd miss the war meeting but would insist on being caught up later. While everything cooked along, I sat with Scout and brought the two feathers out.

"Let's put that sniffer to work. You'll smell me and Steptoe, but someone—or something—dropped these. I'm hoping you'll get a scent and remember it."

He snuffled my hands eagerly, but I didn't know if he was going for the feathers or the dim scent of hamburger from making the meatballs and soap from washing up. He sat, his golden tail sweeping the floor back and forth.

"Good boy." I put the feathers back in my room,

away from whatever controversy they might cause. Steptoe had kept them away from Goldie, and I rather had the feeling that was a good idea in general.

Somewhere between the sauce simmering and the spaghetti becoming al dente, the gang arrived, one by one. Hiram appeared, his heavy footsteps bringing the usual minor earthquake with him. The house groaned at his presence. Steptoe showed up with a faint odor trail of brimstone in his steps. He said nothing when I looked at him curiously, though he dusted his coat sleeves a bit. What had he been up to? Carter came in sharply, as though marching to a drum none of the rest of us could hear. Brian more or less surfed into the room, mellow as could be, and the professor didn't emerge until after the first plate of spaghetti went down enthusiastically.

Strands of noodle without marinara adornment kept disappearing from the table, and I noted that Scout made his rounds underneath, going from knee to knee to knee. When he came to mine, he burped politely, as if stuffed with pasta and sat down on one of my feet. So I scratched his ear instead, while watching the guys eat and talk over idle gossip. Brian led with thanking Carter for running interference for him and did it sincerely. I guess Mom kept hammering on him until it hit home that gratitude was required. Steptoe said little, sitting back in his chair, fingers laced together over his vested stomach, watching the others with an expression of satisfaction. Hiram inclined a chin to him.

"I hear a glop got you."

"And you heard right. But it died, and I got a hand up, and all's well that ends well."

"Good. I think Tessa's going to need all the friends she can get."

I picked up my dirty dishes and put them on the counter till later, coming back with a notebook and pen. They turned to me. "Several key things have happened since the last time we met." I put up a finger as I named them. "One, Brian went to jail and got released with

Carter's intervention. Two, Steptoe got taken down by a glop and got rescued. Three, I went to Silverbranch Academy and—"

"What?" The professor sat up, bristling.

"You were in jail, remember? I didn't have much chance to discuss it with you."

Steptoe offered, "I would have gone as planned but got detained. I did, however, lend her my best coat."

His best one? I wondered what tricks the others could do. I pointed my pen at Brian. "They came to my school with a story that I might be given an internship there this year, and possibly a scholarship later. You know I had to look into that."

"Who?"

"Agents Danbury and Naziz."

Brian's eyes narrowed. "Those two."

"Know them?"

He turned his glare on Carter. "Yes, and he should have warned you."

Carter's brow creased in concern. "I had no idea they'd even heard of Tessa. Did they come to recruit you, then? Or scare you?"

"Recruit. Although I can see where they might act as muscle."

"They are occasionally sent after minor talents to make them cease and desist. Recruitment is only for those the Society desires to bring in and teach." He stopped and thought a moment. "No offense, Tessa, but I thought you were off their radar."

"Some essay packet I wrote drew their attention."

"Hmmm. That wouldn't alert them, that packet is given in response to an alarm, meaning that you were already being watched by the Society. Perhaps the Hashimoto affair caught someone's eye."

It seemed Joanna and her samurai wizard father were still mucking up my life. I made a note. "Moving on, I decided definitely to visit Silverbranch because I'd gotten a vision from Germanigold and thought it directed me to the academy."

Hiram leaned forward, shoving his plate away and

planting his heavy elbows on the tabletop. The dining table dipped slightly in response. "And how would my stepmother know to contact you?"

I cleared my throat. "I, umm, was at the professor's house with Scout when she came out of the ashes. She'd been projecting for the professor but settled for whatever witness she could find. She'd been abducted, all right. Told me she'd been taken by a judge."

"Society?" thundered the professor, echoed by Carter.

"Sounded like it. So point four . . . we're at four, right? Yes." I made another note on my page. "I found her on the Silverbranch campus and released her, after running into a Judge Maxwell Parker." My gaze swept all of them. "He, frankly, seems to be bad news."

The professor shook a finger at Carter. "This, this is why I don't trust the Society. Nefarious and high-handed scoundrels."

"Parker is known to be somewhat of a renegade. I'll pass along word of this latest transgression. He's on probation already."

"Too late. He's already done harm."

"Nonetheless"—and Carter stared down the professor—"he'll be held accountable and by better men than you and I. I'd like to know more about Germanigold."

"Even though Morty died after she'd been taken, she knew about his loss. She grieves for him. She did NOT know about the Eye of Nimora also being missing and took me and Steptoe there—a place where she thought she had it stowed—last night, because she seemed fairly certain it would be safe."

Like a tennis match, now all eyes turned to Steptoe. He shrugged. "Her abode was found demolished and the gem gone. No evidence of who took it, but she is asking about. So will we."

Carter drummed his fingers next to his empty plate. "You've been up all hours, it seems."

I flicked a look at him. "And how would you know?"

"Hmm. The tell-tales let me know when you arrived home last night."

"They did? The bloomin' spies are working for someone else!" cried Steptoe, enraged. "Why I'll pluck their lily-livered stems out!"

"I thought their alarm system was for everyone's benefit." Carter smiled at him mildly.

"Not the Society."

"I may be in the Society, but I don't represent them, nor do they represent me," Carter answered flatly.

Steptoe folded his arms over his chest and continued to simmer but quietly.

"That," said Hiram, "must bring us up to point seven or eight in your notes. Germanigold has returned to her nest."

"Yes. Well, I don't know for sure, but that's where she was headed. The way things have been happening lately, I can't guarantee where anyone ends up." I put a tiny asterisk next to my last note, and debated the wisdom of telling them about Malender. Since Goldie and Evelyn had been involved, it seemed wise, even though I had no way of knowing if Evie had even noticed or if Germanigold would tattle on me.

I made a decision and cleared my throat. "Also, I had a run-in with Malender after leaving Silverbranch."

"You seem all right."

"I am. He wanted to scare me, and he did. He also wants me to convince the professor that he can aid in the restoration ritual." That last I related very reluctantly. But I could be fairly certain Malender would check up to see if his message had been delivered and what the answer might be.

"Does he now, that pompous prick."

Hiram sat upright. "Language!"

The professor blustered an unintelligible word or two before lapsing into silence.

Carter asked quietly, "What happened?"

"A downpour hit the area. It didn't seem natural, but I thought maybe Silverbranch's defenses had set it off, particularly because I'd taken Goldie and made a run for it. Judge Parker suffered an unfortunate blow to his head in the process, got tangled up and gagged when we did."

Carter put a hand to his chin, hiding his mouth, but the professor choked a laugh out. "Buzzard deserved it."

"Looking back on it, I realize I might have made an enemy I shouldn't have. Poor timing. Anyway . . ." I lost track for a moment.

"Rain," prompted Hiram.

"Lots and lots of it. A tree came down across the road, and my car spun out and then into it. I got thrown out—"

"No seat belt?"

"I had one on. It just didn't work right, and then Malender collared me."

"What did he look like?"

"Same as always. Beautifully handsome. Leather and lace. Angry. Not so much of that icky cloud around him, maybe because of the rain, maybe not. He didn't get wet, but I did." I paused, remembering. "He warned me against meddling. And said the professor needed him. Told me he was Fire. And he killed a deer. Disintegrated it into ashes, right in front of me."

"He needed the energy," the professor offered.

"Yes. But he also turned his weakness about into a scare tactic against her. He needed to feed, had to, but did it in such a way as to menace Tessa. Cunning," Carter observed, his face tightly neutral.

Hiram stood. "The beast demeans us all."

"He's not whole," the professor told him. "Gods help us all when he is."

I thumped my pencil on the table like a gavel. "Beside the point."

They all looked at me again. "Malender gets a negative on his offer, but we're still on the clock to find that ruby. What we need to know now is what enemies of Hiram might have taken the Eye or known that Goldie had it and where she might have secured it? Or is it obvious the elves might have taken it to influence their court case?"

"The Eye has little significance, lass, if Malender comes to rule the world."

"But he isn't even close now, and your problem is. Solving it might even deter him, if it keeps the Clans from squabbling. Is there a possibility he could have been the one who took it?"

"Not likely, lass. He's not got the strength. If Germanigold had it secured, it would have been mightily warded."

"Back to enemies, then. Or her family."

Hiram stared at me a long moment before sitting down. "We Dwarf clans get along fairly well. Always have. The Timber men can get a little fractious from time to time, but we have many allies."

I put Timber at the top of my list. "Who else?"

"The Society," growled the professor and put his chin up belligerently as Carter made a dissenting noise.

"Okay."

"There are harpy nests that might," added Hiram.

Steptoe shot a glance at me and then back at his plate. He gathered it up, stood, and began to clear the table.

I wrote down, "Other harpies."

Hiram pursed his lips. "I cannot think of much more."

"The accused elves, as Tessa mentioned," offered Carter.

The professor added, "Yes, they might, indeed, although I admit to being unfamiliar with any current felonies. They like shaking up alliances."

"And how would you know if it was an elf tribe? An elven Mafia, so to speak?"

"You wouldn't, not easily. They're sneaky that way. I've heard some tales of a very powerful boss around here, but I don't remember if he was an elf or not." Steptoe returned from the kitchen. "Noodles are covered and on the counter. I just put a lid on the pot and put it on a backburner."

"Good. Mom will want to eat when she gets home."

If she wasn't home soon, I'd have to remember to put the pot in the fridge. I circled "elves" on my notepad. "Are there any elves around here?"

"You met one of them yesterday. Or, half-elf. Maxwell Parker."

CHAPTER NINETEEN

WICKED THINGS

I DISTINCTLY REMEMBERED the judge, and he hadn't had any black feathers on him, or if he had, he'd disguised them. Steptoe cleared his throat as he watched me; I shook my head ever so slightly. I didn't want to discuss what he'd found, not yet. I have faith in all the guys, but I was beginning to realize they, being what they were, had lives and possibly grudges that stretched far beyond my years. I wrote down Maxwell Parker on my list.

"Anyone else I need to add? Griffons? Dragons? I think a dragon would be cool, but we need to be really cautious dealing with it." I searched around the table.

"Harrummph. This is serious business." Hiram wagged an eyebrow at me.

"I know. I just keep finding out new stuff and it seems surreal. If we think Parker is our suspect, will we have to deal with the Society, too?"

"Stay away from the Society," the professor told me gruffly.

"I agree."

I blinked from the prof to Carter. The two of them in agreement? Stranger and stranger. "I will unless they provoke me, how's that?"

The professor did not react, but Carter frowned at me. "Provoking goes two ways."

"Are you suggesting *moi* might cause trouble?"

"I think you're capable of all sorts of trouble. In the

name of good, of course, but worrisome nevertheless. That's why we're all here, to support and contain you."

I wrinkled my nose a little. "So what's our plan, then?"

"Investigate the elves," answered Steptoe. "Carefully. Very carefully."

"All of them?"

"Likely. But one will probably shake out the moment we begin t' clean the chimney."

Carter cleared his throat as if he thought to add something, but when I flicked a glance at him, he gave a near imperceptible shake of his head. Maybe he'd tell me in private, later.

I looked down at my list and added something to the bottom, before turning to Hiram. "And I have a request. You're probably going to say no, but I would like you to consider it for a day or two before you give me a final answer."

The redwood patio chair creaked under him as he shifted in it, as if bracing himself. "And that would be?"

"Germanigold would like to return to your Hall, briefly, to retrieve what things she has left there, and to give her condolences to you and the clan." She hadn't suggested any such reasons for the trip, but it seemed the best way to get her in for Morty's journals, and if he said yes, she'd agree with the way I'd framed it. Possibly.

He opened his mouth and then closed it sharply. "As you request, I'll think on it a day or two. My first reflex was in the negative, lass, but I know you mean us no harm. Goldie, on the other hand . . ." and he let his voice trail away.

I wrote "maybe" after my last input on the page. I'd wait a few days before nudging him again, then I'd have to figure out how to get in touch with Goldie. I looked up.

"When's a good time to search for elves?"

"Full moon."

"Wouldn't that be . . . werewolves?"

That drew snorts from around the table. "You've been reading too many books."

I could feel the heat on my cheeks. How was I to know?

They hadn't laughed at dragons. In fact, the professor sat looking downright lost in his thoughts. "It won't be a full moon for a few weeks. Next choice?"

"The merest crescent of a moon."

Talk about extremes. I had thought elves might be exhibitionists. Now it sounds like they might be shy. "That will work, too?"

"If you have the right bait."

Carter put his hand over on Hiram's arm as if to shut him up. I quirked an eyebrow at him.

"Nobody is suggesting that Tessa . . ."

I narrowed my eyes. "That Tessa what?"

Male voices suddenly fell quite silent. "Seriously?" I scanned the table. "You're thinking I might decide to be bait? Think twice. I have no intention of running into Maxwell Parker again. He looks the type to insist on getting revenge, and I know I haven't a tenth of the firepower he must have, even if Steptoe gave me all the flash-bangs in the world. Would salt even work on him?"

"Not likely."

"See? I'd be outmatched."

"Not necessarily against the full-blooded elven. They have an . . . erm . . . unicorn quality about themselves. So to speak."

I threw my pencil on the table next to my notebook, glad I had decided on old-fashioned paper and graphite instead of my laptop. There was enough energy flying around the table that it might have fried my computer. "Unicorn? Maidens? OMG. You went there? I'm not going to dignify that remark, and if anyone says anything else even remotely near the subject, I'm going to sic my mother on them."

Someone gasped, and the rest went quiet again.

My scorn swept the room. "How else can we find the elves?"

Looks got traded back and forth. Nobody spoke for what seemed an eternity until Carter ventured.

"They're inveterate gamblers."

"Oh?"

"They like the adrenaline high and many of them have deep pockets."

I scratched my hairline near my temple. Not that I wanted to fall into the same trap as Aunt April and my father, but that could be more workable. I couldn't return to the Hashimoto casino, because that empire, country club and all, had fallen into probate hell after they disappeared from this earth, and too many ghosts roamed there for me to be comfortable. Most particularly not with Joanna's shade stalking me for vengeance. There were a few Indian casinos not too far out of town. One on the Potomac had just opened up to a big fanfare. The food got rave reviews. Problem there: minimum age was 21. Although I could accompany someone.

"What kind of games?"

"Card games and slots. A few like to watch the races."

Horses. That made me think of the horse hair we'd found binding the one black feather, and an even dimmer memory of a horse's whinny across the water at the beach. Elven rider? A highwayman, of sorts, traversing the roads between my world and his? That sounded almost romantic.

"Don't even think it."

I smiled. "All right, I won't." Not anymore. The thoughts had already passed through my mind and been decided upon: Aunt April, it's time to spend a quality evening with your grandniece. I didn't think she'd mind. I checked my phone when it vibrated. Mom texted that she was heading home, and I realized I hadn't finished that last class assignment. College was pretty much an independent enterprise for me, but I liked to keep up and, as mothers will do, she did ask from time to time. "I guess we scatter and see what we can find out and, guys, trade information? I am doing this job for Hiram, but not really, because we're all doing it to help him and the Broadstones, right? And you've appointed yourselves to take care of me, so we all seem to be in this together."

The room filled with the noise of scraping chairs and

hard-soled shoes shuffling about, except for me and Brian who both wore sneakers. Scout went from hand to hand, licking fingers in good-bye, and stood with me at the door as I waved good night.

Hiram trailed the group. I put my hand out and caught him by the elbow.

"Aye, Tessa?"

"Seriously. Why me?" He waggled ginger-red eyebrows. I shook my head. "Don't go looking innocent now. Why did you ask me to find the Eye? Almost anyone at the table tonight is more qualified."

"Not really, although it might possibly seem that way to you."

"Hiram."

He stared at his work boots for a moment. "You have the stone. I thought, but I can't be sure, that it would be attracted, greatly, to the Eye wherever it is."

"Was it before?"

"I haven't ever seen a maelstrom stone and thought any tales told of it were fables, but here you are, and there it is." He looked now at the palm of my hand as I let go of his arm.

"So you thought I might have an advantage."

"Aye, and we need all the benefit we can find. It's an important relic, the Eye, and although many have never seen it, the fact that it exists has kept a number of troublemakers in line."

"So you can't just bluff that you have it."

"It casts an aura that is unmistakable when in use. Again, few have seen the Eye, but its touch can't be overlooked."

"Well. All right then."

He nodded and gave my shoulder a squeeze before going out to his SUV.

It got quiet and stayed that way the rest of the evening, even when my mother came home. Mom seemed a little too tired to make scintillating conversation, so we just hugged and went our separate ways.

Until a little after midnight when I awoke to hear Scout standing at my bedroom window, nails scratching at the sill. He made little, mournful whimpers that I could barely hear but almost broke my heart anyway. When I joined him, his tail whacked against me, but he wouldn't look away. He watched something down below in the backyard. Night pressed in, with purple shadows and little in the way of moonlight. Streetlights didn't throw their illumination past the house and driveway, so I couldn't see much. I didn't want to look. I didn't want to see if Malender had been following me at school and then to the house, or maybe the Society judge, or someone else I couldn't imagine. I wanted my home to be safe.

Scout nosed at me.

"What is it?"

He whined again and pawed at me.

"You want to go out?"

His ears went down and stayed close to his head. No, he didn't want to go out, but then he nudged my hand emphatically. "But you have to go."

He sneezed.

Interpreting one-sided conversations is not easy after being roused from the deepest sleep I'd been in for weeks. I couldn't even remember dreaming. I scratched the side of his neck, just under his collar. "This doesn't seem like a good idea."

He looked up at me, big caramel eyes begging.

"How about I push you out the back door and you go out alone? You can report back to me."

He showed his teeth.

"Oh, no. You don't show those teeth at me, mister."

Scout hung his head.

"Jeez. All right, big baby, I'll go with you. But first, I'm putting on pants and shoes."

He jumped on the bed enthusiastically while I more or less dressed. The glass panes at the window had been cold, so the temperature had dropped. In a few weeks it would dip to freezing, playing with the idea of snow, but it rarely did, although people could hope. Scout, who usually charged downstairs at breakneck speed, came down at my heels sedately. At the back door, we both stood a few moments, hesitating.

I tapped his hard head. "Sure we have to go out there?"

He leaned against me, but he put a paw up and held it against the door frame, pushing.

Hard to misinterpret that one. I looked around and found a long and hefty flashlight, one of those that could crack the average skull wide open if you decided you had to, good batteries in it or not. I wanted it for the weight, not the light. I balanced it in my hand. Tested it. And, by golly, the batteries were okay. Double-threat. "It seems we're good to go." I turned the doorknob.

The door glided open, still smelling of the WD-40 we'd put on the hinges weeks ago. I almost wished we hadn't and that the eerie noise of rusty joints moving would scare whatever it was out of our yard and back where it belonged. No luck.

Scout stayed glued to my right leg. The dew had come in and settled about on the grass but didn't sparkle, the drops just reducing the hem of my chinos to a soaked mess in about six strides. I wanted to flick the flashlight on, but we needed the element of surprise. I heard a tiny rustle and looked down to see Scout flattened, belly to the ground, and crawling toward the garage. I still couldn't see or hear anything, but he had. That did not reassure me.

Lilacs bordered the rear fence and still had plenty of foliage. I went to join them, Scout creeping with me. The side door to the garage banged in its frame and anger shot up in me. We were being burgled. Someone was clearing out the garage!

I thumbed on the flashlight and charged the tiny wooden building. "Stop right there. I'm calling the police."

Steptoe turned around in my spotlight, raised his shaking hands, and froze. I halted in place.

The suit, still dapper. The bowler hat, on his dark hair. The pocket watch, hanging outside of his vest pocket. The brolly, lying on the ground beside him.

But I could barely recognize him for the red flames instead of eyes burning in his contorted face.

He knew me, though. Hands still in the air, he cried, "Don't touch me! Don't get any closer."

I couldn't if I wanted, and Scout huddled next to me, equally terrified, his body pressed as close to me as he could get. Steptoe's blazing eyes held us transfixed. Another source of fire sat in a shoebox on the ground in front of him, itself crowned by a dancing flame, and shooting off sparks that seemed to catch on Steptoe and hang there. Although fire raged in spits and spurts about him, he didn't seem to actually catch. The thought raced through me that perhaps his sort of creature couldn't burn easily. Even if he didn't physically feel the heat, I could tell that whatever it was ate away at him, painfully and dangerously. I could see the agony in his face.

"What can I do?"

"You can stay away from him, that's what," growled the professor behind me. He shoved me aside as he stepped between us. I didn't know what had brought him outside with me and Scout, and wasn't sure if I should be glad to see him. Had the tell-tales told him? "You're out of control, Simon."

"Too right, guv'nor. Keep Tessa away, if you can."

I squinted into the night. "But that's my shoebox." And it was, sitting right there, yet the compelling and foul book it held couldn't be seen. What had Steptoe done? Had he destroyed it, the only link I had between this house and the magic that might have swallowed my father whole? "Give it back, Simon. It's mine."

"Yours?" The professor gave me a startled and disappointed look. "What's yours?"

"A book. I found it jammed into an old desk in the mudroom. I think it's tied to my father somehow, but touching the thing makes my skin crawl so I hid it out here. In that box." I looked at my friend as flames spat up and down his body, sizzling out here and flaring up there. "What have you done?"

The professor took a few paces closer, also pressing for an answer. "Did you invoke anything?"

"Never. Never again, and certainly not here." Steptoe danced uncomfortably in place.

The professor turned back to me. "Does this book have a title?"

"Something about Dark Arts. It's ancient. The ink is faded, the pages are crumbling at the edges and half the words I couldn't even recognize. I put it away, somewhere safe, I thought." I nodded my chin toward Steptoe.

"Oh, ducks. That's what I felt the first night I camped out here. I thought it was a welcome aura, like, for me. Homey. Some place with a spot of welcome. I didn't know it was the dark reaching for me again." Simon dropped his hands to swat at his suit, trying to squelch the tiny blazes. "It started calling to me. Fair drove me crazy, it did, so I finally went hunting it. The minute I grabbed the box off the shelf, it tried to fry me, to crawl inside me. I punted it outside so it wouldn't set the garage alight. Then you two showed up."

The professor moved. "Convenient. I'll just take it, then."

"And let it take you like it tried to take me? No way. It's mine if anyone's . . ."

Steptoe lunged at Brian when he moved to grab up the box and quicker than I could say "Fight!" they were in one, tussling round and round and over and about, the box in between them. The professor might have a young, ab-hard body in Brian, but he seemed to have no idea what to do with it, while Simon seemed disadvantaged by the book itself attacking him. They swung and kicked and thrashed at each other without making many connections. There was no way I would use my bludgeon of a flashlight on either of them.

After a few moments of grunting, heaving, swatting, and general fisticuffs, the two had the box poised between them. I could see the fire reflected on Brian's face. The book reached out to him, as he stood breathing hard, dots of flame coming to life on his flannel shirt and worn-out jeans. He slapped at them. I darted off for the garden hose and came back with the water running when it occurred to me that salt, my universal remedy, might be the better weapon. But I hadn't any on me.

The two men shoved apart from each other. Brian groaned and doubled over, holding his head between his hands.

"Shut it away. It's trying to worm into me. Whatever you do, keep it away from Tessa."

Steptoe shook his head, panting, and got out his answer, "Right-o. We need to close it off then, guv."

And then the two began to work with each other, hands moving in patterns, a cage of silvery strands building about the shoebox and with each weaving, the fire retreated. They grunted with each pass. Steptoe staggered a bit as Brian swayed, but they stayed at work. Their words both clashed and meshed with each other, like musical instruments vying to lead an orchestra. Muttering to each other, hands working in tandem with the other man's, the blazing aura started receding. Scout's ears came up, interested. I hoped then that the tide had turned.

Suddenly, it sent out a flare, a lance erupting and aimed dead center—at me. It struck. I toppled with a sharp cry of pain. My heart pounded as though someone had stabbed me through the chest. It hurt. Ice so cold that it burned shot in and out of me. I folded up, hands to my chest, fingers curled about an orange spear, but I couldn't pull it free. Steptoe and the professor shouted at me, but my ears roared, filling with the crackle of flames. My maelstrom stone lit up, blinding me, and I lost control of my hand as it slid along the length of the object. The stone inhaled the spear noisily, devouring, and didn't stop until I could breathe and hear again. I lay weakly in the grass as Scout tried to revive me with puppy breath kisses.

With a whoosh, the air about the box sucked in and the thing collapsed upon itself until a silvery ball rested on the ground.

"Whoa."

CHAPTER TWENTY

TO GLOW, PERCHANCE TO MAGIC

"SHE'S RADIATING."

"Undeniably, but radiating what? Can you catch the spectrum?"

Steptoe shook his head slowly.

I'd been hit by lightning. Or electrocuted. Or zapped by the biggest static charge ever. Brian and Steptoe looked over me with expressions both dazzled and dismayed.

I tried to stand up and couldn't, every joint in my body like jelly. Never mind the oversized puppy trying to sit on me. Sparks seemed to be showering from me like a Fourth of July firework. I could feel my blood pumping warmly throughout my body, coursing through my heart and back again, my lungs breathing, and the sensation of my nerves pinging. For a moment I wondered if I'd been given some kind of drug that opened up awareness until every impression became almost too painful to endure. Then, like an ocean that must give way to an outgoing tide, it began leaving me. I felt both relieved and bereaved. The last of it left me, except for that stone in my hand. It alone seemed alive and extremely cognizant of everything around me, no longer an odd piece of marble inhabiting my palm. True, it had warmed and pulsated and shielded me and manifested before but only rarely. Now it felt almost like a window into something more. I stared up at the two looking down at me.

"This doesn't look promising." The professor scratched his temple.

"Carter will have our hides. Both of us."

They watched me, assessing. Steptoe's eyes had returned to their normal inky color.

I tried to speak and squeaked instead. I concentrated on breathing.

"Perhaps the maelstrom has converted the energy."

"Or not. I can't differentiate. We could possibly run an experiment or two . . . You read the booklet on it. Any ideas?"

Steptoe considered before answering. "The only hope I can give you is that it matters a great deal who holds the stone." He sounded like the shock had driven his street accent right out of him.

"Well, then, we should be all right." Brian ran a hand through his copper-toned hair again as if his scalp crawled. "It's difficult to tell. I've always had confidence in Tessa, however."

I looked up at the two of them as the damp seeped into every fiber of the clothing I wore and grew shivery cold by the second. Clearing my throat, I managed, "Guys. A little help here?"

"Oh. Oh! Right-o."

They both leaned down and caught an arm, heaving me to my feet, bolstering me up between the two of them. I felt like the filling in a wizard-and-demon sandwich but couldn't have stayed upright otherwise.

"Don't move," I begged. They were warm, and my legs felt like wet noodles.

"Ever?" queried Brian. He grunted when Steptoe lightly cuffed him up the back of the head.

"Look alive, Prof. She needs you."

Brian sighed. "He's tired. Really, really tired."

I looked at the ball of what appeared to be silver string, wrapped around and around and around as it sat next to the shoe box. "Pretty." I reached for it, sagging out of their hold. I felt drunk, and I knew what that felt like because I'd been drunk a few times before deciding that state of being wasn't for me. I liked being able to think and function clearly. What hurt me terribly before now bubbled through me like a sweet and sparkling wine which fizzled merrily. Had the tide come back in? I swayed.

"Oh, no, you don't!" Steptoe pulled back on his grip of me and kept me from my destiny of face-planting as I tried to pick up the silver sphere.

"But I need my book. Is it still in there?"

"More or less."

The object my heart desired twinkled at me, roughly tennis ball–sized. "Looks like less." I could feel my lower lip tremble. "It's gone!"

"No, if it were, you wouldn't want to hold it. But neither is it here in its book form because we had to translocate it to protect the three of us from its influence." The professor gave a hearty sigh. "Not that we were entirely successful, it seems."

"What's all that mean?" I peered at the professor. "And stand still. You keep . . ." I waved my hand. "Floating off."

"This is just an anchor." Steptoe put the edge of his shoe to it. "We can yank it back if we have to, but it's safer that way."

"Oh, who wants to play safe? I don't!" And a giggle floated out of me that threatened to soar with me into the night sky like a kite. Scout let out a low woof and grabbed at the bottom of my jeans leg. I looked down at him. "Good dog. Good puppy."

Brian shook his head. "I'd say the overall influence looks to be lawful or chaotic good. Still. Tessa rules it."

"Pfffff."

Scout put his wet nose to my fingers as if to agree with me.

They both stared at me, so I stopped scoffing at them. I shrugged. I held up my palm with the stone in it. It had settled into a cozy golden glow, making its marble tones even more beautiful. "It looks fabulous."

Ignoring me, Steptoe offered, "We could ask the Society for a review."

That brought the professor standing tall with a vigorous rebuff of the idea. "Never. They'd rake her over the coals."

"Ewww. That sounds like it might hurt." And then I hiccoughed so hard I felt my eyes cross. I looked at one man and then the other. "My eyes crossed. Did they stay that way?"

"No," they answered together.

"We've got to get her inside and to bed. See how she is in the morning."

"Will it fade?"

"Dubious," the professor said to Steptoe. "I think it might be permanent. It's possible we've got a brand-new sorceress here and all we can do is hope for the best. The giddiness, however, should dissipate." He shored me up. "I'll walk her in while you return that to the garage. If you can."

"Got it, guv'nor, never you mind. It'll be put away safe." Steptoe peeled off his jacket and dropped it over the silver ball. "Neat as a bug in a rug."

"But your coat—" I worried as Brian and I began to wobble our way back to the house.

"It'll be fine. I've got a clean one waiting. Get some rest, ducks. You're going to be needing it."

I fell into bed and knew it might be a difficult night. The bed wanted to float off like that kite tried to earlier, and even though Scout jumped up next to me, his weight wasn't enough to keep it steady. At least the room didn't spin. I knew what *that* meant.

Morning tiptoed in like a nearsighted bull in the proverbial china shop. I groaned as my phone alarm went off. Scout rolled over my feet with a puppy moan of his own. The bed, as it should, had stayed in place, more or less, although my throbbing head told me we could have been out tripping the light fantastic anyway. I sat up with care.

The stone gave a little throb. I put my hand to the back of my head, just in case it fell off like it felt it was going to—and the stone hummed a little. The pain faded, not only my headache, but the tightness in my shoulders, too. I put my hand down to stare at the maelstrom.

"Why didn't you tell me you could do that before?"

"Because it didn't have the power." Scout yawned, his long pink tongue lolling in and out, and his eyes considering me.

I jumped.

"You talked."

"No, I did not."

"Doing it again."

"Not doing it again." Scout pawed at his nose. "I'm hungry."

"You're always hungry."

"And I have to pee."

"That, too."

"I'm a dog, what do you expect? C'mon!" He jumped off the bed, tail wagging.

In the hallway, the tell-tales took a look at me and began to jump up and down in their vase in excitement. I shushed them and took him downstairs while he chanted "Kibble, kibble, kibble! Annnnd bacon!" before pushing him outside while I took a shower.

When I returned, Mom had let him in where he concentrated on gulping down a huge bowl of puppy chow while she scrambled eggs for the two of us. Steptoe knocked politely on the side door before coming in to a wave from her.

"Morning, Mary, Tessa."

I sat down with one eye open and the other eye closed. I rubbed it gently before it agreed to join the wide-eyed and bushy-tailed half of me, which seemed to be neither, but I could hope.

Mom gave me a concerned look. "Feeling all right?"

"Scout had stomach problems. We were out several times during the night."

"Oh, poor pup. He seems fine now, though." She smiled as Scout backed away from the empty dish and promptly came over to Steptoe, who was pouring himself a cup of steaming hot tea to go with leftover biscuits. That's the nice thing about biscuits. A day or two old, they are just as good when dunked as they are fresh out of the oven.

Scout seemed to agree as Simon slipped a pinch of crumbs to him. His tail whacked the kitchen floor noisily.

I glanced sideways at Steptoe, who concentrated on sugaring his tea and not looking at me. At least he wouldn't tattle on me, even if he couldn't meet my eyes.

"Can't miss classes today, and don't forget you've got the game tomorrow."

"I'll be fine. I just need to wake up a little more."

Mom looked sympathetic. "Want me to drive you?"

I considered that before declining. "No, thanks. We need milk and eggs, I'll stop on the way home."

"And bacon." She handed me an envelope. "Carter left some funds."

"Right." Always more bacon. I considered forming our group into a union and charging bacon by the pound for dues. We had a budget, after all.

My phone chimed gently. Evelyn, waiting for me.

I snatched up my backpack by the door, waved, and hit the sunlight with my eyes squinted up and my feet half a step behind. Thank goodness it was Thursday. Halfway to the Statler house, I realized I hadn't put on my gloves and that the stone filled the car with bouncy little bubbles that reflected all the colors of the rainbow before they joyfully burst. At the stoplight, I fished around until my soft pink pastel gloves came to hand and donned them before motoring onward. All was right with the world until some idiot in a truck with—not one but two—flags unfurled and displayed in its tailgate came flying through the four-way stop and nearly ran me off the road.

I shook a fist at his disappearing bumper as he soared down the street.

Imagine my shock when all four of his tires blew and he came to a screeching stop in the middle of the next block.

I looked at my hand. The glove seemed fine, but the tips of my bare fingers smoked. Pink smoke.

The last celebratory bubble popped, plinking cheerfully at me as I kept driving until free and clear.

I pulled over and called the house. "Hey, Mom. Erm . . . is Steptoe still there? Or is Brian awake?"

"Yes and not yet." A thoughtful pause. "Are you in some kind of trouble?"

"Not really." They couldn't trace it back to me, anyway, right? I hadn't actually touched the truck. "I just have a question."

I could hear the phone being fumbled around before Steptoe answered. "Allo. What's up?"

"I just blew the tires off an F-150. Or I think it was me. Can I do that?"

"The question is not can you, but should you." A chair scooted across the floor. "Come along, Scout. You need your constitutional."

A little more noise, and then I could tell Steptoe had escaped to the backyard.

"What the 'ell happened?"

"I shook my fist at an offensive driver. Halfway down the road, all four tires blew."

"Interesting. Did you say anything? A chant or a wish or somewhat like that, luv?"

"No. Just strong thoughts. It's got to be the maelstrom stone, right?"

"I think not. You're going to have to be careful. Seems the old prof is right. Welcome to sorcery, Tessa Andrews."

CHAPTER TWENTY-ONE

NEW OR IMPROVED?

EVELYN EYED ME closely. "You're glowing. Did McHotty Carter finally give you a kiss?"

"No and no. Don't even think something like that." I had no intention of telling her about that glorious moment. I intended to keep it close to cherish or until I had several other moments to accompany it. Plus, I was worried that once I started babbling, I might let a lot of other happenings out that should be kept top secret.

She batted her eyelashes. "I do declare," she said in syrupy southern tones, "you protest too much. So give it up. What happened?"

"Nothing. As in, Not A Thing."

"Grumpy."

"Bad night." I clutched my backpack closer. "Practice tonight, so am I still driving you home?"

"Yup, and I've got gas money for you."

"I haven't even had the car a week!"

"True, but my mother insisted, and I agree with her. If you drive, you deserve gas money. Want it now or later?"

"Later."

"Deal."

We separated and saw each other only sporadically during the day. Later, I saw only a glimpse of her at cheerleading practice while I went off to field hockey.

I love the game. It gives me a chance to unwind, kick booty, and growl at people if I feel snarly—and I did.

Hockey stick in hand, I ate dirt, made goals, and generally acted like Wolverine on a good day. After, I cleaned up and waited out front for Evelyn to show.

Phone in hand, I looked at email and some old messages, including a belated "Happy Birthday" from Aunt April. I smiled at her choice of emojis, as it was obvious someone had brought her up to speed. I dialed her up and waited a few rings before her precise and crisp voice answered.

"April Andrews, how may I help you? And if you're calling to solicit remodeling, do us both a favor and hang up now."

My great-aunt, as daunting as ever. "Hi, Aunt April, it's Tessa. Thank you for the birthday greetings and helping with my new car."

"You're welcome, dear. Did you have cake and candles?"

"Not enough, plus I think Mom is waiting for you to come by."

"Ruined the surprise. Tessa, I think you must be half-psychic. I had planned to visit this weekend."

"Great! Are we having chocolate or caramel icing?"

"Some things must remain a mystery," she said sternly. "How do you like the car?"

"It's great. I'm driving everywhere. Can I take you somewhere? To celebrate?" I listened while she thought a bit, and waited for my plan to fall in place.

"A birthday should be celebrated with verve and vigor, not an old lady."

"Aunt April," I told her sincerely, "few people I know have the verve you do."

She laughed. "What did you have in mind?"

"How about going with me and Mom to that super casino? I hear they have an incredible Saturday night buffet?" Complete with elves. I held my breath.

"Oh, that's a bit of a drive. I shouldn't."

"It's a girls' night out!" I wiggled my left hand fingers a little, in case my new mojo might help.

A breathy reply, "I haven't done that in a long time."

"Then it's a date! We can all dress up and everything."

"What about the cake?"

"We'll have that first! You said it was a long drive."

"All right then. I'll be over around three. Tell your mother."

Smiling, I put my phone away. Step one successfully completed. The boys might object, so they could follow us out in Hiram's car if they wanted. And bring Scout. They wouldn't want to do that, but Steptoe would understand when I reminded him about the feather and the pup's nose. There'd be no sense in bringing out the elves without testing them to see if any of them had been involved in bringing down Goldie's vacation home. As for Goldie, I would have to find a way to contact her. If she had found out anything, she'd reneged on letting me know. I hadn't exactly kept her in the loop either but figured she didn't need to know every detail of my life, just about the jewel, and I didn't know much about that. Yet. Saturday night might just break the case open.

Evelyn slid into my car smelling of that new herbal soap and shampoo she'd just bought, something pricey and with a fabulous odor, but she didn't look inspired. Before I started the car, I glanced over.

"Something wrong?"

She shrugged.

I swiveled my head around. "No sign of Dean."

Her mouth tightened.

Her bad boy seemed to be a sore subject, but, hey, if you can't complain at a friend, who can you complain to?

"What didn't he do this time?"

"It's what he did. He came to practice."

"Ummmm. Okay. And then?"

"He had eyes for every girl on the squad but me." She crossed her arms over her chest.

That didn't sound good, but I knew better than to express an opinion. "Mmmm."

She breathed hard three times before adding, "Maybe he just wanted to make me jealous."

Not like I didn't already know the answer, but I asked, "Did it work?"

Evelyn let out a short laugh. "Guess it did. What a fool."

Not being sure if she referred to him or herself, I decided it was best just to start the car and pull out of the college lot.

"So how was your day?"

"A few surprises here and there." I kept my eyes on the road, the streets being perpetually crowded around the community college.

"Any you care to share?" I shot a side glance at her. Evelyn gave a shrug. "Sometimes you are just really tight-lipped."

I hadn't shared much with her lately, not that I had much I could share what with the magic business and all. I decided to give a smidge, despite my earlier self-promise I wouldn't. I wiggled my head a little. "Maybe Carter kissed me for my birthday."

I expected a squeal and a "Birthday kiss!" retort and then examination but what I got was: "And the world turns on this, night to Day as Day to sun. You need the fire, not the ash. There are two, side by side, but neither is the same. Take care you pick the right one."

"Say what?"

She didn't answer. Her pale blue gaze seemed fixed on something out the window I couldn't see.

"Evie?"

Evelyn gave a little shake and she returned from wherever she'd gone. "A birthday kiss! Was it brotherly or steamy?"

"It was definitely an 'I think you're hot' kiss."

"Strong or tender?"

"Both. Strong chin but warm tender lips and no tongue but just a hint of an invitation."

"Nice. And you . . ."

"Kissed him again!"

"That's my girl. For a while there, I was beginning to think you were backward." Her arms unclenched and she looked a lot happier and more comfortable sitting in the passenger seat.

We chatted about nothing else important until I dropped her off and I drove home, thinking. What had possessed Evelyn for that handful of words? I had no idea what she could possibly have meant.

CHAPTER TWENTY-TWO

WITH GREAT POWER, GREAT RESPONSIBILITY, BLAH, BLAH, BLAH

I FOUND MY mom sitting in her study, bent over with her forehead resting on her closed laptop. I hesitated in the doorway, uncertain if I should continue barging in or back out quietly. She lifted her head before I could decide.

"Tessa?"

"Mom? What's wrong?"

She sighed and straightened, combing her hair away from her face with her fingers, before tilting her head slightly. "I've been given this semester and the spring semester. If I haven't made substantive progress, I've been warned I should probably look for another job."

"No!" I sank down on her extra chair. "How could they do that?"

"Because they can. There is competition, always, for any tenured openings, and I haven't earned the right to compete." She gestured at her computer.

"But you're writing. And if you can attend the dissertation boot camps, even the monthly one, you can finish and have it in front of the committee after Christmas."

"If. If." Her blue eyes, usually blazing, looked faded and tired. "I don't think I can do it."

I wanted to object but decided to listen instead. "Why not?"

"This," and she fanned her hands out in front of her, taking in me, the house, and all the nearby surroundings. "I'm writing on magic realism in American history and literature and all this smacked me in the face. How can I write about magic as being surreal and largely subjective, subtly intrusive on the mundane, if influential, when it isn't? It's all around us, isn't it? If the professor wanted to help, or even Steptoe, I could probably gain perspectives on our past no one could even dare guess. Proving it might be more difficult, but I'm certain the ideas are buried in writings, if I only knew where and how to look."

My jaw dropped to offer an answer, but I couldn't come up with one. After a moment of stammering, all I could come up with was: "I'm sorry."

"It's not your fault."

"Well, it is, kinda. I discovered the professor, and then everything else just sort of fell in place with him." I had come in to tell her about our date with Aunt April, but it seemed to be adding insult to her injury at this point. "Maybe you're just a little bit outdated."

"Outdated? No. I'd say I'm completely in the wrong. I should give it up." She took a deep breath, but before she could launch another sentence, I put my hand up to stop her.

"It's not your fault. We know how hard the other side has worked in not being revealed. So we're not seeing, observing, properly. No one has been able to. They have no transparency, they don't believe in it, in fact—just the opposite. The more that gets revealed, the more dangerous it is for them, the other side. They have always been veiled. Hidden. And what we're getting now is still not an open viewing. It's like . . . like . . . like . . ." I stumbled to a halt.

"Like seeing it in a mirror. A dimmed and cracked mirror. Hmmm." And she sat back in her seat.

"Ummm. Yeah. Maybe not quite that diminished but, yeah."

Her eyes lit up. "But you can extrapolate from a mirror's view. Imagine the world turned out and opened up, if you had the vision. If you cultivated it. If you knew what to accept and what to discard." She opened her laptop. "It's not surreal at all. It's coded, encrypted. And you know what you know because they reached out. And then you brought me into it."

Actually, they hadn't reached out at all; I had tripped and fallen face-first into it. "Could be. And all you'd need is to be able to interpret it—"

Mom threw up a hand to stop me. She began typing furiously. Whatever it was, it sounded promising.

I stood up. "Okay, leaving now. But, um, Saturday we've got a date with Aunt April. Going to the new casino for dinner and fun. Maybe seeing elves, if they're out and about, gambling."

She did not look at me as she repeated, "Saturday, casino, Aunt April. And elves."

I wasn't sure if she'd even heard herself over the soft clack of laptop keys and my leaving the room.

Fourth quarter. My jersey clung wetly to my torso, my shin guards felt like they were on fire from the heat, and my elbow throbbed. I threw the last of my cup of water into my face, hoping for a cool-down. Most of the team stood close enough to provide even more heat and sweat.

"I need some blocking," I stated. "That big girl, number fourteen, is all over me." I stared across the field where Abby Jablonski put her head down and glared back.

"All over you? The entire team is all over me." Jheri poked me in the foot with the toe of her soccer shoe. "I can only block so many shots."

I grinned at her. "The number of shots you can block is infinite, so don't try and throw shade. We're covering you."

"Mmm-hmmm. How about stop feeling sorry for yourself and start scoring?"

I looked up at the scoreboard. 2-1. Or, more accurately, 1-2. "I scored."

"Not enough from where I stand." And Jheri shrugged inside her goalie padding.

"Yeah, yeah, I hear you. What about the rest of you guys?"

"They," Kristy pointed out, "obviously know who our best striker is."

"Well, then, they obviously have me covered."

The coach returned from the sidelines where she'd been conferring and stuck her face into our circle. "Break's almost over. Made any decisions yet?"

"We're gonna win this. I just don't know how yet." I swung my stick around in my hands. I looked back over my shoulder where gigantic number fourteen waved at me from her sidelines. Or maybe she was sending obscene hand gestures. Something occurred to me that I should have seen oh, three quarters ago. And the coach, too.

"Almost all their coverage is on me."

"No kidding."

"Shut your mouths and listen. I can pull them just about anywhere I want because they're all over me."

"So . . ."

"So one of you has to hit the goals. If I pull them, there should be a hole somewhere."

"I wondered when one of you would figure that out." Coach beamed. She is not a real hands-on athletic teacher; she likes to let us learn the hard way so that we'll remember it better. This time, it might have been too late.

"Consider it figured. Okay, I'll draw them, but not too obviously. You'll have to thread your way through. Kristy, Beth, you got this?"

"Got it."

We all high-fived each other with the battle cry of "Sky Hawks Soar!" ringing in our ears and prepared for battle.

Number fourteen had badgered me so much that my concentration had frayed. Uncertain of what my newly obtained and untrained sorcery streak could do, other than explode tires on F-150s, I had restrained myself on field. I didn't want to be responsible for concussions or broken limbs and hadn't been as in her face as I could have been. I told myself that I hadn't held back in practice and nothing had blown up or otherwise disintegrated. Odds were that the stone in my palm and whatever it had absorbed this time knew my boundaries and couldn't transcend them unless I forced it. I was in control.

Nice illusion if I could maintain it.

The whistle blew and we were off.

The ball dropped, and I went after it, blocked immediately by Abby, who bared her teeth at me as I tried to flank her and could not. Big she might be, but she was fast as well, and fearless. I, on the other hand, couldn't quite get over the idea that I might snap her legs in two if I thought about it too hard. I pivoted around and dropped to the back field, momentarily giving up. She and another back followed on my heels. We jostled a bit, sticks clacking against one another, the ball angling away from all three of us. I feinted to go after it, drawing Fourteen and two more of her teammates after me. I thought I saw Kristy's heart-shaped face grinning as she darted by, but no time to keep looking. I fake dropped behind in the lane for a pass that I could never have taken successfully because of the coverage on me.

The stone throbbed in my hand under my gloves, responding, I hoped, to my keen desire for a goal and hopefully not to any whims I might have. Like watching Fourteen get a mouthful of dirt when I evaded her so neatly that she would lose all sense of balance and face-plant. It wouldn't happen—she was quick on her feet and at cornering for a tall girl—and if anyone was likely to face-plant, it would probably be me, thinking too much for my feet to keep up with me.

I whirled around and retreated rapidly, still trying to keep up the charade that I expected a backhanded pass annnnny second now.

Lisanne streaked downfield, with only one defender on her, and bam! She took a forward pass and made a shot, so quickly that it had to be seen up close to be believed. I could only see the goalie react to it, bouncing into motion and position—too late.

Goal! And the score stood at tied, two all.

Abby bumped into me solidly as we dropped into line-up for the ball drop. She muttered, "Won't happen again."

What wouldn't? The bump? The coverage? The goal? Think again, my pretty.

Beaming, I moved into my position and waited for the official to put the ball into play again.

She was right, though. Nothing came easy after that, and finally Beth called a time out, winded, her hair plastered to her forehead, her hand reaching for a drink. We paced on the sidelines.

"They're on to us."

"At least we're tied," grunted Jheri. She shook her head, raining drops on all of us from her kerchief-bound curls. Her dark skin glowed.

"All we need is one more." I ran my hands up and down my hockey stick.

"Running out of time," the coach warned.

"We know."

I made a circling motion with my hand, and they gathered in to listen. "Okay. I've been faking it for almost the whole quarter. They figure they'd got me cornered. Well, I'm breaking out. It may cost me another penalty, sidelining me, or I'll get through. Look out, I'm coming." We covered each other's hands. "And break! Sky Hawks Soar!"

The ref positioned to drop the ball. It fell onto the battered grass.

Greta bounded past me, calling, "This won't be pretty," and she angled right at Abby who had the ball, dribbling it down the field toward our net and Jheri.

She hooked sticks. In and out so quickly that the foul, if there had been one, couldn't be seen but heard as wood clattered. She pivoted around, and her shoe struck the ball. It shot out of the hole. I only saw it because I was looking. Staring, actually. Greta bobbed her head, ponytail of streaked blonde celebrating, and she was off.

I saw Michelle head to the ball, cutting it off from the other team, and girls flanking each other in slight confusion. It took me a second to realize they were setting me up. I moved, and almost ran into Fourteen head on. Her eyes narrowed at me.

I did a bump and roll off her, nobody watching us because the ball was downfield, in the midst of plenty of action. I knew it would come shooting back to me.

She probably suspected.

I tried to shake her and almost succeeded. Her ragged breathing and my own filled my ears, the din of the other players and the families and friends in the stands a quiet roar in the background. I'd like to say it was one of those moments like you see in the movies, where everything slows down, and the only thing you know are the heartbeats, slow and steady with all the time in the world before the next beat, and you can accomplish miracles.

Nope.

I tried to shake her and couldn't, not quite, and I could sense that the ball was coming my way any moment now. I needed to be where I could receive it, legally, and drive it on from there. I needed to be *free.*

Running as though my life depended on it, I headed to position, Fourteen on my heels. I could hear her make a noise of effort and, in the corner of my eye, I saw her pass me. She'd block or intercept the pass no matter what it cost, and we were running out of time. The team could survive on a tie—but who wanted to, if we could pull off a win?

My opponent, my nemesis, slashed her stick around in front of me, hitting the ground with a solid THAWK intended to do one thing only: intimidate. Her eyes gleamed defiantly as she did.

The stone blazed in my hand, but I shoved my thoughts back into unknowable land. And then Fourteen did it again, slamming the head of her stick in front of my next step, readying to either stop or trip me.

I swear I did nothing. Not. A. Thing.

Her stick broke. Not just broke, it split in two, lengthwise. Crumpled in her hands.

I sped around in front of her, the gate open, anticipating the ref's whistle—but it didn't sound. The ball came hurtling at me, I caught it, and drove it back, thundering after it. When I caught up with it, I slammed it toward the net.

The goalie dove for it, head down, body parallel with the ground, gloves and arms straining for it—and missed, as the ball sailed into the net's corner.

I could feel the burn of success all the way, from my toes to the top of my head.

But we weren't done yet. There was time to line up, drop the ball again, and drive toward the net, either side. We did so after a brief congratulations while Fourteen trotted to her team's equipment manager and got a gleaming, new hockey stick. Its enameled paint shone in the reflected sunlight. She worked it around a bit in her hands, getting used to its carry and weight and grip. Hockey sticks are all created equal and yet not. I had two, but one was definitely my favorite. She'd already sacrificed her best equipment trying to block me. I had her at a disadvantage now.

My rib cage burned a bit, in the fatigue that a long tough game can hit you with. I'd given most of what I had to give, but I wasn't about to quit—and neither were any of the girls lined up next to me. Michelle gave a huff of defiance.

The ref tossed the ball into the face-off. We all heard the clack-clack-clack of battle to knock it free, one way or the other. When it came slinging by me, I took off after it, my hulking shadow right there with me. We bumped hips and shoulders, muttered at each other, but stayed together as if we had been harnessed. Midfield, the ball came flying, and I missed the pickup. Only by microns, but a miss is a miss and she didn't. She might be a defender, but Abby stood at a place on the field where she could go for a goal of her own . . . and she did.

I flew after to try and stop her. She burst through Kristy and Beth as if they were transparent and then tripped Lisanne off to the side as she dribbled the ball toward destiny. Lisanne went rolling on the ground, but the refs knew dramatics when they saw it and no whistle sounded.

Fourteen lined up her shot and Jheri threw me a look of desperation. The timer on the clock showed us down to mere seconds. There would be no chance after this. I caught up with her and put my stick out, bumping hers just as she pulled back for the swing. The ball flew forward as if winged. My wrists stung from the contact. Fourteen rocked back on her heels to keep from falling backward. Jheri flung herself by sheer instinct to where the ball should be headed.

She was wrong. Our invincible goalie, she of the keen eyes and even greater heart, missed the block.

But no one could have blamed her. It was one of those things.

I'd deflected it first.

The ball shot through the air and hit the goal post, bouncing harmlessly off into the grass and skittering behind the net as the game buzzer went off.

All the good feelings exploded, and we almost poured a vat of cold drink over the coach, but she's pretty fast for her age and we mostly got ourselves. You'd have thought we made it into the finals, but the season wasn't quite old enough. Coach did tell us the win vaulted us into first with the team we'd just beaten right at our heels. After the rest of my team peeled off, headed to the locker room, I spotted my mom, Brian, and Aunt April waiting in the home stands. I trotted over.

"Great game," Aunt April said, her back straight as ever, parallel to the concrete blocks that build the stands. Her hair held a lavender cast from the last afternoon rays. Visitor stands were spindly lumber-built structures, but ours stood sturdily against the elements.

"Thank you! Ready for tomorrow?"

"Naturally." She looked down her nose at me. "I may come over a bit early. There's something hidden away in the house I should find."

Oh? Like my father? I smiled instead of saying anything, though. If she didn't know about my father, she might have a heart attack when she found out. I made a note to stick by her side when she arrived. I waved my stick at them. "Gotta go before they close the locker room!"

The field and opposite stands had emptied when I ducked my head to pass through. The day had sunk deep into early evening shadows and no lights were due to come on. Our game had run long, but this particular field was never lit unless programmed to do so early. I looked into the long and dark shapes and felt a moment—just a tiny moment—of uncertainty before I began moving past the stands. If Joanna showed up again out of her nowhere zone, I had my gear on and my stick in hand and the stone always present.

So it's safe to say I expected the person who sprang out in front of me, except that I didn't. Abby Jablonski leered into my face.

"Good game," she mocked. She hadn't been in the ending lineup when we all congratulated each other, so I figured she'd trudged on ahead to the gym and lockers. Silly me. She'd stood, waiting.

"Actually, it was. You almost had us."

"I had *you*."

"You did," I agreed. "For a while there. I think you guys gave me too much credit, though, and it backfired on you."

I couldn't see much of Fourteen but her face, higher than mine, with the corner of her upper lip curled in scorn. A blue cast lit her eyes. I blinked. I thought they were brown . . .

"Won't happen again," she told me.

"We'll probably meet in finals." I moved to step around her.

"Not if you're on the injured list." And she strode forward to block me, her hands moving into sight, fingers gripping a big cement slab. "A broken bone can be a big inconvenience."

Not to mention a world of hurt. I could scream, but no one remained to hear. I danced backward and she followed, transferring her burden to one hand and pulling her stick out of her gear bag on the ground with the other. That blueness kept blazing from her dark eyes and I wondered what possessed her. What fueled her into unthinking anger. I knew the hit was coming—I knew it, damnit—and still couldn't avoid it. My feet tangled on the stick as I scrambled to get out of her way and I went down, sprawling, and the slab began to descend on my ankles. Both of them.

I threw one leg up to stall her movement and kick her away, feeling the stone begin to pulse along with my panicked heartbeat. I grabbed at my glove, peeling it off frantically. Anger flooded me, forcing out the fear in harsh, stabbing breaths. I wanted to annihilate her. Do what I couldn't do on the playing fields, with all those eyes on me, witnessing. I wanted to teach her a lesson. Who she could bully and who she couldn't! Abby must have been saying something. Her lips moved and her face snarled, but I couldn't hear her through the roar in my ears.

I could feel the earth shift around me in answer to my will. Stone spoke. Wood and iron replied. I turned my face away and, when I realized what I saw, flipped over as she heaved her weapon toward me. I yelled at her.

"Run!"

Abby had a split-second to realize what I meant, and she twisted away. I levered myself to one knee and took off from there as though I were in a sprinting block on the track. We both barely got out from under the stands as the structure heaved up and then collapsed resoundingly where we had just been fighting. Tons of debris covered the spot.

Abby paled. That eerie blue color in her eyes faded out. She jerked her chin at me, yanked her bag out of the ruins, muttered, "Freak," and then jogged off as her team bus honked impatiently for her from the other side of the gym buildings.

I stared at the grandstand. Half of it gone, just like that. My vision blurred faintly, and the feeling nagged at me that I could—I should—restore it if I could only see clearly enough how to do it. There had to be a way . . . My pink glove peered from under the edge of the rubble, and I went to get it from the disaster. Had I meant it, or had it been fear or anger?

Like the F-150 tires exploding.

Like the hockey stick splitting in two. Like I had become dangerous.

CHAPTER TWENTY-THREE

RUNNING IN THE FAMILY

WE CELEBRATED THE win, my team boisterous and pretty well ignoring my sudden silence, before they closed the restaurant and kicked us out. I went home because I had no place else I wanted to be. My mom met me at the front door when I got home, her face haloed by the golden porch light, her hand on Scout's collar so that he couldn't bound out and go for a run while I parked in the driveway. I grinned at her.

"Told you not to wait up!"

"And I suggested no drinking."

"Mom. I can take care of myself." I'd only had two beers because most of the girls on the team are over twenty-one and I got treated, but I'd known when to stop and pizza had soaked up most of the drink before I'd even thought to head home. No way was I going to risk my new car on a stupid buzz.

Scout stood on three paws, one excitedly held up so he could paw at me when I got close enough. I did and he did, so I dropped to one knee.

She let go of his collar while the dog glommed me. "Quite a game."

"No kidding. We might both make it to finals. Gotta say, I'm not looking forward to meeting that Fourteen on the field again."

"Probably just the mom in me, but I'd say you had her number."

"Finally. Took me long enough to figure an angle. Hope you didn't save dinner."

"Nope. I know a pizza night when I see one. Enjoy the metabolism while you can."

I stood up and brushed past her in the doorway, Scout on my heels. "Let me put my gear bag up and I'll take the dog out."

The tell-tales turned to greet me in the hallway as I passed them. Scout put his nose toward the niche and gave a gusty sneeze.

"Was that nice?"

He shook his head, ears flapping, giving me the distinct impression he didn't care if it was nice or not. Apparently, he and the interactive blooms had issues.

Dropping my bag in the far corner of the room, I gathered up my bracers from the windowsill and changed into a pair of well-worn and comfortable sandals. The night air felt brisk and cooling, but until frost blanketed the yard or rain hailed from the sky, I would pick out my sandals. My toes like a bit of freedom now and then.

Although, frankly, if they'd been exposed today, Fourteen would have taken them out, all the way up to my ankles. I'd be lucky to have any phalanges left.

I made it down the stairs in relative quiet, but Scout tripped on the second step and bounced down with a surprised yip or two and other accumulated noise. We made it to the bottom and looked up as Brian hung over the top banister.

"Trying to sleep here."

I laughed at him, his red-gold hair standing half on end and the professor staring grumpily from young eyes. "Sorry."

"Yes, well, I thought you had fallen." He sniffed and frowned at Scout. "The enthusiasm of youth. And dogs."

"Look at you, all of six months old and ready to be aged again."

"Hmmmm." He started to turn away, and stopped himself. "Oh. I think I may have found what we need for Mrs. Sherman and her possession debacle."

"Really?" And at the back of my mind, I wondered if Brian had ever even heard the word "debacle." Seriously, the two of them in that body were polar opposites.

"I've a test or two to run first, wouldn't want to traumatize her if I've the wrong remedy, but yes." He did turn then and waved the back of his hand at me. "Carry on."

"We need to talk."

"We do?" Brian simmered that for a moment. "Out of the house, then, just as well. I could use a walkabout tomorrow. No need to distress Mary."

"In the morning?"

"Good, good."

I watched him back away from the railing and decided he probably had something of an idea what I wanted to talk about. He'd be a pretty poor wizard if he didn't.

Mom had retreated, too, but not to bed. I could hear her at her laptop, typing at a good pace. I hoped it was her paper and not just email as the pup and I went out the door. My muscles had already cooked and cooled, so I moved a little stiffly the first few steps. Scout tugged at me until we settled into a pace something a little less than an all-out run and a little more than a collected jog. If I walked the pup like this twice a day, I'd either be more than ready for league playoffs or maybe the Kentucky Derby. He didn't slow until we neared home again. Most of the downstairs lights were off, with only a flickering light upstairs from my mom's room, meaning she was streaming something on her laptop and quite likely had fallen asleep while doing it.

If she could sleep, all the better. The sooner I found the Eye of Nimora, the sooner I could give her the help she needed beyond what I normally did. I warmed for a minute, thinking of being able to do that. Scout whined slightly and fell back against my ankle.

The fine hairs on my arm rose. The stone already glistened free in the evening air, and my bracers glowed faintly under a harvest moon illumination. Nothing that would draw attention but would definitely give me an advantage seeing in the dark. Not that I wanted there to be anything to see. Collapsing part of the grandstand was already what I hoped would be the pinnacle of my day.

Scout's ears went up, and he all but towed me around to the mudroom door, which stood slightly ajar. I had no idea what his training was telling him. I put my hand on his head.

"Who's there, boy, huh?"

He whined very faintly again, but didn't seem alarmed. I pushed the mudroom door open wider, my bracers softly blooming the small area with light, and Aunt April let out a gasp as she straightened up.

All the drawers except the locked one had been pulled out of the old chest, and she looked as if she'd seen a ghost.

"Aunt April. What are you doing?"

She sagged against the threshold. "Something I shouldn't be, and you've caught me."

"I won't tell if you won't, but—what are you looking for?"

She pressed a shaking hand to her hair, in a vain effort to straighten it up. She beckoned me and Scout inside the door and shut it quietly behind us. "I don't want your mother to know I'm here."

"I guessed that."

"I haven't gambled—much—since your father disappeared. He got me out of quite a bit of trouble, and I've always been afraid I was the reason he had to leave like he did."

I wanted to tell her that she was wrong, it had been me, but I decided not to. I hadn't even been able to tell my mother. Besides, Great-Aunt April had been a contributing factor as well. I needed to know what she knew. "Is this why you talked about coming over a little early?" I looked at my phone. "It's a lot more than a little."

She pursed her lips a moment as if to hold back words that wanted to spill out untidily. Finally, she said, "I gamble compulsively. More than a little. I was a fool for it, and I owed a lot of money. But there was a time when I made money, more than a woman normally could in a man's world, and it gave me freedom. Until it didn't."

"Is that why you sold some of your other properties?"

Aunt April didn't want to look me square in the eye. "They left me no choice. I had to pay down my debts, but with interest and such, I couldn't seem to get even. Your father said he'd take care of it. My streak had gone cold, but his hadn't. I lent him my lucky book and he went off to do what I couldn't, on the promise that I would stop gambling. Imagine my shock when, although my debts were cleared, he left the two of you in poverty and then disappeared. I know he didn't mean to. I must have done that to him, somehow. When luck goes cold."

I'd heard or figured out all that before, except for— "What do you mean, lucky book?"

"It's just a little leather book, been in the family for generations, and it's always brought good luck. I used to tuck it away in my purse, next to my wallet, and it always seemed to bring fortune. One night I won an incredible amount at roulette—$77,000. After I paid my taxes, I bought that lovely little home on the west side, the one with the greenhouse. Years ago, when prices were lower."

I knew that home. Mom and I had hoped that that was the house Aunt April would send us to, but instead it was one of the first to sell after we moved. She'd had it for years. I nodded.

"I stored the book in here. I'd forgotten all about it until recently, and with talk that we were visiting the casino, I thought I might have a go at the luck again. Your father had seen me pull it from here, and I thought perhaps he'd put it back before he ran off."

"Faded, old-fashioned writing?"

"Oh, yes. No one in the family could understand a word of it although we'd had it, for oh, decades and decades."

I shivered. If that malicious thing had brought any luck to the Andrews family, they must have paid dearly for it, and worse, hadn't even realized. I caught her wrist and brought her near to hug.

"You don't need it," I whispered into her ear. "You truly don't."

Aunt April frowned in the shadows. "I blame myself, you know. Your father got into trouble to help me, and it dragged him down. I've done what little I can to help the two of you, but I know it's not enough. I'll never forgive myself, Tessa. When we planned this little trip, just for a moment, my heart leaped up in my chest, and I thought—I can win again."

"The casino always wins."

"But I had hope. I thought, for the last day or two, that I could rescue all of us."

I'd had that idea, too, when Hiram hired me. Here we were, both of us, chasing pipe dreams. "You don't need the book, Aunt April. We've got Andrews smarts."

She kissed my cheek before drawing back. "You're right, I don't. What silliness to drive me out here to find it! One last fling."

"Oh, we'll try a bit tomorrow, but we've both got twenty dollar limits. Deal?"

Color sparked back into her cheeks. "Deal," she said, hugged me, and slipped out the mudroom door. In the kitchen, I could tell by Scout's ears that she'd gone, as she'd promised, before he put his muzzle down to his water bowl and drank noisily.

Heading to my bedroom, I wondered about the cost of magic, good and bad, and if my father had paid for generations of his family in one fell swoop. If so, getting him back could be far more difficult than I'd hoped. I pulled the curtains shut, so the moon, lamppost, and any other figment of bright light couldn't bother me.

And one last, troubling thought tickled at my mind as I slipped between the sheets and into bed.

What sort of price was the maelstrom stone getting from me?

CHAPTER TWENTY-FOUR

PAYBACKS

I BLAMED EDGAR Allan Poe for seriously interrupting my sleep as, for once not fighting an epic battle and actually getting some quality rest time, a tap-tap-tapping woke me. Actually, the first couple of times the sound was so mild that I thought it couldn't be real and scarcely opened one eye, let alone two. And then someone *bammed* on the windowsill and I bolted upright, afraid the glass had split. Both bleary eyes open, I squinted across the room. Something large loomed in the frame, light from the lamppost glaring away the details. Hadn't I shut the curtains tight? Did I want to go see what stared in through the window at me or not?

I did not. In fact, I clearly remembered closing the curtains securely. Now, however, they stood wide open. So that begged the question: what opened them, how, and why? The maelstrom stone gave me no help whatsoever.

I slipped out of bed, padded out into the hallway and, rubbing my eyes awake, stared at the tell-tales. Only one seemed as awake as I was, more or less, and it stared toward my bedroom but not with petals flung outward in alarm. So. Either the tell-tale knew what it was outside my window and didn't fear it all that much, or it had no idea at all and had been magicked into ignorance.

"Big help you are," I muttered and stumbled back to my bed. I had just about sat down when the tap-tap-tapping began again.

I had no wish for whatever it was to wake anyone else. I lunged for the window and plied it open.

Goldie stopped, knuckles paused in mid-rapping, and spat out, "About time." Her wings beat, holding her in the air, a helicopter of a bird woman.

I wrenched my window open as far as it would go, catching the screen before it fell away. She came halfway in, balancing on one hip, her wings tucked tightly in behind her. She smelled of blood, smoke, and sweat as she braced herself in the frame.

"Are you all right?"

Small, precise stitches gathered close a crescent-shaped wound over one eye. I could see bruising around the eye below, and another on the jawline. Her white-and-gold wings looked bedraggled and dirty. It must have been one heck of a fight. I said so.

Goldie smirked. "I am victorious, so I am more than fine." She waved off any other concern. "There were traitors in my home."

Past tense. I decided not to ask exactly what had happened to the traitors. "Congratulations on the victory."

Goldie gave a lopsided smile, but she reached for my wrist and held me tightly. "Listen now. You're in grave danger. We were attacked within and without. My nest, my home, is destroyed, and they knew what they were looking for but asked questions about more."

Her fingers hurt, but I didn't draw back. "More?"

"They know a phoenix is rising. Brandard can't hesitate any longer—he must rejuv as soon as possible, or they'll put an end to him, and that end will affect all of us around the world."

I tried to imagine the professor being that important and failed, but I understand ripple effects on a pond. His death could be one that set off multitudes. "I'll tell him."

"And help him."

"I am."

Goldie's hand began to relax on my arm. My skin tingled as blood started to flow again. "Now for the other matter. The treasonous ones did not take the Eye, but they spilled information that eventually led to the theft." Goldie paused. She flexed her jaw a bit till it popped. She gave a tiny wince. "I'm told it may be in the hands of those who would auction it. Not only does that put the Broadstones at great risk because it reveals that object is no longer theirs, but it means the Eye could fall into almost any hands with enough money. The dwarves have traitors, too. The stakes are high, and you're in danger no matter what you do, as long as you have anything to do with finding it."

"I'm not going to stop." I exchanged a long look with her.

Goldie's wings fluttered a bit. "I thought I tagged you as a fellow warrior. They may have warned us, but they haven't turned us back."

"How do I reach you if I need you?"

"Any owl. Tell them my name and yours, and they will remember it until they find me. I'll know that you sent them."

"Oh-kay." I preferred cell phones, but evidently her realm went for the old-fashioned methods of communication. I watched her scull off the eave of the house, wave, and disappear into the night sky. She flew straight, if labored.

I thought of something and leaned out the window. "Wait. Goldie—who is behind all this?"

Too late.

Back in bed, I fell asleep again, although with a lot more trouble. I couldn't tell if it was my thoughts or lumps in my mattress that bothered me.

"Love the dress, but you're not wearing your bracers with that. Opera length gloves or not."

"But—"

The tell-tales in the hallway niche drooped with me.

Brian frowned at me. "Seriously? You think that the elves and whoever else we might meet won't sense those? You did intend to go in secretly, right? Not that you'll manage it with the stone embedded in you."

"But—I need a distraction, then."

He waved a hand imperiously. "No argument. You can wait till Hiram and Carter get here, but you'll hear the same from them."

My shoulders slumped. "All right. But if I don't have anything to bounce bullets away, you're to blame."

The professor peered at me from Brian's mild eyes. "My dear, you have far more to fear than bullets."

"Gee, thanks. Now I want to go dressed in full-body armor."

"Which might not be a bad idea, if doable. . . ?" His words trailed away as if he might be pondering working up a spell.

"We haven't had our talk yet."

"Indeed. I'd quite forgotten."

No wonder. He'd spent the day making stink bombs in the garage that made Scout howl and paw at his muzzle, and stopped only long enough to devour an early lunch and tell me that Mrs. Sherman's cure was "coming around." I suspected it would float in on a malodorous cloud to announce itself when ready.

"Did Steptoe tell you what I did?"

"Did what? Should he have?"

Great. It was answer a question with a question day. "I blew the tires off an F-150 truck."

"You don't say? And how did you manage that?"

"I was hoping you could tell me. I had a little bit of road rage after the driver tried to blow me off the road, and I shook my fist at him."

His eyes went to my left hand.

"Yup, with that hand."

"And you're wondering if you activated the stone as well as your new power within it."

"That would be it, yup."

Brian exhaled for a long moment, his cheeks puffed up and gradually deflating as he thought.

"You haven't really sat me down and explained this whole sorceress business."

He looked away. "No, I haven't. A sorceress is a bit tricky to define. The magical opportunities and such as well as responsibilities. Put succinctly, a sorcerer or sorceress has the ability to release the inherent or stored magical qualities of an object."

"But an object would have to contain magic to do it?"

"Normally."

"What do you mean?"

"Only that you, Tessa, with the maelstrom stone embedded in you, are far from normal."

I shifted weight. "Okay. I'll give you that one."

"Thank you. The best thing I can do at the moment is urge you to be careful. To realize that every movement, every active thought you have, may have consequences. You've gone from having as much magic as a dried stick to being a new, inexperienced sorceress. Someone who could find the magic, buried or inherent, in an object and call it forth, seemingly out of midair. Wizards are always sinking magic into something or other, using objects to function like batteries to be tapped later. I happened to excel at that, once. You can find those things, often unknown or hidden, and unleash them, invited or not, and whether you were the one who charged it or not. Or, like the maelstrom stone, it has sorcery of its own enveloped and swirled in its being and the two of you use each other." He paused.

"Wow." That was unsettling. "You make me feel like a live bomb."

"On a countdown? That would be accurate. I had hoped to have my own rejuvenation farther along so I could be better prepared to teach you, yet here we are—"

"The blind leading the blind, huh?"

"More apt than you know."

"But how do I release that magic?"

"Will. Will and knowledge."

"There must be more to it than that."

"A sorcerer spends many years in study of those things which naturally have magic buried in them. It's not as easy as it sounds. To gain control of such an object, the sorcerer has to find or create its real and proper name. Its potential has to be seen clearly, and recognized. Once that name is gained, the sorcerer owns that thing. It will be made or unmade as it is told."

I took a deep breath. "I brought down the visitor grandstand at school."

"Did you, now? How did you manage that?"

"A rival player had me on the ground and was thinking of breaking a leg. I panicked. Next thing I know, the ground is buckling and the stand with it."

"Do you remember calling on the earth? The wood? The nails and braces? Anything?"

"All I remember is not wanting to get pummeled."

"But you did not activate your shield?"

I hadn't thought of it then, and the realization now shocked me a bit. It should have been second nature. If I keep getting attacked, and it isn't second nature, I could get demolished. I shook my head. "Too panicked."

"So the stone activated on its own, in response, and what it did was . . ." The professor in him paused. "It reached into the earth itself, upsetting the foundation of the grandstands . . . what would call that up?" His eyebrows beetled. "Ah. Ley lines. It grabbed for whatever power it could, and tapped into those. It must be. I'll have to research my maps later to prove it—"

"Ley lines?"

"Naturally occurring power around the world. Think of them like a net, covering earth, with lines holding force."

"Not a string of orchids."

"What?" He stared for a moment and then sputtered. "Of course not. No. Like magnetic resonance or sound waves that travel through rock and stone . . . but this is power we would term magic, for lack of a more scientific explanation. They are not frequent, but ley lines do exist."

"And a sorceress could touch them."

"And draw upon them, yes." He cleared his throat. Checked his watch.

"One last thing, and probably the most important."

"Oh?"

"Goldie dropped by last night."

And now his "oh" was more of an impatient grunt. He brushed a hand through the air. "Unimportant."

"It is not! Her nest was attacked and wiped out. Traitors who'd given away the Eye's location got exposed, but the raiders were looking for information on the phoenix. She says you need to finish your ritual as soon as possible. You're needed."

"Hmmm." He straightened. "We'll all be needed."

"Maybe you should stay home tonight and review the ritual. You haven't worked on it much, lately."

"I have done far more than you realize, young lady! Under the circumstances."

"Still."

His upper lip waggled as if he still carried his bushy mustache on it, which he didn't, but I guess the waggle stays a habit. "My journal suggests that I need to obtain a pinch of pixie dust. I can't think of a better place to obtain that than from an elf. So my coming along is necessary."

"Pixie dust? What do you need that for?"

"It is highly recommended for the pain."

"Pain of—oh." Burning to death might hurt a lot. I tried to recover. "You're sure you need elves for that?"

"Very. One thing at a time. We both need to make ready for this evening. I hope to disguise that rock of yours in some way."

I took the opportunity to turn on my heel and go back to my room, pull off my bracers, and set them back on the windowsill to bathe in the sunlight. When I came back out, Brian had disappeared, presumably to work on his own appearance and incantations. Mom had found some dress slacks for him and a nice, blue patterned shirt to go with them. I imagined a bottomless closet somewhere, where all Dad's things had gone to live, despite the bags we'd taken to various thrift shops when we decided he was never coming back. Mom had only spoken to his ghost three or four times since I found him last spring. Whatever strength he expended in materializing, he'd become less and less able to use it.

My efforts to find out what happened and how to reverse it gave me few answers. But she'd saved a few outfits, obviously. I noticed that Brian rarely went into the basement (that I knew about—when I went to campus, who knew what he was up to?) but wondered if Dad ever recognized the outfits. Did he think Brian had somehow replaced him?

I shook that awful idea out of my head and rattled downstairs, strappy heels in one hand and dress gloves in the other. The look would blend retro with contemporary, but I could think of no other way to inconspicuously hide the stone. Where I went, the stone went, and no matter what the professor said about the bracers, it seemed the maelstrom stone would be even more outstanding to anyone sensitive. I looked at my palm for a long moment. "Shield yourself," I suggested strongly. Nothing seemed to happen and, frankly, I had no idea if it could work.

Scout met me at the bottom of the stairs, tail in ultimate windup mode, snuffling wherever I would let him, although I batted his nose away a few times to avoid wet nose prints. At that, he sneezed and sat down, although his butt kept wiggling. I massaged his head and ears. He no longer talked, to my great relief, but I could read his body language easily. "You need to be on guard. Not sure if we'll start a problem tonight or not." Who knew, with elves? If I could discover if they were the ones responsible for turning Goldie's beach home to ashes and might have stolen the Eye of Nimora while they were at it, not to mention destroyed the harpy nest, there could definitely be fireworks. I'd need evidence before I could accuse anyone of anything, though. Once I had said evidence, unless it was the Eye itself, would I take it before the Society? I'd probably have to. And if I did, what could possibly go wrong? I know, right?

Maybe I should just go and enjoy the munificent buffet and gamble my twenty and come home before the complications began.

I could hear Aunt April chatting brightly with my mom in the kitchen. The guys had all elected to go in

Hiram's SUV together and my mother was driving us. Carter, Hiram, Brian, and Steptoe had decided en masse that none of them could escort us because they would be a dead giveaway. As soon as I appeared, Carter gave me a look, first, at the dress. "Still a knockout."

"Bad luck to wear it?" I twirled once, and the sea-glass-colored silk swirled with me.

He shook his head. Took a deep breath and exhaled a long sentence that I could feel warm the air about me.

"What's that?"

"A glamour meant to hide the stone." He squinted at me and muttered, "Not sure it'll work."

"Why?"

He shrugged. "You have a glow, Tessa."

"Thanks, I think." I realized none of us had told him about my stone and the book it had absorbed, meaning his glamour worked with a handicap right off the bat. I watched him disappear out the side door to join the other guys.

Now, Scout bolted past me to see if the ladies in the kitchen were eating cookies, biscuits, or anything else of interest (bacon?). He skidded to a stop just before slamming into Aunt April. She wore an evening pantsuit in dark navy, the bottom with swingy legs and the top studded with rhinestones. In addition, she wore three diamond rings and two pearl-and-diamond ones, to match her pearl earrings and necklace. And, yet, she wasn't blingy. She was worth studying to see just how she accomplished that. My mother, on the other hand, had chosen to reveal her knees, legs shapely and very viewable, her black dress short with a skirt, belted, her neckline V'd and her back scooped bare, and she wore a nice gold necklace that I knew had to be costume jewelry because we'd sold everything of value to try and keep our house years earlier. Her ears sparkled in gold and CZs as well. She looked relatively happy although I could see that vertical frown line between her blue eyes seemed to have become a permanent fixture. And that made me scowl, a little, and promise to myself I'd fix that. Somehow.

My chiffon-and-silk sea glass gown had been meant for a charity auction, and although it had seen a lot of action that day (and not in a good way), it had dry-cleaned up just fine—and it's not like I own a lot of evening dresses. It would draw me looks, although with a glamour on me to hide my shine, hopefully not too many. I gathered up my purse and checked the time on my phone.

"Everyone ready?"

"Absolutely."

Scout sprinted out the door ahead of us, and it seemed the guys waiting in the SUV had a door open and he leaped in. He'd plans I hadn't known about. He went to the back window and watched me with puppy amusement.

"I guess Cinderella gets to go to the ball after all!"

Mom passed me, saying, "Brian and Hiram thought he might be useful."

Her words stopped me in my tracks. For what? Maybe finding me if I suddenly went missing? Oh, joy. I caught up with Aunt April and opened the car door for her before sprawling in the back, trying to decide if I felt reassured or threatened by the planning.

Aunt April threw me a questioning look over her shoulder. I shook my head. "Sorry, Aunt April, I didn't find your good luck charm."

"April, I didn't know you'd lost something at the house. I'd have helped Tessa look for it."

My great-aunt slid a blue-veined hand over and patted her knee. "It's all right. I imagine wherever it's gone, it will be quite impossible to find. I shall have to wing it on my own. We Andrews have always been good at that."

Mother shot me a look over her shoulder before she backed the car out of the front driveway. "I've always found that Tessa is my luck."

That gave me a warm and fuzzy feeling, making up for the sinking one that Scout might be needed to track me down sometime tonight. I settled back, enjoying the ride along with the thought that I could have driven if I'd wanted to. The little aches and pains of yesterday's hard-fought game had begun to fade except for one black-and-blue bruise along my shin that would be even worse if I hadn't worn guards. The look on Fourteen's face as the grandstand had collapsed on her heels stayed with me—one of shock and disbelief. Did she think that I'd had something to do with it? I had, but she couldn't have known that. Not unless she had a sixth sense that some of us have, but only if we're different.

So what did that mean for me?

Being damned careful, for one. I had that idea down pat, but should have realized it sooner. I may be slow sometimes, but I am not as dumb as a sack of hammers. Carter hadn't been told of my new ability because of the Society. I had this figured out, or would. Soon. Honestly.

CHAPTER TWENTY-FIVE

KA-CHING

BECAUSE IT WAS near-serious fall weather and the days had shortened, we could see the multicolor gleam of the casino and its lights on the eastern horizon long before we got there. Aunt April tilted her head. "Rather like the northern lights, I should imagine."

"Or a perpetual rainbow. I imagine they're playing on people's subconscious about the whole pot of gold thing." Mom flexed her hands on the steering wheel. "We're close."

I tried to shut my mouth mid-yawn. I could see the glance in the rearview mirror. "Don't worry," I said. "I'm just storing energy for later."

"Right."

I could see her watching me in the rearview mirror and wrinkled my nose at her. I know she remembered the days when I used to sleep through car trips, but that was way back when Dad sat in the driver's seat and Mom at his side, and the back seat had been filled with pillows and toys to keep me quiet. We hadn't been going to casinos then. Sometimes beaches and often forests, to grab a few days of vacation.

As we reached the casino and pulled into the parking lot, we all took a moment of silence to appreciate the money that had been sunk into the place for maximum visual effect. Finally, Aunt April snorted. "Getting back their investments means the machines will be tighter than a virgin."

I tried to stifle my response, but my mother gave a short, startled laugh.

Aunt April looked at the two of us. "It's true," she said.

"I don't doubt it. But we're here for the buffet."

And, indeed, the Saturday night seafood buffet dominated several flashing marquees with tempting pictures of lobster and crab. My mouth watered.

Aunt April bent over and fished a plastic placard out of her purse. "Park in the handicapped."

"You still use that?"

"I needed it after hip surgery. Still do, occasionally. With a parking lot this big, I think it necessary."

Mom steered us across to the appropriate slots and parked us while I looked back to see Hiram's big SUV trailing us and parking fairly close as well. I stroked my gloves into place. Under each, I wore my black leather half-gloves, just in case the opera-length ones seemed a bit much, and there was no way I was going to be cracking open crab claws and dipping into melted butter with them on.

Hiram's SUV emptied, and I thought the guys would be happy to finally arrive, but the looks on all their faces telegraphed otherwise. Carter looked the stormiest. It looked like plans had just gone sideways.

"What's wrong?"

"What's wrong is that I just found out why you look different, a very important happening that *no one thought to mention* to me!"

"Ummm . . . my stone ate another magical relic?"

"Yeah, that would be it." He grabbed up my hand and rolled my glove down. "I should have seen it, but you always look special to me," Carter muttered, and I could feel the heat in his fingers. "You've got a shield on the stone, it appears, but it's still embedded in your system and that radiates—"

"I do?"

He didn't appear to have heard me. "We can't let you go in like this."

"And why not? How does this interrupt my unicornness?"

"That's not a word, and you will be a magnet, Tessa, an effing magnet if there are any elves in there, and I can almost guarantee there will be."

"How's that? I mean, we thought it was a probability, but now you guys are certain. Why?"

"This," and he cupped the side of my face gently, turning me to face part of the casino. For a moment, amid all the cling of the façade, I didn't see it and then . . . well, an archway decorated an enchanting entrance slightly out of the way, and my whole body ached to pass through it. I took a step forward.

"No, you don't."

"But it's an entrance, and look at it—"

"That's an elven arch, and you shouldn't even be able to see it."

"I couldn't until you touched me."

His hand dropped away from my face. I blinked once or twice, almost losing the arch but not now that it had been pointed out, although it no longer looked like a floral arbor and the doorway to heaven.

"Truly?"

I put his hand back to the side of my jaw and turned to look about the parking lot and public side of the casino. It looked far less blingy and yet extremely enchanted, as though Carter's touch magnified all the things I could see and feel. I spared a look toward Hiram's SUV. I could see the guys, the same and yet astonishingly different. Steptoe had a more impish look and his shadow showed a saucy, barbed tail that I knew he was missing. Hiram stood like a rock, solid and defined. Even Scout looked different, leaner and more agile, with a bright glow about his paws as if he stood on ground not quite earthlike. I looked back at Carter, who held the look of being in clear, impenetrable sunlight and power. I could almost name all of them truer than the name I knew them by, if I could only watch them a bit longer . . .

"You can see when I touch you."

"Now I can."

"You're a sorceress without the sight."

"Did you just insult me?"

"No, but I'm beginning to think the powers that create magic have." He rubbed his thumb under one eye gently before pulling his hand away. "You can't name what you can't see clearly."

"Tell me about it! That's the way I feel now, like I have these cobwebs in front of my eyes, obscuring everything that I need to know to fix things—"

He winced. "Fixing may not be exactly what the stone and your powers have in mind."

"I'm still me, aren't I? The maelstrom doesn't own me, I own it."

"That would be a question for the Society. You could do with a lot of training, at the very minimum."

"Brian and Steptoe didn't mention that. But they don't think it's wise."

"No." His voice went flat.

"And you've been yelling at them." Now I understood the stormy faces.

"Because now that I know . . ." Carter swung to me. "Tessa, you're taking a big risk going in, even with us here. Even with Scout. I can try a second glamour to dampen you down, but there's no guarantee it'll work."

"And if it doesn't?"

"Your raw power will draw attention. Attention you don't want. If the Eye of Nimora is here, there are bidders who will be just as eager to own you."

"Wait a minute. Own me?"

"That's what I said and meant."

I crossed my arms. "I can take care of myself."

"Normally, I'd agree. I've been watching you for years, and you have."

"Did Steptoe tell you I blew the tires off an F-150?"

"Ummmm . . . no." And Carter flicked a look over his shoulder at the guys, who were leaning on the front bumper of Hiram's SUV, trying to look harmless. "I'll be taking that up with him later. And you."

"Glamour away and hurry. I'm hungry. Someone promised me a birthday dinner. As for the rest of it, we'll find the Eye first and deal with possibilities after."

"Don't move." He took a deep breath and put his shoulders back. Then, with a quick sketch through the air that left fiery lines, he passed both palms over me.

I could feel something snake over me. I wanted to pull a Scout and shake the excess whatever it was off me, but stood very still until Carter stepped back. He twitched twice. "I think it worked."

"Good. Now what?"

"Stay away from the elven arch. We're putting Scout in the Komfort Kennel for a bit, so we can reconnoiter the casino, and we'll see you at dinner. And, please, don't go running off on your own. We can't afford to lose you." He gave me a quick hug that didn't mean what I'd hoped, for years, it would mean, but I wasn't going to turn it down, and I rejoined my aunt and mother.

"Okay, ladies. We're good to go." Aunt April followed on my heels, and I could hear her remarking, "Is that the Phillips boy? He's grown up well. I knew his grandparents. Good blood and good sense in that family."

The elven arch beckoned to me in the corner of my eye as we stepped toward the massive, sextuple-doored main entrance. I didn't see anyone guarding the forbidden entrance but supposed there might be someone waiting on the inside. Someday I was going to have to come back here and try it. I'd do it before we left today, but I'd hate to give anyone a heart attack.

The doorman at the front doors dipped his head as we came through. "Homecoming?" he asked cheerfully.

"Ummm . . . yeah. And birthday."

"Have a good one!"

I trotted after the relatives wondering why he'd singled me out. Did I still glow? Had he sensed it? Or was I just being paranoid? The fact that he could turn heads himself didn't influence my worry. I felt as though I had a target on my sea-glass-gowned body. So if people went out of their way to take a look at me, was it because I was ridiculously overdressed or because they had pointed ears and a thousand years of magic behind them? I stroked the palm of my left hand once, just to see if the stone happened to be awake and in protective mode. It warmed very slightly, or maybe I just had sweaty palms from being touchy. I jumped when Mom tapped my shoulder.

"Are you all right?"

"Of course."

"Okay. Well, Aunt April says we should make reservations and then wait in the gambling area until our time."

"I gave her a twenty-dollar limit."

Mom's eyes held a little sparkle. "Keeping the old gal in line?"

I shrugged. "Wouldn't hurt."

"Let's head in this direction, then." And she pointed overhead to the neon arrows proclaiming "World Famous Seafood Buffet" in case we didn't know where to go. The carpets were plush and the ceilings in mirrored splendor and the machines rang ka-ching, ka-ching with the noise of coins tumbling from them into stainless steel bins. I didn't actually see any money cascading down, which meant it was all sound effects being piped in. The machines caught my attention anyway as we passed, most of the screens alight with tales of derring do or animal whimsy, with a million ways to play for only a penny a line, which, near as I could tell, added up to almost a dollar a spin if you bet them all. And I don't know how anybody could tell if they'd won anything or not unless coins cascaded into their lap like a damn waterfall or the red siren on top went off. I got the distinct feeling that the games were aimed at maximum entertainment with minimum knowledge of what the gambler was doing. The guys trailed behind me, and I could hear Scout snuffing at something every now and then.

My twenty would go fast unless I sat down at one of the old-time, more standard machines that simply matched bars and 7's until you won or lost. Aunt April pointed at one as we passed it. "At least you know where you stand on one of these."

I pondered whether I'd been talking aloud or if the Andrews family just had a kind of telepathic thing going.

The casino floor plan made it impossible to get to the restaurant by a direct path, a result of good marketing, I suppose, because it led through the machines, the gaming tables, past the sports book with all its huge screen displays of horse races around the country, and deep into another wing altogether. I think we also passed a duty-free shop, or maybe it was just a shopping area for the newly enriched to indulge some impulse buying.

Then we also passed the glass windows of some very nice and very private poker rooms. They must have had a tournament going in one of them because the room held spectators as well as players and a camera setup. The next two rooms were almost as crowded, but it was the last that held my attention.

I wouldn't have noticed if he hadn't looked up to watch us passing.

It wasn't the suit, rich threads though they were, or the marvelously colorful and impeccable necktie with the matching handkerchief, or the way he stood with one shoulder to the wall, one leg crossing the other at the ankle showing off the perfectly cobbled dark leather shoes. No. It was the paler than pale blue gaze that shot to us and fixed on me, eyes that might almost have been silver in color but for the barest tint of blue, sharp and alert and almost painful in their regard. His mass of honey-streaked hair struck me as combed back without a stray bit hanging loose yet looked as if one really, really needed to run their fingers through it to straighten it up just a tad more . . . and that look caught at me.

There stood a man nearly as beautiful and perfect as Malender.

As soon as I thought that name, the connection between me and that glass-walled poker room weakened. I had been slowing down, almost to a stop, but I found my stride and hurried to catch up with my mother and aunt, aware his attention still burned my cheek, the side of my neck, and the curve of my shoulder where my gown revealed it. I moved in between the two of them as if they could shield me.

They couldn't. I felt the sharpness of his look along my spine until the pathway went around another corner which set me free, and I found I'd been holding my breath the whole time.

Another block or two through gambling wonderland and we finally reached the World Famous Buffet where Aunt April put in our names for a seating and tucked her purse under her arm.

"Well. It'll be an hour. Where should we park ourselves?"

We waited while Hiram put his name in for a nearby table to ours, and Scout sat demurely at his feet as though he'd been born with perfect manners. I raised an eyebrow at him, and the pup pawed at his nose.

Signs overhead pointed us to the Bingo room or back to the main casino. I wasn't certain my knees could hold out if we passed that gentleman again. I caught a glimpse of an art gallery/art auction a corridor away with free champagne and beckoned at it.

"That sounds fun."

"It does," my mother agreed. "I could do with some free bubbly." She narrowed her eyes at me. "You, however, aren't old enough."

"I won't tell if you don't."

"You are the designated driver."

"Sheesh." I trailed them down the opulent corridor to the art show. "What about my twenty?"

"You can't gamble either. And if you do, and win, they don't have to pay out."

"Everybody has to rain on my parade. I'm coming back here next year, but I'm not sure if I'm inviting you guys or not!"

Laughing at each other, we entered the gallery where a crowd already milled about, drawn by the promise of free drinks and auction bargains. I took it all in.

"What are you looking for?" Mom, at my elbow, already stood with a champagne flute in her slender fingers.

"Dogs playing poker or Elvis on black velvet or a

white tiger with blue eyes. It looks like these guys are too classy for that, though." As soon as I mentioned the tiger, I felt a new shiver run down my spine. That was what the silver blue-eyed gentleman had reminded me of, how intense and piercing his attention had instantly become, as though I'd walked into the view of a predator. I tried to shake it off without much success.

A tuxedoed man came to the podium. Both my mom and Aunt April reached out to draw me into a chair between the two of them, and I sat down as he began to review the wonders of the art world they were going to show us. He started the auction off; I tried to pay attention, but boredom seeped in around me. The guys stood bunched at the back of the room, bored and talking among themselves. No one had said anything about silver eyes to me, so either they hadn't noticed him—how on earth not?—or he wasn't of any importance.

I looked away from the podium and all the glasses of champagne bubble with their effervescence taunting me, turning about almost completely in my seat, and that's when I saw it.

In the far corner, a display of custom jewelry glittered on blue velvet stands; the prize of the bunch seemed to be either a platinum or white gold diadem band with a rich red gem accenting its center. I could see it from a football field away.

A ruby the size of a goose egg. The thing should have been at Sotheby's, not a casino gallery.

Bingo.

CHAPTER TWENTY-SIX

SNIPS N SNAILS N PUPPY DOG TAILS . . . OH, MY

"I THOUGHT YOU were finally old enough to sit still!" Aunt April whispered in my ear, snapping my head about.

"Sorry." I craned my neck to see if Carter could see the jewelry display from where he stood. It didn't appear that any of them could, and they were having an animated conversation about something, the professor appearing to be scowling.

I knotted my own eyebrows. I had a feeling they were talking about me.

"Fifteen minutes here and then we'll head back to the restaurant. I'll slip them a bill to move our wait time." Aunt April made a soothing sound.

My stomach gave a tiny rumble, and that made her smile. "I'm hungry, too," she added, and patted my knee.

I hardly heard her. I'd spotted the Eye of Nimora, and if we sat here all evening, I'd probably see it auctioned. But to whom? And who had brought it here? And would anyone bidding on it know just what it was, besides a ginormous gem? Did the elves know? Had one of them brought it to sell to another? If so, which group belonged to the crime family giving the Broadstone family grief over the trial: sellers or buyers?

And, because it also seemed important, could I sit through everything before I starved to death?

I swiveled my head about again. Could I possibly

alert them to the Eye without letting anyone else know of our keen interest? I laced my fingers together as they suddenly itched to touch the object of our search. I couldn't be certain but felt fairly confident that the moment I tried to touch the diadem the mother of all security systems would go off. The jewelry cases had to be alarmed. That kept me quiet in my seat as the first six or so pieces of art, just standard landscapes that might have appealed to some people but didn't raise an eyebrow on me, went up on the easels. I pulled my cell phone and quietly tapped in a message, and turned the sound to vibrate for the answer. The auctioneer, partnered with a beautiful young woman who glided back and forth about him displaying canvasses as though we sat at Sotheby's, kept up a nice patter, congratulating the bidders on "knowing their stuff." All the while I wondered if he knew his.

"He's good," murmured my mother as she sipped her drink. "He makes it like a contest and you want to be successful by bidding. Very interesting psychology. Oh, look. It's not exactly dogs and poker, but there you go, Tessa."

The painting depicted a New York brownstone neighborhood on a blustery day, with a guy out dog-walking a dozen or so charges who gamboled about him. It actually appealed to me, the different dogs with vibrant personalities pulling at their leashes and the man who seemed determined to ignore their enthusiasm. We watched it go for a couple thousand, not high for an original whatever the artist's name was. A number of the offerings were prints. They went in the moderately reasonable range, and I could feel Aunt April beside me shaking with mild adrenaline and the desire to bid. I nudged her.

"What house would you hang that in?"

Of all the properties she'd owned at one time, only three remained: our house, her big house, and a small, quaint cottage in the historic end of town that wasn't worth much for the architecture but for the location.

She looked down her nose at me, and the question seemed to quiet her, reminding her just how much she'd lost over the last five years. She gave me a curt nod.

I tried to pay attention. Honest. But that red jewel haunted me, and it took all I could not to turn around again and stare as it burned at the back of my thoughts.

I touched my mother. "Bathroom," I whispered and before she could answer, smoothly exited the row and headed back to where I thought I might have seen a restroom sign, and had definitely seen the Eye. The hem of my dress flowed around my ankles like a sea at high tide, reminding me to walk a bit more carefully rather than like a striker about to wreak havoc on a hockey field. So I settled by walking like a lady but a very fast one. Scout saw me make my move and strained against his leash, but the guys took no notice nor had Carter answered my text. Brian seemed animated enough that his hair stood a little on edge. That must be one heck of an argument. Carter looked up to catch me in the corner of his eye and jerked a nod when I inclined my head in the direction I moved. He gave a signal to let me know he watched.

At the corridor's edge, I halted by the jewelry case to get the look I so desired. A number of handmade, one-of-a-kind, stunning pieces of jewelry caught my eye. A slinky choker of obsidian with a spade finishing it rested on a mannequin next to rings on bedazzled fingers. As beautiful as they all were, the diadem featuring the Eye of Nimora ruby stood out blatantly. For a moment I wondered if it were like the elven arch and only certain eyes could see it. It had to be what Hiram's family had given to Germanigold; there couldn't be two pieces of jewelry like this in the world . . . well, there could, but only if one were a deliberate forgery . . . and I pondered how we could track it. Who had stolen it? How many hands had it passed through to get here, and where might it go? My palm itched, and I put my hand up absent-mindedly to scratch at it, but of course it was the stone demanding my attention.

It not only warmed, but pulsed gently, as if sensing

the Eye. "Stone, meet Eye," I muttered softly. Not that I wanted it to get too close, magic-devouring thing that my stone seemed to be, and there was the high probability of a very sensitive alarm system on this window case. But the possibility came to me that the stone definitely had vibrations for the jewel, and that might come in handy. I came as close as I could to touching the glass, saying the item's name in a soft whisper, and for the barest of a second, it sat crystal clear and alone in my thoughts, a brilliant stone with a depth of facets. Then the clarity faded and although still beautiful, the Eye sat in its place looking a bit . . . ordinary. Not that I thought for a minute that it was.

Just beyond the cases sat a doorway into a small office area. I leaned over for a look. No one presided at the desk and computer. Folders, most open, appeared scattered all over. The desire to snoop took over, and I glided in after a look or two to make sure I couldn't be seen.

Nothing met my glance immediately, and then I saw a glossy picture of that choker necklace. I nudged it aside and under it sat the object of my search. The picture looked as if someone had taken it on their phone and printed it out from there. They had also written along the edge but I did not recognize the script, let alone what the words might have said. One good picture deserves another, so I got my phone out. As soon as it snapped the shot, I heard voices drifting my way and high-tailed it out of the office before being discovered.

Out in the corridor, I saw no one who could have spoken, let alone two someones. Pondering, I drifted back to my seat in the middle of a bidding war for a "mystery" painting, its back to the audience, and found my aunt with her hands buried under her thighs to keep herself from making an offer. Mom and I traded looks. She leaned against me.

"Aunt April is resisting temptation."

"It looks tough."

"Adrenaline junkie."

We nodded to each other. I leaned the other way, toward Aunt April's ear. "Almost dinner?"

"Yes, thank god."

The auction hammer came down. "That's $750.00 for this stunning painting. Let's see what you have won!" And the pretty assistant turned around the painting to reveal the Eiffel tower in the rain, its lights glowing, and two or three young couples in love wandering the rain-glistened streets before it. Quite winsome, actually, and the gallery audience oooh'd because it evidently was 1) an original and 2) a steal at that price. Aunt April pounded the side of her chair with her fist. I nudged her.

"That's $750 we didn't have."

"True." She deflated a bit and checked her watch. "Five more minutes and we can go check in for the line."

"Great!" I sat back, thinking and growling, my mind and stomach both working furiously. I stopped when a feeling crept up the back of my shoulder blades and buried itself in the nape of my neck as though a target rested there. As though a predator watched.

I wanted to turn around and look. Every nerve in my body twinged, sending tiny shocks here and there that would stop if I just looked. I froze in place. Something told me that if I did, if I turned about, a line would be crossed. A test passed that I didn't want to pass. A feeling of danger settled about me like a net; I fought to keep from shrugging it off, from springing to my feet and heading for the nearest exit. My body tensed until it hurt.

I had to look. I let my purse slip off my knee to the carpet and, at a snail's pace, bent to retrieve it. Glaciers move faster than I did, although I tried to do it naturally and look behind us. Even upside down, I recognized the beautiful man with the silver eyes from the poker rooms. He wasn't watching the room. His gaze had locked on the three of us. I slid back into place and pulled my phone out of my purse cautiously. I wanted to take a picture but knew if I did, all the care I'd taken to be unaware and oblivious would be blown away. Still, I sent a text to Carter with his description and interest and where we were. He hadn't answered the first text yet, which bothered me. Had he gotten mine? Or was the signal blocked? Neither possibility sounded promising.

Aunt April's foot pushed the side of mine. "I've had enough. Let's head for dinner."

The three of us stood together, bowing out as quietly as we could as another "mystery" objet d' art rested on the easel. Bidding this time seemed to go through the roof, drawing everyone's eager attention, even that of ice-cold eyes.

Although I could swear the moment we passed by his stare followed our steps until the corridor turned, taking us out of sight. My flesh tingled with feeling, and when I looked down at my arms, goose bumps covered them.

I told myself I should do something heroic, like point him out to the guys. But I'd been warned, most emphatically, not to do anything solo or stupid. If anything, my guys would want the element of surprise. My stomach took over as we passed the restaurant and marched me into line because I felt like I was starving. With the phones not working as they should—and for all I knew the casino might be dampening the signal to discourage cheating—I hoped they were right on our heels.

Mom bravely held the table while Aunt April and I went cruising the buffet line. I'd seen pictures of dinners like this but hadn't ever attended one. I grabbed one plate and filled it full of crab legs while my second plate held more demure offerings of rare roast beef, Virginia ham, and au gratin potatoes. Mom gave me a look when I sat down. I contemplated the plates, trying to determine her disapproval.

"I'll get salad next round," I promised her. "And shrimp."

With a laugh, she stood and marched off to do her own conquering while Aunt April brought back two ewers of clarified butter with her own dishes. She had the balancing act down pat and smiled at my envying look.

"Experience, dearie, experience." She passed me one ewer and we began to eat. I'd almost cleared my crab plate before my mother rejoined us.

She lifted an eyebrow at me. I pointed a seafood fork at her. "I have been waiting all day for this."

The guys filed into the restaurant about then, Scout with them, prancing in his Service dog jacket and looking about as helpful as he could. One ear twitched my way, but he stayed with Carter and took a place under the table as Carter signaled him to down and stay. A few people approached them, but Carter shook his head and explained that dogs in training and service shouldn't be distracted. Both fans and pup looked disappointed as he fended them off.

My own appetite quashed, I got to watch as Hiram laid assault to the buffet, a wondrous thing to behold, because Iron Dwarves can nearly eat their considerable weight in offerings if they put their mind to it. I think I heard one of the floor managers moan softly as she ordered a new platter of crab legs to be brought out. Carter didn't disgrace himself either, or Brian, although I noted that Brian preferred the beef to seafood, and he had one enormous plate of salad and exotic-looking vegetable dishes. Maybe the seafood was left for dessert.

Mom poked the back of my hand with the tip of her knife.

"What?"

"You're staring."

"Sorry. It's like watching Godzilla devour Tokyo." I swiveled slightly in my chair to turn my eyes away.

"He does have a prodigious appetite," noted Aunt April. "Reminds me of a gentleman I dated when I was young. Had the enthusiasm of a Paul Bunyan—"

"Paul who?"

Aunt April shook her head at me. "Never mind." To my mother, she added, "Thought you were giving her a classical education?"

Mom just shook her head before skillfully stripping a crab leg of its delicious meat.

I stacked my empty plates to one side before standing. "Back to the front. Desserts this time." My mother side-eyed me. "And salad. Definitely salad."

The dessert end of the buffet bars sparkled with a

hundred or more different jewels of deliciousness. I hovered over them in indecision, knowing I could only taste maybe half a dozen or so without getting more killer stares from my mother and great-aunt and wondering if I could possibly stuff two or three down before I got back to my table. Sugar is definitely my weakness.

So the strawberry and whipped cream topped meringue thingy called a Pavlova definitely found a spot on my plate. Then a caramel and chocolate frosted mini-brownie. Most of the desserts came in mini size, which was a good thing, I told myself. I could always get another one if I wanted. Poised over the éclairs, a movement in the kitchen beyond caught my attention. Someone watched from behind the scenes. I wouldn't have blamed a worker for sneaking glances of Hiram's Herculean-sized portions, but my skin chilled when I identified the spy.

Once seen, it took all I had to look away and find another pastry, but I could feel the knife-edged sharp watch of chilly blue eyes on me, and on our tables beyond me. Had he come looking for us? Trailed us to the restaurant? And did he have any inkling who Hiram, Brian, and Carter might be? Or was that steely attention fixed on me, because of the maelstrom stone or worse? Something told me I really did not want definite answers to any of my questions. I snagged a chocolate caramel éclair bite and sauntered back to my table where I promptly ignored the towers of goodness on my plate while I got my phone and texted Carter two tables away, hiding my actions. I then waited to see if he showed any reaction that my phone message had reached him.

None.

It seemed the casinos, in strategic areas anyway, had phone reception blocked. Not cool. I could rush to his side and tell him everything, but I'd spoil the trap. The Keno board lit up, and a young lady not much older than I was stopped by the table to collect our cards. I grabbed a crayon, scribbled a message on the back of the playing slip and gave her five bucks to get it to the other table. She pocketed the cash, went to two or three other tables first, and then sauntered by the guys. Credit to Hiram, he even stopped eating long enough to smile gently at her, and Carter sat up straight in his chair when he'd finished reading. Scout lurched to his feet.

Brian leaned over to listen when Carter tapped his arm, and both of them looked serious for a few minutes, then Hiram flashed a nod my way before pushing aside a plate of devastated shells and heading back to the buffet. He positioned himself strategically so that he could check on my report, so skillfully done that I couldn't have told that anything but the fresh crab legs and a bin of chilled and peeled shrimp interested him. He returned to the table and then three things happened:

Hiram reported to Carter and Brian. Carter put a hand down under the table, unsnapped Scout's leash, and said something. Scout launched himself at my table. He bounded into a table leg, upsetting a tower of emptied platters waiting for pickup, and they tumbled into my sweet tea glass, which dumped right into my lap. Okay, maybe five or six things took place. I jumped up as the ice-cold beverage swept across my good dress and began dripping down my legs. I didn't have to fake the gasp of surprise and dismay.

Carter swept to his feet and darted over, apologizing. He dabbed me all over with a napkin and muttered, "Get yourself, your mom, and Aunt April out of here."

"But who is that?"

"Someone we don't want to meet. Trust me!"

I let out a strangled, "My dress!"

Both women got up and wrestled me away from the pup and tried to console me. Carter finished off with a promise to take care of the dry cleaning, tucking a business card in my mother's hands. We'd already paid for our meals before we went in, so bolting from the restaurant wouldn't raise any eyebrows. Mom did say, several times, "Cold water will work the stain out just fine," as they pushed me down the hall back to the bathroom. The guys sauntered a little more casually after us, as if they weren't part of the group. I thought I heard a sigh of relief from the buffet workers in charge of refilling the seafood bins at the sight of Hiram departing. Aunt April began to lag a little, as if the call of the casino machines filled her ears.

I took her by the elbow. "We've got trouble. Carter says to head to the car."

Aunt April protested. I put my hand on Mom. "Both of you."

So they retreated, grumbling a bit, but they went. I went with them despite the fact I had a jewel to reclaim, if the guys would run interference for me.

And everything would have been grand, Carter getting us out of harm's way, and the object of our hunt having been located, at least for the moment.

Except we ran into a heist in the hallway.

CHAPTER TWENTY-SEVEN

DUCK AND RUN

IF IT WASN'T a heist, then these guys looked pretty ridiculous running out of the art gallery with guns drawn, black hoods over their head, skin-tight black pants and shirts, and black silk pillowcases bulging with goodies in their free hands. Guns pointed. Words were snarled. They cut through us like a herd dog through sheep, separating us. My mom and Aunt April took to their heels and ran for the nearest exit door, while I took up the rear, wondering if I should summon my stone to life or try to keep it hidden. I considered running for it, but the guns pointing in my direction made that a terrible decision. I made the additional mistake of looking behind me.

"Freeze!"

I could hear the metal fire door exit clang into place and hoped my mom and great-aunt had gotten out as I flung my hands up and froze, back to the wall, expecting them to blow by me and out the nearest exit door. Gun barrels waved at me. I could hear the slow plops of iced tea draining from my gown onto the carpeted floor. I could also hear Scout's excited yaps in the near distance, just around a corridor corner.

What I didn't hear were alarms of any kind, surprising me as the sound of glass breaking and collapsing to smithereens continued, and two more men joined the exodus from the gallery. A final case cracked open, and the last perpetrator turned the corner, his prize in hand.

Only this guy didn't wear a black hood, bandanna, or even sunglasses. The Eye of Nimora in its diadem hung from his fingers. He stopped short and then gave me a smile that held absolutely no humor or warmth whatsoever. His smile simmered as cold as his eyes, and I no longer had any desire to smooth his blond hair off his forehead. I didn't even want to be sharing the same casino with him.

"I wondered if we were going to meet."

"I didn't."

I could feel the stone in my palm hiccough. I know marble can't hiccough, and the stone isn't a living or breathing thing (I do know that, don't I?), but if it could have, it did. Or maybe it was a gasp. The only saving grace was that my glamour still held and hopefully Blue Eyes hadn't noticed it because something had startled it as much as he'd startled me. How did he get from the back of the kitchen to the art gallery?

Then I realized that those trays of champagne offered during the auction had to be filled and carried from somewhere behind the scenes, and that would have undoubtedly been the kitchen. Silly me for forgetting these modern resorts had as many secret tunnels and back ways hidden from the public view as old and historic castles. I could barely breathe, let alone think.

He sauntered up to me. Far prettier than Legolas had ever been, definitely more chill, and taller, he put his gun hand out and traced my chin with his index finger. I held very still, praying the gun had a safety or maybe even wasn't loaded, but there seemed little chance of that. That's when I realized that our trap for which I was the bait had been successful. Here was our elf. I guess I'd known it since that first sight but hadn't fixed on it. No wonder Carter had told me to hustle myself out of the casino.

"Do you know what this is?" He waved the Eye of Nimora slightly.

I shook my head very carefully, averting my gaze a bit, just in case he could read lies easily.

"It's something interesting. I'll spare you the details,

but I collect interesting things. At least until I learn their value, and then I may keep them or pass them along, whatever serves my purpose. There's a bit of curiosity about you, as well. My employer and I have noticed you."

"Me? I just like to look around. A lot." Employer? He struck me as all-Boss, but I stored that away for when I could think again.

"Not what I meant, but I think you know that."

I shook my head. "I'm just a lot of trouble. Not worth it." Or at least, I intended to make it a lot of trouble. My frame tightened in readiness to unleash whatever problems I could muster, starting with an ear-piercing scream and unleashing the stone.

"And you're modest, too. So many interesting attributes. I think I'll take you with me." He swapped his gun to the hand holding the Eye of Nimora, which winked up at me with its dazzling crimson facets, and dipped his fingers inside his jacket. He moved, faster than I could draw breath for that scream, hand up. When he touched my brow, something sparkling drifted down, a rainfall of glitter. Surprise drove my intended yell from me, and I said instead, "What are you, an effing unicorn?"

He only smiled wider and colder as a numbness rained down over me. Words skittered away from my lips before they could be spoken, and all my little aches and pains of the day and the day before where Fourteen had hammered me on the hockey field just melted away. I felt as though I could fall asleep standing up and be perfectly happy to do so. I blinked rapidly, but the glitter caught on the tips of my eyelashes just spun out and on down my body where it disappeared like sea foam on wet sand. I couldn't think of anything else important to say. There had been something, but I'd forgotten . . .

Nothing seemed important. If this nice man wanted me to go with him, I would. Surely nothing wrong with that. Pleasant bubbles floated through my head. What a beautiful evening it seemed to be. I could drift forever, almost boneless, certainly worriless.

"I've tarried a bit too long. You will make an appropriate shield, I think, not that I expect too much trouble. Your friends are watching and holding back to see what I do with you." He took my elbow, and my left hand jerked up as though he'd stuck a hot poker into my palm.

Popping bubbles exploded in my skull and my foot swung up, kicking him sharply in the ankle as I pulled loose and swung my weight across the hall. A string of colorful words burst from him, words I had no way of recognizing, but I put my hand out, just in case they carried more than ordinary cursing, in elven.

Footsteps pounded our way, sight unseen but not unheard, and he grabbed for me again. I shrugged him off, body still not quite obeying what I wanted to do, but responding as well as it could. Resistance seemed to be the best option.

So I dropped. Fell like a sack of wet noodles to the floor, never mind dignity, never mind that he grabbed a handful of hair as I went down because I knew he was never going to get dead weight up and motivating in time to make good his escape. Or, at least that was the idea.

He ground out a few words and my body rose horizontally, shakily, like one of those ladies levitating in a magic show illusion, only I didn't have hidden wires pulling me up. Fake Legolas had me like a balloon on a string and this time, stretched across midair, I had no leverage to strike back. Tugging me after him, my hair still firmly wrapped about his hand, we made our way through the corridor toward the main portion of the casino and the nearest emergency exit. I only knew that because my chin pointed at the ceiling and I read the neon sign as I floated under it. Emergency. Exit. This way. I struggled as he wrapped his hand deeper into my hairline until it felt as though he might scalp me. My body bobbed up and down like a cork in water, and he laughed. A mean, quiet, to-himself chortle as he steered my course.

But I had no intention of going quietly. I sucked in a long, slow, determined breath. I couldn't feel my body very well, but I reached for the rock in my palm. I knew it rested there, a small, warm core in my otherwise lukewarm and becharmed body. Nothing happened. I might as well have been nothing more than sea foam floating on the air. That wouldn't do. I inhaled deeper. The stone had picked me out. Embedded in me. Given me all sorts of trouble. It had shielded me in chancy times. Ate up Brian's cursed ring. Blown tires off a truck at fifty miles an hour. Swallowed a book on Dark Arts. I knew that gorgeous hunk of marble hadn't moved. I dug down deep, a drive from inside me where I reached when I wanted to, had to, score.

It felt like touching bottom as I sank into a lake without end. I bounced off it, thrusting myself upward, back toward the sunlit surface, back to where I needed to be.

It hurt to dig so deep, feeling as though I'd turned myself inside out. The magic, when it answered, stabbed. It began to sputter, like a spark catching fire reluctantly in a wet and heavy wind, flickering, and then catching. The lake of nothingness surrounding me began to burn. Power seared the inside of my eyelids and my mouth went dry. The maelstrom stone poured heat into my hand and up my arm and over my shoulder, like sinking into a hot tub full of energy. I could feel the lethargy bursting in tiny pings as warmth spread, and my floating body bobbled a bit.

It did not keep me from going out a doorway into the dusk, the casino lights dazzling overhead. It did not halt a slow but steady float toward that elven arch, the one I was told never to go through. The stone burned brighter until I feared it would set my glove—and me—on fire. Not only would that hurt, but my secrets would be cracked wide open.

I tried to lick lips now split and hurting, so dry from the heat that burned through me. I could save myself if only I had a little help, the slightest of pushes that could bring me back to my feet and then I could take over. Sound came as if I were a glacier inching toward a melt. Not fast enough. Not soon enough. I had no idea where the guys were or what kept them, but if they didn't show up soon, I was going to be floated over the rainbow. Or, rather, under it, to forbidden territory. Then it hit me that they could have already come running—and been met by a firefight none of them would have been prepared for. Except Carter, that would be, his military background would have more than readied him, but the others—no. A handgun against a magic wand was no contest at all. I might already have lost more than I knew. But surely I would have heard it, wouldn't I? My gaze flicked back the way he'd pulled me, but all I saw was the immense side of the casino building with a door still halfway open. Nothing and no one came through it.

My mind sped ahead, thoughts racing and then . . . then . . . we hit a snag.

Actually, it felt like I hit a brick building. Or maybe an Iron Dwarf.

But I hadn't. My head turned, and I saw Malender standing in his cloak of dark ooze, his hands spread, his garb of a rogue swordsman or bard in full costume unmistakable, his eyes blazing jade green, and he looked unstoppable. He'd a hand thrown up, and that had been enough to bring icy-eyes and me to a thumping halt. I would have yelled whiplash if I could speak. But I couldn't . . . so how did he show up?

I hadn't called his name, had I? And certainly not three times. If I could have called anybody, it would have been Carter or Brian. They were detained by caution behind us, and I had little doubt Carter was making plans faster than he was breathing to free me and the Eye of Nimora. But my throat felt locked down, my voice stifled. I hadn't even thought of Malender, yet here he stood.

My feet lowered to the ground. I stood, although not on my own, my head tilted back as the hand wrapped in my hair tightened and my captor snarled in words I wasn't meant to understand. He yanked me back toward him, a shield.

The corner of Malender's mouth twitched. "You're not taking her anywhere. I've marked her." And his hand brushed the side of my face, by my temple, and into my hairline and I could feel an answering prickle of skin as though he'd awakened a part of me I hadn't known existed.

"Interesting. Does Nico know? Possession and all that," the elf answered. His breath grazed the back of my ear, as icy as the color of his eyes.

"You possess nothing."

For a moment, my upright form swayed between them, caught in a nameless tug of war of will. I wanted to shake myself loose of both of them, and yet, beyond, that forbidden archway beckoned to me. If I could get to it on my own, I'd be freed.

My foot stirred.

"You would be better served to retreat gracefully while you can." Malender's cloak shuddered a bit around him as if it had a life of his own. I saw an edge of pain shoot across his expression. He shuttered his eyes quickly and when he opened them, that telltale emotion had disappeared. I wondered what I might have just witnessed.

Icy-eyes spoke bitterly. "I never retreat. You have to have lost to retreat, and I haven't lost. Meanwhile, the world has all but forgotten you . . . and you still wear a cloak of imprisonment."

That last sank in, and I hoped I wouldn't forget it as the haze of numbness tried to grip me afresh.

"Ah, but it diminishes, and I restore while you fight to run in place. Your age has passed, yet you are too blind to see it. Know this. I will protect what I must and destroy what deserves it." Malender brushed his hand over my face, and my senses reacted in sudden, dazzling liberty. I understood right then and there how mad a wet hen could be and threw my hands up to tear away the elf gripping me. Fingers ripped from my scalp.

Malender caught me by the wrist and twirled me away, spinning like a dancer, back against the casino building while he lunged forward. Shadows leaped up to cover him. For a blinding second, I saw the elven archway in clear relief, but that wasn't the door Malender had taken.

Then I heard a snarling growl and a rush as a door clanged wide open and we were hit by the cavalry. Blue-

Eyes went to his knees, my body jerked downward in answer, and I could smell dog—Scout, bless his heart—surging all around us. Malender disappeared into shadow with a sidestep, but I had no chance to worry about it as I fought for control of my body. Wet noodles had nothing on me. The spell broke, and I fell to the floor where I rolled to my hands and knees. Scout whipped around the elf like a golden whirlwind, teeth clashing and feet scrambling. The gun tumbled to the ground and then the Eye as Blue-Eyes fought to protect himself. Carter's voice cracked like a shot.

"Stop right there!"

For just that moment, no one moved. Scout dove for Nimora's crimson glory, retrieving it even as the elf reached in his pocket and pulled out another handful of glitter. He threw it.

My dog fell over, limp. Blue-Eyes scooped him up, jewelry and all, and ran. The elven archway winked as he leaped through it. Carter flung himself after but came to a halt himself as the parking lot filled with uniforms and other familiar bodies and shouts and I put my hands up, just in case. A silk pouch lay on the asphalt, and I scooted one knee over to cover it as everyone surrounded me. A babble of voices whirled about, and I could only see one face clearly, that of Carter, and in the evening dark, he shone like the sun. Djinn, Steptoe would have whispered in my ear if he'd been with us, but he wasn't, and I didn't know what powers Carter had, but I was afraid to look at him. He'd come for me. As Malender had done. The rescue left me blinking in wonder.

It seemed hours, but it wasn't, until Carter got everything sorted out. Brian brought me a bracing cup of tea in a cardboard cup although we both agreed china would taste better. Hiram toured the building to see if he could ascertain exactly where the other elves had exited because it seemed a certainty they didn't just spill out into the parking lot like ordinary folk. He found residual traces of another, temporary elven gate. Brian's face tightened, and his eyebrows knotted together like a storm cloud as I could see the professor inside fighting off anger.

Casino security finished with us eventually, and we all stood in the parking lot under a half moon, although with the blinking bling of the signs, the nighttime sky seemed very muted and far away. Carter took my hand.

"Are you okay?"

His warmth felt good on my skin. "Disappointed."

"I didn't think we'd walk out of here with the Eye of Nimora. Did you?"

I shrugged. "Maybe. At least we found it, though, right? Except Blue-Eyes has it."

"Blue—oh. Tessa, that was Devian."

I'd heard the name before but couldn't quite remember where. "And he's a big shot."

"A big, bad shot."

"And Scout saved me."

"Looks like. It would have been very, very ugly, if he'd tried taking you through the arch." The off-side cleft in his chin deepened as he frowned. "I would have stopped him however I could."

"Good thing you didn't have to try. He had the stone muffled, mostly, don't know how since he didn't seem to be aware of it, but I broke through in time to put up a little bit of a fight." I hated lying to him, but I didn't want to mention Malender, and I still had some thinking to do about what I'd seen and what he'd said. My fingers went to my hairline behind my right temple and rubbed gently. A patch of skin tingled in answer. Against the curve of my ear, a whisper sounded. *"Tell the professor I am his Fire!"* I jumped but saw no one. I needed a mirror and privacy.

"Muffled?" Brian straightened up. "But you don't think Devian was aware of it?"

"I have no idea. None. He stunned and levitated me, and then—"

"Levitated?"

I put my hand out, illustrating. "As in, horizontal and floating about three feet or so off the floor." I winced. "Hope casino cameras didn't catch that."

"According to security, they weren't able to catch any of it."

"Oh, really? Convenient. Anyway, the stun wore off when the stone woke up." I lifted my hand and looked at it. "From the palm outward. I was just drifting out of the levitation when Scout attacked." Also, both Devian and Malender had treated that envelope of ooze about him as something meant to imprison him. That stood out crystal clear in my slightly befuddled thoughts. Every time I saw him that I could, the shroud got liberally doused in salt. Was I freeing him, bit by bit? No wonder he seemed to refer to me fondly as Tessa of the Salt. That reminded me of the other stuff, and I turned abruptly to drop the drawstring pouch I'd retrieved into Brian's hand, which he had raised to make a vigorous point, and the gift surprised him instead. His mouth opened and shut a few times.

"What is this?"

"That," Carter said tightly, "is pixie dust, unless I am greatly mistaken. If you let Tessa set herself up as bait just to obtain that—"

"I did no such thing although I did suggest it might be helpful to find out where it could be obtained."

Their argument was interrupted by my mother and Aunt April joining us in the parking lot.

"Are you all right?" My mom hugged me tightly.

"I am. Not sure about everyone else."

"They robbed the casino?"

"Seems like. Smashed the jewelry cases and took off. Stampeded right past me." I frowned at Carter, Brian, and Hiram to tell no more. Hiram cleared his throat and said he'd retrieve the SUV.

The other two stared at each other, nose to nose, and I realized that the professor stood nearly as tall as Carter. Or, at least his new body did. Brian took a step back as if realizing this was no place to start another fight.

I just stood, my mom on one side and my Aunt April on the other, my mom knowing a little of what went on and my great-aunt a little stunned though listening closely. When all was said and done, and a local constabulary came out the exit door one last time, he told Carter we could go home.

Aunt April dusted herself off and said, “Oh, my.”

I hugged myself.

“Are you all right?”

I looked at all of them as I realized the one true loss of the evening, and my eyes misted up. “No. They took my dog.”

CHAPTER TWENTY-EIGHT

HUSH PUPPY BLUES

THE DRIVE HOME seemed a little too quiet until Aunt April finally spoke up. "I can't blame you for not telling me much, I would have thought you both batshit crazy, but what happened this evening? And don't tell me it's complicated because I sure as hell can tell that." She swiveled around in the front seat to peer at me, but I didn't know what to tell her. She stared at the side of my mom's head as she attempted to drive. "I'm no bump on a log. Talk, the two of you."

"Yes, ma'am." I cleared my throat. "Well, it seems there is a little bit of magic in the world—"

"Are you going to pussyfoot about that? Of course there is! Do you think I won thousands of dollars gambling—and lost it, too, for that matter—because I had a pretty face and a sharp nose once? No. I had a few good luck tokens about me, and however they got charmed, they *worked*. Your daddy now, before he disappeared and cell phones got all popular, he always knew when the phone was going to ring and who'd be calling. The mind and the senses are powerful things."

"It's a little stronger than that, Aunt April," my mom noted. "We're talking actual magic and things we can't explain. Like, for instance, John's ghost lives in our basement."

"John? Our John?"

My mother nodded. My great-aunt went as pale as a sheet of writing paper. "Ghost? Oh, no."

I leaned forward and put my hand on her shoulder. "He's not dead. Just not here in the traditional sense, and I plan to get him back."

"What's he doing as a ghost? How could that happen? And what do you mean, get him back?"

"We don't exactly know, which is why we haven't been able to undo it, but that's how he disappeared without a trace. He slipped into a kind of twilight zone."

She inhaled sharply as if she'd just remembered how to breathe again. "So that's why that old house makes all those strange noises. He's a haint."

"Yup." My mother skillfully took a curve in the night-cloaked road. "We didn't find him until a while back, ourselves."

"After the new cellar went in."

"Pretty much."

I swallowed. "And that's not all."

"There's more?" Her voice went a bit higher, as if she really couldn't take more, but I forged ahead.

"Professor Brandard didn't die in that house fire."

"Oh, glory be. I couldn't bear to think of him dying that way. Where's he gone, then? It's been months. You tell him to get in touch with me. We're old friends. Used to play cards at the club all the time, and I miss his irascible old self. Not that he could beat me, that is, but we made good partners."

"That's a little more complicated."

Her mouth tensed into a thin line, and before she could tell me that she'd told me not to bring that up as an excuse, I said, "Our house guest is the professor, reincarnated. We think. It looks like it." I left off the wizardly part of it. Great-Aunt April may be a trooper, but I didn't want to give her more than she could handle.

"Reincarnated?" She let out a long exhale. "Well. Well, well." She gave a sniff. "Isn't that special."

Her words fell like a large rock into a still pond, and then I began to laugh. She followed and then my mother. When we could finally draw our breaths, she gave a little snort. "Leave it to a man to get a new body. Usually, he goes for a trophy wife instead of trading himself in, but the professor always thought high and mighty of himself." She drew a lace-edged handkerchief out of her purse and dabbed at the laughter tear in the corner of her eyes. "I take it he doesn't remember much. He's not a good enough actor to pretend he's forgotten me."

"Not much, but he's working on that. There's a magic ritual involved."

Her purse snapped shut after she'd folded her handkerchief and put it back where it belonged. "So what happened at the casino? You were quite taken by the jewelry, Tessa. Something of note there? A cursed amulet or such? Something the professor needs?"

"Something like that. A diadem caught my eye, but I didn't plan on getting caught in a heist! I was just playing tourist."

A very, very long moment of silence followed. I didn't break it as my mother concentrated on keeping us in a smooth flow of highway traffic and my aunt settled back against the car seat. She turned her head to watch the roadway go by and after another long pause said, "Live and learn, ladies. That's what it's all about. Live and learn."

She folded her blue-veined hands in her lap and that was it until we pulled into our driveway.

A caramel-iced sheet cake awaited us, my aunt having learned that there would be more than three people digging in, but we'd had ours and Hiram's SUV still hadn't parked out front, when Aunt April took me by the hand.

"Come to the basement with me."

"I will, but you won't see him. He's very weak."

"Ah." An expression I couldn't identify passed through her eyes. "Still, I'd like to go down there."

"Of course."

The new lighting system flooded the room, and it didn't look a bit like the creepy old place Hiram had fallen into. Walls, floor, and ceiling all gleamed brightly. She shook her head as we stood in the center, the professor's boxes piled off to the side and the only familiar thing the old wooden cabinet where the maelstrom stone had been waiting for me. She crossed to it.

"This old thing. I'm glad you all didn't haul it out and get rid of it. Belonged to my grandmother." She stroked the paint-faded wood. "Now there was a lady who probably had a touch. She lived back in the days when people made their own medicines because a good doctor was often a few days away, or more, by carriage. She was known for it, she was—Potion Polly, they used to call her. She could cure you of melancholy or a cough or even most cases of arthritis, but then she knew all about willow bark before aspirin got compounded." Aunt April smiled softly in memory before dropping her hand. She drew herself up. "All right now, John Graham Andrews. I'm talking to you. I'm sorry, mighty sorry, for sending you into my sea of troubles, but I'm fine now and this family of yours survives and thrives. So you hang on, you hear, until this outstanding daughter of yours comes and gets you!"

No one answered. I hadn't expected them to, although I could feel a cool mist swirl about us. I nudged her. "Feel that?"

"A draft? I do, though I can't tell where it's coming from." Aunt April looked about.

"It's him."

She made a sound. Then, "Good. I hope he heard and does what's needful."

She didn't hear it, but I did as we turned about and began climbing up the stairs. A voice at the back of my neck, hollow but recognizable, murmured, "Yes, ma'am."

The guys piled in the door after we'd settled back in the kitchen and decided that the evening had settled cool enough for hot tea instead of sweet iced tea. I'd changed clothes and hung my gown on my closet door, as a reminder to get it to the cleaners sometime Monday. Since that was a game day, it might have to wait until Tuesday. As I came downstairs, I saw Mom had put the coffeepot on, anticipating, with a stack of paper plates and nice but decidedly plastic forks to the side. She'd finally gotten tired of doing dishes, I noted.

Aunt April dipped her head at each of them as they pulled up kitchen chairs, and then Steptoe drifted in from the backyard as well. He doffed his bowler. "Madam."

"Indeed," she answered. "It seems cake calls to everyone. Pull up a seat."

"No doubt o' that and it smells scrumptious. Mary, did you concoct this?"

"No, it's one of Aunt April's specialties. Made-from-scratch yellow cake with caramel icing."

"I can barely wait." He sat down next to Hiram.

Because Mom was brewing, I got up and started slicing the rectangle into neat squares. I knew they'd give me disappointed looks when they saw the size, but I figured they wouldn't hesitate to ask for seconds, anyway. I stopped midway, cake knife in my hand. I missed Scout nudging and begging at my knees and my breath caught in my throat.

"Where's th' pup?" Steptoe asked, even as Carter shot him a look across the kitchen and I let out a small sniffle.

"We're getting him back."

Simon considered Carter for a moment before looking down and retrieving his paper napkin. "A-course you are. No tears now, Tessa. What this man promises, he means, and we'll all help. Any success in the rest of the evening?"

Aunt April tilted her head thoughtfully. "A regular mob you've got here, Mary, and I was no more the wiser. Well," and she scanned all of them. "I've been let in on the secret."

Voices broke out then, all round, noisily, and I managed to quiet them a bit as I passed out cake squares perched neatly on their little plates and said, "Not quite everything." The din died back a little. "We may have trouble with elves."

"Elves?" she repeated. "Nasty little tiny pisks or high elves?"

"High and mightily arrogant." Steptoe reached for his dessert with a beaming smile and set the cake down in front of him, coal eyes gleaming. He rubbed his hands together eagerly.

"Aunt April," my mother interrupted, "is a bit new to all of this. And, you all must admit, it's a lot to take in."

"Certainly, certainly," Hiram's deep tones rumbled. "I don't think I've seen a finer cake." He held his fork in anticipation, and his waiting stopped Steptoe just before he dug in.

They all paused, albeit a tad impatiently, while my mother got drinks poured around and put cream and sugar on the table. As soon as she took a chair, they dug in.

I would have, too, but I sat on my phone. I didn't butt-dial anyone though I dug it out of my rear pocket and stared at it a moment before remembering the pictures I'd taken at the art show auction. I thumbed them up and sent them to the printer in Mom's study before putting my phone down and listening to the talk around me as they discussed why the security system at the casino had failed to capture the robbery (or me floating through the air). They said more than my Great-Aunt April seemed prepared for, but she took it in, adding a salient point about the community in general when necessary, and it seemed she knew more about casinos and security than most people. Even Carter gave her an appraising look as she shared. Of course, she'd spent enough time in them, both private and public, than was healthy for just about anybody.

But she also knew how to make a fine cake. Moist and tasty, with the icing melting in my mouth like a rich, decadent fudge, I was definitely right that everybody would demand seconds. And we had enough to provide that, with a couple of extra slices for me and Mom tomorrow. Hiram could have inhaled them, but he tightened his belt and made do with just the two pieces. An ant couldn't have found a crumb on his plate, though. Mom swept to her feet and gathered up the debris while I made a beeline to the printer, determined to see a big picture of the snap I'd taken of the sheet on the Eye, with that strange-looking writing. I'd managed to take five pictures in quick succession without knowing. My phone has a hair trigger, evidently.

I brought in the five pages and dropped them in the middle of the table. "Whoever sent the Eye of Nimora to the casino to be sold left us a little bit of a trail."

Hands reached out to grab them. Carter caught the main printout first.

He frowned. "Elven. Probably."

The professor said, "Let me see that."

Steptoe huffed a little. "As if you remembered enough to read that."

The professor started to draw Brian's hand back but countered with, "I might."

Carter passed it to him. Shoulder to shoulder, they both considered it. Carter looked up briefly, "We know who took it. Information came to them from Germanigold's nest, and they acted on it and passed it to the casino for resale. They are aware of some of its value but not all. They thought the gem might be an attractor for other jewels, the Broadstone propensity for mineral wealth considered."

The professor interrupted. "But there is no direct connection to Devian although it is speculated that he might be interested in a private purchase if it didn't sell at auction. In so many words. The Eye of Nimora has not been seen in centuries outside of the Broadstone clan. Few know what it looks like or how it is presented. Devian wanted to bid for it, but it could have been anything as far he knew. Hence the massive jewelry grab." He stabbed at the paper. "We put word out that the ruby is a dwarven talisman to locate gems, and they want it back."

"What's the plan, then?"

"We tell Germanigold and her nest of the informant—"

"She already knows and has dealt with the problem," I interrupted. I got several side eyes on that and waved a hand. "I'll fill y'all in."

"All right then. We give her names and let her deal

with that fallout. And tomorrow, Sunday, we try to entice Devian to make a deal."

I stared at Carter. "A deal?"

He lifted one shoulder and let it drop. "He doesn't know what he has. Yet."

"He thinks he has a magical Geiger counter for precious gems?"

"That about sums it up. If we explain that it's running low on charge and will shortly be totally useless to him, he's likely to give it up."

"And what would you all trade to him for it?"

Hiram stood with a clearing of his throat. "Me."

We all turned to stare at the Iron Dwarf. He put his chin up a little defiantly. "I could be his hound for a fortnight, in exchange for the woefully inadequate ruby and the pup."

"You'd invite him to test the Eye to prove to him its prowess greatly depleted." Carter grinned at him.

"Naturally. He should accept the word of a Broadstone, but elves, being duplicitous themselves, are a suspicious lot."

"Damned tricksters," Brian muttered.

"A bit of flash and no substance," Aunt April agreed. Mom and I both stared wide-eyed at her. She pulled a bit of a face. "Well, they are. I've met one or two. At least, as I look back on my years of experience, I suspect they were elves."

"No doubt." Carter stood up next to Hiram. "If you're up for it, I'll back your idea, but we'll need to have a failsafe."

"Naturally, neither I nor the gem will work on the other side of that arch." Hiram arched an eyebrow at him.

"Devious and perfect. I think we can handle that. We'll get word to him, but when we do, I want Tessa protected and not out of anyone's sight."

"Done."

I could feel a frown setting in. "I want to be there. Scout might need me." And I hated being left out.

Carter shook his head. "Not wise. He knew he wanted

you before as a hostage and if you're exposed to him again, he might figure out exactly why."

Aunt April frowned. "Why would he want Tessa specifically?"

"Because of this." I showed my palm to her in all its marble-embedded glory. My great-aunt sat back rigidly.

"Great Matilda," Aunt April snapped. "Did you do that to yourself? Like a tattoo or one of those spools?"

"Ah. No. Not exactly. It's a talisman, like a charmed ring or something."

"But it just happens to be a piece of marble sunk into your hand."

I beamed at her. "Exactly."

And then Hiram, Carter, and Brian leaned forward, talking all at once and trying to explain to her it wasn't as bad as it looked but that the elves might think it intriguing, which would not be a good thing, and I think she understood that but also thought there was more than they were saying. She took it in, anyway, not bad for a beginner in her first night of learning modern magic. Of course, with Potion Polly for a grandmother, Aunt April might have had a leg up on the whole learning process.

Steptoe, however, had gone curiously quiet. While everyone else discussed the proper timing to reach Devian and make their offer, he slid the remaining photocopies over to himself and studied one intently. He seemed to pale, which caught my attention. His hand, when he lowered it over the main copy, shook.

"How could you not tell me?" he asked me quietly.

"Not tell you what?"

He moved his hand, revealing the copy. "This wot." The picture was of that obsidian choker, the jet necklace that curved about, ending in the token of a spade. I hadn't realized I'd snapped that shot.

"That was another piece of jewelry in the case with the Eye. Clever, isn't it?"

"Clever?" His voice rose above everyone else's. "Clever? That necklace, that cunning bit of jewelry, is my tail—barb and all!"

"Your tail?"

He glared at Aunt April. "Did you not 'ear me? Tail! Mine! Barbed as any demon's tail should be, and you," he glared at me. "Didn't think to tell me you'd found it!"

And that's when my great-aunt keeled over.

CHAPTER TWENTY-NINE

DEARIE ME

"I THOUGHT SHE did marvelously well up until that last bit."

The kitchen had cleared, everyone had departed, my mom had driven Aunt April home and returned, and we sat in the living room with our heels on the coffee table. Marvelously fragrant and hot, mugs filled with tea and brandy and honey rested in our hands while Brian rattled around doing something or other upstairs.

"A demon is a bit much for anyone."

I blew across the surface of my mug before taking a bracing sip. We wouldn't have had brandy with our teas, but Mom had gotten it out to fortify Aunt April and we decided that sounded like a good idea, so here we were fortifying ourselves as well. Mom sat with her fingers circling her mug.

"I just wish he could have refrained."

The tea felt so good going down my throat and warming my stomach. "He was in shock, I think. That I'd found it and not told him. Or overlooked him or whatever." I tilted my head. "I really would never have recognized it for his missing tail."

She put her mug down. "We did hit her with a lot tonight."

"Absolutely. Ghost in the basement and all."

"She did ask."

"But," and I paused to take another sip. "I don't

think she realized what she had asked for. The extent of everything." I drew a ring in the air.

"True."

I leaned forward to put another shot of brandy in, and my mother tapped the back of my hand. "No."

"No?"

"You're in training."

"Oh. Right." I knew there was more to it than that. Her side of the family had a few permanently drunk uncles, and she didn't want to see me go their way, but seriously? I'd had enough drama for the night, though, so I let it go. To be fair, she didn't freshen up her tea either.

Finished, I took the mugs into the kitchen and nearly dropped them in the sink when Steptoe appeared out of the corner.

"Simon!"

"Sorry, ducks."

"Are you . . . are you all right?"

He gave a half bow. "I am . . . most . . . apologetic. I thought the worse of you, just for a moment. Old 'abits, I'm afraid."

"You've had centuries being with the worse, so I guess it's understandable. We'll get your tail back."

"Did they take it?"

I thought hard before shaking my head slightly. "I don't know. It was in the case with the Eye, and Devian might have filled his pockets with other items, but the only thing I saw him carrying, for sure, was the ruby." I rinsed the mugs out and put them to the side. "He probably would have recognized your tail, though?"

"I would think so. Be a stupid bloke if he 'adn't. Not that he would have known it was mine, but he'd 'ave known what it was."

"Not stupid, but he was a bit occupied." I put a hand on my hip. "So we don't know if Devian's crew took it or not."

"From th' snaps you 'ave 'ere, it was in the same case."

"Yes."

"Then 'e probably took it. The bastige would have known 'twas something worth 'aving."

I knew Steptoe was either really tired or really worried because his accent came out so thick I had a little trouble understanding him. I went to the board in the hall where the car keys hung, took mine off, and tossed them at him. "If you need to go look."

The keys bounced off him and hit the floor. "I can't go in there. I'd never get past their sniffers."

"I don't think anyone else is in any shape to go with us."

He bent over, picked the keys up, and put them on the counter. "You're not up to it?"

"I barely got out of there last time. Mom and Carter would have conniptions if I went back without a lot of protection with me."

"Too right, that." He gave a heavy sigh.

"Although," I began, thinking. "Neither of us needs to get out of the car . . ."

"Wot?"

"You should know if your tail was there or not if we pulled into the parking lot, shouldn't you?"

Steptoe considered me a moment before nodding. "I should, indeed, ducks. I should, indeed." He snatched the keys up again. "Then let's give it a go. You're with me, right?"

Thinking I should just go to my room and try to catch up on my sleep, I answered, "Of course, I am!"

For some reason the second trip out went much faster than the first. Maybe it's because I knew the way or maybe it was because Steptoe drove as if AC/DC was his copilot. Heavy metal blasting in our ears, we flew down the road, windows down, my hair streaming behind me. It was midnight dark when we pulled in the lot, with the moonlight rising right in our eyes, the casino's neon on full illumination. Simon snapped the radio off. We sat in absolute quiet a moment while the car made settling noises, little pops and squeaks. I imagined it was complaining about the drive, compared to the little use the professor had made of it when he owned it.

Steptoe said nothing. I finally turned to him. "Well?"

He needn't have said it, I could tell from his expression, "Nothin'. Not a cursed thing."

"Now we know." I nudged him.

"Devian has it."

"Somewhere. And he hasn't made use of it yet because you'd know if somebody pulled your tail, right?"

"Damn right, I would." That brightened him up. "Now, 'e wouldn't know if the demon belongin' to that tail was 'ere or passed on, not until 'e tested it out a bit, and 'e hasn't, so . . . we've got to get it back. Before . . ." and Steptoe went silent.

"Before what?"

"Before I go chaotic evil or some such." He wrapped his hands about the steering wheel, his knuckles pale.

"He can make you do that?"

"Not exactly. He'd have to get ahold—look, ducks. The less you know the better."

I didn't want to not ask questions but I had to respect that. "Home, then. And neither of us to worry unless the glop shows up in our backyard. Or whatever manifests. All we have to do is figure out how to get Devian to turn over the tail when he gives us the ruby and Scout."

"Nothing like a threesome," Steptoe said, as he put the car back in gear and steered us toward the highway.

About halfway back on the road, he said, "Smelled the professor lately?"

I'd been almost asleep but that snapped me awake. "Smelled Brian?"

"Like that, yup."

"As in . . ."

"Aromatic. He's wearing that jacket about, right-o?"

"Well, yeah. It's getting cooler nights, so Mom dragged one of my dad's old coats out. He'll probably get a knit cap in a few weeks."

"But he smells. Like . . . like redwood and juniper."

I had to think on it. "Likeeeee . . . well, yeah, juniper I guess. Kind of like a holiday spice. Shouldn't he?"

"I've been thinking on the way things 'appened at the casino. Now I can see why Carter didn't attack Devian mano a mano, as it 'twere. He's got a Society leash on 'im, that lad does, so he has to be very circumspect about magic and wot he uses and how and against whomever, so to speak."

"He does?"

"Oh, aye. Carter can be very, very powerful. He denies it, but I still swear he's a djinn. He's got that ancient sun and desert magic about him. The Society is a little bit afraid of 'im so they give him a long lead, but he knows one misstep, and he's under their lock and key. He must be very, very careful."

No wonder he seemed uptight. "They can take his power away?"

"Not exactly, but they can try to put it down, see? Shut it off. Not that I think the lot o' them can manage it, but it would lead to quite a brawl, and Carter wants t' avoid that."

"Okay, so Carter could have taken on Devian but held back. What about Brian and his smell?"

"The old man could have taken on Devian as well. Couldn't have held him long, but tripped him up, no doubt. Even as Brian, he's remembered enough tricks to try it. He's always been a wily old cuss."

"But he didn't."

Steptoe gave me a quick glance. "No? Then who freed you?"

"The stone."

"Lass. We be friends here. You may not tell anyone else, but you can tell me."

I fidgeted in the passenger seat. I knew, though, if I asked him, that he wouldn't tell the others. Not unless he suddenly went rogue or something, if his tail got yanked. "I reached for the stone."

Simon shook his head. "I can still see the glitter on your eyelashes, like. He pixied you."

"He did." I took a deep breath. "All right then. Malender showed up. How or why, I don't know. I couldn't get a word out. If I could have, it wouldn't have been his name. Suddenly, there he was, staring down Devian. I just happened to be in between them."

"Now that makes a bit o' sense."

"It does?"

"Indubitably." He thought heavily for a bit.

My head throbbed for a few seconds while I wished we'd just left the heavy metal channel echoing in the car. It would have been easier on me than this conversation. I tried again. "Why?"

"Because someone had t'up and rescue you. Because Carter can't use his power the way he wants, an' the professor won't."

Trying to keep up, I added, "Because of his smell."

Steptoe laughed. "No, no, not right, that one. Because he's a bloody coward."

"Why would you say that?"

"Because, luv, he's got all that he needs to do the ritual, he carries it about in his pockets, but 'e doesn't have the nerve to go through it."

"But—we still have to find everything."

"No."

"He told me we did."

"That was months ago. He's been busy wi'out you."

"You mean he can build his phoenix pyre now?"

Steptoe didn't answer until two cars blew past us going the other way, then he said, "Pretty sure, I am."

"But you don't know."

"I haven't asked him. Have you?"

Outside of the need for pixie dust, we hadn't really talked about it for weeks. If he were hiding it, I don't think he'd answer a direct question from either me or Steptoe. I wouldn't look forward to the fire either, but, truth be told, I didn't think I'd have the nerve to be a phoenix wizard under any of the conditions. "No, I haven't. What makes you think he's gathered everything he needs?"

"Th' desk in his 'ome."

"We went through that."

"Oh, you just thought you did. Secret drawers and all that." Steptoe gave me a sly look.

"Didn't find any."

"'Course not. Secret."

I could see freeway exit signs telling us that Richmond was not far away at all now.

"You knew they were there."

"Bet your brass buttons I did. Like my tail."

"I thought you sent your lads in to ask him where the tail was!"

He took one hand off the wheel and laid a finger alongside his nose. "A wee bit of a lie, that were. I had finally peeled back some of the protections and could tell the old cuss had 'idden it there . . . think of it . . . for decades! Hidden it away from me. But I needed him to fetch it out of the house, from wherever he 'ad it secured. He wouldn't do it for me. I'd begged him once or twice, so I sent me lads in. Now I know that one was working against both o' us, for Zinthrasta, and forced events. The house and the professor went up in smoke. Wards still held, I could not get to my tail—and then it disappeared."

"Someone went through the study before we did?"

"Too right."

"When?"

"I'd say soon as th' ashes cooled. Maybe even a touch before. I was too busy chasin' down the professor's head or new body to check the 'ouse out. By the time I did, the desk had been popped like a safe. That particular drawer, at any rate."

"Think the professor knew that?"

"Had to 'ave."

I sat without words while he negotiated the right exit ramp and tooled us onto the residential streets of our end of town.

"Why wouldn't he give you your tail back?"

"Said 'e wanted to keep me bound. I told 'im I was tryin' th' redemption side o'things, but he didn't believe me, quite. Can't say as I blame him. You believe me, though?"

Tail or no tail, Simon *was* a lesser demon. However, he'd had my back in a number of bad situations, and I called him a friend. I knew he'd taken a chance telling me about the professor, not able to predict how I'd take it. I patted his shoulder. "I do," I said.

He beamed at me. "So wot are you going to do?"

"Well, I'm not going to set him on fire, even if he asks."

"No?"

I waggled my head. I had far more doubts about Malender than I did about Steptoe, however, and it seemed probable that the professor might feel the same. I don't know if the professor had turned cowardly because he feared doing the hard thing that had made him a wizard throughout the ages, or if he wasn't ready even if the demon thought he had everything lined up. It's not like he would have a second chance to do a fiery rebirth over again if he did. "No. He has the right to decide if he's going to do it, and Malender has already told me—and him—that he's the spark. So whatever the professor decides, it's Malender he'll answer to and not me. Keep your peace about it, Simon. He'll either rejuv himself—or he won't." Of course, with that came the realization that I might never get the information I needed to revive my father. Not unless the Iron Dwarves let Germanigold back into their lives so she could get Morty's journals for me, and that seemed a real long shot as long as the Eye of Nimora stayed missing. I sighed.

"I don't like th' odds o' that. We need him, and soon. Th' elves are getting bold, and I am thinkin' that there are grave and dark times coming. A'course, th' professor knows that as well, being himself or not."

He pulled into our driveway, stopped the car, and turned the headlights off. The evening shrouding us seemed to echo his gloomy statement.

CHAPTER THIRTY

TEXAS REDHEADS

I FELL INTO bed with the hope that I could sleep through whatever was left of the late hours and not go to battle with whatever might show up in a nightmare. Sunday morning meant I could sleep in. We used to be churchgoers, Mom and I, but all the whispers drove us away. They used to be: "Wonder if she killed him?" and now it was, "Poor woman. He's never coming back. Wonder if they'll find a body?" I couldn't remember if we'd acted like that about other members of our parish, but I hoped not. Surely we hadn't gone to church to be petty. So, Sundays meant late hours, catching up, and slow afternoons.

Sleep did take me in, soundly and warmly and cozily—but someone forgot to tell the professor about my morning plans.

The firm but quiet knocking sounded on my door insistently until I staggered to it and yanked it open. Brian stepped back, his eyebrow quirked, as if suddenly aware I might be in a bad mood. It could barely have been dawn.

"What?"

"Did I wake you?"

My hair stood on end, my pajamas twisted about my body, and my chin still had sleep drool on it. "Seriously?"

"It wasn't my idea." He shuffled from one sneakered

foot to the other. "Honestly, the professor knocked and then just left me standing here."

"And you let him get away with it. Why are you *here*?"

"It's time to take care of Mrs. Sherman."

I scrubbed my eyes to clear them. "I am hoping you're not thinking about rubbing her out."

"I . . . don't think so. He usually doesn't have malicious thoughts about ordinary people."

"Fine. I'll shower and get dressed. You go downstairs, quietly, and make some coffee." I started to close my bedroom door and then stopped. "Both of you know how to do that, right?"

"Yes."

I shut the door. The professor might have popped back in as soon as I did because I heard a snarl or two at the tell-tales in the hallway before the stair steps creaked lightly. By the time I was pulling my damp hair back in a ponytail and shoving my toes into a pair of clean jeans, I could smell the coffee. Tea is great and I love it, but sometimes what the gut needs is a hearty kick, and I definitely needed one this morning.

Brian's body had mugs, sugar bowl, and the creamer lined up at the kitchen sink as the coffee maker settled into rest, its work done for the day. I looked at it.

"Lucky you. Your day is finished."

"You're not talking to the coffee maker."

"I am, and in sheer envy." I muffled a yawn while stirring the fixings into my mug and stopped when I caught sight of the clock. I counted up. That made all of four hours of sleep. "Seven- ten AM? Good god, Professor."

"I thought it best to catch her before she went out for the day."

"What are we doing? Digging a lion pit in the front yard?"

"You *are* cranky. Drink your coffee."

I took a long, hot, gulp. It didn't chase away the mean feeling coursing through my body. "I think you're still in trouble."

"Maybe. But this way she gets her remedy and has

the whole day ahead of her, feeling radiant and relieved. She seems a naturally pleasant woman, unlike some others I could reference."

I shook a finger at him. "Better make sure some of that remedy, whatever it is, is left over so I can 'feel radiant.'"

The professor smiled behind his coffee mug. "I don't think I made it strong enough for that."

"Damn right." I finished my drink and poured half a cup, straight and black, into a paper container. "Let's go."

He paused by the row of hats, hoodies, and hanging car keys. "Aren't you driving?"

I looked him up and down. "You want that body to stay toned? Then you'd better start walking."

We didn't talk, but half a block from her little house, I realized that, over the aroma of freshly brewed coffee, I could smell redwood, pine, juniper, and cinnamon. The pockets of Brian's jacket bulged slightly, and I knew that Steptoe had been onto something. Whether it was the stuff phoenix rituals or dreams were made of, I didn't know, but I could be fairly sure I wouldn't get a straight answer if I asked. That made me ponder if our demon friend could be right. Why hadn't he told me he'd come this far? Was Brandard too cowardly to finish what we had started?

I could understand, but he'd been doggedly determined a few months ago. Had he been compelled rather than motivated? There didn't seem to be a way for me to know. I might be a so-called sorceress now, but I had no idea how that worked or what I could do with it, other than defending myself now and then and—after the casino heist—not even when it counted. Study seemed in line, but no one really wanted to step up. Remy had been a sorceress and desperate enough at what she did to get tangled up with several different and dangerous bosses. It had not ended well. So if I were looking for a role model, I'd look elsewhere.

Steptoe had left me with the distinct impression that the professor wouldn't be up to the task either, at least not until he transitioned. That left the dubious Society.

If I did decide to go there, were they keeping Judge Maxwell in check and would I have a chance of getting an impartial education? But, like they say, if you have to ask . . .

The professor said abruptly, "I don't think we can throw Simon's tail into the bargain with Devian." He patted his vest as if searching for his pipe. I pointed at his left pants pocket. "It's probably there."

He confirmed and pulled it out. "Thank you."

I would have said, "Think nothing of it," but he didn't give me a chance. He plowed ahead.

"I know Steptoe's upset, and he has a right to be under the circumstances, but that object was one of the first things I went back to retrieve, and it has been missing from the get-go."

"But you didn't tell him that."

"No. My mistake, probably, but I have been busy lining up friends and foes."

"That, he would understand."

"No doubt." He gave up searching for a tobacco pouch and just clamped the stem between his teeth, pipe unlit.

I pointed at Mrs. Sherman's neat, sturdy little stucco house. "Anything I have to do?"

"No, not really, other than being a person she would trust. I do hope she's up and about."

I drained my paper cup of black coffee even though it had gone cold. Might as well complete the punishment for the day. "Her fireplace is working." And, indeed it was, a little spiral of thin, gray smoke winding out of the chimney. It seemed a little early in the season for that, but she'd always been a woman well-bundled up and maybe she just liked being super cozy.

We trudged up the porch and I stood at her door for a minute before looking at the professor. "What kind of excuse do I have for being here this early?"

He dipped a hand inside his coat and brought out Scout's harness and leash. "Your pup is missing."

My eyes brimmed immediately. The professor gave me a scathing look. "No crying."

I choked it back as I took Scout's things. "Right." I knocked on the cheery white door.

It took a few long moments to be answered, but we could hear noises headed our way and then Mrs. Sherman and her vibrant red-bewigged head looked out at us. "Well, land sakes. Whatever are you doing here, Tessa?"

"Scout got loose. Sorry, I know it's early, but I thought he might have come by here. You fed him cookies. Have you seen him?"

"Dear me, no. Come in, come in, I just took a coffee cake out of the oven. I meant it for circle meeting this morning, but my ladies are all getting a little pudgy as it is. Better we eat it ourselves." She ushered us in. The kitchen sang with the smells of her baking, overwhelming even the professor's fragrance, which I had begun to find a bit much. Vanilla, butter, sugar, and other good smells promised better things.

She cut us significant portions, with half a measure for herself. She had a teapot steeping and we got a cup of that as well, although I already felt as if I floated in hot beverage.

She waited until we'd each had a forkful. All I could get out was, "Oh, yum!" and the professor remarked, "Absolutely divine, Mrs. Sherman."

The baker beamed. "What good manners. But it *is* good, isn't it?" She ate two bites and then put her attention on me. "As for your concern . . . How long has the dog been gone?"

"Most of yesterday and all night."

"Missed his dinner, did he? That's not good. Well, you can't call the pound on a Sunday, but you should check first thing in the morning, just in case." She wagged her utensil at me. "Not that I've seen the city's jail truck about, thank heavens. Does he have one of those thingies? Trackers in him?"

I tried to remember if Carter had said so. "I think so. Not sure. Trouble is, I haven't had him long enough to change the address info."

"Still, they'll know just to look at him that he isn't

some poor stray. Such a shame it is, all the homeless on the streets."

I wasn't certain if she meant people or animals, so I just returned to eating my divine coffee cake.

The professor cleaned up every last smidge on his plate and looked up, hopefully.

"Another piece?" she offered. "You're a growing boy, after all!"

"That would be wonderful." He held his plate out.

The moment she turned about, he pulled out an envelope and dumped its contents into her half cup of tea, managed a quiet stir, and leaned back in his chair. I could smell a bit of lemon and more vanilla, but nothing like the noxious fumes which had been emanating from the garage for days while he perfected whatever tonic this might be. He gave a satisfied sniff as she handed him a newly stocked plate.

She sipped the tea, and then took a deep, long swallow. "Sometimes," she noted, "a good drink is very bracing, don't you think?"

"Nothing like it," the professor told her. "Quite enjoyable."

She beamed at him before saying to me, "He has the best manners. I definitely approve."

My drink went down the wrong pipe, and I sputtered and coughed for a few minutes until the professor thumped my back, hitting the right spot because, I assumed, he'd had centuries of practice rescuing choking people, and I could finally breathe again. I wiped my mouth and chin with a paper napkin.

"Oh, it's not like that, Mrs. Sherman." And I crossed my fingers she wouldn't gossip around about it.

"Well, then, it should be. Good looks and good manners are a winsome pair." She paused then. "My husband had both. First husband. Second wasn't so bad either, come to think of it."

I froze, waiting for melancholy to descend over her again, but she shook herself and said, "Oh, look at the time. I believe there's enough for me to make another coffee cake." She winked at us. "There's a widowed and retired gentleman who comes to services every other Sunday, and I'd like to make a good impression on him." She straightened her wig. "Out with you now, and if I find your pup, I will call you, Tessa."

"Um, thanks!" And I found the two of us being hurried outside in unseemly haste, while the snatch of a song broke out in the house behind us.

"Think it worked?"

Brian smiled, and the professor answered, "I can guarantee it did." He dusted his hands off. "It's about time we had a win, don't you think?"

CHAPTER THIRTY-ONE

WHO, INDEED

OUTSIDE MY BEDROOM window, in the beginning light of day, an owl sat on a branch that came close to the house. It blinked at me as I started to draw the curtain, thought better of it, instead opening the window and leaning close to the screen. "Tell Germanigold that Tessa needs to talk to her."

The large golden eyes closed once, twice, and then the bird ruffled up his feathers and flew off. I'd no idea if I'd done it right or if I was an idiot talking to strange owls, and I was too tired to worry about it.

Staying dressed, I collapsed diagonally across the mattress, uncaring if the covers wrinkled under me or not. With any luck, I could catch a couple of hours before Mom got up. I drifted off, thinking of Malender and his coat of inky darkness and stinky odors and if I was creating some kind of prison break every time I hit him with salt. Somewhere in my dreams, Malender morphed into Carter and I was leaning forward, hoping for another kiss with a bone-melting hug, but he began to shake all over and buzz irritatingly loud—

And my phone woke me up. On silent, but vibrating and buzzing with the intensity of it and it wouldn't stop. The call stopped and then began again and then a third time while I wrenched it out of my pants' pocket.

Evelyn's number popped up and I caught her on the fourth call back.

"About time!"

"Sleeping."

"I'm at the hospital. Please come pick me up."

I lowered the phone a bit and stared at the number, just to be sure the whispery voice came from Evelyn and the phone ID matched. It did. I raised the phone again. "What do you mean, you're at the hospital? Are you all right? What happened?"

"Bumped around and my leg looks like somebody went after it with a crowbar, well, actually somebody did, but I'm okay."

I had two thoughts and the first one I blurted out. "I'm going to kill Dean."

"No. No, no. He had nothing to do with it, well, he did, but . . . just come and get me and I'll explain."

My second thought followed. "What about your parents?"

"They don't know yet, and I have to figure out a way to explain it to them. Pleeease, come get me. I hate these places." Her voice choked up a bit.

"Where at the hospital?"

"ER, but I'll be in the lounge. They've already released me." A sniffle. "Thank you, Tessa. And hurry."

So I did, and true to her word, she was sitting in the lounge waiting for me. Her jeans were torn, and not artfully as if they were meant to be, and she held a disposable ice pack to her shin. I helped her to her feet. Her eyes glistened with tears waiting to be shed. I grabbed a tissue from a box at the check-in desk and handed it to her as we limped out the door. Once in the car, she sat back with a quavering sigh. I put the key in the ignition but didn't turn it.

"Home?"

"Not yet. I've got to get a cover story."

That started to boil my temper. "Then it is Dean's fault."

She waved a hand at me. "No. Not really."

"You can't sit there looking like someone battered you and tell me it wasn't really his fault. That's the syndrome, you know. Making excuses for the inexcusable."

"You think Dean did this? Oh, hell no. One of the protestors got me."

I turned the car on then because the interior held a chill, and I didn't want her to start shivering along with everything else that bothered her. "Protest? You got caught in a protest?"

She pointed out the windshield. "Drive. Your place. Please."

"Just what kind of a cover story do you think will work? What protest and where and what makes you think anyone involved won't tell your father what happened?"

Evelyn shifted her ice bag to a slightly different spot on her leg, hissing a bit in pain, and began her story. "Dean picked me up for a late hamburger, and we heard on the radio that there was a midnight protest against that big old Confederate flag just raised on the edge of town. We went there to support taking it down. It was something I wanted to do, and Dean agreed. It seems important."

"Mmm. But your dad supports removing those."

"He does. But he doesn't support my getting involved in it. Some of the believers are pretty nasty on social media and stuff—" She peered down at her exposed leg. "In person, too, I guess. Anyway, there were candles and singing and it was pretty peaceful, if tense for a while. Then tempers flared up and—good golly, Miss Molly—we had a riot. Dean took off—"

"He what???" I was back to killing Dean mode. "He left you there?"

"I thought he'd just gone to get the car, but he never came back. I got surrounded. There was no place to go, and fists were flying, and then this big ole guy came through swinging a crowbar." Her eye leaked a slow tear. "He did leave me, didn't he?"

"Sounds like it." My hands tightened on the steering wheel. "In fact, I think there is no doubt about it."

She blurted, "He just burned his last bridge."

It was not the time to ask about the other bridges, but I would hear about them, eventually. I looked at her. "I don't think there is a cover story that will handle this.

It's bound to get back to your father, even if there were no hospital bill showing up, but there will be, and pictures and maybe even a podcast that will place you on the scene. You're pretty identifiable as Evelyn Statler."

She brushed her light blond hair back. "He'll be upset."

"Yeah, dads who care about you are like that."

The gray early morning lifted into a brilliantly blue day with high, wispy clouds as we turned into my neighborhood. It would be a crisp, clear day. I added, "Look. Have breakfast with us, then call home, and if they can't pick you up, I'll drive you over." I felt pretty certain the Statlers would be over in a flash and she might be in for both a lecture and an embrace. "And if you are ever nice to Dean again, I'm cutting you off as a friend."

She laughed at that. "You wouldn't do that to your partner in crime."

She reminded me that I had never told Carter or the others about her going to Silverbranch with me. I protected her whenever I could, unlike Dean. "I would certainly think about it, though. Honestly, whatever made you do it?"

"I wanted to be badass, like you."

"Me? You wanted to be like me?"

"You don't stand down, Tessa. No matter what life hands you. I want to be worthy of being your wingman, and I need to toughen up."

"Oh, Evie. I don't want someone tough. I want someone understanding, and you fit that pretty perfectly."

"I do?"

"You've stood by me through thick and thin. That's enough for me."

She took a deep, quavering breath. "Still . . ."

"Nope. No, no. Not an argument. I'm the one who tears down a hockey field, pushing people out of my way left and right, one goal in sight, and I tend to do the same thing in life. Meanwhile, you stand on the sideline, cheering the good guys, whoever they are . . . and I need to be reminded of that. There are good guys everywhere."

She put her hand up. "I am swearing off men."

"I would note that time and date, but I know it won't last."

Her nose wrinkled. "Too true." She moved the ice pack again. "I think this is about done in." She waved the limp thing.

"Mom probably has one in the fridge." I negotiated the turn into the drive.

We were into a batch of newly baked biscuits when Mom came downstairs. She raised an eyebrow at the sight of Evelyn sitting at the kitchen table, her leg up and one foot resting on the seat of another chair. She steered to the fridge and made herself an iced tea. "Trouble . . . or should I even ask?"

"You know that Confederate flag—"

"The great big one? The only thing good about it is that the loblolly pines hide half of it."

"It's down."

"Oh, really?" She toasted Evelyn. "Then you fought the good battle. I respect Southern pride, but I have a stopping point." She sat down carefully, leaving the next chair empty so as not to jostle her leg. "Battle injury?"

"Riot."

"Oh, my. Your father know yet?"

"He has a business and prayer meeting this morning, but he'll be over soon."

"Be sure and tell me when the thundercloud gets here."

Evelyn and I grinned, and I passed Mom the biscuit plate. She sliced one open deftly and slathered it with butter. "If he gives you any trouble, Evie, I'll run interference."

"I think he already knew and my mother already has, but thanks."

"Any time." Mom traded looks with me. The guys should be showing up any time soon to make Eye of Nimora retrieval plans. The strategy session would have to be postponed until she left. I gave her a slight shrug, which Evelyn didn't catch because she eyed the biscuits.

"You've only had one," I told her.

"One should be enough."

I fingered the tear in her jeans. "Oh, like you're busting out all over."

She snorted.

I pushed the plate over. "They're small."

They weren't. We don't make small biscuits at the Andrews house. We make ginormous biscuits that would fill Hiram Broadstone's palm if he held one. Not to mention mouth-meltingly good.

I passed along some fine, homemade peach jam to go with. And sat back to watch Evelyn do battle with herself, glad that she had something else to fret over.

She'd just about devoured all but a few crumbs when the house trembled slightly. I could hear the front door opening.

"Hello the house."

"Hiram's here."

Evelyn grabbed for a napkin to wipe her mouth and fingers off. She would have bolted to her feet, but instead let out a little cry when the foot of her injured leg hit the floor as she tried to stand. She pitched my way, and I grabbed her up even as Hiram came in.

Their gazes met across the room.

I realized I could no longer say that I didn't believe in love at first sight because I was seeing it happen. Hiram, taller than the average Iron Dwarf, straightened in his black, shiny boots and working man garb, put his chin up and his hand out long before he got close enough to touch hers, as if he couldn't resist. His auburn hair curled neatly behind his ears, just above his shoulders, and his warm brown eyes took her in as though no one else stood in the room with them. Evelyn pushed away from me a little bit as if she intended to stand on her own two legs, her blond hair swinging about to tangle gracefully down her back. Her makeshift ice bag dropped, forgotten, to the floor. Her gray-blue eyes locked onto his face and stayed there, and her hand drifted up to take his in response.

"Mmm. You don't want to be doing this."

Neither of them heard me. My mother's iced tea glass clattered in the kitchen sink as she put it there, and it sounded like a firehouse alarm bell, but they didn't notice.

"I'm Hiram Broadstone," he said, deep tones ringing. "A friend of the Andrews." He made it sound like a testament to his good standing, and maybe it was. Neither Mom nor I suffered fools, but still . . .

"You must be a linebacker." Evelyn smiled, a genuine smile, the first ray of true happiness I'd seen from her since I picked her up.

"Sorry, no, miss. I'm in construction and mining. Broadstone Family Enterprises?"

"Oh! I've heard of you. You're doing part of the restoration on the Washington Monument!"

A becoming blush tinted his face. He'd had a small, neat auburn beard until very recently. In fact, I'd guess that he'd clean-shaved just that morning, and his face bloomed slightly. It was almost as if he'd known he would be meeting his own true love. "That would be us."

She limped forward a step. "I'm Evelyn Statler, Tessa's friend."

Their hands touched. His engulfed hers tenderly, and his eyebrows drew down in concern. "But you're injured. Please, sit down."

"Oh, it's nothing." Evelyn fidgeted with the torn flap of her jeans a moment, but it didn't look like "nothing."

He ushered her to the nearest chair and settled her. "You're hurt! Tessa, what happened?"

"It's all right, Hiram, the hospital released her this morning. It's a heavy contusion, but she'll be fine—"

"Miss Statler is not fine if she's in pain." He let go of her hand and strode to the base of the stairs. "Brian! We have a guest who needs you. Bring something for pain down with you!"

The house shivered again, in vibration with his voice, and then it was Evelyn's turn to color, her face warming.

Brian came down hastily, almost took himself out on the bottom step as he saw Evelyn beyond in the kitchen, and Hiram took hold of the envelope in the professor's hand.

"Just a half teaspoon," he cautioned. "In a drink of some kind. And, ah, good morning, Evelyn."

"Hi, Bri," she answered faintly, her attention still on Hiram as he got a glass and fixed her a cold drink with the potion shook into it, the guys knowing our kitchen just about as well as anybody in the household. She took it and began to drink.

I grabbed Brian by the shirtsleeve and asked quietly, "You're not stoning her or anything."

"Of course not. It's just soothing."

"And how soothed is she going to be?"

Brian watched, eyes getting a little bigger, as she basically chugged her entire glass without taking a breath. "Very. But that will pass."

Good lord. I didn't need to have Statler breathing down my neck because his daughter was higher than a kite.

Hiram swept her up out of the chair. "I think the couch is the best place for you, to keep the leg elevated." He took her into the living room where he deposited her gently, the rest of us trailing behind.

Brian whispered to me, "What just happened here?"

"You have as much of a clue as I do." I looked at Brian then, thinking of both the souls in one body, and amended, "Or maybe you don't. But I think they fell in love." He stumbled, jolting into me. I gripped his shoulder as he straightened himself out. "I know."

"This can't be."

"Tell me about it. Her father's coming to get her, but I think it may already be too late."

He raised his hand and whispered, "Somnus."

Evelyn suddenly yawned. "Oh, excuse me."

"Think nothing of it." Hiram leaned close and touched the back of her wrist. "Rest, it will do you good," whereupon, as if she'd turned into Sleeping Beauty, Evie dropped into sleep. Hiram squinted a suspicious look at Brian as he turned around and passed us going to the dining/conference room.

Muttering, "Wish I'd thought of that," I met my mother in the kitchen, cleared breakfast things up, and sorted items out for lunch. Hiram excused himself and came back in with two grocery bags brimming with goods, recognizing the expense of feeding a small army, or at least a couple of guys who could eat like a small army. "I almost forgot that I'd brought these." He helped Mom put everything away and by the time they were done, Evelyn's father arrived, we exchanged information over her condition, and he escorted her to their very nice and expensive sedan out front.

Evie waved a hand at Hiram, ignored the rest of us, and promptly went back to sleep in the front seat. We watched them pull away, Statler's forehead creased in concern, with no one conscious to yell at.

"How long is that going to last?"

"The somnus? Maybe another fifteen minutes. The potion should be in effect most of the day. That will be all right?"

"That'll do," my mother told him. "Although you should have done it sooner."

Brian coughed. "I'm getting the Andrews in stereo."

He stopped grumbling when the smell of home cooking wafted through the house. We almost had everything ready and Carter had joined us when I heard the hoot of an owl coming from somewhere in the backyard.

The professor's eyes met mine.

"Is there something we should know about?"

CHAPTER THIRTY-TWO

COMPANY

I TOSSED MY NAPKIN on the table. "Company's here. I think."

"An owl rarely hoots at midday."

"I know, right?" I got up and scooted out the backdoor. The screen door clattered a second time and Carter caught up with me, saying, "I'm coming with."

"Don't trust me?"

"Protective."

Heavy dew still sparkled on the grass and dampened the toes of my sneakers as we strode across the yard, him matching steps with me. "Which reminds me, I need to discuss a theory Steptoe has with you."

He looked down at me. "What theory might that be?"

"Something about the professor."

"That should be interesting." His attention moved. "It's definitely Germanigold."

And indeed, the harpy leader sat on the edge of our garage roof, her wings folded, and booted ankles crossed, watching as we drew closer.

"You expected her."

"I hoped. She told me about the harpy communication system."

We both craned our heads back, calling out our greetings. She sketched a wave. "Tessa and the young lion. Good morrow."

I shot Carter a tiny look. He didn't appear lion-ish.

No amber eyes, no wavy tawny hair, nothing in that offset tiny scar in his chin . . . maybe something in the way he moved. Was she watching his shoulder muscles ripple under his shirt the way I was? Or was it something else? I wondered if she knew something I didn't.

"You asked for a word with me?"

"In case you hadn't heard, and I know you have a network, but I thought you should hear it from me—we located the Eye last night, but it was taken by Devian and his crew."

"I understand you lost a skirmish. It's no wonder . . . the elves have been quiescent for a while now, and it is easy to underestimate them." She spoke directly to Carter then. "You have plans to reclaim the item?"

"We do."

"I wish you fortune on that, then. We both know how vital it is, but the family Broadstone has kept its virtues secret for many decades, so it's possible Devian doesn't quite know what he has, even though there is a bounty on it and a decree to obstruct justice. He may think he simply has an enormous jewel worth a king's ransom."

"We're banking on that."

"Excellent. I have news for you both, as well." She hopped down from the roof's edge, landing lightly. "We have elicited a few interesting facts. There was a betrayal in the House of Broadstone although I have no definitive name yet, but information was given out that I had the Eye of Nimora. Less than a handful of people, that I'm familiar with, knew that was Morty's bridal gift to me."

"Would Hiram know the others?"

"Tessa, he is one of the five. I would not count him out of trouble, and I will not confide in him of the other names I know. Are you certain of his loyalty?"

"Any day." I would trust Hiram as I had his father Mortimer, but a tiny voice inside reminded me that Morty had betrayed us on that fateful trip to New York City. Was I as sure as I thought? But, as far as naming names, I'd discovered the hard way years ago that there were always more people in on a secret than there were supposed to be.

"From House Broadstone, then to my nest, where my sister eagerly plotted a coup of her own to displace me and put me in the hands of Judge Maxwell, bring Mortimer to a downfall, and turn the Eye over to an agent for sale. From what I gathered from her coconspirators, she never knew exactly what it's capable of, but she knew a treasure when she saw it."

"She just wanted the money?"

Goldie gave a little smile my way. "It takes money to fund a coup. More money to build a new nest. Property is expensive here in the northeast."

So . . . they didn't actually build nests somewhere. They bought houses, probably big ones, since their family sounded like a commune, and you bet that could be expensive. I kicked myself mentally for thinking of twigs and such making a harpy's home.

Germanigold stretched an arm out. "Remember these five," and she recited the names. I knew two, but the other three meant nothing to me, nor did they to Carter evidently who made a noncommittal *hrmmm* when she finished. I did find myself relieved that most of Hiram's home redo crew weren't on the short list. I'd liked all of them who'd come to work on our cellar. I found it hard to believe that Goldie thought she'd found a traitor in the Broadstone dynasty. Perhaps she'd been led astray. The magical side of the street didn't operate all that differently from the human side, I'd discovered. Petty grievances, lying, envy, and so forth seemed universal. There seemed to be an imbalance, though, because I hadn't really found any saintlike qualities on their side. Not that we had all that many on ours, but a few hit the commendable roll.

"When are you making your move?" she asked of Carter.

"Tonight, I believe. We really haven't any time to waste. If Devian considers breaking the ruby up to make it easier to sell, he could destroy it as a magical relic. We've given him a decoy use for the gem, based on what he already supposes, and we're confident he'll take the bait."

She nodded. "You do what you must, and if you need me, there are ways to reach me."

"Besides owl?"

She winked at me. "The lion here knows many ways to reach those he has to." Then, with a leap, she launched herself up, her wings came out, and she soared off over the canopy of trees dotting the neighborhood.

Carter and I watched her go before I turned to him. "Suppose anybody saw that?"

"She has her own ways of being seen and unseen." He reached down to hold my hand as we walked back to the house.

"More protective duty?"

"No." His scar deepened a little. "Because I like it." He walked a bit more deliberately, forcing me to keep pace. "Now what's this about Steptoe? What's he said that's got you thinking?"

I punched him lightly in the bicep. "I think all the time, thank you very much."

"Not what I meant and you know it." Carter stopped and turned to face me.

"He has a theory about the professor."

Carter waited.

"He's seen Brian hang back. Hesitate. And says he can smell the herbs and relics on him. He thinks he's carrying the element for a pyre about with him, but . . ." My voice trailed off. The more indistinct my words got, the higher one of Carter's eyebrows rose. "He thinks the professor has what he needs to do his ritual and is too cowardly to follow through."

"Even with the pixie dust?"

"That's what he thinks."

Carter looked away from me then, over my shoulder to someplace I couldn't see, maybe even across a vast Egyptian desert somewhere where he'd taken me once to try and show me what he'd been through and what magic had done to him. Finally, he said, "Could be."

"If it were just him, I could leave it be, but I can't, can I?"

"Why do you say that?"

I dug a sneaker toe into a grass clump. "There's too much going on. This is a world that didn't—couldn't—exist, but it does. It gets more complicated every day, and I can see that there's trouble. You, they, whatever, stayed hidden, but you can't stay that way much longer. Something really nasty is coming along and we have to be ready to stop it."

His voice tensed, just a bit. "You've seen it?"

"No, but it stomps through my dreams every night. I don't think it's Malender." I shrugged. "I'm tough and can take it, but what if it comes after my mother? Or Evelyn? It's already taken my dad."

"We don't know what happened to your father."

"I know that he's a ghost without much hope of going back or moving forward unless we can help him. What we don't know is who did that to him or if he did it to himself, doing something he wasn't supposed to, or if he fell into some kind of trap, or . . ." I stopped. I could see in Carter's expression that my words were almost as painful for him as they were for me. "Anyway, things keep getting stranger and tougher."

"It's not a one-way street. Things also get more wonderful." He leaned forward, and this time there was no mistaking the intent as we kissed again.

It warmed me from the inside out, uncurling and streaking through me until I could feel myself grinning instead of kissing, and he pulled back a little, with a short laugh.

"Think this is funny, do you?"

"No. Yes . . . no, it's fun. Not funny. Just . . . fun." And I grabbed his collar to bring him close again and, well, we didn't move for a few minutes until we heard Hiram and Brian coughing from the back porch. We stopped and returned to the house.

"That really was an owl hooting, Professor," I said as we passed them.

"No doubt. But he must have had quite a lot to say. Volumes. We got curious."

"We have news."

In the end, we didn't tell the group everything Goldie told us. Without consulting each other, we left the names named out of the conversation, only that she hoped to have confirmation of the traitor soon. Hiram looked thunderous, resembling his father more than I'd ever seen him before. Mom stayed quiet and pensive, but I could tell she took things in and weighed them. I decided for myself that, despite what Germanigold had said, he couldn't have gone Benedict Arnold on his father and family. Not just for myself, mind you. Evelyn was involved in it now, too, whether I wanted her to be or not, and neither of us needed to be disappointed in Hiram's honor.

Our plan stayed simple: contact Devian. Offer a trade for Scout and the Eye of Nimora (which would simply be referred to as the Queen gem), with a contract for Hiram's services as a locator in its place. Hopefully, in the short hours between last night and today, Devian hadn't had a chance to verify exactly what he had in his possession and what its true worth might be.

Steptoe didn't make an appearance until the last of our little convention, hanging back and leaning against the doorjamb. I didn't think I'd ever seen him turn down a meal before. Or stay quiet. Marveling at these two things, I'd just cast a look at him when Carter said, "Don't like admitting it, but I can't see a way to get your tail into the negotiations."

"Likely not, guv'nor."

The two considered each other across the room. Hiram opened his mouth to say something, but Carter stopped him by putting up an index finger. "The way I do see it is that we are putting up a hell of a distraction while you go in and retrieve what you need. He'll be watching us. You'll be invisible. Devian will have exposed his cache, probably left it unlocked while he brings out the Eye, and that gives you the opportunity to get in and out, undetected."

Steptoe considered it, looking as if he sucked on a sore tooth before asking, "What's in it for you?"

"He won't know what hit him until after the deal is done and over. Then, realizing he's lost the gem, he's likely to go through the remaining treasures to see what he has. When Devian realizes he's missing a few items more, he'll be unhappy and impatient and at odds. Distracted and off-balance. The longer we can keep him that way—"

"The 'appier we'll all be," Steptoe finished. "A'right then. I know where I stand. When do we leave?"

"Soon as Devian gets an answer back to us."

Steptoe moved to the table, pulling up a chair. "Any lunch left?"

"Of course," Mom said. "But then you all are on your own. I've a paper to work on."

"Yes, ma'am," we all answered.

My phone rang, and I turned away from the table to answer it. As if she knew she might be interrupting, Evelyn whispered a quiet "Hello" in my ear. And a yawn.

"How are you feeling?"

"Sore. If I hadn't gone to the ER, I'd think it was broken. The only good thing is that Dad isn't upset too much with me, and my mom is waiting on me hand and foot, at least until I go to bed. I slept all the way home, but I'm still a bit (yawn) drowsy."

I covered my mouth before I gave a yawn myself. "Well, I'm glad you're home and the dust has settled."

"Not quite." And her voice changed a little, just enough that when she started talking again, the hairs rose on the back of my neck. "You're in trouble, Tessa Andrews, in the eyes of a foe far more dangerous than any of you and yours can imagine. Take care before you take harm."

The tone of her voice took an icy dive into my inner self. "Say what? Is that you, Evie? What are you talking about?"

A slight pause before she coughed a bit and said, "Sorry. Falling asleep right in front of you! Talk to you later, and I want you to tell me everything you know about Hiram."

Fat chance of that. "Sure," I soothed her. "Later."

The phone clicked silent. I thought a moment before shoving it aside and facing our gang of good intentions. My insides still felt chilled. "So. Devian mentioned a boss. Any idea who that might be and if these guys have any relation to the big evil baddie we've been told might return? 'Cause at this point, it's my opinion Malender is not our guy."

You'd have thought I dropped a conversation bomb in the middle of the table. Voices broke out at once, and Hiram's deep voice shook the commotion into silence when he finally yelled, "Quiet!"

I sat very still, hoping my mother would not come out of her study unhappy. Or at all. Hiram looked about the table. "Decorum," he suggested, before sitting back in his chair and crossing his arms over his chest.

"Precisely," the professor said, looking squarely at me. "What is this about?"

"Not that I wasn't grateful and glad to see you guys, but you weren't the first to come charging to my aid. Malender was, and I've no idea how or why he did, because it was all I could do to breathe, let alone call anyone. And Devian threw the name Nico in his face."

That brought the voices up again, and I put my hand out. "Can't tell you that," I answered Hiram, who wanted to know if he knew about the Eye. "Or that," I said to Brian as the professor grunted, "Why didn't he blast Devian into smithereens?"

But it was Carter who caught my attention, the expression unreadable on his face, eyes intent and that offset cleft going white against his jawline. "Was anything else said about Nico?"

"No, although it seemed he might have a hold on Malender somehow. So . . . what is this black cloud that's around him? Is it of his making or did someone curse him with it?" I leaned on my elbows.

"We don't know, and it's nothing you should be investigating. We only have some very old familial memories of Malender, and they all suggest that he is a powerful being none of us should be involved with if we can help it."

"He stopped Devian in his tracks. I was being floated out of the casino toward the archway when I thought I'd hit a brick wall. So even if he didn't turn the elf into dust on the asphalt, he did stop him long enough that you guys could catch up, and that was more trouble than Devian wanted. And he had a reminder for the professor about being the Fire he needed."

Brian had a mild coughing fit but blamed it on the sweet tea going down wrong. The rest of us stared at one another.

I finally added, "But who is Ni—"

"No one you should worry or ask about." Carter's gruff tone made it an order rather than a suggestion.

"Oh-kay then. Our minds are full and our plates are empty, so we wait to see what kind of rendezvous awaits us." I smiled brightly in hopes their stormy faces would clear.

I didn't get much of a response as I stood to clear the table, so I leaned over Hiram. "Evelyn wants to know allllll about you."

He brightened. "And, lass, you need to tell me about her!" And he talked about his impression of my bestie until the room cleared in self-defense.

Devian's choice of a meet wasn't anywhere near the casino, or anywhere else in town. He chose an area near the Powhatan Mills Quarter golf course, west and a bit north of town, a quiet area with quiet money. Green and forested, with beautiful two- and three-story gray-stoned estate houses laid back off the looping roads, it looked too peaceful for a devious elf and nefarious plots. But there we were, about to meet one and step into the other.

CHAPTER THIRTY-THREE

THE DOG BARKS AT MIDNIGHT

HIRAM BROUGHT HIS SUV to a stop at the curb. The house and meet in question stood elegantly set back on what was about three acres of ground with a three- or maybe it was a four-car garage behind it. A stable and arena occupied a good deal of the side acreage, but no sign of equines, not even a pony. On the other side of the winding brick drive, stood a tiny house that turned out to be a chicken coop, complete with an outdoor run protected by chicken wire. Steptoe made a tight noise.

"Chickens."

"Looks like. Maybe elves like really fresh eggs."

"They'll sense me."

I looked from Simon back to the henhouse. "Oh. You think?"

"Bloody feather mops. Geese are worse, but they'll cluck their 'eads off."

"When Scout sees me, he'll start barking. That should set them off anyway, right?"

He shrugged, his face sagging in a disheartened expression.

"This is going to work, Steptoe."

"It's a big 'ouse, innit?"

Carter said, "He's right. Time isn't on his side."

I stared down the driveway, looking for icy-eyes to make his appearance. "I have an idea."

The other three said, as one, "No."

I sat back in the car seat, carefully folding my arms over my chest. The bracers had stayed home because everyone had agreed that Devian liked sparklies and would have negotiated for them, somehow, in the bargain. Brian, however, had been okayed to bring his blasting stick, the crystal knob on the cane not yet clear and diamond-like, but definitely improved to a slate-gray appearance. He'd deemed the minor magical setback in its restoration worth the risk and that it would not attract the elf's attention too much because of its impaired state. Never mind the oddity of a strong, good-looking twenty-year-old leaning on a cane. If Brian couldn't use it, I had plans for the sturdy stick.

Steptoe squeezed my elbow. "Never mind, ducks, it'll work out." He slid out of his coat and began turning it inside out. A second later, he disappeared from sight.

"How is it you do that?"

"Trade secret." A muffled moment later, he said, "Open the car doors, so I can get out."

So we did, and that's when I spotted the figure at the far end of the driveway, pulling a golden lump behind him on a leash. I jumped out of the back seat and an unseen hand stopped me in my tracks.

"Easy, luv. Too eager and 'e'll take advantage. The pup is likely a'right, just stubborn. Wish me luck."

"Luck, Steptoe."

"Too right."

And then he was gone. Or I think he was, not seeing him and all. The chickens that had been pecking around in their fenced yard did throw up their heads and begin to cluck a bit and beat their wings about. I whistled at Scout and, bless his heart, the pup threw his head up and began barking sharply back at me. Who knew exactly what had disturbed the poultry?

I could see the man at the driveway's end clearly now, although not the color of his eyes, but Devian couldn't be mistaken. Dressed sharply, like a country gentleman, he approached us deliberately, and the Eye of Nimora dangled from his free hand.

I breathed in, saying to myself, "Don't. Drop. It." The brick expanse we trod might be infamously damaging to the ruby if they met suddenly. Scout had gone from being dragged to bounding ahead of Devian and pulling furiously at his leash. I trotted out a few steps ahead of the guys.

"Scout! Good boy, there you are!"

Ears flopping, tail wagging, tongue lolling, he bounced around gloriously at the end of his lead, yanking the elf this way and that way. Devian lost the arrogance to his gait and fell into simply keeping on his feet and following after the dog.

I bent over and slapped my palms on my thighs. "Who's a good boy? You are!"

Chickens and pup went wild. Scout lunged toward me.

Devian fell to one knee, and I could hear a sharp command that crackled through the air like lightning. Scout yelped and somersaulted. When he got up on his paws, he whined loudly and strained to get to me. I think I might have growled in response. Brian held his cane out, blocking me.

"Not yet."

Scout's piteous noisemaking shook me, but I knew Brian was right. So I steadied myself and waited. Devian untangled himself, dusted himself off, and drew close enough for me to clearly see not only his icy-blue eyes, but the deep anger in them. He took a breath as if to steady himself.

"You keep appointments promptly."

Carter barely inclined his head in agreement. "We're ready to fulfill our bargain." He looked past Devian, assessing the estate, and I wondered if he, like I did, caught the nearly silent opening and closing of a side door. "It might be easier on you to let the dog go first." His gaze dropped to Scout, who had stopped jumping but sat at the length of his lead, which was stretched taut between them.

Devian took a leisurely moment to look down at his arm, and hand, and then the dog, as if deciding. "Does she know," he asked, raising his gaze to look at me, "where he comes from? His heritage and his breeding and training? Does she," and he gave a slow, mean, smile, "does she know that he's a hound of the Huntsman? What will happen when his true owner comes to take him back?"

I heard a hiss of breath to my flank but had no idea who it came from. "What Huntsman?"

"Have you never heard of the Great Hunt? Gentlemen, you are remiss in her education!"

I cut my hand through the air. "Heard of him. Seen real hounds, and he's nothing at all like them, if I even believed in the Hunt. Do you lie? I heard elves couldn't."

"We cannot."

But he didn't say they couldn't deceive by bending the truth, a nice dodge on its own. The hand I'd cut through the air I now fisted. "Give me back my dog."

"All in good time. I believe we are bargaining."

"Bargaining?" I swung around on Carter. "I thought this was a done deal."

"Easy," Carter said, but his mouth quirked to one side as if he realized the game I played. "There may still be a few details to iron out." At Devian's wince, he amended, "Straighten out."

Hiram rumbled at me, "Elves don't like the thought of iron."

"Oh, so that rumor is true?"

"More or less."

"Mostly less, or we would not still exist here," Devian stated.

"Still, it's an interesting concept."

The elf would not look at me. "Carter, I thought when you came to treat with me, you would keep the riffraff out of the process."

Brian straightened, and the end of his cane thumped the bricks. "Riffraff, are we? While you were playing gather ye rosebuds while ye may, I was studying how to better the world."

"And forgot all you learned and then some, from the looks of you." Devian's cold silver scorn swept over Brian, lingered a moment on the cane, and came back to Carter and Hiram. He fastened on Hiram. "You, I take it, are Mortimer Broadstone's son."

"I am and proud to acknowledge it."

"Dwarves and elves have long stood apart, but your father had a good reputation among my people. It's unfortunate I do not agree with them."

Hiram might have taken a step forward, but Carter's tall frame blocked him.

I couldn't let that one go. "You're just full of good things to say."

"You were in my power once. It won't take much to put you there again." And he pulled back on Scout's lead and I finally saw what he had done. The leash was little more than a rope with a slip knot, the loop around Scout's neck—and every time Devian yanked on it, the noose tightened. Evelyn wanted to be like me: a badass, and I decided I wanted to be all over that elf-man for hurting Scout.

Now Carter blocked me. "Terms decreed this to be a peaceful parley. We need to honor that."

"He's already broken it! He's strangling my dog!" I grabbed Brian's cane and, with a yell, launched at the smug elf. I didn't expect to reach him, pixie dust being at his disposal and all, but then Devian didn't seem to realize I'd throw myself at him in an all-out tackle until too late. I hit him and laid him low, cane at his throat like a hockey stick in my hands, before anyone even knew I had moved.

Except for Scout. He jumped at the same time I did, and went for his enemy's ankles.

To be fair, Carter had put a pretty heavy glamour on me, none of us wanting Devian to get a feel of the maelstrom stone in my hand. To be even fairer, I thought it was worth it to knock his ass down. A stunned silence hung in the air for about five seconds.

And then the fight started.

I've been in some good brawls in my life. Most of them started on the field in high school because I walked around in a lot of anger for those last two years, and I don't like people who think they can get away with bullshit. I've grown since then, but sometimes those old skills just come in really handy. Devian threw me off, I rolled over and began to swing cane, fists, and feet while Scout dodged in and out, growling and yipping in excitement, fangs flashing. If the elf had a magic spell he could use, he didn't have time to prep it, let alone send it my way. He tucked the ruby inside his fancy broadcloth shirt and came back at me. We rolled over and over on the fancy bricked driveway, in an old-fashioned donnybrook. He slapped me once hard enough to make my ears ring. I recoiled, gathering my strength, watching his eyes to see what his next move would be. Devian had no fear about hitting a woman. Or maybe it was because I was human riffraff. I knotted my muscles and went after him with a haymaker, knew I'd miss, and ducked away from his parry, contacting instead with his rib cage with all I could muster. The wind exploded from him, and he reeled back, eyes closed, fighting for breath. That sort of thing can counteract most spoken spells.

About then, Carter and Hiram got into the fray. Brian stood back, visibly shaken, hands empty. Hiram took hold of me about the time I thought of the flash-bangs I had on me, wondering if elves could swallow them. Or should.

Hiram held me in midair by my shoulders as I glared down at Devian.

Carter had the other, on his knees, arms behind his back. That beautiful blond hair looked frightfully mussed and not at all alluring, and the expression on his face told me he was mad enough to spit nails. Blood trickled sluggishly from a split lip.

I'd drawn elven blood. Or Scout had. The pup scooted over to me, rope trailing behind him, and sat down on Hiram's boot.

Devian breathed hard. "The deal is off."

Carter told him, "We're getting what we came for. You broke with terms first. The pup was indeed mishandled and injured."

I looked down and saw the swollen welts on Scout's neck. I'd been somewhat angry before; now rage coiled up in me, hot and nasty. "Let me go."

"No," Hiram told me. "Not until you cool down."

"He hurt Scout."

Devian laughed. "Take the cursed dog. See how you feel when the Huntsman shows up on your doorstep and wants his creature back." He spat a crimson blob to one side in disdain before flicking a look at me. "Damn, woman, you've got a fist on you."

"I can fight for what I want." I handed the cane back to Brian who'd dared to come a little closer. "Consider that payback for the way you treated me at the casino."

"I saved your life. But never mind that. Humans have always been ingrates." Scorn poured out with his voice. "Why do you play with your inferiors, Broadstone? I think we shall have to renegotiate your little contract with us. No Queen's gem until you prove yourself, and the length of term will be considerably longer."

I didn't feel the least bit cooler, and now Devian was threatening Hiram. "Let me at him!"

"You're right," Hiram agreed and dropped me on top of him.

By the time Carter had us all sorted out again, one of Devian's scornful eyes sported a nice purple shiner and I had lost a shoe. We'd all gotten to our feet, eying each other with high suspicion, but no one held anyone at bay. Scout helpfully picked my sneaker up and stood with the item in his mouth, sad caramel eyes watching all the fuss. Lest you think this should be beyond a Southern lady, think again. We invented vengeance.

"Reparations!" shouted Devian.

That must have been a magical spell because suddenly, elven henchmen surrounded us, and we had no place to run.

Hiram dusted his hands. "Now that's the sort of elven deviousness I expected." He gave a piercing whistle and behind the elves, ranks of Iron Dwarves emerged from the verdant and vast trees lining the roads and country properties, and closed in.

CHAPTER THIRTY-FOUR

OOOPS

FORGET NOT SEEING them. I hadn't felt them either, not the slightest vibration in the earth, and I knew a dozen Iron Dwarves stomping about could make you think the world was coming to an inglorious shake, rattle, and roll ending. I would never have associated stealth with any of their movements, and I made a note for the future: Iron Dwarves can tiptoe with the best of them. Carter looked about him quickly and then his expression became one of relief.

It took me a moment to figure out. Having backup was more than welcome, of course, but then I realized that not one of the dozen who appeared had been named by Germanigold, except for Hiram. So that was good. I leaned over to retrieve my shoe and remove the disgraceful rope from Scout's sore neck. I rubbed his ruff gently and told him again what a good dog he was. He knew it and agreed, wiggling butt pressed against my leg. His golden hide warmed up against me, and his size reminded me that he was still, after all, a puppy. Overgrown a mite, but still. He stayed up close while I put my foot back in my shoe, just like Cinderella, and tightened the laces.

I fingered a soft ear flap which he enjoyed for a moment before giving a low whine as if that, too, might hurt him a bit. I settled for a few strokes down the center of his head.

Hiram indicated the troops. "Feel free to negotiate

whatever you think best. I think the terms will be agreeable to me." He held his hand out, palm up. "Hand over the Queen's gem, as agreed upon, and we'll proceed."

"I think not. We have made other arrangements."

"What have you done?"

"What I must. Tsk. One would think you'd never dealt with elves before." Devian lowered his eyebrows a bit and looked at Brian, Carter, and Hiram. "I must admit that I have not really met any of you in the last few centuries except for a brief skirmish at the casino. So perhaps you are operating outside your sphere of experience. You didn't think I'd give it up that easily, did you?"

"You lied."

Devian shrugged. "Elves cannot lie. Make what you can of that. I thought we'd already discussed this."

"We are all well aware that you will circle around and about whenever you can."

He smiled at me, busted lip and all. "You should have brought Malender with you. That one would make an opponent." Silence greeted his declaration except for me. I didn't speak, however. My face heated, especially that cheek where he'd slapped me roughly. Devian pivoted about to look at the others. "Oh, dear. She didn't tell you, did she? Before you all came rushing in to save her, Malender took her from me. She really didn't need saving by any of you."

But I had told them. I just hadn't expected Devian to rub their noses into it.

He took a step closer, but Carter moved to block him. "Witness. Still protecting her. I had hopes. Plans. Something about her intrigues me and not just that she did not mention her rescuer to you. Why is that, do you suppose? She wears his mark, he told me. He told me to stay clear of her, but I can't do that. She draws me. It looks as if she attracts all of you, as well. We should investigate what it is we find so alluring. Besides the obvious, of course."

I really wanted to wipe that smile off his face.

"She calls us friends, as we do her," Hiram answered.

I wanted to remind them that I stood right there, but

there seemed to be a battle behind the words that I was not entirely aware of, and ought to stay away from. Not that I like being talked about, but at least it wasn't behind my back. I knew it wasn't the maelstrom stone that made us friends. It couldn't manufacture loyalty; its strength is chaos.

Devian tossed his head back. "Yet you haven't introduced her to your little Society. Again, why? Tainted, perhaps?"

"We won't respond to your baiting," the professor told him. "Honor your agreement, or we'll withdraw." He raised his cane into blasting rod position as if he, and it, were fully loaded. I was happy to hear that he still operated somewhere inside of Brian.

"Not quite a society of fools," Devian returned. "But no brilliant geniuses, either. As you wish." He fetched the diadem and ruby from inside his shirt, held it up—and dropped it.

Carter pitched forward in an all-out dive. He missed.

It hit the driveway and shattered with a noise of splintering chimes, scattering red fragments everywhere. The hard smack of Carter belly flopping on the drive followed immediately after. Hiram uttered a moan of dismay, and Brian stepped smartly back behind me.

Carter rolled over. Crimson shards filled the hollow of his palm. He exhaled, and the crystals floated off, disappearing. "Fake." He stood and dusted his hands off. "Not a move I would suggest making, considering you're surrounded."

"Me? Surrounded?" Devian gave a short, bitter laugh and Scout shivered against me. "Have at it if you think you've got me. As you might say—bring it on." He raised both hands in entreaty.

Brian let out a professor-infused curse, but no one moved.

Then, almost quicker than the eye could follow, Devian began to melt until nothing more remained of him than a pool of mercury on the red brick driveway. The silvery-gray puddle caught the slanting rays of late afternoon sunlight. His henchmen dissolved after him, not even leaving a memory behind of their existence. Hiram's fellow Iron Dwarves called out to one another in alarm, as behind them, a ring of elven archers appeared, with drawn bows in hand and a target sighted. They wore black and gold, each of them handsome is as handsome does, cold and deadly so, and their arrowheads shone as though honed within an nth degree of death. Now these guys looked like true elven.

It began to occur to me that this fellow had magic my guys couldn't even anticipate—and we could all be in serious trouble. The bowmen knelt poised for orders, yet no one stood to take that command. A shimmering at the far end of the drive opened up, and I sensed the tug of an elven archway as it did. My heart felt as though it slid sideways when Devian materialized next to it. He looked almost the same except more slender and taller. Imposing.

"Pity. That doppelganger had its uses. He failed me at the casino, however. He could have had you instead of the ruby. He had a chance to learn your mystery and failed. I don't intend to fail." He put a hand out to me.

Beyond the rainbow arch, a land lay in full autumn color: red, orange, yellow with carpets of green still at the trees' roots, and the sky pulsed a clear, eye-burning blue. It looked incredibly beautiful and yet sharp, like a glass of lemonade promising a cold, sweet drink and betraying the tongue when found to be pure juice, acid and bitter. A wind rippled the alien landscape, or perhaps something immense moved behind the branches, sinister and unseen. I hated that I wanted to enter and that fear kept me from moving to it.

I knew better, but my right foot shuffled into a step. Scout whined and threw himself against my ankle.

Wrong foot. Now the left paced forward a half measure.

"Don't," warned Carter.

"I know. Trust me, I know." And I did, but still my heart kept slipping sideways, falling toward the elven arch. I grabbed at Hiram's hand as I passed him and for a moment, the Iron Dwarf anchored me. He felt solid and reassuring, and his hand engulfed mine. For a fleeting minute, I held the surprising image of Evelyn's hand in his, her very slender and elegant fingers all but disappearing forever in his gentle grasp. Then the tug came at me again and I let go of Hiram—I couldn't drag him in after me, the pull too powerful for even Hiram to resist if I kept hold of him.

I thought to strip my left-hand glove off and reveal the stone, as if a cord strung between me and Devian, and I could slice it away as I had carved up the bonds holding Germanigold. But Carter's glamour weighed too heavily on me, closing the stone as much away from me as from others. I couldn't reach it or sense it.

Carter began to glow around the edges.

"Best not."

He did not look back at Brian's soft words, but he did straighten as if constraining himself. I gave them both an unhappy look over my shoulder as I took another three steps in Devian's direction. Not that I expected anyone to save me, but it would have been nice if Carter dissolved the glamour so that I could unleash the stone and let the havoc fall where it may.

I didn't know what held all of them back. If they waited for me to make a defiant move, I failed. The only thing I could do was walk toward the autumn face of Faerieland. I could smell it, like cinnamon with a sharp tang of something more potent and maybe even poisonous behind it. A faint mist edged it, a creeping fog bubbling forth from the portal's arch. I struggled to another halt, and Scout wrapped himself about my legs, rope tangling both of us. He couldn't keep me in place and I knew it, but I'm not sure the pup knew it. He looked up at me, brown eyes bright and expectant. He licked my hand, tongue rasping against my fingers. It brought me back from wherever my thoughts had suddenly drifted, and Devian made a loud, scornful sound.

"Pay attention, Tessa."

My gaze snapped back to his sharp-planed face, the eyes now not icy-blue but a blazing blue, and it jogged something in my memories. The recognition thudded harder when his shadow threw off a darker image: a prancing fox on hind legs with three tails, wielding a katana. There is no mistaking that silhouette. *He was the one.*

"You've got Joanna." I thought Malender had gathered up her evil soul but no.

"*Naturellement.* I'm not inclined to bring her out. She has been a naughty failure, that one, and does not deserve to breathe freely. Not yet."

The shadowy girl-fox shape rippled and then reluctantly allowed itself to be reabsorbed into Devian's own shade. I looked back at his face. "You pretended to be Malender once."

He placed the palm of his hand over his heart. "Me? Or a doppelganger? More than once, actually. It would be enlightening to know when, would it not?"

Was it, then, or was it not Malender who'd gathered up Remy . . . Joanna . . . Hashimoto at their great defeat? Or had it been Mal, and then Devian had wrested them away from him? I'd just seen the evidence that Devian bossed Joanna. Either way, I had no way of knowing who'd been in charge when or who had not. What I did know was that after Joanna had come after me, it had been the false Malender I'd then encountered. All other meetings, as far as I knew, were authentic. Even when the stag had been killed that night. It was not a Malender that I wanted to know, but that seemed to be the nature of our relationship. He appeared, I thwarted and threw salt on him, and he disappeared. The sum of all those times did not make him into the Great Evil the others feared coming.

Devian on the other hand . . .

"I grow impatient."

Imagine how I felt, waiting for him to give up or someone to make a big move.

He lifted something in his hand, something he'd been holding lightly that I couldn't see, nor could I see it all that well in full sunlight. It looked like someone had tried to make a cloth doll, scraggly and limp, out of a handkerchief and a bit of hair. "My doppelganger didn't serve me as well as expected, but he did manage to obtain a souvenir from the other night, one that, properly invoked, gives me quite a bit of influence." He waggled the dolly. "A few strands of hair, only, but that's all that is needed. When this doll crosses the threshold, you will follow. You'll have no choice."

My scalp tingled.

I felt a bit relieved that my compulsion to move did not come from a fatal weakness. He'd been using magic on me. Magic and I had been doing battle for months now, and I'd managed to hold my own. I respected it, and I think I'd fought it enough times to a standstill where it held the same modicum of respect for me.

At least, that should be how it worked. I might have known better. In fact, I supposedly had the potential to be a kickass sorceress. So why was I ambling across the driveway like a nearsighted possum hoping to make it across the highway yet in no hurry about it?

Carter caught up with me, wrapping a hold about my elbow. "Don't do it." He still glowed, catching the aura of the late sun and its heat, too. It hurt my eyes to look at him and my skin stung where he touched me.

"Carter . . ." warned the professor.

"I'm not letting him take her."

That made me feel better in spite of the possibility of being strung out between them like a tug of war at a college kegger. I shrugged him off gently. "Remove the glamour."

I heard the professor mutter an objection, but Carter only watched my face as he asked quietly, "Are you sure?"

"He's seen a little bit of what I can do, so we're not hiding anything." Not true. Actually, we were hiding quite a bit, but if Devian was unprepared for that, so much the better. I felt it the moment the glamour let go . . . as if iron shackles had just dropped from my wrists. I chafed both of them lightly, immensely glad for the sensation of freedom, and wishing for my bracers. I turned my face slightly to him. "Why are you glowing?"

He gave a very small shake of his head.

"Not good, eh?"

Carter sighed. "It's either very little or full-on nuke. And the professor doesn't seem to want a nuke here. Something about the portal." We both glanced at the elven arch and silently agreed with each other that the professor could have a point. Blasting a portal of elven power might unleash a deadly amount of magic loose. On the other hand, this was *me* we were risking.

Devian jerked his arm, throwing me off my feet and toward the portal. It pitched me forward, and I had to catch up with my impetus or fall flat on my face, arms akimbo. From the corner of my eye, I saw something dark and twisty wave in midair. It jerked up and down before disappearing, the vision giving me a jot of hope.

I caught up with myself, opposite Devian. He exhaled as if he'd just inhaled a deep essence of my very being.

"Ahhh. I can taste you now . . ." He walked around me. "A veritable Pandora's box of magic relics embedded in you. Delightful. At the moment, I'm most concerned with the book. That book belongs to my family; we want it back and have been trying to obtain it for a few decades now. We shall have to negotiate, but things will go better over the threshold."

His words freed one of my options. If he already sensed it, why not use it? I engaged the stone, looking for that knife-sharp boundary that I'd used to cut Goldie free, narrowing my vision to see what sort of binding he had on me. It could cut both ways, and I might damage myself more than I'd free myself depending on how the magic held me, but I'd no intention of following Devian anywhere. Then I spotted it: a taut red line from me to the doll in his hand. Would I bleed if I sliced it away? Goldie hadn't, but then, harpies are a different breed from mortal flesh. For all I knew, this cord had been spun from my heart and soul itself. With a twist of my left hand, I began to saw away at it and nearly fell over.

Agonizing spasms froze my chest until I couldn't breathe. My stomach went rock hard and my heart stopped a beat or two before fluttering on. I felt as though I'd been hit by a pile driver and the wind knocked out of me. Someone with a nasty sense of humor followed it up with a spear of agony deep to the chest. It buried itself in me.

The red cord bounced against the maelstrom stone's edge. I sawed at it again, praying for it to fray or cut through before I stopped breathing altogether. My walk stiffened down to nothing, my whole body now one vicious cramp.

Devian didn't seem to notice. Almost blithely, he kept talking to me. "I'll hold on to the Queen's gem because it doesn't enter into the terms for the book, but I will concede that I do have the advantage. In all things. Come along now." And he waved the doll broadly through the air, it and his hand disappearing into the mist edging the portal.

A string of the red cord parted, snapping through the air, and I could inhale again but lost it in a gasp as Devian's yank propelled me headlong toward the archway.

My world exploded. Something big and bulky hit me hard, twirling me away, and I caught sight of Hiram's body hurtling past and colliding into Devian. But something unseen had already hit the elf, spinning him about and tearing the doll from his hand, leaving him open to Hiram's tackle. The doll drifted toward my feet even as I began to collapse in a truckload of hurt. Devian and his attackers disappeared into the elven archway, fog boiling up, and the autumn lands disintegrated with a loud hiss.

CHAPTER THIRTY-FIVE

HOW MANY FINGERS . . .

". . . AM I holding up?"

Vision fuzzy, I glared at the hand hovering over my face. "None," I answered triumphantly as Scout nudged the hand away and moved in to lick my nose. He whuffled at me anxiously. I sat up slowly, duly noting that I had meant to be kickass, not get my ass kicked. We were definitely short on supporters—I counted only Brian and Carter, plus myself. Dwarves had gone as silently as they'd appeared. And the drop-dead archers were nowhere to be seen, although about a half dozen of those lethal arrows were stuck in the driveway around us. Impressive, sunk into the stonework. I saw crimson leaking from Carter's left bicep where he'd tied a strip of cloth about it tightly.

"What's that?"

"Flesh wound. What about you?"

"Did we win?" I sat up groggily. I so wanted a win, for once.

"Not quite."

"No?"

"You didn't get dragged in, but we lost Hiram."

"And Steptoe," I muttered.

"Steptoe?"

"We stalled long enough that he found his tail. Didn't you see him flash it at us? He hit Devian first, knocking the doll away. Then Hiram clocked him. And seriously? Do you think I would lower my head and charge in like a bull in a china shop unless I'm stalling for someone?"

"I've watched you play field hockey."

"Really? When?"

"More often than you know. If you played on ice, you'd be called an Enforcer."

Brian stood with his head to one side, considering, and patted himself all over as if searching for the professor inside him. "Hmmph. She's right, he's retrieved his tail." He scratched an earlobe at that. "Inside Faerie or not, he'll be fine as long as he's intact. He'll have many of his powers restored."

"But is he still bound to the church?"

The professor stared down at me. "The lad has been mighty chatty."

"He has to talk to someone." I didn't let the professor off the hook as Carter reached down and gave me a hand up. "Doesn't he? And is he?"

"Bound for the moment." Brian turned his back on both of us, head down, pretending to study one of the elven arrows. He bent over to pull one out and as his fingers grazed it, the lethal missile dissolved into ashes, much as the ruby had when Carter touched it, tiny particles drifting away on the wind. "Hmmm," he said and reached for a second as if performing a scientific experiment, and the next arrow disintegrated harmlessly as well.

I wobbled over to the doll lying on the bricked way and kicked at it. It did not disperse. In fact, it kicked back. I clutched at my stomach. Scout lurched into a bracing position at my knees as I gulped.

That got Brian's attention. He pointed at the fetish. "I believe your skill will work best on that."

Carter obliged by aiming his hand at it, and a gout of flame ate the doll in a split-second, incinerating it into oblivion. I felt a moment of heat graze me and then nothing. Staring in amazement, I murmured, "I thought he said no nuking earlier."

His scar-cleft deepened as he looked embarrassed. "That was just a tap. With great power comes . . ."

"I know, blah, responsibility, blah." My body still in rebellion, I pivoted and headed back to Hiram's car. "Anyone have the keys or did Hiram take them with him?"

They trailed after me, searching pockets uselessly, trying the vehicle's doors (locked), and then Carter reached under a forward fender and found one of those little magnetic boxes affixed to the undercarriage of the SUV. The key would open the doors and start the ignition, but we couldn't pushbutton the accessories.

As we settled inside, I passed around a bottle of water I'd found in the door's side pocket. We all drank deeply and I made a cup out of the palm of my hand for Scout. He drank messily and not nearly so deeply, but at least he wouldn't drop dead of dehydration before we got home.

If home we went. I leaned forward between the front seats and said, "So, we can track Steptoe if he's still bound, right?"

No one answered for a very long minute. Carter cut Brian a look. "You should have known that."

"As should you. But she is indeed right. Simon's whereabouts can be traced." He pulled on the flaps of his coat, unsettled. "Right, indeed."

"Will he know it, or will they be alerted if we did?"

"Yes, and probably not, sounds appropriate."

Carter pulled smoothly away from the curb and down the street. "You sound uncertain."

Brian scratched the side of his nose. "Information is still hazy and has unfortunate gaps in it. Huge gaps."

"As it will be as long as you're half-baked." I felt Scout settle down beside me and put his head across my thigh. "Carter, you're still bleeding."

"Am I?" He didn't spare a look, but I could see the makeshift bandage on his upper arm leaking blood. A lot of it. "I'll take care of it later."

"Half-baked?" Brian repeated.

"Until you finish your ritual."

"I wouldn't quite refer to it in that manner. Sounds a bit flippant."

And he sounded a bit petulant, making me ponder if

Steptoe had indeed been correct with his little theory. He hadn't exactly stepped in to help me very much, but then we all knew his skills were nowhere at the level they should be. But cowardly? I didn't like thinking of the professor that way. With that thought came the distinct feeling that he wasn't sharing with me anymore, if he had been in the first place. Exactly what was our late great wizard up to these days?

The stone in my hand warmed slightly beneath my glove, and I peeled it off to see if the battle had harmed it in any way. I didn't expect to see it changed, and I didn't. Stone is stone, after all, or marble, or whatever material comprised this one. I thought of it as marble, with the colors of ivory, caramel, and obsidian swirled together with flecks of gold. It had its beauty. Could I compel it to give up the dark arts book as ransom for Hiram and, possibly, Steptoe? It hadn't exactly swallowed the whole book, not in the way it had the professor's cursed ring. Was I a sorceress because it had absorbed a bolt of power and shared that with me, or had it transferred it, meaning that if a day came that I lost the stone or had it taken away from me, what would that make me? Plain old Tessa, as before? Not that I'd become so spectacular now, not understanding most of my so-called abilities or knowing how to use them. But it was the feeling, I suppose, that I walked around with this untapped potential and I could snap it into use and—I don't know—slay dragons or whatnot.

I curled my hand into a fist, hiding away the enigmatic stone. The professor used to like to tell me it all came from the will. Seemed to me that one had to know what they wished for, have the determination to reach for it, the guts to ask for and pay the price for it, and the strength to take it when magic offered it. And I'm sure there were a half dozen other conditions I couldn't begin to guess at. There were no magic wands in my world.

I put my head back against the seat and watched the countryside unspool around us, the sun dipping low in the sky, and the edge of a storm cloud rolling in from the west. I didn't like leaving anyone behind.

* * *

Mom came out to meet us when we parked. She had a pencil tucked behind one ear, so I knew she'd either been writing or working on students' tests, and she made a face as she saw the car didn't hold as many of us as it had when we'd left.

"What happened?"

"Operation unsuccessful." Carter held one hand cupped over the wounded arm. "Have you hydrogen peroxide and bandages?"

"Good lord—who shot you? Shouldn't you go to the hospital?"

"It would be difficult to explain, and it wasn't a gun, and no, I don't think they can help me." Carter looked to Brian. "Surely you have something?"

"Mayhap. Elven wounds can be tricky, that I do recall. If the arrowhead was magicked with everbleed . . . you'd be best off headed to your Society friends and see what one of them can do for you."

Carter's forehead crinkled. "They will be asking questions."

"I should hope so—oh. Yes, I see what you mean." Brian ran a hand through his hair. "I'll take a look at my *Remedies* book, see if I have the herbs."

"Appreciate that." He trailed after my mother into the kitchen, and I took Scout out back to hose him down quickly and get a better look at his ruff. Something about the thought of seeing Carter Phillips bleed made me a little queasy.

Scout danced around a bit under the cold water, but the lab in him came out and he eventually started enjoying it. My phone buzzed insistently until I deigned to answer it.

"OMG," said Evelyn. "Why didn't you tell me about him?"

"Him who?"

"Hiram!"

"I . . . didn't think he was your type?"

"How could he not be?"

I had thought it rather obvious, but held my tongue.

"Or are you interested?" Evelyn poked at me.

"You know me better than that!"

"I know. Carter's the one you lust after. But Hiram . . . wow. Is he the kind of guy who won't call you back? Tell me he's not. I can't take ghosting. I can't get a hold of him, but he said he had a meeting and then errands to run, so I can't keep calling, but I wanted to hear his voice again . . . so low and powerful . . . like that singer who's dead now, but your mom and my mom loved him . . . Barry White? And such a gentleman!"

"Barry White?"

"No! Hiram."

"He is, that. And busy tonight, so if you can't reach him, don't worry or be insulted. I'm sure he'll call you soon." *Soon as we break him out of Faerieland.* I cradled my phone between my ear and my shoulder while I toweled Scout dry. It was almost dark, and the wind had come up with a chill in its touch. Scout nosed at me as I worked carefully about his wounds. They weren't awful, but they weren't good either. Bastard must have kept him tied up and tightly. As for that nonsense about being some kind of hound of the dreadful Huntsman . . . who did Devian think I was? Some country bumpkin who just fell off the turnip truck?

"Don't you think? Tessa! Are you listening?"

"Of course I am." I hadn't been, though.

"Oh. Okay. It's just that he's in business and I'm still taking classes, but I didn't think he was that much older."

Oh, Evelyn, you have no idea. And neither did I, frankly, but I had come to the conclusion that Iron Dwarves probably had a life span of about two hundred years, give or take, dependent on wars and bad magic and other problems. The family enterprise would meet her father's examination, though, and Hiram himself presented well, even if he could shake the foundations of any building he walked into. Should I encourage her or not? Undoubtedly, Hiram and his family could handle a mild infatuation. On the other hand, his father had married a harpy and nearly started a war.

I let her babble for another few minutes, reminded

her to ice that leg off and on, and that it was nearly dark and I was trying to finish giving the dog a bath. She signed off reluctantly.

I stowed my phone in a pocket. Had I ever gushed like that over Carter? Probably not. He'd come into my life as an investigator on my father's disappearance and although he'd decided for himself quickly enough that neither me nor my mom were ax murderers who'd done away with Dad, he couldn't not consider us suspects that quickly. He had protocol to follow. And, in the months after, he'd dropped by periodically as things kept spiraling downward. So I'd noticed him. Crushed on him. And avoided him whenever I could because he was, after all, an authority figure and a reminder of a very traumatic time period. And significantly older. But he wasn't anymore.

So, no. No gushing. Maybe a longing sigh now and then. What I hoped we could have between us had definitely looked up.

Maybe I *could* spare a little gush.

I returned to the house to find two strangers flanking Carter as he sat at the kitchen table. Mom shot me a *be quiet* look as she finished filling two glasses of sweet tea for them, a man and a woman, both dressed a little formally for an autumn evening just after dusk. If I hadn't suspected otherwise, I'd peg them as Bible thumpers but because of their interest in Carter, I decided they were likely Society.

The man, hair slicked back like a New Yorker, not old but not young, cashmere sports coat over dark brown pants and light tan shirt, asked, "How long has it been bleeding?"

Ah. Explanation seemed the professor had given up and reinforcements had come in.

"Not long. Just before sunset."

"Long enough," the woman remarked as she shrugged off her light cardigan and accepted her drink. "My thanks. Is it all right if we tend to him here? There shouldn't be any contamination. Or do you have a downstairs bathroom big enough to hold three people at once?"

She offered a tentative smile as if in apology for dissing our house. "Here is fine," Mom told her. "Shall I leave you all to it? I have classes to prepare for." She didn't; she was extremely organized as a professor, but I sensed the new people made her uncomfortable. She looked back over her shoulder, once, but I just gave a tiny shake of my head. I wanted to leave as well but couldn't think of an excuse and thought I should really stay, in case they tried to make off with the family silver or something.

I nudged Carter lightly. "You're not going to bleed to death, are you?"

"Not this time." He pointed to the man and woman. "This is Raymond Bialy and this is Natalie Chandler, both of the Societas Obscura."

"Catchy name. I'd be a tad more excited if it was Societas Lucida, but you work with whatever you've got, I guess."

"And you must be the young lady who has such an unconventional way with magical relics." Bialy took his gaze off me long enough to watch Natalie clip off the old bandage and then scissor away the shirt sleeve to look more closely at the wound. Blood wasn't spurting alarmingly or anything, but it kept welling up determinedly no matter how many times she blotted it dry. It did look like a slice mark across his bicep.

"Definitely everbleed." Natalie seemed to have decided to ignore me, for whatever reason. Maybe she had more designs on Carter than simply attending to that wound. She snapped open her purse and brought out a purplish vial. "Should I ask how? And would you tell me if I did?"

"Arrow."

"All right." She blotted some liquid onto a new gauze pad and began to briskly attack the wound with it, wiping it back and forth, while I watched Carter's lips tighten rather than admit her ministrations were less than tender and appreciated. When she finished, she said, "That might sting a little."

"Thanks for the warning," Carter returned dryly and relaxed on his chair.

Quickly and efficiently, she wrapped the bandage and tied a neat little knot to keep it fixed in place. "If it starts bleeding again, let me know. You may need a second application."

"Now that's done," Raymond Bialy leaned forward. "How about letting me have a look at you."

"Me?" My gaze met his.

"I've heard a rumor that you've bonded with a maelstrom stone."

"There's more than one?"

He chuckled. His brown eyes had crinkle marks at the corners and, frankly, he looked like an okay person. "I hope not, but there's always a possibility. Willing to let me examine it?"

"No." Carter answered for me.

"It would be better here than formally in front of the Society."

"That would give you a leg up on preparing."

"Nothing wrong with that, is there?"

I looked back and forth between them. Scout, who'd been lying quietly on my feet, gave a short and very soft growl. "I'm not interested in the Society."

"Ah, but we're interested in you."

"I suppose the two of you teach at Silverbranch?"

"Actually, no."

"Good because at this point, the academy is a deal breaker."

"Judge Parker?" asked Bialy.

"Judge Parker," I confirmed.

"He's on suspension."

"Guarded suspension," Natalie added to Bialy's statement.

"Meaning?"

Carter opened his mouth as if to object to the conversation and shut it when I glared his way.

"Meaning," Natalie said, as she cleaned up the first aid supplies, "that we put him under guard until his suspension is served. We don't just let a magic user run around willy-nilly once they've gone rogue."

"Was that before or after he abducted a harpy?"

Bialy leaned forward even more avidly. "Are you the one who breached the campus and let her loose?"

"I think it's your turn to answer."

He let out a short bark of a laugh. "By gods, Carter, she's a live wire. Actually, as we had it explained to us, the harpy had entered into a partnership with Parker and into an agreement she later reneged upon. He held her pending a change of mind and cooperation."

My turn. "Yes."

"Yes?"

"I let her loose."

"I see."

"I don't think you do. I believe her claim that she was betrayed and then kidnapped. Parker may have had an agreement with a harpy, but it wasn't the one he imprisoned. That particular harpy was a traitor."

"That," muttered Natalie, "changes things."

"It certainly does." Bialy tapped the tabletop. "How did you even know about Silverbranch?"

"Two agents, Naziz and Danbury, recruited me and I decided to take a look. I already knew Germanigold was being held somewhere, and the campus seemed a good place to investigate."

"Parker isn't near as clever as he thinks he is," Natalie commented with some satisfaction. She dropped her purple vial into her purse. "The first person to look for her found her almost immediately."

"The question being: why didn't somebody look sooner?"

She stood up, so close to me I could smell the very faint scent of Chanel No. 5. Or was that on him? "Our position is to stay neutral. The other races prefer to be quiet and independent. So we stay . . . *obscura*."

"Nice if it works, but it didn't. At least, the judge is under observation."

Bialy stood as well. "Certain you won't give me a look at that?"

"And have you join the legions who want to take it from me? I don't think so."

Bialy smiled down at Carter who stayed in his chair. "You walk a dangerous road, Phillips. First the professor and now this one. Sooner or later, you're going to have to give an accounting."

"It'll have to be later, then. I prefer to know all I can and who is on what side before I present anyone to the Society."

"Cynical of you to think there are sides."

"Naïve of you to think there aren't." Carter watched Natalie pull her purse up onto her wrist and walk to the kitchen threshold. "Being who and what we are, there are always sides. Thanks for the nursing."

"Don't mention it. And we mean that literally. There is enough tension rising now, and we can't risk confrontation with the elves. We don't need any rumors that you were elf shot."

They left, and the two of us looked at each other. Carter reached out and took my hand.

We'd have to be extra careful about what we planned to do to get Hiram and the Eye back lest we start a war.

CHAPTER THIRTY-SIX

BOTHER

THE PROFESSOR CAME out of the stairwell shadows as soon as the door closed on our visitors' heels.

"I remember them as being more pompous."

"Them in particular or just the Society as a whole?" Carter asked.

"All of them."

I rubbed my hands together. "Should I have let them see the stone, then?"

"Absolutely not. Carter was right that Bialy would have prepared for the inevitable formal unveiling and that might include suggestions for schooling, usage, perhaps even containment or removal of the item. Better to catch all of them off-balance if and when you have to let them evaluate what you've got." The professor's excitement reflected in Brian's faint blush.

"Be thankful they didn't start in on you."

"Bring it on."

That made me snicker and Brian caught it. "Well," he said, "you know," sounding as if the professor had abandoned their body and left him holding the karma bag.

I gathered up the first aid supplies and returned them to the kitchen shelf where we kept them. "Did that stuff work?"

"Seems to have." Carter examined the snow-white wrapping. "So far."

"Can it, like, break loose again?"

"It can. Everbleed is an anticoagulant. It can be

deadly if the hit is hard enough. Even if not, the constant bleeding isn't good."

"I wouldn't think so." I put my hip to the counter. "Does it work on elves, too, or just everyone else?"

"Anything that bleeds, more or less. It can even affect trees, with sap lines. It's nasty stuff."

"And rare and expensive, which makes one wonder why Devian's men had it and why they used it against us." The professor was back.

"Unless he was bluffing."

"Why would you think that?" Brian shifted his weight at Carter's statement.

"The arrow you examined disintegrated. A fake. He had a body double. Another fake. Most of those archers could have been mirror illusions."

"He can do that?"

Carter answered me, "That and more. Devian is powerful, and he's not operating independently. I would question why he'd do it more than if."

"Then I'd answer that he's conserving himself. He plans on bigger battles to fight and hesitation on our parts to do so against an overwhelming force." Brian began to pace.

"What is he preparing for?"

Neither of them answered me. Scout put a paw up, and I shook it absently. "Power. It's always power, isn't it?"

"Usually. Or some version of it."

"We need to get Hiram out of there. Is time the same for him behind the arch? All those folk ballads seem to think a hundred years can pass overnight? The Rip Van Winkle effect?"

"That can happen, but I think Devian has synchronized times, in order to carry out whatever plans he has. He doesn't want or need for decades to fly by here. I'd be willing to say that if they did, if there was a massive time difference, he'd lose his advantage."

"So the skirmish today built his reputation."

"He hoped and planned for it, too. We may not have dealt with Devian before this, but neither are we unsophisticated or untrained."

I beamed at Carter. "Thanks!"

"I don't think he was referring to you." The professor stopped pacing.

"You don't know he wasn't."

Brian started to argue but Carter moved in between us. "Prepared to track Steptoe down? He's likely allied with Hiram or, if he's lost his invisibility, imprisoned with him."

"I'll get on that. It may take more than what I've got available." Brian dodged around both of us and hit the staircase running. Scout caught the fervor and went bounding upstairs as well before turning around and returning to me with a look on his puppy face that seemed to ask what had just happened. "You were faked out," I told him, and rubbed the top of his head. He didn't seem to mind.

Brian leaned over the railing and called down, "I'll likely not be ready until tomorrow night." He disappeared before anyone answered.

"It's home for me, then. I've a full schedule next week, but it's days."

"What are you working on now? Your time seems to be really flexible."

He hesitated a smidge. "Undercover."

"Narcotics?"

"Not exactly. I'm dealing with anomalies they don't know how to handle."

"Magic shit they don't understand or need to know?"

He shifted his weight uneasily. "Something like that."

"And you can't tell me either."

"Tessa . . ."

I put my palm up. "Believe it or not, I understand. Sorta."

"Good. I am worried enough about you. Stay away from Malender if you can."

"I have a theory about him."

"Wait until this is all handled and discuss it with me." He waited until I gave a sharp nod. "Classes and practice tomorrow?"

"Yup. The coach is gonna run my ass off, too. I missed a bonus practice yesterday morning."

"Bonus?"

"Optional."

"But if she makes you make up for it . . ."

"Then it's not all that optional. Thanks for playing!" I grinned at him. "I'll text you if the prof comes up with anything."

"Do that."

The house seemed a lot emptier after he went through the door. At the back of the first floor, I could hear the very quiet tapping of Mom on her laptop. That gave me a warm feeling.

We flopped across my bed and did some thinking. Well, I thought. Scout snored the faint, whistling snores of a puppy. Darkness as complete as it be could surrounded the old house. Had Devian, in some scheme to score the old magic book from the Andrews, plotted my father's downfall? It seemed likely, but not likely that he'd directly confined him as a ghost between dimensions, or Devian would have been here, trying to find where the book had gone. No, that had come about through some other accident after the book had been hidden away in the old bureau in a forgotten corner of the forgotten cellar. I needed Morty's journals to know who might have been involved and how it could have happened, and to get those journals, I needed Germanigold to get permission to enter the Broadstone home and retrieve them, and for that I needed Hiram, safe and sound. And the Eye. Mom and I needed the money that rescuing the Eye could earn us. Things seemed to be going around in a spiral.

And then there was Malender who had somehow earned Devian's scorn. Those two had evidently squared off against each other before.

I thought of the little souls that died, in the thousands, each time Malender appeared—but I hadn't seen that at the casino. Had his manifestation been so quick and uneventful, he hadn't needed to pull power? But he'd used a wallop of it against Devian, or Devian's doppelganger, and ought to have needed to replenish it. I hadn't gotten a straight answer about his cloak, which made me think no one in my gang knew one way or the other.

So what, then? Had it been Malender or Devian acting against the body double, just to mess with my mind and trust? I couldn't put it past the elf to be that twisted to have stepped in against himself. And then I had my own and Goldie's observations about Malender.

I needed to know. I looked at my phone. It was late to be creeping around outside, but my task seemed important. So I got up, put my shoes back on, and left my dog sleeping soundly on my bed while I went to make my own supernatural preparations.

The air hung still and quiet about me. My heartbeat drummed a little too loudly in my ears. Did I dare do this? What if I'd thought things over and came to the wrong conclusion? Would Carter be able to forgive me? But what if I could pull Malender in with us as firepower against Devian? We could use that.

"Malender," I whispered. The night drew close, draping itself upon my shoulders, and I knew it listened. Dew crept in to wet my shoes and chill my feet within them. A small breeze began to stir, pulling at my hair and tossing it about my face. "Malender." The lilac bushes hanging over the backyard fencing rustled and far away an owl hooted, once, before beginning its soundless sweeping flight over the neighborhood. A streetlight buzzed like a hornet before winking out, light expired. Burned-out bulb or . . .

"Malender."

And then he was there, shadows splitting apart to reveal him, in his troubadour garb, the color of his eyes unknowable in the late hour, but night couldn't hide his slow, answering smile or dampen the stink of the insidious gunk trying to swallow him whole.

"Tessa of the Salt."

"You may or may not forgive me for this." Without

further explanation, I dug my mother's sugar scoop into the 40-pound bag at my toes and showered it over him and that oily cloud hanging about him. Dip and shovel and shower, dip and shovel and shower.

"What do you know about my father?"

He stood pale and still as the crystals assaulted him. "Only what you know," he answered quietly.

Another scoopful.

"Tell me about Devian." I didn't know if my actions held him at bay, or if he stood and bore it, but I had far more questions than I had salt, and I'd started with forty pounds of that.

"Much of my memory is lost in time, but I do know that we are old enemies."

"That doesn't put either of you on the side of good."

He swayed. "No. It does not."

I moved as quickly as I could, trying not to give him a chance to duck or back away or retreat altogether, and he did not. His breathing roughened, and he curled in upon himself slightly, but he endured. Salt crystals bounced everywhere until the ground looked as though a hail storm had opened up on a four-foot patch. Grass wasn't going to grow there again for a very long time, I thought, regardless of whether the Romans actually salted Carthage in its defeat or not. Salt, invaluable then, and cheap now . . . I'd paid about $7.00 for my bag of crystal salt . . . had never lost its storied punch against evil.

"I can't ask you to do this."

I raised an eyebrow. "But you won't tell me not to."

He shook his head weakly.

I'd gotten a few more questions asked, and terse answers that helped me not at all. The bag lay exhausted, nearly empty, when I realized the last shower bounced off Malender's wavy hair and shoulders, avalanching down his leather coat and pants, trailing off his boots. His inky cloak covered him no longer.

He stood, withdrawn, shoulders tense and arms pulled close to his sides, face lowered, as if hiding and in pain, but wordless.

"No ooze."

He looked up. Put his arms out and turned his hands up and over, stretching, examining. He stomped his boots on the ground, and more salt crystals cascaded off him, and he shook his head, then his whole body like Scout after his bath. Tiny white rocks bounced everywhere. His eyes widened.

"Do you know what you've done?"

"I hope I do." I dropped the sugar scoop. I let him have my theory and hopes full force. "That gunky stuff wasn't you, wasn't your emanation as a being of nastiness . . . that was your prison? You broke away from your anchor, but you couldn't wash that away. And all the souls that got sucked in, that wasn't you drinking them down for power, that was the prison renewing itself? Perpetuating itself, keeping you bound. And the salt working on it all, because that's what salt does, ate away at it anyhow, partly because of its properties and, I hope, because of my intention to fight the malevolence of your very presence. Naïve, on my part, but maybe that's what ate away at the curse. A kind of innocence. At least, that's what I reasoned out because you kept seeking me out. So I decided on an all-out assault. And if I'm not right, if I just did away with an essential part of you, I'm really sorry." My words faltered because he didn't answer me. He just stood quietly, his gaze on me, and I couldn't tell what he thought at all because the night still shadowed him.

CHAPTER THIRTY-SEVEN

DUEL

I BALANCED ON my chilled toes, ready to run, although the idea swept over me that there really wouldn't be any safe place to go.

He reached a hand out toward me, then withdrew it, and instead brushed his hair away from his forehead and deep-set jade eyes. As salt rained down, he chuckled faintly and shook himself again. He half-turned about. "I must go."

Had I expected a thank you? You bet your barbecuing reputation I did, but it obviously wasn't forthcoming. "Did it work?"

"I believe so. My prison fed off my own essence as well, so I am greatly weakened. I cannot stay, Tessa of the Salt. Nor will I be of much use to you."

"What was that thing?"

He hesitated as if he wanted to withhold his answer. "A vampiric cloak. It fed off me and whatever life essences it could grab. I am, perhaps, even more surprised than you that salt would have had any effect on it and eternally grateful it did."

"But you're free now."

"Let us both hope so."

I persisted, saying, "I need your help. At least your knowledge about Devian—"

He wavered and for a moment, I could see right through him as if he did not exist. "I have no help to offer but the one idea I gifted you, and you have only to remember it to have all you need. I am not a being you choose to take your side. Remember that of me, if you recall nothing else."

"What the hell is that supposed to mean?"

"It means that you cannot call on me as you do the sun lion and the phoenix and the demon."

"Oh, that's great. You left out Hiram."

"Good-bye for now, Tessa. You have my gratitude."

And then he left, shimmering apart like a soap bubble bursting, transparent and prismatic one second and gone the next.

I picked up the limp plastic bag of salt remnants. "I'm buying another bag," I told the thin air. "Just in case."

I couldn't count it as a win, but it didn't seem like a total loss either. He said he'd left me something if I could remember it. Great.

My dreams that night didn't involve a fight for my life although I thought I heard Steptoe whispering, not once but twice, "Hurry, ducks. Hurry."

Coming out of the mudroom, I heard muted voices from my mother's study. For a wild moment I thought my father had broken free of his basement prison and had come upstairs to talk with her, the talk sounding intimate. But as I approached, I recognized the professor speaking to my mom.

"I've read the last few pages, Mary. It's encouraging that you've had a break-through and the paper is progressing well . . ."

"But."

"Yes. But. You're taking a stance that ultimately could be very harmful."

"And it's obvious from the casino incident that you won't be rushing in to save anyone."

"Yes, well, as to that—I'm not at full strength, and even if I were, magic has its limits."

"Courage appears to be one of them." A sound came from the laptop being pushed along her desk slightly, and I could sense her leaning back in her chair and giving him a look. One of those "you let me down and you know who you are" looks. A momentary silence followed.

"Be that as it may, and I have no intention of explaining myself to you, I have to caution you against this dissertation and the direction you're currently taking it."

I could barely hear her respond.

"This is not wise, Mary. For you and Tessa. Your paper touches too closely on the boundaries between our worlds, and the one I inhabit, the one that I know best, doesn't want to be revealed."

"Professor, I'm not writing truth that will be taken literally."

"You don't know how it will be taken."

"I know that, after reading *Winnie the Pooh*, people didn't really expect their stuffed bears and donkeys to walk around and talk."

He made a gruff sound. "You are playing with fire."

"And look who's talking." A chair scraped the floor. "I've gotten quite a bit written, and I'm running out of time to gain a permanent position at the university. I can't start over, not again, and whether you think so or not, Tessa and I have a stake in this. You invaded our lives, and I discovered a truth in that which threads through much of our history, written and lived. You can't deny that."

"You don't have proof."

"It's not a scientific paper. I can build my thesis on the backs of other literary works, and you know that the theme runs throughout human existence. We've always seen a bit of the sparkle, the cast of a shadow where there shouldn't be one."

I pressed back into the hall as sounds came telling me my mother had closed her laptop and was locking it away in a desk drawer for the night.

The professor made a near inaudible sound. "I can't dissuade you."

"No. And it would be horribly selfish of you to try. I'm trying to establish a future for my daughter through my scholarship, and I'm close. Very, very close."

"Very well, then. But if I should choose to offer more advice—"

"I don't promise to follow it, but I will listen."

And steps sounded, so I scampered back up the stairs quietly and went to bed, feeling achingly proud of my mother, who sounded absolutely unbent by the circumstances we'd found ourselves in years ago. I managed to sleep.

Chemistry class had a brief quiz. My instructor sounded foggy and interrupted class twice to get a throat lozenge, complaining that students bought more germs to campus than completed assignments. We complained that he was unduly vindictive, but I knew the basic compounds pretty well, and it seemed auspicious that the test paper started off with NaCL.

English assigned us an 800-word essay on cursive writing and whether it should be continued or abolished in elementary teaching. History talked about something or other in the past.

And, as predicted, my gym teacher and coach tried to run our behinds off on the field, her eyes squinting as she chanted, "Just because it's posted as optional, doesn't mean it is! Is breathing optional?"

"No!" we chanted back as we thundered past her.

Evelyn, leg outstretched and elevated, waved cheerily at me every time I passed until her arm got tired. By the time I sat down at the bottom bleacher, towel around my neck to mop my face, I couldn't talk. I hadn't the breath.

She could.

"I haven't heard from Hiram."

Speaking still evaded me. I waved a hand in the no harm, no foul signal before pointing at her shin.

"Better. It's going to stay the most awful purple for another week or two. I'll have to wear ice skating tights to hide the marks. Shona Barrett is taking my place on the squad. She's so excited she hasn't stopped bouncing."

We both smiled at that. Shona was a pixie of a cheerleader, normally second squad, whose diminutive size and enthusiasm made her the natural top of any pyramid, although her inexperience made her more of a daredevil than she should have been. Evelyn sighed. "She'll learn. Right now, she's just a brown blur, rushing everywhere. She'll be an asset." She adjusted her ice pack. "I have asked the squad to include her whether I come back or not. She just needs more practice."

"You'll be back. I think my eyelids are melting," I managed to answer.

"Ewwww. You do look all red and sweaty."

"Thanks."

The coach jogged up. "Back to work, Andrews."

I stifled a groan as I stood up, dropped the now soaked towel somewhere near the team bench, and lurched back out on the track. It got easier as I fell into the rhythm. I could thank jogging with Scout for the additional stamina in my legs or I didn't think I would have survived. When the coach signaled we were done, I staggered back over by Evelyn, who started chattering again as though we'd just had a brief recess.

"Dad wasn't too upset with me, considering, although he is having videotapes in the area pulled to see if the police can identify the jerk that did this. They, of course, are too eager to help, just in case he wins the election and they have to be on his good side, although I think they should be interested in justice and all that. Suppose he bashed someone else?" She eased the ice pack into another sore spot. "I kind of hope they find him and kind of hope they don't. My dad can be a real Papa Bear. Needless to say, I didn't answer Dean's calls today except to tell him what an asshat he was, running off and leaving me. Baby, that bridge has burned!" She made an emphatic hand gesture.

"Of course, I know you really didn't like him, and you were right, but thank you, ma'am, for not telling me. I had to find out for myself. Lesson learned and all that."

I merely nodded.

"So tell me about Hiram."

Oh, hell. I needed to be able to breathe better to do that. My teammates saved me by gathering me up by the elbows and trotting me off to the locker room to shower and get more presentable. Not to worry. Evelyn, on crutches, waited for me at the exit doors when I'd finished.

She talked all the way to the car, where her father had a nice demo vehicle from the luxury dealership and driver waiting for her, and I had to ponder if I had enough skeletal strength left to pilot my little red vehicle home or if I'd turned to jelly. I waved her off as she made the usual "call me" sign at me. When I could breathe.

The sun had broken through early morning clouds and my car's interior felt a comfortable toasty warm as I sat down and got my keys ready. I enjoyed it for a few minutes before starting the motor up. Just in case it might work, I chanted Steptoe's name three times, but it didn't. Sometimes the magic world seems to have no rhyme or reason. Then again, if it were easy, anybody could do it.

I came home to a quiet house. Scout came downstairs yawning, looking as if he'd just woken up, his puppy hair standing out all over while I took him outside. He didn't want a romp, which worked out well because I didn't think my knees had one left in them. He sat down by his empty dog food bowl and gave it a longing look.

"I'm pretty sure Mom left it filled when she went to work this morning. I saw her with the kibble bag when I left for campus."

He pawed it disdainfully.

"You're gonna pull that, huh?"

He flattened himself, propping his chin on the empty dish. Those big, soft, puppy eyes stared at me.

"Really?"

He chuffed.

I relented. "All right, half a bowl full because you must have been starved the few days you were a captive."

Scout sat up spritely and devoured the kibble as I poured it in the bowl. I think I should have put the middle man aside and just gone straight down the gullet, but a dog needs to chew, doesn't he? Strong teeth and healthy gums and all that.

I went upstairs to change into something less rumpled than I currently wore and saw the tell-tales in their vase had all slumped over. One or two managed a look at me.

"It's all right, guys. We're gonna get Simon back."

If they understood, they didn't brighten up any. I changed, checked the weather, put on waterproof shoes, and got a hoodie out of the closet. Sunny today, but evening warned of a storm cloud or two drifting in, and rain might not be out of the question.

When I poked my head out of my bedroom, it occurred to me I hadn't heard the professor moving about. On the first floor, I cast around, looking to see if the house were as lonely as it felt, getting confirmation that it was just me and Scout. I was rummaging in the pantry looking for something easy to fix for dinner when the door bounced in its frame.

The odor of ash and soot drifted through the house before his soft footfall did. He sat down wearily, sighing.

"You went back again." It wasn't a question. It was obvious Brian had gone back to the ruins of the old house.

"It's gone," he told me. "They bulldozed it today, down to the foundation. Another rake or two by the backhoes, and there will be nothing left, not a brick, not a stick, not even a twisted rod. Sometime tonight, it'll be a patch of mud."

"We knew it was scheduled."

"And does knowing the exact march of time heal the hurt? No, it does not." He put his hands on the table, turning his smoking pipe over and over in them. He rarely smoked it anymore, in deference perhaps to Brian's reborn and healthy body, but I doubt the professor was even thinking about tobacco. He mourned a life he'd lost before he was ready.

"We've saved what we could."

He threw his pipe across the kitchen. It clattered into the corner and rolled over on its side, unbroken. "It should never have burned in the first place!"

I stayed silent.

"That insufferable Steptoe. He pushed and pushed at me. None of this ever should have happened. Now it's gone, years upon centuries of study, booklore, compilations and gatherings, objects that don't even exist today. Even if I could remember how to recreate it all, and I can't . . . destroyed. Fire, water, and now by bulldozer. The days of youth stretch far behind me, of my own and the civilized world's. I ought to be able to recall them, and I can't. I can't even imagine how to rebuild, and I don't want to. I feel old."

He scratched at his ear, seeming surprised not to feel that old familiar tuft of hair that used to stick out from it, and paused. "I can't even teach you what you need to know, Tessa. You're a sorceress, but to work your talent, you need to know how to discern the true nature of things, so that you can Name them and call on their will. You need to be able to recognize the magic that lies within all objects and how to make it rise up in answer to you. I can't give that knowledge to you now. Not that I was ever known to be a great teacher, I suppose. Everyone seems to remember me as a crusty old loner, set apart by choice rather than circumstance. It was what I wished."

"Not entirely. You made friends with me."

He grunted. "I do recall a bit of that, and it seemed to be far more effort on your part than mine."

"You called me for help."

"And you answered." He looked up at me then, squarely. "Would you answer today, I wonder?"

"I would. Even as I intend to answer Hiram and Steptoe and whoever else needs it." I rubbed at an itchy eye, stifling a yawn that had nothing to do with the seriousness of the topic. "I raced out to help Evelyn the other early morning."

"How is she, by the way?"

"Sore and enjoying the attention. And asking after young Mister Broadstone." I pulled up a chair next to him. "Should I nip that romance in the bud?"

"Don't see as how you can. They both looked struck by lightning. Some rivers have to run their own course."

I stumbled over the mixed metaphors. "But—"

"No buts. If there is one thing I do remember, it's how stubborn the young can be about living their own lives."

"Even if they get hurt?"

"Especially then." He got up quickly to retrieve his pipe, checked it over, and then stuck it in his coat pocket. The smell of crushed herbs rose as he did.

"Steptoe thinks—"

"That demon thinks a lot of things, most of them incorrect, including that it was time for me to release his binding. Two hundred years of being centered to Richmond and he'd only just begun working to redeem himself and right the kinks he'd been busy twisting. I might have considered it in another decade or three."

"You do remember some things."

He started to bluster and stopped abruptly. "Some," he admitted.

"Can you show me how to bring out the book? I think that's going to be what we need to convince Devian to turn over Hiram. Steptoe . . ."

"Simon will be fine. If he sees the tiniest opening, he'll plunge through." Brian fidgeted once or twice. "The book will be difficult. Simon did most of the translocating on it, after it charged you; I just assisted with the boundaries."

My gloves had been peeled off the moment I hit the house, and I rubbed the stone. "Illusion?"

"Probably the most likely, but at the same time, Devian will be most sensitive to that. He appears to deal heavily with manifestation, so he has talent and training in that area."

"Then we'll have to find a way to flash the real thing at him."

"You could do that, but it would still be connected to you, and if the elf grabs it, he'll take you with it. That would be most undesirable. Your very life counts on staying out of his reach. He's one who would not hesitate to kill you to take the stone."

"It wouldn't work for him that way."

"We are told that it wouldn't, but the stone is chaos. It will do what it wants. It makes a good argument for us to say it can't be taken, but I wouldn't count on it. Especially not when you and your soul are concerned."

"I've got to be able to produce the book, at least enough for him to think he can have it."

"Sleep on it. Perhaps something will come to you, or me."

I stared him down. "If you did rejuv, would you be able to handle Devian?"

"Restoration, from what I gathered in my journal, isn't spontaneous. It is more like a river which has been dammed up and then freed, filling the waterways below. It might take me seasons or possibly years to be renewed to the point where I even know what questions I must ask to be the man I once was."

"So the answer is no?"

"The answer is I don't have one. And don't be like Carter and think if you ask the same thing, but in a different way, you'll get another response. I don't know what I am missing, only that I have this abyss, this ache, inside of me and nothing I can do seems to fill it. And . . . as might have been suggested . . . I am afraid."

He got up then and left me sitting alone. I'd been hungry, but now I wasn't. I stayed, trying to design a way to get Devian to come duel with me so that my friends could go free. The stone grew warm and warmer in my hand as we conspired.

CHAPTER THIRTY-EIGHT

CHICKEN

CARTER CALLED BEFORE I left for the morning's lab class. "How are you doing?"

"Fine. A little leg-weary."

"Field runs as you expected, then?"

"Oh, yeah." I shouldered my backpack. "Why did the chicken cross the road?"

"Hmmm . . . why?"

"Because the coach was chasing her." I checked the time. "I'm just going out for class. Talk to you later?"

"I might be able to. A full moon is coming."

That sounded as if he thought it significant. "Oh-kay."

"A good time to breach a portal." He had thought it important.

"If I can still move after practice today, I'll consider that."

"Good."

The call disconnected, I rubbed Scout's head goodbye and fingered his wounds lightly. They felt almost entirely healed although the hair in his ruff seemed a little coarser than the rest of his puppy coat. "Don't beg for a second breakfast," I told him. "You're getting chubby."

He made a disagreeing noise but wagged his tail as I went out the door.

I enjoyed lab, puttering around and taking notes for my partner as well as myself while she got to wear the ugly goggles and gloves and risk smoking the place up.

Language lab is a horse of a different color but bound to be useful someday if I ever get to travel to a foreign country where it almost doesn't matter what language I've learned as the hosts know five or six.

And then there was Evelyn, frantic as a chicken with a fox in the henhouse, because Hiram hadn't called back. I invented a family business top secret diplomatic trip, with phone blackout, to cover for his disappearance. I don't know if she believed me totally or not, but she stopped checking her messages every five seconds like she had a nervous tic.

Hockey practice, though, was brutal. We started with stretches and then moved into lines, sprinting back and forth and hoping I didn't blow an ankle doing them while the coach yelled, "Faster!"

Then she held a sparring match and we did okay, Jheri her usual fantastic goalie self on my side, but the coach pulled me over just when I thought we were all done.

"I want to work on your striker technique."

Since I had gotten into Sky Hawk CC on a partial athletic scholarship because of my abilities, that took me aback. She guided me downfield where hammering and sawing work by the construction class filled the air with raucous noise. Their new project seemed to be rebuilding the grandstand I'd collapsed.

"You're good," coach said, "but that number fourteen had you collared last week."

"I didn't know a colossus could move that fast."

"Many can. So what you need to know is a little judo."

Visions of my doing a Karate Kid on her and flattening her filled my head, immediately followed by lots of whistles from the referees. "Penalties?"

"Not if you handle yourself correctly. Look, she's going to come straight at you if she can, giving you the perfect opportunity to use her weight and momentum against her. You have to step aside at the last minute, like a matador with a charging bull . . . but you need to put your hip out. You're a tall, slim girl, but I know you have a butt. You do, don't you?"

Unless I'd forgotten to slide it into my jeans with the rest of me this morning, you bet I had a butt. I gave the affirmative.

"You angle it this way and when you hit, which you will, let her run push you, and you will also push her thatta way. We don't hit the way the guys do, their center of gravity is in their shoulders, ours is in the pelvis. I'm going to come at you, and you try it."

There are few things I'd faced lately more frightening than the sight of my middle-aged coach running at me like a freight train. She intended to steamroll me. I stood my ground, wrapped in my gear and with my stick in hand, thoughts stampeding through my mind, and took a half second to wonder if I were dreaming. Then I could hear her breathing and the thud of her track shoes. Put my hip out, and prepared to pivot away.

A little rough. I staggered more than spun away smoothly, but it worked. She blew by, mostly, and I went off on a side angle, free of her path and on my own. It looked as though I could break relatively free but not being in an actual game, it seemed theoretical.

The coach came trotting back to me. "Not bad. Again."

And before I could brace myself, she circled off and launched herself at me, twice as hard as before.

I decided she'd been possessed and swore I could see little red flames dancing in the pupils of her eyes as she came at me. Her jaw squared. Her shoulders looked twice as wide as her waist. The noise of her approach even drowned out the busy construction crew at the grandstand.

I had nowhere to hide.

"Run at me! You're a striker!"

Orders I dared not refuse, I dropped into my familiar mode of intimidating the enemy and quite possibly threatening to bash their head in unless I got the ball and pass. My ears filled with the noise of our headlong rush. Then, before she could knock me aside, I put that hip out and rolled off her body, coming about at an angle she couldn't possibly follow as she straggled to a halt, defeated.

"Excellent." Coach grinned at me.

"Thanks."

And she waved me off the field with everyone else, me trotting in after because not only had she taught me something a little new, but she gave me an idea.

At week's end, we conspirators gathered to make plans on Friday after the away game—and eat pulled pork sandwiches laced with bourbon BBQ sauce and baked beans. I'd also made about a dozen or so deviled eggs which I put atop a little green salad plate for each of us. Sky Hawk had won again, which put us squarely at the top of our division, but only by half a game. Fourteen was right that we'd probably meet in the playoffs. Hunger banged at my ribs and I sat down eagerly to devour the last flavors of an Indian summer. Brian and Carter ate heartily, but I saw no sign of my mother. Unexpected office hours? That could, and did, happen from time to time, so I fell into supper with the rest of them, missing Hiram and Steptoe more than usual.

After dishes were cleared (bless paper plates), I said, "I think I can produce the book. Give me the silver globe, and I think I can cut the binding ties."

"Not a good idea."

"I can't think of any reason Devian would agree to meet with us otherwise. Other than a feline tendency to toy with us."

Brian tapped the back of my left wrist. "You're too vulnerable with this."

"I don't think so. Because you two are making a fundamental mistake."

Carter wiped a touch of bbq sauce away from the corner of his mouth. "What mistake?"

"That it's just a stone."

"We know it's not just a stone, it's an elemental of chaos, charged, and capable—very—of absorbing more." He wadded up his napkin and dropped it.

"That's not it."

Brian made an impatient gesture. "What, then?"

"It thinks. It partners with me, it reacts, and it often

works with me. Yet it's a stone and an inanimate object when it's not part of me."

"When it wishes. I don't buy that it's sentient. It's . . . instinctive."

I shifted a bit uneasily. "That's true. But it didn't absorb the book, just a bolt from it, and it might be just as enticed by the possibility of more power as Devian is."

"Tessa, you can't play 'button, button who's got the button' with both the elf and the maelstrom stone. You're playing with fire."

"I think if we retrieve that dimensional cage Brian and Steptoe made for the book, and I carry that, the stone will unleash it at my command." More probably, I'd cut it loose, but they didn't need to know that part of it. I added helpfully, "To get a better sense of it, if nothing else."

"Good gods." Brian sat back, looking as stunned as he possibly felt. "You're talking about dangling a fish in front of a great white shark."

"Not quite. The stone answers to me."

"Until it's taken or is ready to move on. What makes you think that Devian's power alone isn't enough to entice it to leave you and go to him? What if Devian offers more?"

"Because it thrives on chaos, and whose life has been more disrupted than mine? Every day I bounce off a new crisis. Losing my father, my chance at a good college, plunging into debt, trying to keep my head above water, falling into magic . . . the list goes on."

Carter said quietly, "It's not been all bad."

"It's been a roller coaster, and I love where I am now, but this stone craves possibilities, the more out of the norm, the better. As I see it, I offer an infinite number of them. A foot in two crazed worlds."

"Let's see what you've got, then."

We adjourned to the backyard, for safety's sake. I rubbed my bare hands together as the night's edge toward winter fell around us. I set my feet and extended my palm, willing the stone to produce the frayed, leather volume of the old book. I could see it in my mind's eye as well as if I held it and expected to see it materialize in my fingers. I could smell the musty scent of it, hear the slightly crisp pages crackle as I turned them, see faded ink that made deciphering its language even tougher.

Nothing.

I rubbed my stone lightly, feeling like a gambler at a craps table rubbing his dice. That made me grin a little. The casino had sunk deeper into my blood than I knew. I blew gently across the marble surface. "Come on. Work with me."

I put my hand out again to summon up the book or at least a reasonable illusion of it, not caring if I had the real thing or a fake. I didn't intend to let Devian get hold of it, let alone keep it. Perhaps the anarchic bent of the object would entertain the idea of faking Devian out. The stone grew heavy. I don't remember its weight becoming terrible before, but now my entire arm and shoulder ached and trembled as I stretched out. My whole body quivered with the effort. Was it testing me? I squared myself off. "I have to be able to do it."

Brian and Carter watched me like hawks on a field mouse in a cornfield. I could feel their intensity while, even in the cooling night, sweat dripped from my right temple and slipped down to my neck. Instead of my inner self seeing the book, I looked into a mass of dancing light and shining obsidian, folding in and out of itself over and over. Was that me? My confusion or knowledge? The thought made me sweat more, and the stone heavier, and the night oppressive. The stone hadn't felt this way when I called on it at the casino. Was it being stubborn? Or did it now have a darker purpose? Or was I looking into my own soul, which, heaven knew, had its black corners?

That thought stung. I quickly pulled my hand back and tucked it into my waistband for a moment, till the muscle fatigue left. My observers said nothing although Brian searched for and found his pipe. Again, he didn't light it but stuck it in the corner of his mouth and clamped down on it. I shook both arms out, trying to loosen the tightness I'd begun to feel.

Then I considered the maelstrom stone again. I had to get this done. It was the best, perhaps the only, bait we could offer Devian for another meet. He wouldn't be too eager to let go of Hiram in his role of mineral prospector, but this book . . . he'd mentioned it himself. He'd been looking for it. He wanted it.

And I wanted to be able to dangle it in front of him. Only the guys wouldn't let me attempt to free the real thing. Therefore, I had to create its essence out of nothing. No, not quite right. I knew the sight of it, the feel, the ominous mood that descended on me when I'd tried to read it, and the smell of old ink, old paper, and the brown wrapper that held it.

This time a slow cloud of steam, condensation against the evening as if I'd breathed it out, formed. And as it turned, it gained a rectangular form. I could hear the professor chomp on his pipe stem.

"She's almost got it."

"Not near good enough. It's only fog." Carter folded his arms across his chest. He didn't look happy.

"She'll get there."

With my second hand, I traced the edges of the illusion, correcting the shape of it, and whispering to the stone that I wanted leather, aged brown leather. For a brief, fleeting moment, I had exactly what I needed floating above my hands.

Then, poof!—and it was gone.

"You did it."

Sweat glued my hair to the back of my neck and threatened to make my eyesight blurry. Swiping my wrist over my face, I tried to clear my eyes. "Would it fool him?"

"If you can hold it for a good three or four minutes, I think so. That was closer to twenty seconds."

"I'll work on it." I inhaled deeply. "What if I had the cage in my pocket?"

Carter and the professor said "No" in unison.

"But—"

"We can't afford for it to be returned from its location, not until you yourself are stronger and trained. It wants you far more than you want it."

Brian's words sent a shiver down my back. "It's hunting me."

"If it is freed, it will be."

Not a question from me, but a statement. "It's that powerful."

Brian and Carter traded a look before the professor told me, "Not nearly as powerful as the stone, but we can't discount the effect it could have on you. It acted to enhance you, and now it needs to possess you. The stone, on the other hand, has always been a sort of partner, not a possessor."

"Then I have to perfect the book and hope the elf thinks I'm giving it over. He'll come to a meet for that."

"If you're right, and I don't concede that you are, how would that stop Devian?"

"While he's looking at me, you two have to hit him with everything you've got. I'm the decoy, you're the attack."

Brian twitched an eyebrow. "Not likely to kill him, but yes, we could very well knock him from one side of Faerie to another, with the power of an exploding portal behind us. Delay him for a few years on whatever he has planned. What about Hiram and the Eye of Nimora?"

"He'd have to produce them before I show the book. Once outside the arch, Hiram can take care of himself, right?"

"Likely."

I watched him fidget slightly. Was Brian ready for an epic confrontation?

Carter shook his head. "I don't like you being within reach of Devian. Or whatever doppelganger he might be using, or near an edged weapon with everbleed, or—" He halted abruptly.

"That's where my coach comes in. I learned a little lesson earlier this week." And I told them what else I had in mind. They were listening closely when my phone rang. I didn't recognize the phone number.

It was my mother. When I answered, she said tersely, "Put it on speaker."

"Where are you?"

"Do as you're told, Tessa."

So I did.

My mother's voice choked up, then Devian's voice came over the line smoothly. "Good evening, all . . . I assume I'm speaking to your little cadre? If not, I trust you'll relay all the pertinent information. It's a new moon coming at week's end, an auspicious omen for many projects, particularly new starts. I suggest we meet accordingly. I'll text the location and timing. And precisely what it is I expect you to trade."

I didn't want to sound eager, so I answered, "What if I'm not ready?"

"Then get ready. I have both Mary and April Andrews with me, and—frankly—I don't think they're enjoying themselves." The phone went silent.

CHAPTER THIRTY-NINE

NOW YOU SEE IT

I WANTED TO smash the phone. Carter reached out and snagged it, examining the information about the call, which didn't appear helpful, name and number successfully blocked. He set it back on the table. "I could take this into the Society and they might be able to wring its secrets out of it, but that will take time. And neither Brandard nor I have a lot of confidence in them at the moment. I'd say it's up to you, but I don't think you have a choice now."

My throat dried and I couldn't talk for a second until I picked up my glass and took a hefty swallow of weak sweet tea and melted ice cubes. Then my voice squeaked out. "How did he get them? And he didn't say what he wanted to trade for. Yet." A text would be coming, but would we have time to make preparations?

"He could have used any number of tricks to get them to come to him. Speaking from my experience at the department, it's likely he told them you'd had a car accident and where to meet him. Then he just took them." Carter paused. "As for what he wants, I think we can assume it's the stone, or you and the stone, and the book."

"And we have to do this."

Carter met my stare. "You were ready to do this before."

"That was different! This is my mom and Aunt

April we're talking about. Why don't we—what about the FBI?" Quantico was only a ninety-minute drive from Richmond, and they seemed handy.

"Tessa."

"Or the Society? What use are they if they don't help at times like this?"

"Tessa."

"It's my *mom.*" I tugged at a string of my hair that couldn't decide whether it would hang in my eyes or where it belonged tucked behind an ear. "This is different."

"Not really," Brian answered me, his voice low and even.

My world was ending. I thought then of Malender and my dream of days and days ago as he told me how the world ended. A ripple of decision passed through me. High stakes and I couldn't afford to bow out. Now was when I needed all that I could muster. I folded my arms. "Right."

"We can put him off, possibly."

"No. I'm ready. I will be ready. He just shook me."

"As he intended." Brian stood up. "I've a few things to get from the basement."

As he descended the stairs, I called after him, "Don't forget I have flash-bangs!"

"Oh, right!" he called back up. "I had forgotten! Those, my girl, can make the difference!"

I felt a little better.

"So we're still on for the illusion and switch?"

"I don't know any other way to play it."

Carter reached out and put his arm around my waist. "We'll get them back, and he won't be taking you. Not if I have anything to say about it."

"Since we don't have Steptoe or Hiram, I'm going to pull in Goldie."

"Will she fight for you?"

"I think so."

He nodded. "She might be a good ally."

I couldn't let him see the tears in the corners of my

eyes, or the doubt I felt coursing through my body. He'd do all he could. I would do all I could. I didn't know about the professor or the other person in our plan. All I could do was hope.

When Brian returned, he put his hand out. "Give me a flash-bang."

I went up to my room to retrieve a few, but he solemnly counted out just one and told me, "When I return it, mark it as the first one you throw. Put it somewhere you won't forget which one it is."

"You're going to alter it."

"Of course, I am. Devian deserves all we can toss at him." And he gave me a professorial wink before disappearing to his workroom in the garage.

I sat down on the cellar stairs. The house seemed dreadfully empty without my mother; even though I'm used to her working hours, knowing she would return home at some time filled the place with her presence. I don't know how Devian had gotten his hands on her. Or Aunt April. I'd placed them in jeopardy without knowing. It was fine when I thought it was just myself who needed to be on the lookout. I should have felt Devian watching us, learning about us. The tell-tales and Scout hadn't protected us.

The pup in question sidled down the steps after me, and curled up under my knees. He'd grown big enough that a single step couldn't hold all of him anymore. I looked at an outstretched paw and calculated his potential size. As Carter and I had discussed, he would be on the small side for a Lab, which was good for me, and he hadn't the sprung rib cage of a big retriever, either. He'd be neat and quick on his feet. But I couldn't imagine him as a hound of the Great Huntsman and the Hunt. Devian seemed to be the kind of ruler who ruled best by fear, and he'd done what he could to strike that deep into me. I didn't want to be afraid of my dog, and I wouldn't be.

Not that I'm the bravest bear in the woods, but I'm not the most stupid either. Unfortunately, I cannot tell when the magic is real or a bluff, and that would put me at a distinct disadvantage. Carter and Brian reacted to Devian as if he could be a real nasty customer, and that worried me.

A slight chill swirled about me. This is the time of year when Richmond settles into autumn. Frost at night. Ice, sometimes, after the rain. Trees that shed don a flare of color before going shockingly bare, in advance of winter, and their bare moments had hit. I can't ever remember getting much in the way of heavy snow here, but we do get winter, cold and achy, and it does snow now and then. I couldn't tell if the essence around me teased of the coming season or if it was my father haunting me.

"Hey, Dad," I said to the cold air. "Don't try to talk, just listen. I'm just thinking things over. Making plans. There's a high elf, Devian. He's not a nice guy and he's taking hostages. I'm just trying to figure out a way to get Mom and Aunt April home safe. If we can work things out, I might even be able to get my hands on Mortimer's journals. There's a possibility he worked with you, even if briefly, and knew what had you all knotted up, and who might have done this to you. Iron Dwarves keep thorough records, supposedly. If I can get that information, I'm one step closer to helping you. One step closer to bringing you back. Devian might have had a hand in it, too, but I'm betting he won't answer any questions, and we intend on putting him out of reach. So I'm not sure how I can bring you home." Or send him on, which was a possibility I didn't want to consider, but might have to, when that day came.

The cold air developed a misty wing which enveloped me and then faded. A hug, I guessed, the best he could do right now. He'd been so weak lately. Or perhaps the stone kept him a little out of reach as it protected me. I couldn't ask either to determine which. I stood up, tugged on my jeans' waistband, and decided it would all work out because it had to and I had no other choice.

Brian met me at the top of the stairs, dropping the flash-bang in my hand. "Slam dunk it."

I couldn't mistake it for any of the others. It glittered like one of those rainbows that had greeted my twentieth birthday, but it had a skin around it, rather like saran wrap, to protect it. I knew when I tossed it, the flash-bang would have to hit the ground hard or it wouldn't explode.

"Got it."

He cleared his throat then. "I'm going to prepare."

He went upstairs where I could hear the floorboards creak faintly as he moved across them.

I paused at the door to my mom's office. Her laptop was in place on her desk, so at least that hadn't been abducted along with her; her work was safe. From what I could tell, work had been moving right along on her dissertation, finally. She should be here, too, safe at her desk. If I hadn't decided to go after the Eye of Nimora, she would still be where she wanted to be—home. Out of habit, I plucked the computer up and stowed it in her desk drawer although I left it unlocked, in case I needed to retrieve it.

My phone let out a little chime indicating a text was received. I thumbed it open and then forwarded it to everyone who counted. I Googled the time. Just before dawn, when the new moon would fade into the sunrise, and in a part of town I did not know. I immediately heard from the professor: No, absolutely not.

I queried back: why?

Not to our advantage, he told me.

Advantages could make the difference, obviously, but I wasn't sure what he objected to. So I asked.

And he texted back: Midnight or dawn. Location is unimportant, it's the time.

It came back so quickly I realized that Brian used the phone and he'd more than just learned two-thumb texting, he'd mastered it. But it was the professor behind the words. Before I could ask more questions, Carter weighed in on the group text: The time will be fine.

And the two began to go back and forth on the merits of the rendezvous while I just listened to the texts ping and kept up. Finally, the time and place were begrudgingly accepted, and I let Devian know.

The guys told me to get whatever sleep I could. Nice advice, if I could take it. I didn't think I could sleep a wink.

Next thing I knew, I dreamed.

And the fight started.

I had almost forgotten what it was like to do battle in my sleep. Maybe Scout's presence soothed me or maybe I'd just been too dog-tired, pun intended, to dream, but I hadn't been up to a fight in days. Or, more accurately, nights. Yet as I stood alone, in downtown Richmond near where bricks lined the streets and quaint lampposts decorated the corners, I knew I wasn't alone nor would I be left alone. Something or someone hunted me.

And, dollars to doughnuts, I knew exactly what.

So, since I was going to be out here on my own, I decided I knew what I wanted to be carrying, and named it. Before I could blink, I held the professor's blasting rod in my hands, his wooden cane with its faceted crystal in the handle, and it glittered like a clear and perfect diamond in the dream light. The stone in my left palm clicked gently against it as I righted it and gripped it tighter. Even the sound of it radiated confidence, not to mention the heft.

The thought nagged at me: why the cane and not the professor himself?

Because he wasn't himself, not at all, and the cane did not have the weakness of a mortal being. My dream self knew what it wanted to rely upon, even if I was uncertain. I was new. Untrained but not untested.

I wandered along through stores and businesses that had been gentrified from dockside business, where once nobody respectable would have strolled. Many had brass plaques identifying what historic period they'd survived and what, if anything, significant had happened there. A surprising number had leaned upon one another since Revolutionary war days, reinforced with modern beams and roofing but not refined, little changed where possible, and now holding storefronts with a certain cachet. At the end of the block, near a curve of the James, a sign swung out. The Cutting Block, it read, and although it was a dream, I recognized a popular college bar and grill that often didn't check ID as it should. Rumor had it that the building was haunted and that it had been a butchery in its first life, livestock driven into it and carcasses of meat hauled out. I'd been in there once or twice despite being underage but didn't believe the common urban legend that blood could still be smelled or the sad and low cries of animals heard as their lives ended.

As I approached it, that disbelief fled. The heavy copper tang did infiltrate my senses, but I heard no sound, the entire street deadly silent except for my own steady trespass. It made my insides feel quivery and cowardly. Then a quiet wind swung the sign as I approached and paused under it; it should have creaked, but it didn't. The front door stood ajar, just enough to offer an invitation. Nothing else on the street attracted my attention or looked like it should. I hesitated under the sign for another long moment, deciding.

Then I toed the door wide open.

The door should have creaked, too, rusty hinges and all, but it didn't. It swung smoothly inward, and the streetlight from outside, with a gas instead of electric flame, cast my shadow across the threshold. My breath hitched as I felt Evelyn with me, or her shade, or her essence, going to the doorway with me.

"Live and learn," she told me. She glowed as I passed her by. It wasn't much of a casting, as the interior seemed to swallow it up, but I took a deep breath and entered anyway.

I know. Places like this aren't meant to be entered. I mean, I seriously realize that. Every nerve in my body screamed at me not to go into the Cutting Block. Before I finished crossing the border from street to building, I let go of the professor's cane and wished it back home safe, where it belonged. Because I dreamed it, it went. I could only hope that safe became part of it as well.

Once inside, my eyes adjusted; I discovered I wore my bracers, with each of those golden stones, topazes, softly lit. I couldn't see a lot, but what I could see, I didn't want to. What should have been a hipster bar reverted back to its original, grisly occupation. I could smell the blood and odor of freshly cut and ground meat. It roiled inside of me, and my stomach clenched, overwhelmed, halting me in place.

Then the meat hooks and racks caught my attention. Row after row of them, suspended from the ceiling, crude chains and thick heavy ropes holding them, sides of beef and pork waiting to be chopped down. And beyond them . . .

Human forms hung from the racks.

More grotesque in their own way, they swung back and forth slightly in a nonexistent wind, clothed as they would be in real life, but at the mercy of the meat hook that held them. And they were not lifeless. Far from it. As I approached them, they opened eyes to watch me. Lifted their heads. Opened their mouths to try to speak to me, and I knew what they wanted. To be taken down. To be freed.

One managed a whisper as I passed her: "No voice but yours." I looked up and recognized a fourth grade teacher from Franklin elementary school. Another lifted a hand, and his shirt cuff brushed my sleeve, the owner of the little pharmacy on the corner. A begrimed car mechanic from the garage that had kept my mom's car running for years. Good people, as I remembered. So what were they doing here? This was not some insane dream idea of physical therapy, they were prisoners.

And they looked at me now, chins turning, eyes imploring, as if they thought I could be their savior. I wanted to say, not my popcorn, not my circus, but I couldn't. I sidled by one of the economics teachers at Sky Hawk CC and he managed to say: "The stone."

That caught on. It sighed through the cavernous building, echoing back from the high rafters and faraway corners. Stone. Stone.

My left hand tingled vigorously.

How did they know? Why did they hope?

And who was behind this army of distraught people?

Then I saw the hanger who was more shade and darkness than mortal flesh, the girl-fox with three tails I knew as Joanna Hashimoto. She spun about on her hook, and her katana lashed out at me, missing by a scant inch. She spat and hissed at her failure to cut me. She'd been pretty once but now anger and pain contorted her features.

She kicked at me, spinning about on the rack, and shreds of inky nothingness peeled off her body, disintegrating as they hit the old flooring. Her katana slashed about as she spun, a silver crescent that moved like lightning. I knew who her puppet master had to be, so I ducked around her, careful, because I did not intend to meet Devian in this place of horrors. Not without my crew and the plans we'd tried to carefully make. In the corner just beyond Joanna, I saw her father, who did little more than open his eyes and glare at me as I went down the aisle. His katana stayed in its back sheath and his hands remained quiet by his sides, but I could feel the hatred boiling out of his stare.

Beyond them, I encountered Judge Maxwell Parker. His eyes narrowed in anger at me, one of them still purple and greenish above the brow and down into the temple. He reached for me and missed, hissing in disappointment. That gave me pause. How good could the Society be if it was unaware of Parker's fall? Or perhaps they knew full well and kept him as a small fish to lead them to the bigger fish. As I circled widely past, I could feel the emanation of hate coming after. Even with no idea why he'd taken Germanigold, I knew we'd made an enemy and would have to watch our backs if the Society couldn't. I had a more immediate problem, though, as the scent of the butchery rose thickly.

The smell of blood worried me. What bled here, and how much, and why?

The old wood floor creaked under my feet. When I

looked down, I could see clouds of stains, old blood and worse, no doubt from the past. But dry now, gone for all intents and purposes, long gone. The butchery floor held its own resonance and gore from its past, but I told myself it couldn't touch me now. I hoped I was right.

Then I saw Remy. Her once-elegant form twirled about slowly on its hook, and blood dripped from her seemingly lifeless form. I remembered her as slender, long-nosed but beautiful, hair done up, movements as graceful as they could be deceitful. Her turtleneck sweater hid the arch of her throat, soaked with blood that looked more black than crimson in this lighting, and her eyes, already open, showed no hint of awareness. A blood drop fell from a limp hand and as it hit the floor, rippled into a small puddle of the same, I saw her rib cage lift and fall in a breath. I stood for a minute or two but did not see another exhalation.

I moved away, thinking that she both lived and died at an excruciatingly slow rate. Tortured, unlike all the others, and in ways far worse.

Illumination from my bracers flickered, growing dim. If I wasn't careful, I'd be left in the dark here, and I definitely did not want that.

I was about to turn away and leave when I saw two final captives. The sight froze me for a split second, and then hot tears filled my eyes and I moved down the row heedlessly, because nothing could keep me from my mother.

Sweat or rain had wet her blond hair to her skull, and she wore a cream silk blouse that was one of her favorites. This time she'd paired it with her navy slacks. I couldn't see a bit of red on her, but that didn't keep my heart from thumping in my chest so loudly she had to have heard it. Aunt April hung next to her, ankles crossed primly and her arms folded over her chest, eyes shut tightly as if she couldn't bear to see about her.

I glided to a stop next to my mother. She put out her hand and held me as I tried to reach up and pull her down off the hook. "It is not," she whispered into my ear, "what you think."

"You," I told her, "are displayed like a meat carcass in a butcher shop. It can't be much worse. Stand on my shoulders, let me see if I can lift you off." I tried to heave her up, but she fought me, feet flying and the two of us circling about each other futilely, her telling me to leave and me telling her to stand up.

Aunt April said quietly, "Listen to Mary and get out, while you can." Her eyes flew open. "It's a trap."

Seriously, she didn't think I knew that . . . and she also thought I'd leave her and my mother behind?

My mother shook herself hard enough that chains rattled and ropes sawed and a bit of dust flitted from the eaves down about us. I batted the debris away from me and saw, just for a flash, a bit of glitter about it. I looked up. Moonlight shined through patches in the roof where boards had split open, and rain had wrenched a pathway down, and I watched the colorful motes drifting to the floor, like pixie dust.

And beyond, in the corner, something monstrous spread cloaklike wings, and a face as pale as a moon stared out at me from the dark, and he—whatever, whoever it was—laughed. He put a hand out, waggled a few fingers and all the chains and pulleys answered to his movement, bodies dancing like grotesque puppets as the rainbow dust swirled closer to me.

"Oh, hell no," I said, backing away quickly. I wasn't going to be beguiled by that stuff again even as I realized my mother and my aunt might not be my mother and aunt.

I turned and ran for the door, far in front of me now, its thin edge of an opening falling radiant across the blood-stained floor to guide me.

The door, scarcely open before, began to close. Thanking my coach for making me run sprints, I raced for it. But a body occupied the threshold for a moment and I saw Evelyn, beckoning, holding the time and space for me.

"Hurry!" she urged me. "The jaws are closing!"

I stretched my legs and dug for all the strength I had. Then I put my left palm down and fell into a baseball diamond runner's skid, a slide meant to carry me across the plate, and asked my stone for an extra kick of speed. Evelyn faded as I slipped through her form.

We, the stone and I, made it through as the doorway slammed shut behind. Dream over.

CHAPTER FORTY

. . . NOW YOU DON'T

SLEEP IS A wonderful thing. I managed about two hours of it before Brian and Carter knocked politely on my bedroom door and told me to get the lead out, time to leave. I wondered where southern chivalry had fled. I hadn't bothered to undress for the night so I'd be on my feet and all set.

Scout rolled over on his back, stretching all four paws into the air as he yawned.

"Like you have anything to complain about!" I shoved him off the bed. He came back for my pillow, yanked it out from under me to the floor and plopped his puppy body down on it, engulfing it.

Finding my shoes, I got them on, despite the big stumbling block taking up most of the floor space in my room and returning to doggish snores. He had to know I was going out when I reached for my sneakers, but he didn't put up a single protest when I started downstairs without him. I did a U-turn in the hallway and came back, grabbing one of his soft ears anyway. "You're going out before you go back to sleep," I told him and so he did. The light from the mudroom back door fell upon a still, very unawake backyard.

Carter had coffee waiting in three big containers from one of those fancy coffee shops in town. He pointed at the one marked with a T. "Coffee mocha with cream and sugar and an extra shot of chocolate."

"Be still my heart," I said as I took it up and tested

the heavenly goodness. Still very hot but not enough to scald the tip of my tongue. "Sweet and free, just the way I like it."

Now that he had returned inside, Scout began hopefully nudging his empty food dish.

"Too early."

He sneezed.

Relenting, I dropped a handful of kibble into the stainless steel realm. "Still early for a full feeding. That will have to do."

He settled for it, but when he finished, it was Carter's foot he came and sat on, not mine. I got a baleful look, instead.

"Have we got all that we need?"

I had the special flash-bang in my right pocket and that was about all I had to carry. Brian's jacket pockets bulged with whatever it was the professor thought he needed, and Carter had a long knife that I'd never seen before lashed to his left thigh.

"Wow. Know how to use it?"

"I do. If necessary."

"Let's hope it's not," put in Brian. "I have what I wish to bring."

I turned and inspected. "No blasting rod?"

"No. Odd thing, the crystal appears to have cleared, but I cannot count on a full charge, nor do I wish to chance it falling into Devian's hands. Therefore, it stays home."

"Wise. All right, let's go. With no traffic on the road, I'd say we'll arrive early, but I imagine he is waiting for us." Carter held up Hiram's SUV key. He couldn't start the car remotely without the electronic key fob, but we all wanted to drive a vehicle that could hold the lot of us, and the SUV fit the need. We piled in.

I heard a faint *Arooo* from the house. "Is that howling? Is he going to do that all morning?"

"Doubtful. Go back in and tell him to guard the house and garage."

"He's a dog; he should do that anyway. It's natural to bark at intruders."

Carter gave me a "don't argue with me" look. "Just tell him."

When I unlocked the front, Scout approached me, head and tail down. "No howling," I told him. "Guard the house and garage. There are relics here that need you on watch. Got me?"

His ears and tail came up. He dipped his nose down to his toenails and then sat, on alert, in the foyer.

"Good boy."

I went back out to the SUV.

"Well?"

"He's guarding."

"Don't ever forget what you've got there," Carter told me seriously. "I wouldn't put it past Devian to have a team go through this place while we're distracted."

"And now they won't."

"Not without a great deal of trouble and a lot of pain."

"What about the tell-tales?"

Brian waved a hand in the air. "They can react forcibly as well."

"How?"

"Among other things, they emit a fragrance that can stun."

"I smell roses."

Brian grinned a little. "They're happy. Trust me, they can turn nasty if they must. That's why Steptoe gave them to you."

I watched out the windows as Carter drove through streets empty of everyone but the newspaper carriers, their cars burning yellow-white lights in the gloom. "I thought they were just an alarm."

"What good is an alarm without an offensive action?"

"Not much, I guess. Stunning scent, huh?"

"Very."

I counted myself lucky that Scout and the tell-tales hadn't set each other off. We sat in relative silence the rest of the way, sipping at our paper cups full of goodness as the drinks cooled, and I had no idea what the other two thought.

I know what I did. That Devian had people hooked, in one way or another, struggling to be freed, and we had to knock him out of his game. Whether we had game enough to do it was another matter altogether.

I hadn't worn my gloves or my bracers. Like the professor, I thought the Iron Dwarf–gifted item too valuable to lose, so I'd left them behind. As the car plowed through a very dark night, I worried I'd been wrong. The new moon, sunk very low on the horizon, revealed little of the streets and the streetlights dimmed in preparation for the coming day, which seemed to be delayed.

We passed a sign for Chippenham Hospital, and Carter turned there. I rubbed an eye and leaned into the front seats. "Tell me it's not the hospital."

"It's not."

"There's a subdivision here, brand-new . . . I don't see this as being secluded."

He pointed. "Powhite Park."

And there it was, a gem of a park, tucked away off the freeway, between the roads and new homes and condos, looking as pristine and green as it could be. It was just off the road and yet as far away as it could be. I'd never heard of it even though I knew my mother and I had driven the freeway past this area a number of times.

Tucking my now-empty drink away in a cup holder, I said, "How big is this place? There are trail markers."

"I believe it's about a hundred acres, and much of it is wooded. Nobody will be about this morning, and I doubt later, because Devian will have shielded it. At least until after the confrontation."

"No witnesses, huh?"

Brian answered me, as he pushed his car door open and got out, "None at all."

Cycle tracks crisscrossed the dirt and grassy flat, leading up small hills and through thinning woods. Leaves too damp in the dew and mist rustled instead of crunched under our steps. Sunlight would dapple through the trees after dawn but for now, the park seemed hushed. The three of us trotted down a trail until a sign stopped us at a small, slat-wooded, and nearly flat bridge. Carter consulted his phone and tapped the sign. "One hundred feet in."

I read it as we passed: Wilson Memorial Bridge, Eagle Scout Project 2002, Thomas Chapman Troop 705. The sign had weathered better than the bridge, and I wondered when the troop would muster up a new effort to restore their legacy.

The professor started to talk to himself. I couldn't catch his words, low and soft and somewhat mumbled, and Carter didn't seem to hear him at all. From somewhere in the woods about us, an owl hooted softly. I looked up but didn't catch sight of it. I wouldn't if it were flying, a silent presence, soaring between the canopy of the forest and the autumn-covered ground.

"She's here," I said quietly.

"Good," Carter answered. He knew a little of what I'd planned but not all of it. I hadn't dared to tell him.

I yanked a scrunchie out of my pocket and pulled my hair back into a ponytail, but a low one at the back of my neck. Summer being gone, at least I didn't have to worry about mosquitoes because I could smell bog somewhere up ahead. The cold snaps at night were setting in and driving the biters out.

"Watch out for glops," Carter called back, and I jumped at the break in the quiet. He chuckled at me and dropped back to catch up my hand. "Nervous much?"

"Nervous a lot."

He squeezed my fingers. "But better now?"

"Yes. Always." I paused. "How much chance do we have?"

"It depends on how well you can manifest the book. I don't mean to put pressure on you, but we needed a diversion at the very least, and an outstanding illusion at the best."

"I'll try for the illusion." I moved my free hand behind my back, crossing my fingers.

"Like I said, no pressure. I intend to go in like a marshal, remind him of the bargain we had . . . he's got Hiram now, regardless of how, and the Eye needs to come back to us. He has no reason to involve mortal flesh like your mother and aunt and should release them immediately."

"And our deal?"

"That's on you, voluntarily. He'll insist on your fulfilling it, of course, and I will insist you shouldn't have to."

"Sounds like you've been talking to the Society."

"I have their backing if not their backup," Carter said, his tone aware of the irony. He observed the sky. "No sign of our silent partner. Devian thinks he has us at a great disadvantage."

"So does the professor."

We looked at Brian trudging ahead of us on the trail, his shoulders bowed as if he thought he were an old man, despite his new body. He ran a hand through his thick head of hair and now Carter could hear his rambling, too.

"What is he talking about?"

Carter held up a finger to quiet me and listened.

"What is it?"

"Nothing," he told me in that way people do when it's definitely something, but they don't want you to know or worry.

"Not working."

Carter squeezed my hand again. "Don't interrupt him."

I thought about my dream, and Evelyn's near-oracle advice to live and learn. I bit the corner of my lip.

"Carter."

"Hmmm?"

"Would Devian present himself as . . . oh, I don't know . . . a vampire or something?"

He tripped. Caught himself up and swung around to face me. "Why would you ask that?"

"Just a stupid question."

He schooled his expression, but I'd already seen the alarm jump across his face. "Not Devian."

"Nico?"

"Not here. Not now. You don't want to call that name. Ever. Remember? I told you."

He had.

But I had looked and learned. Seen a puppet master in the corner of my dreams. Melted a vampiric shroud off Malender. Knew that as bad as Devian was, something worse lurked behind him. The only question was: would we meet that personage today, or was Devian overconfident?

So we let the professor ramble on as I sank into my own thoughts and dodged out of the way of low-hanging branches as they slashed across the path at us, as if the trees had suddenly come alive and hated us.

Perhaps they did.

Ten more minutes in, on a slope that doglegged abruptly to the right, with a steep and rocky ascent that looked like it might give a trail biker a real thrill when it jumped off, Brian halted. Carter and I caught up.

I couldn't see it, but I could hear the faint, jagged music of an elven archway and another world. An aroma came from the red cedar junipers nestled in the brush around us, driven by our trespass. I found I couldn't remember what the other doorway had smelled like but knew I would recognize it the moment I did. I let go of Carter reluctantly and flexed both my hands.

Carter checked his watch. "Ahead of time."

The professor's chanting under his breath grew even more inaudible, but he did not give it up. I began to feel a bit freaked. I would have nudged him to get his attention, but I thought I could tell he was fully aware of where we walked and what was happening. His steps seemed steady.

Devian's sulky tones filled the clearing. "Not even dawn, yet the early birds are determined to catch their worm, as they say."

He stepped out of the lee of a tree, dressed in resplendent black and silver as his bowmen had been garbed a few days before, but in a suit and greatcoat, silky shirt and pearl-gray tie. He saw me assessing him. "Like it? Bespoke, of course. Nothing quite like it to be found anywhere, on this earthly plane, that is. Come with me and I'll have a gown tailored just for you, one that will win you hearts the world over, spun of magic and spider silk." He held out his hand to me. I didn't answer, and after a long moment he dropped it. "No? An experience you shouldn't miss. Perhaps you had a rough evening."

"He's goading you."

I gave Carter the side eye. "No kidding. I thought you were going to come on like a boss."

"We're here for the return of the Queen's gem and the Iron Dwarf known as Hiram Broadstone. We also expect Mary Andrews and April Andrews to be handed over immediately, as they are mortals you have no quarrel with and no right to be detaining."

"All that in one breath. Admirable." Devian looked behind him, and then we could all see the portal opening behind him, the same shocking colors of a vibrant autumn, and just after dawn there, but then the doorway stood to the east. Did they even have the same sun? Devian arched an eyebrow up, looking quizzical. "Did we not make a new agreement?" He spread both of his arms. "Carter Phillips, you have far less authority with me than you have with others. I treat with young Tessa."

"Not if I don't allow you to."

"And who would stop me? You?" He shifted his gaze to Brian, who had not stopped his near-silent chanting. "Him? Both failures at what you seek. Nothing compared to the untapped potential of our little sorceress here."

I put my hand out slightly, concentrating on illusion, my fingers curled to hide the stone as I reached for the awareness I had forged within it. It warmed in answer. As I strengthened our partnership, that owl—or perhaps it was a different one—gave a soft hooting nearby. I nodded in response to its question. A leather booklet arose from a gathering mist in my hand.

Devian inhaled tightly. As both Carter and the professor warned me, he could sense it—taste it, he would say—and its reality. His silvery blue eyes watched me eagerly.

"My mother and aunt. Hiram. The jewel." I spoke short sentences and words, trying not to break my focus.

"For the book?" He looked back over his shoulder.

"Not a good trade for me. The women, agreed, and the jewel is no good as it is—but the dwarf stays with me. He has a contract to fulfill."

"No," answered Carter.

Devian looked from me to him and back. A shape behind him moved, flashed, came into being and then stepped backward into autumn country again, but I had seen it and so had Carter. He scrubbed a hand across his chin to hide his expression.

"You don't deal in good faith and have not from the onset. Fulfill what you vowed or take the consequences."

"Brave words from a mage without his Society, and powerless in the night." Devian shrugged him off and returned his attention to me.

I could see my mother and Aunt April in the elven doorway, both pale and drawn, holding onto each other as if a storm wind threatened to tear them away. Mist began to boil up, frothing and wild, clutching at them. It must have stung, too, for Aunt April cried out and Mom . . . well, her lips went tight and she winced, but she wouldn't make a sound, her bright gaze fastened on me. My hand shook from the effort to hold the book's illusion.

A thin and shiny obsidian rope slid around their waists and began to quietly draw them forward out of Faerie. My mother fought the tug for a half-second, and then seemed to relax and go with it.

We needed a distraction, and now.

I flipped my hand. The illusion disappeared with a spit and hiss like an angry cat. "No. No deal to liars. I have but one thing to trade for the whole kit and kaboodle, and you take it or leave it."

"And what might you have more than that book which, it seems, was but an illusion." Devian's lip curled in a sneer.

"Oh, I have the book, but that's off the table." Carter stirred, and I put a hand out to stop him. "I have this."

And I put my hands out and took the maelstrom stone from my palm. I waved it at him, glamour gone, power shining through my fingers. It had leaped out of my hand at my bidding, just as I had hoped.

Gasps filled the air. Carter swung wildly toward me, but I stepped aside.

"Done!" Devian cried in triumph.

The doorway opened wide and Hiram thrust through, on the heels of my mother and my aunt. My aunt, I could see now, wore the Eye of Nimora perched atop her head and a stunned look on her face. Did she see the truth as I did when I touched it? She stumbled slightly. The obsidian tie around them both drew them safely off to the side and they scarcely seemed to note it, but I did.

"Here." And I threw the stone up, arcing through the air, like a three point toss for a basketball rim from half court. It tumbled over and over on itself, gleaming in its ivory, caramel, and jet tones, beautiful in the twilight before dawn. I saw it all and the flash of Malender and his golden voice telling me, *This is the way the world ends . . .*

Not if I had anything to say about it.

Devian leaped for it, as graceful as a stag soaring over a fallen log and even as he did, I felt myself caught up, and his voice in my ear. Two of them, in simultaneous places at once.

"Now I have both you beauties. Cannot learn, can you, between the fake and the copy?"

"Take it!" I yelled, but the owl already had plunged into flight, white-and-gold wings wide spread, talons out. She dove and plucked the maelstrom stone cleanly out of reach of grasping elven fingertips and carried it off.

I dragged a hand free as Brian shouted, "Throw it, and Carter–you know what to do!"

The flash-bang left my hand in a smash among the broken stones that littered the forest path. It detonated in a dazzling blaze of light and smoke, noise and showering glitter at Devian's smartly shod feet. He reeled back, vision stunned.

Pixie dust fountained upward and then fell over him like a cloudburst. He did not freeze entirely but swung about in excruciatingly slow motion, his hand beginning to trace a sigil of red fire in the night sky.

Too late. Brian grabbed him in a hug and could not be shaken off, imprisoning the two of them together.

Carter, bathed for a few blinding seconds of pure light from the flash-bang, let out a shout. He threw a flare as only he could. Fire, pure flame as bright as the sun, blazed from his pointing finger, striking the professor and Devian.

They went up like dry kindling. The clearing exploded in sound and fury as flames shot skyward. The explosion knocked them backward through the arch, and a bigger conflagration roared, illuminating Brian's body and I thought I could see the professor transposed over it, for just a split second before everything went white-hot.

CHAPTER FORTY-ONE

AFTERMATH

"BLIMEY." STEPTOE APPEARED out of thin air, unlashing his tail from my mom and aunt. "Got them out in the nick o'time." He bowed to them, bowler hat in hand, and a saucy grin across his face.

I staggered, going to one knee, as my doppelganger captor disintegrated in a flash. The gate, gone. Faerie, gone. Devian, gone.

And Brian and the professor nowhere to be seen.

I expected Carter to give me a hand up, but he dropped to a knee beside me and threw his arms about me.

"Are you all right?" he asked me as I asked him, "What was that?"

"That was your young lion," Goldie remarked, as she stepped from the forest behind us. She dropped my stone into my hand where it quickly reset itself in my palm. She added, "Sun lion. Carter. Or didn't you know? As far back as ancient Ra, the sun god, had two lieutenants to aid him."

"Sun lions."

"Yes. Almost as powerful as Ra Himself. And you had no idea?" Goldie smiled down at me.

"Evidently not," I flustered a bit. "Is that why the professor didn't want a before-daylight meet?"

Carter's breath tickled my forehead as he answered. "Yes. He thought I could not be at my full strength, but I didn't need to be. All he needed was a spark. And you could have told me exactly what you had worked out with Germanigold."

"That meant I would have had to tell you what I'd planned, and I didn't think you would be okay with that. Freeing the stone and all."

"You'd be right." My young lion held me closer, warm and strong, his lips against my temple. "What if he'd been a better jumper?"

Goldie made a scornful noise. "I would simply have flown faster."

I put my head back to view Carter's profile. "What do you mean, all the professor needed was a spark?"

"I didn't know what he had planned, but I recognized the phoenix ritual when I listened. He chanted it all the way in, and that was why I told you not to interrupt him. The consummation by fire is extremely powerful, and he evidently decided it was his only way of stopping Devian."

"The two of you nuked him." So Brian *had* been carrying his pyre in his pockets all these days, afraid to do what he had to until he had no choice.

"Basically."

"Then where is the professor?"

We all looked about. No sign met our search.

Hiram gently took the Eye of Nimora from Aunt April's brow and hung it about his wrist like a massive and priceless bracelet. He and Goldie kept their distance as we beat the brush, looking for a newborn wizard. We called his various names, over and over, as the sun came up and then cyclists and trail walkers began to fill their park.

And we found nothing. Not a scrap of clothing. Not a shoe. Not a pipe.

Days later, we survivors convened in the basement. My mom. Carter. Hiram. Germanigold. Steptoe. Scout trotting from one to another, tail wagging enthusiastically. Our circle stayed incomplete. Hiram still carried the Eye of Nimora, this time in a plush velvet drawstring bag. He pulled a thick envelope from his vest and handed it to me.

"Your payment, hard and deservedly earned."

I took it. Thick and heavy and stuffed with as much hope as it held money. I hefted it.

"I'll trade this."

His jaw dropped. "For what?"

Germanigold's gaze met mine across the room. I licked dry lips. "For permission for Goldie to visit the Broadstone home and retrieve her things and borrow a few things of her late husband's, Mortimer Broadstone, his journals in particular. To be returned."

"You asked before, and I took counsel on it, and aye, permission granted. But not for a price of money, not from you."

I didn't quite understand. "What, then?"

"Forgiveness. From both you and Germanigold, for my family being thick and rusty about the way things should be."

"Oh, most forgiven," cried Germanigold, and her wings came up in a spread of joy.

I hugged Hiram. "Always forgiven."

"Good. Good." He gulped down a relieved sigh.

Steptoe leaned against a stack of boxes. The professor's perdition stick cane rested in his empty room, the crystal clear as he'd told us, and it waited, as did these treasures stored here.

The demon had his tail looped about one wrist, rather like the handle of a dapper cane. Steptoe flicked a nail against the barb of said tail. "Well, 'e's not gone. That I'd know."

"He's not here."

"True, that. But I've still a binding on me, which means th' professor exists. All we've got to do is find 'im, ducks."

I grabbed Steptoe's shoulder and shook him lightly. "Does your tail know where?"

"Not likely."

I handed my mother the envelope. "This," I told her,

"is for a sabbatical and the finishing of your dissertation. And maybe six months of my car insurance."

"Tessa. You went through all this for that?"

"For us? For the future? You bet." I cupped my hands around hers. "It's you and me against the world, right?"

She tilted her head at me, and pointed at everyone surrounding us.

"Okay, well, maybe it's you and you and you and you and us against the world."

Hiram opened his bag and took out the Eye of Nimora.

"Why did you bring that?"

He dropped his chin. "You worked for it. I thought . . . well, I thought you deserved a look at it. To see what you fought for." He placed the diadem gently on my head.

And I did see. I swept my gaze about the cellar and saw all of them revealed, for the briefest of moments, in the truth of themselves. Even my ghostly father who stood in the corner, a clear expression upon his face. The moment swept over me, like a tidal wave cleansing a beach, and then the vision dissipated. It wasn't mine to keep.

Feeling a longing that matched what I'd seen on my father's face, I removed the Eye of Nimora. "It . . . it's awesome. Thank you, Hiram." I passed the jewel to him. "I know your family will use it wisely."

He took it. Scout leaned against his knees as he did. Nothing stands as sturdy as an Iron Dwarf. I swear he had a firm hold on it. *Deedle deedle deedle dum deedle dum.* The strains of the *Für Elise* ringtone sounded from his shirt pocket. "That's Evelyn!" Cheeks pinking and words suddenly flustered, he reached for his phone. The Eye of Nimora jumped. He juggled it. We held our breaths. The ring tone stopped, but those massive hands seized. Then fumbled. The precious talisman slipped.

And then the gem, the real one, diadem and all, fell. Hiram and I stabbed for it, both missing.

It hit the cellar floor with a sound that shivered into my bones and teeth. It didn't bounce but lay there as if dead. Shards split off and littered the tiles.

"Oh, no. No."

Hiram and I bent over as one to gather it up.

I came up empty, my hands outstretched. He came up with the gem and the diadem, two separate pieces but the ruby mostly, miraculously, whole—except for two bright splinters shining up at me.

My left hand twitched. Sounding like a dread vacuum cleaner, the maelstrom stone gulped them down before anyone else could move. In a split-second, they disappeared.

"Oh, my," said Steptoe. "That can't be good."

I blinked. My eyes watered a bit before my vision straightened out, and I could see again.

Everything.

The truth as it stood around me. Everything bright as day.

The aura surrounding all the professor's boxes. The wards tying them in place. The enchantments the Iron Dwarves had sunk into the very foundation of the house when they'd rebuilt the cellar. The web that kept my father in place and out of time. And more. I thought I could begin naming True Names and wondered where that would lead me.

I looked down at my stone where two crimson eyes seemed to stare back at me. My vision improved past imagining.

This was going to be interesting. And beyond me.

"I am definitely," I stated, "going to need some instruction on this new, improved sorceress business."

Don't miss the thrilling conclusion,
available June 2021 from DAW:
by Sara Hanover

THE WAYWARD MAGE

Read on for a special preview.

HAVING MAGIC WOULD be awesome, if only there weren't people willing to kill me for it.

There are, as far as I know, and my knowledge is like Swiss cheese with a number of holes in it, only three ways to naturally have Magic. It can be studied and practiced for years on end to gain skill, or one can simply be born Magical like an Iron Dwarf, harpy, or an elf. Don't ask me about Vampires, I've been told they're extremely rare and no one likes discusses them.

My friend the professor, wherever he is, has learned several lifetimes' worth of skill, being a Phoenix Wizard who can rejuvenate himself when time weighs too heavily. He has unlimited lifetimes to spend learning his spells. I can't pontificate about those born with it; I'm just learning about the different folk who exist in a world I never thought possible.

And then there's the third, reviled way—theft. Out and out stealing magic from those unsuspecting or unable to defend themselves. The professor wouldn't tell me how it's done, but I gather it's really something terrible, like stealing a soul.

There are articles which can store power in their core, but they are few and far between, and someone has to have charged them in the first place, so the magic in those items is simply transferred.

As for me, I've been possessed. A relic known as the Maelstrom stone has decided to imbed itself in the palm of my left hand and there it stays until I give it away or die, which is why I've been hunted. Now the stone itself has power which it lends to me when needed, and it also absorbs other relics, increasing its ability almost at will. I could easily be convinced that it is alive, somehow, and . . . well, hungry. One of those relics made a sorceress of me, but don't ask me what happens if I lose the stone. I don't know. I don't even have a good guess, unless I lose it in the most drastic way possible—over my dead body.

What I do have is a healthy respect for self-defense. I'm an enforcer for my college field hockey team, meaning I can run, and I can hit, jar, bump, trip, tackle (discreetly) and scramble at will. Off the field, the stone can help me throw up a defensive shield and so can the awesome bracers the Broadstone dwarven tribe gave me for my twentieth birthday. As a sorceress, my power lies in recognizing the Magic sunk into other objects and calling that power up for my use. This is a little dicier than it sounds because I didn't used to have the Sight necessary to recognize and name power so I can own it. I do now, thanks to shards of the Eye of Nimora which my stone absorbed. That's another magical object possessed by the Iron dwarves, which they use in their judicial system. There was a minor accident when I retrieved the Eye for them (it had been stolen) and it broke when dropped. Not much damage, thank goodness, but two distinct splinters snapped off and my Maelstrom stone didn't hesitate to gobble them up. They reside in the stone and are a little temperamental about opening and viewing, but I think we've reached an agreement. I would have given them back so the Eye could be whole again, but their loss doesn't seem to have weakened the original relic and my stone has never regurgitated anything it's swallowed. And so my power grows.

So, no, I don't rest easy, even at night.

Especially then.

I wasn't surprised when something woke me. Nights are the worst, because things can creep in and out through the veil of dreams, the sort of things that nobody wants to deal with.

So when I rolled over in the dead of night, in that still, silent, and frozen week after Christmas and New Year's, an unwelcome presence took me right out of my sleep. It ran across the edge of my conscious thought like a tiny beast with razor sharp claws and ice-cold toes.

I blinked up at the ceiling, and listened. Had something entered the house? It shouldn't have been possible, but the professor no longer lived here and his wards might be weakening. My overgrown pup, Scout, snored from the corner of the mattress. Whatever I'd heard, he hadn't. My bedroom felt cold outside the covers and I didn't want to leave them. I pulled them up under my chin until I realized that I'd already passed the point of falling asleep again. I hate it when that happens. I slid out of bed quietly and found the bedroom floor as chilled as the air. It could have been the weather, with snow that comes and goes, and icy rain following it in, and everything seems interrupted and left for dead.

My robe didn't hang on its usual hook by the closet. My mom must have taken it to wash, so I grabbed my favorite oversized tee-shirt and pulled it on over my boy shorts and athletic bra. I don't sleep in cozy nightgowns or pjs in case I have to react quickly. In the faint light from the hallway, my shirt proudly read: We Ar the Champi ns. I tend to wear my favorite shirts to smithereens.

Once in the hallway, I still heard nothing but something hung in the air. It smelled moldy and musty, and left a slimy feeling down the back of my throat. I'd never encountered anything like it before and wasn't happy about sensing it now.

Just past my doorway, there's a niche in the hall wall. A vase and a bouquet of what looks to be budding red roses about to open, resided there. They're not flowers. They're tell-tales, a mostly reliable alarm system and as I approached them, I could see that every flower had opened wide, looking like daisies scared straight. I put a finger out and stroked one of their velvety petals. It shivered under my touch and then leaned into it. Something had definitely alarmed them.

They looked toward the street side of the house.

I turned and made my way slowly down the hall, trying to avoid squeaky boards. Scout joined me, a little sheepishly, his golden tail hung low in an apologetic wag for letting me explore the unknown alone. I put a hand on his head. "Quiet."

He gave a little snuff of understanding.

I opened the next bedroom door, which had been the professor's room, although it had been empty for months. The bed stayed made and no dust lingered on the wardrobe or nightstand, but the area had that smell of being unoccupied. Or maybe the musty smell from the hall had followed me in. I looked at the bed where his walking cane with the large quartz decorating its handle caught a bit of starlight through the curtained window, and glowed like the diamond it resembled. I smiled to see it so bright and clean. It had been through a lot, that crystal, turning dark and opaque, and we'd thought it would never recover. I guessed that's why the professor left it behind. It's one of those relics I mentioned.

I stepped around the single bed and headed to the window. The curtains were askew the tiniest bit and if I were careful, I could look outside on the street without being caught spying. I positioned myself and Scout promptly sat down on my left foot to anchor me.

Down below, a mist danced along the street and sidewalks, up and down the block, and I could see frosted patterns on the ground. Lights up and down the block seemed a little dimmed, and the shadows they cast were barely there. I could see two porch lights turned on down the block but no lit windows. Everyone in the neighborhood but me seemed to be safely asleep, but it was the street light directly below that drew my attention. It cast shadows where none should be, shaped like nothing I'd ever seen before, shadows that didn't belong there. How can something cast backward silhouettes?

The curtains at the window wiggled a little as I pulled one aside, just a slit, to better look down at our street. It's odd, but our street lights change intensity. They burn brighter once warmed up. On a winter night like tonight, with a heavy mist that might turn into a light snow by morning, the street lights barely seemed to cut into the evening. Midsummer was like that too, as though the day had been long and bright enough, that we deserved a milder, gentler illumination at night. Tonight, though the streets lights seemed to be pitching a losing battle against the cloak of evening. I could see little more than outlines, although many were longer and deeper than expected. That hair tickling feeling didn't go away. Something leaned against a lamppost out there.

I leaned close enough that my breath fogged the window a little. I watched it for the briefest of moments, trying to separate true shadow from illusion, and then—it seemed as if I had caught its attention as it looked up at me.

I wouldn't have seen it, if it hadn't moved. Stretched and turned, it seemed, as if suddenly becoming aware of my study.

Instinct jumped me backward. I dropped the curtain, breath thudded out of my lungs for a brief moment as my heart did a skip and a thump, and I fought to inhale. But the thing I found watching . . . in a brief and hasty glimpse before I retreated . . . had looked up with blazing red eyes.

I'd seen Steptoe like that once, when he'd lost control over his demonic powers, and I'd hoped never to see such a sight again.

I stepped back two, three steps from the window, just in case my silhouette could somehow be visible. I didn't want to draw attention. I took a ragged breath or two. My hand remained in the air and I stared at my palm, my left palm, where the Eye of Nimora often looked back at me, and as I watched it awoke.

Two, small red slits opened to observe my world. But these eyes held absolutely no resemblance to what I'd just seen below. They showed no malevolence, no sinister aspect, but on the street—I'd felt a wave of malignance turned upward, toward my window, toward me, as the thing below searched.

My foot took a step of its own accord. The rest of my body wanted to follow. To go see what the hell was going on, what sat on my street by my front door and driveway, and glowered at the world. I knew that would not be smart. I could feel the icy presence of malice drifting outward from it, whatever it was. I stared at the curtains, transfixed, while my heart thumped heavily.

What had I just seen? Like watching a train wreck, I couldn't stay away from the vision.

What was it doing here?

Eyes narrowing, I stared at where it had been. I finally spotted it among the spiked silhouettes. Something near impossible to see.

Not a wisp of the curtain moved. I hadn't given myself away but it had caught me . . . or had it? If it was surveilling the house, it could be gazing all over, not just where I stood. I waited until my heartbeats steadied and Scout went from sitting on my foot to lying down on it, paw across his nose as if he too could smell the evil odor creeping through the upstairs. When I leaned close to look again, the shadows had scattered—splintered across the road and sidewalk as if they had never been out of the ordinary and grotesque. It had disappeared or melded into the evening. I couldn't detect it even though I *felt* it. Slimy. Rotten. Evil.

So I did that thing that one should never do—I went downstairs, determined to go outside in search of what might have been happening. Nearly every gothic horror tale ever written or filmed warns you against that. Do Not Go Out Wandering. It's deadly. It's exactly what the enemy wants. It is usually fatal. But this was my house. We'd been driven out of our other home by poverty and addiction and found refuge here, and I wasn't about to let it happen again.

I went anyway, my dog tucked against the back of my leg as if knowing what I planned to do and hoping

I'd change my mind. Scout is smarter than the average dog, being of exceptional bloodlines—half elven, half Labrador retriever—with a predicted longevity of thirty years or so. His devotion to me is endless, except now he took a corner of my droopy tee shirt in his jaw and didn't want to let go when I got to the door. He had no intention of going out the front door and worked to keep me from accomplishing it.

I pushed him aside with a stern "off" and he retreated with a whine, his eyes sad and his ears drooping. The moment my bare feet touched the porch, I nearly turned around and bolted back inside. Cold radiated upward as if attacking, and my whole body went icy, setting my teeth to chattering. I'd explore but in a damned hurry, I decided. Something inside me, probably my common sense, tugged at me to go back.

I didn't.

The shadows had all shrunk to normal size and dimensions, with no sign of what had been there. Something wicked had been here . . . I could feel it in every tingling nerve . . . but it had passed, and I was no closer to knowing what it was.

I walked about the lamppost and watched the shadows dance as I did, all normal, no grotesque rendering. I peered at the iron structure itself, to see if anything had been left behind but hoarfrost and saw nothing. Even that smell had dissipated or I had gotten used to it, because it no longer hung on the evening air. Yet . . . when I looked at the ground, I saw one distinctive shoeprint outlined there. It seemed to be fading even as I studied it. I hadn't brought my phone with me, so I had no chance to take a shot. It looked like a boot print, long and narrow with a distinctive heel but definitely man-sized, and then . . . it disappeared into the mist.

I retreated back to the safety of the house and had trouble closing the front door because of Scout's relieved and exuberant welcome. My feet tingled in the warmer air. I tugged on his neck.

"Enough already. Back to bed. Let's not disturb anyone else, I don't want a lecture."

And I could hardly wait to shove my toes back under warm covers again.

As I passed the tell-tales upstairs, they had lost their exaggerated pose and slumped back into sleepy buds as though nothing had ever been wrong. I wondered if Steptoe, my friend who'd given them to me with the express purpose of having an alarm in the house, had even noted their panic. If not, then something dread had been watching the house—and almost nobody knew it. What measures we had in place hadn't been enough to protect us. That would have to change.

As I pulled the covers back up, and Scout arranged himself alongside, I thought of how we'd been forced out of the home that had been my safety and haven for most of my life. If not for Aunt April and her generosity, we wouldn't have the place we did, rickety structure, old fashioned plumbing and all.

Once upon a time, I had had a father. I thought him awesome until he caught the gambling bug, so I killed him. And no, I didn't shoot him or take an ax to him although half my high school at the time thought I did when he disappeared suddenly. We had a shouting match when I found out he'd cleaned out my college fund and I shoved him away. Magic's greedy jaws swallowed him whole and he hasn't been seen by the general public since. I didn't believe in him or Magic then. In the ensuing years, my mother and I lost our house, our savings, our credit cards but at least we had each other.

If I'd known then what I know now, I might have done things differently. Yes, he had an illness, and Magic had a grip on him as well, for he'd used it to increase his luck which fed his addiction. Can't do that. The House always wins.

Magic has a price and when it comes to take its due, it can be fairly messy. It's not pretty. Don't ever believe it is. It is the stuff of blood, sweat, and tears. Add a little cursing—but that will lead you into the dark side. Avoid that, if possible. Because the price is high enough as it is. I lost a father . . . and gained a family I never expected.

Power imbues all of us, like sunlight and shadow, and those who can see it, sense it, or bend it hold a definite advantage over those of us who cannot. I want to use it to right those wrongs in my life that changed everything but Magic doesn't work backward, only forward. There's a balance to the powers of life, and then there's chaos which thrives on the messy bits. The forgotten pieces. The ragged overlaps.

I wouldn't have Magic at all, but it chose me for reasons I have yet to understand. Chaos decided to burrow into me and stick. It seems permanently attached, and don't think others haven't tried to take it any way they can, including over my dead body. As for devouring, well, my stone has inhaled a cursed ring, a Book of Dark Arts, as well as those bits of the Eye I mentioned. As for why the breaking of the Eye of Nimora didn't really seem to hurt it, well, the darn thing is a gem big enough to choke a horse.

Sorcery struck me, not that differently from a bolt of lightning, but forgot to leave me with a set of directions and I've been struggling ever since. Lightning not only struck twice, it darn near incinerated me.

There's a steep learning curve to dealing with my new reality and, if not for my sake but for that of others, I'm running out of time. The power I have to manipulate is stubborn, sometimes angry, possessive, and impatient. Chaos stones are adept that way, I've been warned, although it has its excellent moments. I've also been told by those who know that magic mirrors the person who wields it but I don't think so. Maybe. Maybe not.

Magic can't mend things, well, magically. Not in reality. It's like pulling a piece of elastic to change its shape. The form will change, but conditions alter and ofttimes—abruptly—everything snaps back. The snap can be killer. Like super glue, power is best used in small, very careful doses, trying not to get your fingers stuck together. I can't trust Magic to do the ordinary stuff I need done, but I have this situation.

Two floors below me, in the basement of this creaky

old house, I found my missing father, fallen into a crack between dimensions. He's out of place. I drove him into that jeopardy, and I need to get him free. I'm fairly certain a conjuring put him there, and it's going to take the same to pull him out, and it needs to be soon. He's a poltergeist in our cellar, and he's fading. I can't get him out without knowing how he got in, and I haven't been able to determine what happened. It's time for me to go visit my father and see how he's faring. It's one of those not pretty, very messy moments I hate.

I fell asleep in a tangle of thoughts and emotions and didn't wake until Scout put his damp nose to my cheek, signaling he needed to go outside and be fed. I got up and prepared for my day, and decided I could wait no longer to check on my father.

I sat down on the cellar steps, pulled my glove off my left hand and put my palm out, hoping the little red slits highlighting the marbled stone set in my hand would open which they often will not do. They glow red. They also bring heat into the marble of the stone. One sees, the other consumes, and all of it is a pain in my existence. I hadn't known about any of this until I met Professor Brennus Mordicant Brandard, a crusty old guy on a charity senior meal route. When he set his house (and himself) on fire, the Phoenix wizard called me for help, and I answered. I've never been certain why it was me he called. Maybe no one else answered his first or second attempt, but then I showed up. Life has not been the same since. I've met a host of magical beings, good and bad, and been infested myself. It's rather like having a virus that can cure one fatal disease but gives you another, highly troublesome one, in exchange.

While I sat, hand open in the air, and thoughts stampeded through my brain, I took stock of my current situation, including the apparition which had awakened me.

Other life projects loom in front of me, besides rescuing my father, which include falling in love with Carter Phillips, finding our now missing Phoenix Wizard professor, establishing world peace, and curing childhood hunger. Oh, and declaring my major at Sky Hawk Community College. I really don't count on any other burdens, because these seem tough enough as it is. Well, Carter isn't tough. I mean, he is tough, but loving him isn't, and I've had strong hints that he might feel the same way.

So I sat in a moment of quiet and searched the cellar for my father. I felt it the moment the Eyes open in my palm, and a subtle warmth traveled from my hand to my face and eyes. What had been dim was now illuminated. Storage boxes piled hither and yon glowed with magical possibilities—they belonged to the professor and were all we could salvage of his former life and burned out house, and although the boxes are battered and look like ordinary cardboard, I can see the auras that dance about them. Tiny motes of starlight have drifted in from upstairs and they whirl about like fireflies. And there, in the corner, stood my transparent father. He lifted a hand in greeting. A green haze surrounded him and if he were a tree, I might think that was good. But he's not, and it looked sickly to me.

"Dad."

A small gust of cold air surrounded me. "Don't try to talk," I tell him. "I'm just checking in. Goldwing and I are visiting Broadstone manor tomorrow, so I'm hoping to finally get some of the information on how this happened, so we can undo it."

The ghost didn't react at all. Did he understand what I said? I waved my palm. "Goldwing is the Harpy who was married to Mortimer. She knows he kept journals, and he told me once he thought he knew how all of this might have happened, so I am thinking he noted it down before he died." My dwarven friends were detail oriented and the Broadstone clan was a pillar of their community. I counted the late Mortimer as a friend and his son, Hiram, a close friend.

My see-through dad cut a hand through the air, a negation, a warning, a signal to stop, as emphatically as he could.

"No? Why not? This is good news."

He drifted closer, but stopped halfway across the cellar as if the Maelstrom stone put up a barrier he could not cross. And it might. It's a very defensive item and has saved my life more than once. Now I needed it to save his. I might add that any saving it had done was probably self-preservation of its own interests and not necessarily mine.

But he halted and shook his head.

"The Broadstones are friends. So is Goldie. I'll be fine. You can't wait much longer, and this is the only break we've had."

The air about me grew so chill I expected snow or hail to start falling.

"I did this to you," I tell the apparition. "We fought and I sent you away, and you got into some kind of trouble and shoved between dimensions and this is all my fault, and I'm the only one who can fix it. I thought . . . I thought you'd taken everything away from me that I'd planned, but what I have now instead, is . . . well, it's better. I have friends I could never have believed even existed, and Mom is doing well, finally, and we not only survived, we thrived. But you belong here, as part of us, and I have to find a way to bring you back. I won't lose you again. So, you better get used to the idea that I intend to undo what I did."

My father held both hands palm up and stood watching me.

"You're not going to talk me out of this. If I do nothing else with the magic I've got, I will free you. I will."

He sliced a finger across the air again, an unmistakable gesture, killing my plans.

I stood up abruptly. "Look. I know what I'm doing. I'll be fine. You're the one I'm worried about, all right? I have the stone and my bracers for protection, and a Harpy warrior on my side, and the Iron Dwarves, not to mention Carter and Steptoe, and you've no one but me. I'd say I'm in good shape. I'll check in with you tomorrow when I get back."

Upstairs, I heard Scout's toenails clicking on the

floor as he scrambled to go bark at someone at the front door. I closed my fist, shutting down the Eyes and although I could feel the ghost-touched cold, I couldn't see him anymore.

"I'm doing this," I finished. "And you'll be happy I did."

Tanya Huff

"The Gales are an amazing family, the aunts will strike fear into your heart, and the characters Allie meets are both charming and terrifying."

—#1 *New York Times* bestselling author
Charlaine Harris

"Thoughtful and leisurely, this fresh urban fantasy from Canadian author Huff features an ensemble cast of nuanced characters in Calgary, Alberta.... Fantasy buffs will find plenty of humor, thrills and original mythology to chew on, along with refreshingly three-dimensional women in an original, fully realized world." —*Publishers Weekly*

The Enchantment Emporium

978-0-7564-0605-9

The Wild Ways

978-0-7564-0763-6

The Future Falls

978-0-7564-0754-4

Celia Jerome

The Willow Tate *Novels*

"Readers will love the first Willow Tate book. Willow is funny, brave and open to possibilities most people would not have even considered as she meets her perfect foil in Thaddeus Grant, a British agent assigned to look over the strange occurrences following Willow like a shadow. Together they make a wonderful pair and readers will love their unconventional courtship." —*RT Book Review*

TROLLS IN THE HAMPTONS
978-0-7564-0630-1

NIGHT MARES IN THE HAMPTONS
978-0-7564-0663-9

FIRE WORKS IN THE HAMPTONS
978-0-7564-0688-2

LIFE GUARDS IN THE HAMPTONS
978-0-7564-0725-4

SAND WITCHES IN THE HAMPTONS
978-0-7564-0767-4

Katharine Kerr

The Nola O'Grady Novels

"Breakneck plotting, punning, and romance make for a mostly fast, fun read." —*Publishers Weekly*

"This is an entertaining investigative urban fantasy that sub-genre readers will enjoy...fans will enjoy the streets of San Francisco as seen through an otherworldly lens."
—*Midwest Book Review*

LICENSE TO ENSORCELL
978-0-7564-0656-1

WATER TO BURN
978-0-7564-0691-2

APOCALYPSE TO GO
978-0-7564-0709-4

LOVE ON THE RUN
978-0-7564-0762-9

WORLDSHAPERS

For Shawna Keys, the world is almost perfect. She's just opened a pottery studio in a beautiful city. She's in love with a wonderful man. She has good friends.

But one shattering moment of violence changes everything. Mysterious attackers kill her best friend. They're about to kill Shawna. She can't believe it's happening—and just like that, it isn't. It hasn't. No one else remembers the attack, or her friend. To everyone else, Shawna's friend never existed...

Everyone, that is, except the mysterious stranger who shows up in Shawna's shop. He claims her world has been perfect because she Shaped it to be perfect; that it is only one of uncounted Shaped worlds in a great Labyrinth; and that all those worlds are under threat from the Adversary who has now invaded hers. She cannot save her world, he says, but she might be able to save others—if she will follow him from world to world, learning their secrets and carrying them to Ygrair, the mysterious Lady at the Labyrinth's heart.

Frightened and hounded, Shawna sets off on a desperate journey, uncertain whom she can trust, how to use her newfound power, and what awaits her in the myriad worlds beyond her own.

Worldshaper

by Edward Willett

978-0-7564-1346-0

DAW 178